TO CONQUER PRIDE

TO CONQUER PRIDE

A PRIDE AND PREJUDICE VARIATION

JENNIFER ALTMAN

Box Hill Books

To the one and only Jane Austen,
for creating such memorable characters,
and for allowing me to take them down a slightly different path.

Amor vincit omnia.

~ Love conquers all. ~

CHAPTER 1

U nder different circumstances the rocking of the carriage might have been soothing; however, on this brisk November day, the motion offered little comfort to the compartment's sole occupant.

Fitzwilliam Darcy stared out the frosted windowpane, but his thoughts were far removed from the passing Kent countryside. From the outset, he had dreaded this journey. Indeed, if it were up to him, he would not have come within fifty miles of Hunsford for as long as he lived. But despite the accusations leveled at him in that very village, Darcy was a man who knew his duty, so when Lady Catherine had requested—nay, demanded—his assistance, he had come. Even so, he kept his visit as brief as possible, arriving yesterday morning and working late into the night. He spoke to no one, save his aunt's steward, going so far as to take meals in his chambers. And not his usual chambers, either. No, he had made a point of requesting a different apartment. Never again would he step foot in the room where he had dared to dream of a life spent happily with Miss Elizabeth Bennet. The room where he had poured out his soul in that ill-conceived letter...

Releasing a rough sigh, Darcy pressed his forehead to the cold glass. Seven months. It had been seven months since his previous trip to Rosings. Seven months since he had last seen *her*.

Darcy's head fell back against the cushions. Just thinking about Elizabeth was like a spill of salt to an open wound—and yet he could do nothing to *stop* thinking. God knows he had tried.

Oh, it had not been difficult at first. After leaving Rosings, he had gone straight to London to set things right with Bingley, and then there was Wickham to contend with. That endeavor had proven a bit more challenging, but at least it had kept Darcy from dwelling on his disappointed hopes. By mid-summer he was back at Pemberley, and though he made every effort to throw himself into the management of his estate, even the brandy he had taken to consuming on a nightly basis did little to dull his memories. For no matter what he did, Elizabeth Bennet haunted his dreams, both sleeping and awake. Sometimes she would appear to him the way he wished to remember her—her smile radiant, her expression bright with humor. But other times he recalled the way she had looked at him the day of his disastrous proposal—her fine eyes dark with anger.

Had you behaved in a more gentlemanlike manner...

An icy wind swept into the carriage and Darcy started,

realizing they were no longer moving. Turning to face the open door, he regarded the footman silhouetted against the lead-gray sky. When Darcy spoke, his voice was tight.

"Why are we stopping? I thought I made it clear I wished to travel straight through."

Despite his master's black expression and clipped speech, the footman's countenance remained carefully composed. "I beg your pardon, Mr. Darcy. This is the last coaching inn before we reach Town. I believe Mr. Johnson thought it prudent to check the state of the roads."

Darcy lifted his gaze, cursing under his breath as he took in the fat white flakes rapidly descending to join the thick snow already blanketing the ground. Blast! His mind had been so preoccupied; he had not even noticed the worsening conditions.

Turning to his footman, Darcy immediately relaxed his tone. "Of course. Forgive me, Thomas. I had not perceived the change in weather. Johnson was correct to stop."

His man offered a deferential nod and Darcy moved to the door, exiting the carriage. In the near distance, he could see the retreating form of his driver, heading for the mews. Addressing the footman, Darcy issued instructions to have the horses watered and rested before stalking off in the direction of the inn. Despite his protestations, he was glad to escape the confines of the coach. His legs needed stretching, but more than that, he required a distraction. Anything to keep from continuously reliving those horrible moments at the parsonage.

No, he did not welcome the delay, but perhaps a

change of scene would help banish Elizabeth Bennet from his thoughts, even if only for an hour.

Elizabeth Bennet pressed through the thickening crowd, the note clutched tightly in her hand. She should have known something was amiss when her uncle was not waiting to meet her. Moving to the nearest window, she stared out at the blowing snow and her shoulders slumped. What had she been thinking, releasing the carriage without being certain someone had arrived to collect her? But before the thought was fully formed, she already knew the answer. She had simply been grateful to get away. Away from Hunsford. Away from Charlotte's happiness. And most of all, away from the parsonage, where she could still see Mr. Darcy standing before the empty hearth, professing his admiration and his love.

Of course, he had said other things, too. Hateful, horrible things. About her sister. About the inferiority of her connections.

And she had replied in kind.

Elizabeth shook her head and a soft sigh escaped her lips. More than half a year had come and gone since that awful day, and Mr. Darcy clearly had no intention of being in her company ever again. So much so that he had not even bothered to attend the wedding of one of his closest friends.

Not that this had come as a surprise to Elizabeth, given his feelings about the match.

Well, there was nothing to be done for it. Mr. Darcy was out of her life, and despite her desire to leave the area as soon as may be, she would have to remain at the Bell until tomorrow, along with what appeared to be half of Kent.

Elizabeth's gaze swept the cramped parlor, but every seat was taken. Circling back the way she'd come, she threaded her way towards the outer corridor. Perhaps she would have better luck in the dining room.

Entering the Bell, Darcy paused, allowing his eyes to become accustomed to the dim light. The air around him felt overly warm after the outside chill, and a steady clamor of voices reverberated off the low ceilings. Darcy frowned, already regretting his decision to come inside. Although the inn was no worse than most, and quite a bit better than many, this type of public room filled with strangers never failed to make him uncomfortable.

Shouldering his way through the crowded vestibule, he headed for the saloon, pacing to the front window and staring out at the falling snow. He could only hope the road to London was still passable. He did not wish to be stuck in Kent one moment longer than necessary.

A chorus of restrained titters at a nearby table drew his attention and Darcy turned away from the glass. A congregation of women stared back at him with obvious interest. Darcy's skin prickled, and he pivoted on his heel, hastily retreating to the relative quiet of the corridor. He would find the proprietor and hope that in spite of the weather there was still a private chamber where he could rest and take tea, or possibly something stronger, while he waited for news.

Crossing into the dining parlor, Darcy scanned the tightly clustered tables. As if by instinct, his gaze shifted to the corner of the room and an odd buzzing filled his ears. Darcy blinked. Were his eyes deceiving him? Could merely thinking about Elizabeth Bennet have conjured her into existence? His gaze settled on the delicate curve of the woman's neck and a bitter laugh rumbled in his throat. No. If he had such a power, surely Elizabeth would have been thrown into his path long before now.

The woman turned, and Darcy's heart lurched inside his chest. He stepped forward, and before he could think better of it, her name was on his lips.

At the sound of her name, Elizabeth's eyes lifted and the fine hairs on the back of her neck immediately stood on end. *Merciful heavens! Mr. Darcy!*

Staring back at her, Darcy momentarily froze before propriety propelled him forward to offer her a rigid bow. Elizabeth returned the greeting, her cheeks warming with a vivid blush.

Darcy looked away and Elizabeth suspected their thoughts were both on that long-ago April morning—the last occasion they had been in one another's company. The day he had handed her a letter, his expression as dark and stormy as the windswept sky.

Elizabeth forced a shallow smile. She knew that one of them must speak, and if past interactions had taught her anything, the first overture would likely need to be hers.

"Mr. Darcy, this is an unexpected surprise. I had no notion you were in Kent. You are visiting your aunt, I imagine?" Even to her own ears, her voice sounded unnaturally bright.

Darcy frowned, answering in the affirmative. Several seconds passed before he seemed to realize something more might be required of him and he haltingly explained that an urgent matter at Rosings had necessitated the trip.

His voice trailed off and Elizabeth studied him from the corner of her vision. "I see," she answered, wondering if the urgent matter had anything to do with the cousin he was expected to marry.

They stood in silence for some moments before Mr. Darcy cleared his throat.

"You are well, I hope?"

"I am, sir. And yourself?"

"Quite well. I thank you." Darcy paused, tugging at his coat. "And your family? I hope they are all in good health? Your parents... and all your sisters?"

Elizabeth tilted her head. Despite the awkwardness of the situation, she could not prevent the half-smile that captured her lips. "Yes, they are all well." She hesitated before saying, "Perhaps you have heard that my eldest sister is newly married?"

Elizabeth thought she saw him color, but when he spoke, his voice was unaffected.

"Yes, of course. Pray, allow me to offer my congratulations."

She attempted to read his expression, but as was often the case, his face was an inscrutable mask. Elizabeth lifted her chin. "I thank you, sir. Jane and Mr. Bingley are very happy."

"I am glad to hear it."

Once again, conversation faltered and Darcy's gaze drifted to the edges of the room. "Are you traveling to Hunsford?" he finally inquired.

"No, I am just returning. My cousin and Mrs. Collins have recently welcomed a baby boy. Lady Lucas was kind enough to allow me to accompany her on a brief visit."

"Ah, I had not heard. I hope you will give Mr. and Mrs. Collins my best wishes."

Elizabeth indicated that she would and the air around them grew still.

The scrape of cutlery mingled with the clatter of dishes at a nearby table. Somewhere across the room a glass shattered and the din was punctuated by a sudden burst of laughter.

Darcy shifted his weight. "Forgive me for taking up so much of your time, Miss Bennet. I am certain you are anxious to rejoin your companions. Would you allow me to escort you to them?"

Elizabeth's stomach tightened, and she quickly looked away. "I thank you, no... That is, there is no one with me at present. Lady Lucas and Maria will remain at the parsonage for several more weeks. I chose to leave early so that I might spend some time in London with my relations."

Darcy's brows drew together. "You are alone? Are you traveling by post? I did not see a coach outside."

"No. Mr. Collins was able to procure a carriage to deliver me to Bromley. My uncle was to have met me here, but I have just learned that he has been delayed due to the poor weather. He will not be able to send for me until tomorrow."

Darcy's frown deepened. "Is there not a maid or a footman accompanying you?"

"No, sir. Mrs. Collins sent one of her maids with me as far as the Bell, but she has departed with the carriage." Elizabeth could see the tick of a muscle in Darcy's jaw.

"Miss Bennet, surely you do not plan to stay here overnight, unchaperoned?"

She stared back at him, slowly raising one delicately arched brow. "It would appear, sir, that it is not a matter of choice."

Turning away, Darcy expelled a breath. "That will not be necessary. I am returning to London and will escort you in my carriage. We will depart as soon as I am assured it is safe to travel."

Elizabeth stiffened. "I thank you, Mr. Darcy but I am afraid I cannot accept your generous offer. My uncle has already made arrangements to collect me tomorrow afternoon."

Darcy lifted his hand, raking his fingers through his hair before pacing several feet away. When he returned,

Elizabeth noticed that his expression had softened. "I beg your pardon, Miss Bennet, but I cannot leave you in such difficult circumstances. If you will not accept for my sake, think of your family. Bingley would never forgive me if I did not offer you my protection."

Elizabeth's resolve wavered. As much as she resented being ordered about, she had to admit there was sense in his suggestion. And it did seem rather silly to refuse him out of spite. No doubt the journey would be uncomfortable, given their history, but if Mr. Darcy was prepared to treat her with civility, certainly she could manage to do the same. Still…

"Mr. Darcy, truly, that is not necessary," she began, but the words were scarcely out of her mouth before the gentleman interrupted.

"Forgive me, Miss Bennet, I beg to differ. If you will not allow me to accompany you to Town, you leave me no choice but to remain here until your relations arrive tomorrow."

Elizabeth's eyes widened. *Would he really do such a thing?* But she could already see by the firm set of his countenance that he most certainly would. His honor demanded it, and he would brook no argument.

Seeming to notice her hesitation, Darcy stepped back. "Pray, take a moment to consider. I am traveling alone, but I would be happy to engage a maid to act as chaperone. In any case, allow me to speak with my coachman."

Before Elizabeth could respond, Darcy bowed, striding towards the door. Elizabeth followed at a gentler pace, trailing after him until she reached the vestibule. Shaking her head, Elizabeth turned away from the window. What curious twist of fate had placed them both here at the same moment, after so many months apart? And now it seemed she was destined to remain in Mr. Darcy's company for the foreseeable future. It was only up to her to determine whether it would be a few short hours in a carriage, or an entire night spent together in this inn.

Moving to a wooden bench tucked into a nearby alcove, Elizabeth sat. For seven months, she had anticipated this encounter with equal parts desire and dread. But now that the initial meeting was over, Elizabeth reflected that Mr. Darcy seemed, at least in essentials, much as he ever was: aloof, arrogant, overbearing. He had certainly been indignant when he learned that she was traveling unaccompanied. No doubt further evidence of her total want of propriety.

And yet he had been, if not kind, unquestionably polite —inquiring after her family, congratulating her on her sister's marriage, extending his best wishes to Mr. and Mrs. Collins. And of course, offering his protection. Insisting upon it, despite everything she had done. How ironic that the man she had once accused of behaving in an ungentlemanlike manner turned out to hold a stronger code of honor than anyone she had ever known. Oh, how that comment must have rankled!

And she had noticed something else in his behavior today, a sort of quiet sadness, a strange sense of vulnerability. Or, perhaps it was remorse.

When the front door opened a short time later, Elizabeth's mind was made up. Standing, she walked rapidly in his direction. "Mr. Darcy, I have decided to accept your offer of transport, if you are still agreeable?"

The gentleman rewarded her with a curt nod. "I am. And my coachman assures me the roads are passable. I shall speak to the proprietor about securing one of his maids."

He turned to go, but Elizabeth reached out, catching his sleeve. "I thank you for your concern, sir, but there is no need." Glancing around the bustling entryway she added, "I doubt a maid could be freed from her duties under the present conditions."

Slowly, Darcy lowered his gaze, staring down at Elizabeth's gloved hand, which still rested upon his arm.

She thought she could see him swallow before he lifted his eyes to regard her with an impassive stare. "Pray, do not concern yourself, Miss Bennet. I am certain something can be arranged."

Elizabeth looked up at him, a slight frown puckering her brow. Could he not see that the inn was overcrowded and servants in short supply? Clearly, there were no maids to spare. But just as she opened her mouth, understanding dawned. Of course. Anything can be arranged when enough money changes hands. Her mouth turned down at the edges. Although she knew the presence of a neutral third party would make the journey more pleasant for both of them, she had no intention of allowing Mr. Darcy to spend an exorbitant sum, simply to ensure her comfort.

"I appreciate your concern for my reputation, Mr. Darcy, but I assure you, I do not require the services of a maid."

For a moment, Darcy paused, and Elizabeth watched as a mixture of emotions played across his features.

"Very well," he eventually answered. "As you wish, Miss Bennet."

Elizabeth released his arm, and Darcy stepped away.

"I shall see to your luggage. The carriage is already prepared."

And without a backwards glance, Mr. Darcy headed for the door.

CHAPTER 2

Ignoring the presence of his footman, Darcy steered Elizabeth through the crowded courtyard, opening the carriage door and handing her inside.

"A moment, Miss Bennet," he murmured, before retreating to converse with his driver and footman several yards away.

Inside the coach, Elizabeth slid across the thickly padded seat. On the opposite side of the glass, scattered snowflakes continued to swirl, but it was not the weather that held her attention. Her eyes remained fixed upon Mr. Darcy and a strange sensation settled in her stomach.

Hastily she lowered her gaze. It would not do to be caught staring! Seeking a distraction, Elizabeth turned to survey the spacious compartment. Much she would have expected, Mr. Darcy's coach was comfortable and well-appointed, but neither was it gaudy nor overly ostentatious. Thankfully, it bore no resemblance to the barouche-landau that Lady Catherine de Bourgh had condescended to send them home in when the party from the parsonage had dined at Rosings and a sudden rainstorm had prevented them from returning on foot. On that occasion, Mr. Collins had been so overcome with her ladyship's generosity, as well as the elegance of the equipage, he had scarcely been able to contain his effusions. But for Elizabeth's part, the vivid red upholstery and gilded interior had been enough to bring on a headache. Looking around now at the deep-green cushions and gleaming wood paneling of Mr. Darcy's carriage, Elizabeth noted that it was much like the gentleman himself—stately, yet unassuming—and she felt herself begin to relax.

A noise outside pulled Elizabeth from her thoughts and she turned to see Mr. Darcy entering the coach. Tucking his tall frame into the rear-facing seat he allowed the footman to latch the door before removing his hat and reaching up to brush a dusting of snow from his shoulders. An unexpected warmth spread through Elizabeth's body and she quickly looked away. Through the glass, she watched the coachman approach the box, and for the first time it occurred to her to wonder how Mr. Darcy had explained her presence to his attendants. Did they think it odd that he had entered the inn alone and returned with an unaccompanied young lady? Her cheeks grew hot at the thought. Perhaps she had been too hasty in refusing the gentleman's offer to procure one of the Bell's maids... But before she could dwell any further on the subject, her companion rapped upon the roof, and the carriage lurched forward, causing Elizabeth to release a breath. Well, she would simply have to make the best of things. It was only a few hours, after all.

Darcy sat with his right side pressed against the carriage door, his entire body stiff with tension. How he was going to make it through the next few hours, he could not possibly imagine. Turning away, he drew a shallow breath and his pulse quickened. In the tight confines of the coach, Elizabeth's scent enveloped him—a mixture of wildflowers and citrus, and something else he couldn't quite name. Closing his eyes, he stifled a groan. God help him, he was still in love with her. Despite his initial ire, the passage of time had done nothing to alter this simple fact, nor had it served to diminish the power she held over him. *If she only knew...* If she only knew, she would laugh herself silly. What kind of besotted fool persisted in loving a woman who had made it abundantly clear she detested the very sight of him?

As if to emphasize his thoughts, Elizabeth released an uneven sigh and Darcy winced at the sound. Devil take it! He should never have insisted she accompany him. Having her in such close proximity now that he knew her true feelings was the worst type of torment.

Against his better judgment, he shifted his gaze, and the air seemed to leave his body. She was even more beautiful than he remembered. Out of the corner of his vision, he studied her, instantly drawn by her magnificent eyes. When he had first made her acquaintance, he believed them to be brown, but in reality, they were a deep hazel-green, with flecks of amber radiating outwards from the pupils. When she was angry, they seemed to darken, but here in the mid-day light, they sparkled like cut crystal. He knew he should look away, but it was impossible. Instead, his head swiveled in her direction and he drank her in—like a drowning man granted a breath of air after too long beneath the surface of the sea.

A handful of hours. That was all he had before she would be gone from his life forever.

Elizabeth turned away from the snow-flecked glass. Across the carriage, Mr. Darcy was staring at her, his expression rigid. *Likely already regretting his decision to have me accompany him,* she thought ruefully. At first, he did not appear to notice her returning his gaze, but after a moment his eyes refocused and the intensity reflected in his expression caused Elizabeth to shiver.

Darcy blinked. "Miss Bennet, I beg your pardon. You are cold. Here… there are some rugs beneath the seat."

Without waiting for an answer, he removed a thick blanket, reaching to tuck the soft fabric around her legs before withdrawing to his own corner of the compartment.

Elizabeth murmured her thanks, but quickly looked away. Outside, an icy snow continued to pummel the carriage as her own words echoed mercilessly inside her head.

From the very beginning of my acquaintance with you... your arrogance, your conceit, and your selfish disdain for the feelings of others, were such as to form... an immoveable dislike...

Elizabeth cringed. Of course, she was aware of her quick temper—goodness knows her mother had criticized her for it often enough. But Elizabeth had always considered herself to be fair, and above all, kind. Yet, when it came to Mr. Darcy, she had jumped to conclusions without possession of the facts, and in so doing had caused the gentleman who sat across from her the worst sort of pain. A gentleman who, Elizabeth now suspected, rarely made his true feelings known to anyone, had bared his heart, and she had trampled on it in the most callous manner. What did it cost this man to set aside his pride and wounded feelings? To offer his assistance now, after the way she had treated him? For while it was true that his proposal had been insolent and offensive, her response had been spiteful and cruel—and this she could not condone.

Straightening her shoulders, Elizabeth turned away from the door.

"Mr. Darcy, I hope you will forgive me, but I am a selfish creature, and therefore unable to continue further without apologizing to you for the uncivil words I spoke... when last we met. I have regretted my behavior for many months. In truth, I cannot think of it without mortification."

To Elizabeth's surprise, an intense flush colored Darcy's cheeks. He lowered his gaze before meeting her eyes with a serious expression. "Miss Bennet, I am the one who is to be sorry. My manner of address on that occasion was inexcusable. You had every right to speak to me as you did."

"I am afraid I cannot agree with you, sir, but I thank you for saying so." After a moment she added, "Since reading your letter, I have been ashamed of holding Mr. Wickham in such high regard. I was taken in by his empty flattery and was quick to judge a situation about which I was woefully ill-informed. I deeply regret any pain I may have caused you by defending him."

Darcy grimaced. "I fear, again, I owe you an apology, Miss Bennet. It was wrong of me to present you with such a letter. At the time, I was not even certain you would read it. In truth, I have often hoped that you did not."

"I was not certain myself when you handed it to me," Elizabeth answered. "I was still very angry."

"And, may I ask... did you read the letter in its entirety?"

At Elizabeth's nod, Darcy looked away. "Then again, I must beg your pardon. I do not remember all that I wrote, but I know I dwelt on things that should not have been said once, let alone repeated. The only part of that letter about which I feel no remorse is the accounting of my dealings with Mr. Wickham. I believed it essential that you were acquainted with the truth about that gentleman, not only to absolve my own conduct, but so you might guard yourself against him."

Elizabeth sighed, shaking her head. "I was very foolish, about so many things. I wanted to believe Mr. Wickham because he flattered my vanity. My judgment was faulty in every particular and I am glad to have an opportunity to acknowledge it. I had hoped to do so months ago, at my sister's wedding, but you were not in attendance."

Upon uttering this last, she regarded him curiously, and Darcy flinched. "Yes, I... Unfortunately, estate business made it impossible for me to travel at that time."

They continued in silence for several minutes before Darcy leaned forward, saying softly, "You must not blame yourself for anything to do with Wickham, Miss Bennet. The man is a practiced deceiver. A great number of discerning people have been taken in by him."

"That is kind of you to say, sir. In truth, after reading your letter I dreaded coming into contact with Mr. Wickham again, and had resolved to avoid him as long as possible. However, soon after my return to Longbourn, the militia removed to Brighton, and not long after that we received word that Mr. Wickham had gone missing from his unit. To my knowledge, he has not been seen since."

Across the carriage, Darcy tensed. "Oh?"

Elizabeth waited for him to continue, but when he remained silent she said, "There was some talk of Mr. Wickham owing debts to many of the local shopkeepers, but after the gentleman's disappearance, they were mysteriously paid by an anonymous benefactor."

In truth, the report circulating was that it had been Mr. Darcy who had paid off Wickham's debts, but of course Elizabeth did not say so. Though if his reaction to her inquiries was any indication, she was inclined to agree with the rumors.

Darcy frowned. "Mr. Wickham is a clever man. He

generally manages to find others to do his bidding. I am only sorry that my own negligence enabled him to take advantage of the good people of Meryton in the first place."

"Mr. Darcy," Elizabeth answered quietly, "Mr. Wickham is not your responsibility. In any case, I ceased thinking about him long ago and would prefer to put the entire business behind us. Perhaps we can agree to a new beginning?"

Darcy's eyes widened and a small smile lifted his cheeks. "I would like that, Miss Bennet."

Elizabeth returned his smile but their dialogue lapsed, each of them at a loss as to how to navigate this new and unexpected truce. The rattle of the carriage mingled with the steady beat of the horse's hooves, filling the air left empty of speech.

"Miss Bennet, pray, do not feel it necessary to keep up a conversation. You are more than welcome to rest, or read if you like. I have several volumes here, if any would be of interest?" Altering his position, Darcy reached down, extracting a stack of books from a basket underneath the seat and offering them up for Elizabeth's inspection. To her surprise, the titles varied to include a history of the Roman Empire, a book on animal husbandry, and a fat tome entitled *Letters from an American Farmer*.

Studying the spines over Elizabeth's shoulder, Darcy's complexion heightened. "Forgive me, it has been a while since I replenished the collection. I thought there might be some poetry..." he began to root through the basket, but Elizabeth laughed, relaxing into her seat.

"Do not concern yourself. As it happens I enjoy many types of books, and would not hesitate to pick up any of those titles, however, as I am known to be a *great reader*, you must realize that I would never travel without something of my own." Turning to her open satchel, she produced a worn leather volume and Darcy leaned forward.

"*Gulliver's Travels?*"

Studying his expression, Elizabeth nodded. "As you see. Have you read it?"

"Of course."

"But you are surprised that I should be reading it." It was a statement and not a question.

"No. I...."

"What were you expecting, Mr. Darcy? *Clarissa?* Or perhaps *The Romance of the Forest?*"

Darcy instantly colored and Elizabeth laughed again. "Very well, if I am honest, I enjoyed both those novels. As I said, I take pleasure in many types of books."

"Do your sisters like to read as much as you do?"

Elizabeth shook her head. "No. Jane enjoys gothic novels and some poetry. My sister Mary prefers scripture. But my two youngest sisters do not read at all."

"That is a shame." Darcy paused. "And how do you find Swift's work?"

"Oh, I like it very well. I have read this particular volume before, but I am finding new meaning upon a second examination."

Darcy studied her for several moments before asking if

she made a habit of reading books more than once and was rewarded with a look of genuine astonishment.

"Of course! I believe it takes several readings to fully comprehend the nuances of any book. And when I am traveling, I always bring along an old favorite as opposed to something new. I find it comforting, even if it does severely hinder my progress."

Darcy angled his head and Elizabeth continued, "You see, many years ago, I set the goal of reading every book in Papa's library before I was..." Elizabeth flushed. "That is, before I left Longbourn. At the time, it did not seem like an insurmountable task, but my father has continued to add to his collection, so I now find myself woefully behind."

Darcy appeared to be holding back a laugh. "That is indeed a lofty objective."

"You needn't be alarmed, Mr. Darcy. Papa's library is nothing to Pemberley's, I am sure. But then there are quite a few volumes in French and Latin, and I find my language skills have not been up to the challenge."

Darcy did laugh then, leaning back against the squabs and stretching his long legs out in front of him. "And which have been your favorites?"

"Oh, dear! That is like asking a mother to choose her favorite child. However, if pressed, I am quite fond of Shakespeare, particularly his comedies, and I have enjoyed Defoe's work a great deal." After a moment she added, "*Tom Jones* has been a recent favorite." She cocked her head, waiting for Mr. Darcy's censure, but he only looked back at her curiously and so Elizabeth continued, "I know it is not Plato, but as I believe I have mentioned, I do dearly love to laugh."

"Have you read Plato, then, Miss Bennet?"

"Certainly, sir. *The Republic* is one of my father's favorite texts. I was practically raised on it."

Darcy opened his mouth to answer, but a loud crack caused them both to start. The carriage slid sideways and Elizabeth gasped. Before she could fully comprehend what was happening, Mr. Darcy threw himself across the compartment, grabbing her roughly by the arms and pulling her away from the door. The ground beneath them gave way and the carriage tilted, crashing onto its side and rolling them over. Elizabeth's head hit the ceiling, and a scream tore from her throat.

And then there was nothing.

CHAPTER 3

Elizabeth shivered, turning onto her side. Why was she so cold? She must have left the window open, or perhaps she had forgotten to bank the fire. She stretched out a hand, groping for the bedclothes, but what her fingers found was not warm and soft, but rather cold and wet. Her eyes opened and she peered at her surroundings. Where was she? Not in her bedchamber at Longbourn.

No, she was outside, surrounded by trees. And it was snowing.

She struggled to sit, suddenly mindful of an intense throbbing in her temples. Looking around the small copse, she became aware of high-pitched screams echoing in the distance. Not human screams. No. These were the pitiful cries of an animal in pain. But there was another sound, too. A deep moaning coming from somewhere nearby. Pulling herself to her feet, Elizabeth began moving as rapidly as she was able in the direction of the second sound. She had not advanced many steps when she spotted its source—a man lying on his back. Elizabeth closed the space between them in several quick strides and her breath seized inside her throat. Mr. Darcy! Then she remembered. They had been traveling together in his carriage. And there had been an accident.

"Mr. Darcy?" Dropping to her knees, she placed her hand lightly upon the gentleman's shoulder. His eyelids fluttered, lifting briefly and then closing again. "Sir, can you hear me?"

Darcy turned towards her voice and his eyes gradually opened. Confusion clouded his gaze. "Elizabeth?"

Startled by the use of her Christian name, Elizabeth's own eyes widened, but she was too relieved that he was conscious and sensible to be overly bothered by the lapse in propriety. "Yes. How do you fare, sir? Are you injured?"

Darcy blinked up at her through the falling snow. "I... Where are we?"

"I cannot say, precisely. Somewhere in Kent, off the London road. There was an accident. Can you sit up?"

Darcy responded with a short nod, but when he attempted to raise his body, a sharp cry drew from his lips.

"Shh, do not move. I will go for help."

Elizabeth attempted to stand, but Darcy reached out, staying her movement. "You are bleeding."

Angling her head, Elizabeth studied her appearance. Her pelisse was ripped at the shoulder and her clothing wet and dirty, but she could see no evidence of blood.

"Your head."

Lifting her hand, Elizabeth winced as her fingers came in contact with the raw skin. Darcy fumbled with the buttons of his coat but instantly sucked in a breath, pain contorting his features. "There is a handkerchief. In my inside pocket."

Elizabeth hesitated and Darcy frowned. "Miss Bennet, you are injured. I would remove it myself if I was able to do so."

Elizabeth gave him a small smile and nodded, glad to see that he was back to addressing her in a more formal manner. Leaning forward, she tentatively stretched out her hand, slipping it inside his coat and feeling for the inner-pocket. Her fingers brushed the soft fabric of his shirt where it covered the muscles of his chest. Beneath that, she could feel the steady pounding of his heart. Locating a corner of the kerchief, she hurriedly withdrew her hand, pressing the folded cloth to her temple. Mr. Darcy gazed back at her with a stark intensity—his pupils dilated and his breathing rapid. Elizabeth opened her mouth, but the crack of pistol-fire silenced the words in her throat.

Their eyes locked and Elizabeth surged to her feet, running towards the sound. Nearing the road, she took in the wreckage of the carriage. Beside it, one of the horses lay on its side, a dark stain pooling in the fresh snow. Mr. Darcy's footman stood next to the animal, a pistol held limply in his hand. Only then did Elizabeth realize that the screams had stopped.

The man looked up. "His front legs were broken."

Elizabeth nodded, staring past the footman. Several feet away, the remaining horse was tethered to a tree, tossing its head. Her gaze continued to move in the direction of the road, stopping when it reached the place where a dark shape marred the snowy landscape. No, not a shape. A body. Elizabeth's breath hitched and her strangled cry echoed in the frosty air.

Slipping the pistol into the waistband of his livery, the footman stepped forward, gently taking her elbow. "Come, miss. There is nothing to be done here. We should see to the master."

Numbly, Elizabeth nodded, allowing him to lead her a short distance before stopping to peer over her shoulder.

"Miss?"

Elizabeth blinked, realizing the footman had been speaking to her. "I beg your pardon, I was not... What did you say?"

"Mr. Darcy, miss. Have you seen him?"

"Oh! Yes, of course." Elizabeth shook her head, snapping out of her daze. There was nothing more to be done for the coachman, but Mr. Darcy was badly injured and in need of immediate attention. She should never have left him on his own! A ripple of alarm made her quicken her pace, the footman hard at her heels.

When Mr. Darcy came into view, relief swept through her. Somehow, the gentleman had managed to pull himself into a seated position, although his body was slumped, his lips pressed into a flat line.

As soon as they were within earshot, Darcy spoke. "Thomas, what happened? I heard a shot."

"One of the horses, sir. His forelegs were broken. I had

to put him down. The other animal appears to be uninjured, merely frightened."

Darcy nodded, glancing over Elizabeth's shoulder. "Where is Johnson?"

Elizabeth's eyes darted to the liveried servant who shifted on his feet. After a moment, the footman shook his head.

Darcy drew a ragged breath and his eyes momentarily slid closed. "What caused the accident?"

"I believe the front axle cracked, sir. I suspected it from the sound, but the carriage is badly damaged now from the crash."

Darcy nodded, staring off into the distance. When he spoke, his voice was gruff. "Thomas, you must get Miss Bennet safely away from here. Walk to the road and wave down a passing carriage. If no one is about, you will have to take the horse and go for help."

The man nodded, preparing to depart, but Elizabeth held up her hand, staying his progress. "Mr. Darcy, the road is quite deserted and we cannot leave you here."

"I will manage. Please, it will be dark soon."

"All the more reason not to abandon you to the elements." Elizabeth turned to the footman and spoke with quiet authority. "Thomas, if you would be so good as to fetch the horse?"

The man's gaze drifted to his employer and Darcy nodded his consent. When the footman had gone, Mr. Darcy turned back to Elizabeth. "How is your head?" he asked quietly.

Elizabeth explored her brow with the pads of her

fingers. It hurt quite a bit more than she cared to divulge, but she schooled her features into a neutral expression. "It appears to have stopped bleeding." Eager to change the subject, she continued, "We should try to get you on your feet. Do you think you could stand if I were to assist you?"

Darcy looked momentarily doubtful but responded with a nod. Slipping her hands beneath his arms, Elizabeth attempted to pull him up, but immediately released her hold at his howl of pain.

Studiously avoiding her eyes, Darcy murmured, "Forgive me, Miss Bennet. Perhaps we should wait for my man to return."

The two sat in silence until Thomas reappeared, leading the remaining horse by a piece of rope he had tied to the animal's bridle. Handing the lead to Elizabeth, he crouched beside his master, carefully hauling him to his feet. Darcy hissed in pain, pressing his back against a nearby tree. Taking a moment to steady his breathing, he turned to face Elizabeth. "Miss Bennet, I appreciate your consideration, but I fear my leg is broken. I will not be able to mount, especially without the aid of a saddle."

Elizabeth glanced nervously from one man to the other. If it was true that Mr. Darcy was not able to lift his leg over the horse's back, she could see no way for them to move him in his current condition. However, she would not leave him here to fend for himself. She would simply insist on waiting while the servant sought help. But before she could say as much, Mr. Darcy's footman stepped forward.

"Leave it to me." Leading the gelding a few paces away,

he reached inside the pocket of his coat, producing an apple and a silver flask.

Darcy wrinkled his brow. "Are you proposing to intoxicate the beast?"

"No, sir. The brandy is for you. Even if we are able to get you onto the animal's back, the trip is bound to be painful with your injuries."

Darcy started to object, but seemed to think better of it, accepting the flask and taking a small swallow.

Meanwhile, the footman approached the fractious gelding. Speaking in gentle tones he patted the animal's neck, holding the fruit just out of the horse's reach. Tugging on the bridle, he motioned to Elizabeth, instructing her to simultaneously push down on the horse's withers. She hesitated only a moment before stepping forward to do as she was asked. It took several attempts but eventually the gelding's front legs buckled and the animal staggered into a clumsy bow.

"That is remarkable," said Darcy. "Where did you acquire such a skill?"

The footman shrugged. "My father, sir. Generally speaking, it is not an advisable way to mount. It will be difficult for him to stand, especially with your weight on his back. But given the circumstances, I do not believe we have much choice."

Thomas came to his master's aid, but even with the animal lowered to its knees, Darcy could not raise his injured leg high enough to get it over the horse's broad back.

"Forgive me," Thomas apologized, "but I think you will have to sit sideways."

Darcy frowned but eventually consented, allowing his man to assist him up.

Even with this small movement, the pain was obviously severe and Elizabeth could see that it took everything Mr. Darcy had not to cry out. When he was finally situated, Thomas tugged on the bridle and the gelding lurched to its feet.

The horse took a few tentative steps with Darcy clutching at the animal's mane. "Thomas, I appreciate your help, but I am not certain I will be able to go any distance in this position."

"Aye, I would have to agree, sir. If I may, when I went to retrieve the animal, I noticed a small cottage through the trees. It is farther from the road, but perhaps we might take shelter there until the weather improves. It may be some time before another carriage travels this way and the nearest inn is at least ten miles off."

Elizabeth studied her companion as Darcy massaged his forehead. Thomas was undoubtedly correct. From what she had observed, there was no way Mr. Darcy would be able to travel ten miles. In truth, he did not look as though he was in any shape to travel ten steps.

"Yes. I think that would be best," Darcy finally answered. Tilting his chin, he indicated that the footman should begin leading the horse and then reached into his pocket, removing the flask. After a few moments, he allowed his eyelids to close, but they snapped open at Elizabeth's sharply drawn breath.

The party drew to a halt.

Before them lay the shattered carriage and the fallen horse. Several feet away, a still form was shrouded with one of the blankets from the coach, the thick rug already coated in a fine dusting of snow. The footman turned, clearly intending to lead them in the opposite direction, but Mr. Darcy's voice cut through the frigid air.

"Thomas, stop."

The footman did as he was directed, glancing up at his master.

Darcy's gaze returned to the body of the coachman. "We cannot leave him here. Not out in the elements like this. Can you place him inside the compartment?"

Thomas looked back at the broken conveyance, which was tipped precariously onto its side. "I believe so, sir, though it would be better if I could right the carriage."

Elizabeth stepped forward, and Darcy tensed. "No. I will do it. Thomas, help me down."

But Elizabeth continued walking in the direction of the coach. "Mr. Darcy, need I remind you that you can barely stand? You will stay where you are. Thomas... "

The footman paused before casting an apologetic glance in Darcy's direction and joining Elizabeth.

Darcy frowned, but remained where he was. Elizabeth and the manservant worked together, finally managing to roll the carriage to an upright position. Then Thomas carefully moved the body.

Elizabeth watched in silence, brushing at the tears that swam at the corners of her vision. When she glanced up, Mr. Darcy was staring at her, his jaw rigid.

Turning away, Darcy offered his footman a brisk nod. "Very well. Thomas; pray, lead on."

CHAPTER 4

E lizabeth trudged through the driving snow, the sharp wind biting at her neck and cheeks. They had been walking for less than a quarter of an hour, but her boots were already soaked through and she could no longer feel her feet. Every now and then she glanced up at Mr. Darcy, but his eyes remained tightly shut, his expression wooden. She was about to ask the footman how much farther they had to go, when she spotted a squat cottage nestled amongst the trees. Her gaze lifted to the thatched roof. No smoke rose from the stone chimney.

The party drew to a halt and Darcy opened his eyes. The footman approached the door, rapping loudly on the rough wood. Elizabeth stepped up to the front window, but the glass was shuttered from the inside.

From behind her, Mr. Darcy barked out instructions.

"Thomas, go around the back. If the door is locked, break a window."

Elizabeth shivered, for once not put off by Mr. Darcy's domineering manners. Surely whoever owned the cottage would understand their need to take shelter. The sound of breaking glass cut through the gloomy silence and moments later the latch was lifted and the door pulled open.

Darcy shifted on the horse's back, turning to face the entrance to the modest dwelling.

"It appears to be unoccupied, sir."

"That is not surprising. Given where it is situated, this is most likely a hunting retreat."

The footman moved to help Darcy dismount, half carrying him across the threshold and settling him into one of the wing-backed chairs facing the hearth.

Pulling in a shallow breath, Darcy allowed his head to collapse against the back of his seat. Staggering pain assaulted him from all directions. It took every ounce of strength to keep from calling out. Lifting his gaze, he turned his attention to where Elizabeth stood, just inside the door. In the low light, her narrow shoulders trembled, and her breath made soft white puffs in the icy air.

Darcy's jaw tightened as he moved to face his footman. "Thomas, see if there is any dry wood. We need to get a fire going at once." Looking back at Elizabeth he added, "Miss Bennet, you must remove that wet cloak. You will become ill."

His voice seemed to snap Elizabeth out of her lethargy and she moved further into the room.

"I thank you, sir, but I will assist with the fire first."

"There is no need. Thomas is more than capable."

"I have no doubt of that, Mr. Darcy, but with two of us working, we can accomplish the task that much faster."

Darcy released a slow breath, wincing at the pain that seared his ribs. "Very well. But let my man handle the fire. Perhaps you might attempt to locate some candles? It is already growing dark."

Elizabeth opened her mouth, but quickly closed it again. Nodding her acceptance, she quit the room, returning a short time later with two long tapers. Setting them upon the mantle, Darcy watched as she shrugged out of her wet pelisse.

"Miss Bennet, come and warm yourself," he said, indicating the small blaze that Thomas had just started in the stone hearth. "You must be frozen."

Elizabeth approached the fire and the footman turned to face his employer.

"Sir, if I may, I think it would be best for me to ride to Bromley. You require a physician, and if I leave now, I believe I can still make it by nightfall."

Darcy tensed. He had already lost one man under his protection today. He would not risk another. "No. I will not have you out in this weather. We will all wait here until morning."

Thomas was silent, but his lips turned down at the corners.

From her seat by the hearth, Elizabeth cleared her

voice. "Thomas, would you be so good as to start a fire in the kitchen? I saw a tea caddy when I went in search of the candles. I believe we could all use some refreshment."

The footman readily agreed, withdrawing from the room, and Elizabeth slid to the edge of her chair. "Mr. Darcy, forgive me, but you do not look well. Now that we have taken shelter, I believe we should examine your injuries." Pulling up a footstool, she inclined her head in the direction of his injured leg. "May I?"

Darcy startled but after a moment nodded his agreement and Elizabeth carefully lifted his ankle. White-hot fire shot up his leg, and Darcy's grip tightened on the arms of his chair.

"Where is the pain?"

"Just above the ankle," he hissed, and Elizabeth nodded, catching her bottom lip between her teeth.

"I believe we must remove the boot, but I do not wish to pull on it."

Steeling himself against the pain he knew would follow, Darcy reached inside his coat, removing a small penknife. Elizabeth accepted it, opening the blade. Their eyes met before she turned her attention to his black Hessians. Darcy remained silent while Elizabeth worked, but after a few moments he was unable to prevent the muted groan that slipped from his throat.

Elizabeth looked up. "Forgive me, Mr. Darcy. I know this must hurt, but I can see the leg is already swelling. We must get the boot off while we still can."

Not trusting himself to speak, Darcy gave a short nod, and Elizabeth returned to her task. Eventually she had made a rough slit in the soft leather. Setting aside the knife, she cautiously tugged at his heel.

The resulting gasp caused her to jerk back in alarm, looking away as Darcy swore under his breath.

Snatching up the flask, Darcy removed the stopper, taking several rapid swallows. When the pain finally receded enough for him to speak, he glanced in Elizabeth's direction. "Forgive me, Miss Bennet. I am afraid I will not be able to remain silent. It would be best if you removed the boot as quickly as possible."

Elizabeth nodded. Once again, she lifted his foot, yanking backwards with such force she soon found herself on the hearth rug, the boot still clasped tightly in her hands.

Darcy let out an anguished cry, and seconds later Thomas arrived at a run from the other room.

Elizabeth scrambled to her feet as Darcy turned to face his man, assuring him through clenched teeth that all was well. The footman surveyed the scene before offering a bow and retreating to the corridor.

Setting aside the boot, Elizabeth placed her hands on Darcy's leg, gingerly exploring the firm muscles of his calf through his fine wool trousers. "I do not feel anything, and there is no blood. But I believe it would be best to view the injury to be certain." As soon as she said the words, Elizabeth's cheeks flushed scarlet and she quickly stood. "I will fetch Thomas. I am certain you would feel more comfortable with your manservant attending you from this point forward." She turned to go, but Darcy captured her hand, surprising them both.

"Miss Bennet, I am not opposed to you continuing, if it does not make you too uneasy?"

Elizabeth swallowed. "No, not at all." Taking a breath, she knelt once again beside the footstool, pulling the fabric of Darcy's expertly-tailored trousers away from his ankle and retrieving the penknife. It took only a few moments to open the seam up to his knee.

Peeling back the fabric, Elizabeth's eyes skimmed the exposed flesh, and Darcy wondered if she would now give up and fetch his footman. But a moment later he felt the gentle press of her fingers against his bare skin, and a moan rumbled in his throat.

Elizabeth's eyes lifted. "Forgive me, Mr. Darcy. The leg is almost certainly broken, but the bone is not protruding —which is good. But I would agree that the sooner it can be set by a physician, the better."

Darcy nodded numbly, grateful that Elizabeth had misinterpreted his reaction. In truth, while his leg burned like the very devil, Elizabeth's delicate fingers caressing his skin had given rise to an entirely different sensation. He forced his attention away from such thoughts.

From the doorway, Thomas coughed into his fist, causing both Darcy and Elizabeth to jump. Neither of them had noticed his return.

"Sir, I think it would be best if I went for assistance. If I can make it to the inn tonight, I can have a physician here at first light. Besides, there is nowhere to shelter the horse, and I do not like the idea of leaving him outside in this weather."

"Mr. Darcy, I would have to agree. You need medical

attention as soon as possible. It would not be wise to delay." Elizabeth's eyes moved to the window, and Darcy followed her gaze. Thomas had opened the shutters and even through the frosted glass, it was clear that the snowstorm had not abated. If anything, it looked worse than before.

Darcy frowned. After what they had already endured, he had serious qualms about sending his footman out in such treacherous conditions—not to mention the chance Elizabeth would be taking with her reputation if she remained alone with him overnight. He looked at her now, but if she had any misgivings, they were not apparent in her expression. His fingers moved to rub his brow. The unrelenting pain in his leg and ribcage were making coherent thought increasingly difficult.

"Miss Bennet, are you certain this is agreeable to you? I will understand if you would prefer for Thomas to remain."

"I am perfectly agreeable, Mr. Darcy. After all, if Thomas leaves now, we shall be rescued that much sooner."

Darcy's spine stiffened. Of course. She could not wait to be free of him, regardless of the method employed to achieve that end. He felt the muscles inside his neck tighten and he briefly looked away. God, what a fool he was. Rhapsodizing over the feel of her fingers against his skin, when she was only doing her duty. In truth, she wanted nothing more than to escape this nightmare as soon as humanly possible.

"As you wish, Miss Bennet."

Thomas shifted his attention from Darcy to Elizabeth and back again.

Tension hung heavy in the air and Elizabeth stood, moving in the direction of the corridor. "I am certain the two of you have matters to discuss. If you will excuse me, I will...have a look around." And then, like the worst sort of coward, she hastily quit the room.

It did not take Elizabeth long to explore the remainder of the small cottage. Besides the front parlor, there was one bedchamber, sparsely furnished, a cramped dressing room, and a surprisingly large kitchen where she found a well-stocked larder. After filling an old copper kettle with snow collected from the back garden and hanging it over the fire to heat, she made her way to a corner of the room, lowering herself into one of the high-backed chairs surrounding an old wooden table.

She had made Mr. Darcy angry. She hadn't meant to. Was it simply that she had sided with his footman about going for help? Or was he offended by her impatience to be away from the cottage—away from him? She shook her head. No, she could not believe it. Certainly he would be as eager as she was to remove himself from such an awkward situation.

The soft whistling of the kettle tugged Elizabeth from her ponderings. Crossing to the pantry, she raised herself onto the balls of her feet, reaching for the tea caddy which had been placed on one of the upper shelves. But before her fingers closed around the lacquered box, a sharp pain caused her to flinch. Elizabeth pushed up her sleeve, stretching her neck to peer over her shoulder. To her surprise, a lengthy gash ran down the outside of her arm where an angry bruise was beginning to form just above her elbow.

A sudden movement drew Elizabeth's attention to the center of the room. Mr. Darcy stood framed in the open door, his tall figure blocking out the light from the passageway.

Elizabeth jumped, tugging at her sleeve. "Mr. Darcy! You should not be walking around!"

Darcy took a shaky step, gripping the handle of the fire-iron he was using for support, but his eyes remained fixed on Elizabeth's sleeve. "You are injured."

Elizabeth colored. "It is nothing. Only a scratch. Pray, sit. I was just preparing our tea."

Darcy dropped into the seat Elizabeth indicated, his mouth flattened into a firm line.

"Did Thomas leave?" Elizabeth asked, retrieving the box of tea and busying herself with the kettle. "I thought I heard the door." Elizabeth looked up and Darcy offered a terse nod. "Oh. I had intended to offer him some refreshment."

"Do not concern yourself. He was impatient to depart."

Elizabeth reached for a teacup, surprised to see that her fingers trembled.

Narrowing his gaze, Darcy pulled himself to his feet. "Miss Bennet, I think you should sit."

Elizabeth blinked at him before slowly sinking into a

chair on the opposite side of the table. "I… I do not know what is the matter. I feel rather dizzy all of a sudden."

Darcy frowned. "The events of the day are catching up with you. You have had a shock." He reached for the teapot, splashing hot liquid into a cup. Pulling the flask from his pocket, he dispensed a generous amount of brandy into the tea before passing the cup into her hands. "Here, drink this."

Elizabeth looked at him for a moment before wrapping her fingers around the heavy porcelain and taking several rapid swallows. The warm liquid scalded her throat but she continued to drink until the cup was empty.

Darcy drew his chair alongside hers. "Let me see your arm."

"There isn't any need. I told you, it is only a scrape."

Darcy gazed back at her, his expression unyielding. "Miss Bennet."

Releasing a soft huff, Elizabeth pushed up her sleeve.

Darcy stretched out his hand, gently running his fingers along the rough skin and Elizabeth's pulse fluttered inside her throat.

"You are correct, it does not look serious. But you should clean the wound. Have you more water?"

Swallowing her discomfiture, Elizabeth nodded, moving to the fire and filling a small basin. Returning to the table, she reached for one of the linen towels resting on the sideboard, but Darcy pulled the cloth from her fingers. Dipping it into the water, he pressed it gently to the abrasion.

"Does it hurt?"

"No," she whispered. "Not much."

"How about your head?"

Elizabeth touched her temple. "I will confess to a bit of a headache, but otherwise I am well."

Darcy set aside the damp cloth and Elizabeth slowly rolled down her sleeve. They regarded each other for several moments before Darcy released an anguished groan, dropping his head into his hands.

Elizabeth stood, a knot of fear instantly forming in her chest. "Mr. Darcy? Are you in pain?"

He shook his head, but when he lifted his eyes, Elizabeth could see genuine torment reflected in his gaze.

"This is my fault. I never should have suggested that we travel in this weather. If it were not for me, you would be safe at the Bell." He paused before adding in a choked whisper, "And a good man would not be dead."

Instinctively, Elizabeth stretched out her hand, allowing her fingers to settle on his shoulder. "Sir, you take too much upon yourself. It is indeed a horrible thing that a man lost his life today, but it was an accident. That axle could have cracked just as easily if the weather were fair."

"You are too generous, Miss Bennet. The fact remains that you were injured because I insisted you accompany me."

Elizabeth opened her mouth, but as she did, a memory prickled at the corners of her consciousness, and her breath stilled inside her lungs.

"You grabbed me. In the carriage. Right before the crash."

Darcy's head jerked up, and his countenance visibly paled. "Dear God. Did I hurt you?"

Slowly, Elizabeth shook her head as everything came flooding back: Mr. Darcy's strong hands drawing her to the center of the compartment, shifting their positions to put himself between her and the door as the carriage rolled over on its side.

"You pulled me away from the window. You switched places with me."

"But your injuries... The bruises, on your arm..."

"Mr. Darcy, you did not cause me any harm. I think you may have saved my life."

"Miss Bennet, were it not for me, you would not have been in danger in the first place."

Elizabeth began to speak, but before she could gather her thoughts, a low rumbling filled the air, breaking the tension.

"One of us is hungry, I think."

Darcy colored, but seemed glad to have a turn in the conversation. "It would appear so. I do not suppose there is anything to eat inside those cupboards?"

"Oh, but there is!" Hurrying to her feet, Elizabeth disappeared into the larder.

"Miss Bennet, are you well enough for that? I would not have you go to any trouble on my account."

"'Tis no trouble. I am quite recovered," she called, returning several minutes later, her arms laden with parcels. "Besides, you are not the only one who is hungry."

Turning back to the sideboard, Elizabeth surveyed her

haul: a sack of lentils, four slightly withered carrots, one large bag of onions, two turnips, and a length of dried meat. She gave this last a tentative sniff. Venison? Or possibly mutton? Not that it mattered, so long as it was edible.

Filling a pot with what remained of the water, she carefully hung it above the fire. Surely something that passed for a meal could be fashioned from the assembled ingredients. Reaching for a knife, she began to peel the onions, sending up a silent prayer of thanksgiving for all the days she had spent hiding out in the Longbourn kitchens.

Behind her, Darcy shifted in his chair, and although he remained silent, Elizabeth could feel his impenetrable gaze upon her back.

The onion she had been about to cut skittered across the worktop. Darcy leaned forward, catching the wayward vegetable before it could hit the floor. Elizabeth flushed, taking it from his outstretched palm and murmuring her thanks before hastily returning to her task. She worked in silence for several minutes before Mr. Darcy cleared his throat.

"Miss Bennet, is there anything I might do to assist?"

"No, no," she answered quickly. "I have things well in hand." Taking up the sack of lentils she scooped out several large spoonfuls, hesitating briefly before tossing them into the pot.

A smile twitched at the corner of Darcy's lips. "Miss Bennet, do you know what you are doing?"

Elizabeth twisted around to look at him. "Certainly."

From his place at the table, Darcy leaned back in his

seat. "Do you mind if I remain here while you cook?" he finally asked. "I would not wish to make you uneasy."

"No, I am happy for the company. In any case, you should stay off that leg. Oh! I have totally forgotten!" Dropping the knife she had been using to chop carrots, she crossed the room, returning with a small bundle of toweling. "Ice. For your leg." Elizabeth smiled. "At least that is one thing we have in abundance."

Darcy relaxed back into his chair, accepting the cold compress, and Elizabeth returned to her task. When she had finally hung the heavy iron pot over the fire, she took the seat opposite Mr. Darcy, and the two spent the next hour in quiet conversation. Elizabeth rose several times to tend to their meal, and eventually a rich, earthy aroma settled in the air.

"You seem to know your way around a kitchen, Miss Bennet," Darcy offered, as Elizabeth used a long wooden spoon to stir the thick stew that was now bubbling over the embers of the fire.

"Does that shock you, Mr. Darcy?" she asked.

Darcy opened his mouth to answer but Elizabeth's laughter stilled the words on his tongue.

"Indeed, I suppose it *is* rather shocking," she said, covering the pot and coming to take the seat across from him. "My mother would die of mortification if she knew anything about it." At Darcy's confused expression, she continued, "If you were to speak to my mother, she would tell you that we were well able to keep a cook, and that none of her daughters had a thing to do in the kitchen." Elizabeth laughed. "What my mother does not know, is that I used to retreat to the kitchens at Long-bourn when I was a child and the weather did not permit me to go out of doors. Eventually, our cook took pity on me and agreed to teach me a few simple skills. I always thought the knowledge would be useful one day... and now you see it has been. Although I must confess, I always preferred assisting with the desserts. I'll have you know that I make an excellent pie, Mr. Darcy. Alas, the ingredients I require are not present. Perhaps some other time I will have the opportunity to bake one for you."

Darcy blinked back at her, but it wasn't long before Elizabeth's smile slipped and her expression grew somber. "Mr. Darcy, I feel I should apologize for what happened earlier. I assure you, I am not normally prone to swooning."

"Believe me, Miss Bennet, I never thought you were." Elizabeth dropped her gaze and Darcy leaned forward, his voice low and intent. "I know of no other woman who could have born up so admirably under today's circumstances. You have nothing to be ashamed of."

Elizabeth gazed back at him and warmth began building in her belly. Quickly, she slid out of her seat. Returning to the hearth, she lifted the cover off the pot and a savory aroma filled the kitchen.

"I believe our feast is ready, sir," Elizabeth announced, keeping her voice light. Darcy watched her as she ladled out the thick stew and set two steaming bowls upon the wooden table.

"You will have to pardon the simplicity of the meal,

Mr. Darcy. I am certain this is not what you are accustomed to."

"Not at all. I actually prefer simple food, and this looks excellent."

Elizabeth surveyed the dish in front of her as Darcy lifted his spoon. If she was being honest, she wasn't quite as confident as she had let on. While it was true that she had often assisted their cook, Mrs. Doyle, in the kitchens, she had never prepared a meal of any type entirely from scratch. And to think that for her maiden effort she was serving a stew of mysterious meat and questionable carrots to Mr. Darcy! Good heavens, the man probably had a French cook.

Across the table, Darcy swallowed his first mouthful and his eyes lit. "Miss Bennet, this is delicious."

Elizabeth flushed at Darcy's praise, and the two ate for a while in companionable silence. When Mr. Darcy had devoured the last morsel, he sheepishly asked for more, and Elizabeth stood to refill their bowls. Turning away from the hearth, she was surprised to see Mr. Darcy grinning back at her.

Elizabeth's brows lifted. "Might I ask what you find so amusing, sir?"

"Forgive me, I was just imagining how I would have fared if I had been stranded here with Miss Bingley rather than yourself. Besides the fact that it would have been a most unpleasant experience, I cannot think that I should have been treated to a meal such as this. As a matter of fact, I am quite certain we would have starved."

Elizabeth's bright laughter filled the air. "I am afraid

you are likely correct. I somehow doubt Miss Bingley has ever seen the inside of a kitchen!"

Elizabeth soon regained her seat and she and Mr. Darcy conversed amiably for the remainder of the meal. When they had both finished, Elizabeth stood to clear their dishes, taking them to the stone basin in the corner of the room. Rolling her sleeves, she proceeded to the hearth, heaving up the large pot of water she had hung there to heat.

Watching her, Darcy's expression sobered. "Miss Bennet, may I ask what you are doing?"

Elizabeth tilted her chin. "What does it look like I am doing, Mr. Darcy?"

"It looks like you are preparing to wash dishes."

"You are very perceptive, sir."

"Miss Bennet, that is not required of you."

Setting the pot back over the fire, Elizabeth turned to face her companion. "Oh? Have the servants arrived from Pemberley? Forgive me. I did not see them come in."

Darcy blew out a frustrated breath. "Miss Bennet, cooking is one thing. But I will not have you scrubbing pots like a scullery maid."

Irritation prickled beneath Elizabeth's skin and her expression darkened. Folding her arms, she attempted to regulate her temper. "Mr. Darcy, I realize that you are accustomed to having a large household to see to the less pleasant necessities of life, but as we are stranded here without the benefit of servants, I am afraid we must make do."

"I think you misunderstand me," Darcy replied, stiffly.

"What is there to misunderstand? Clearly you think this type of work is beneath your station, and my own. If it offends you to watch, pray, feel free to leave the room."

Darcy's eyes widened. "Is that what you think of me? That I believe honest, hard work is in some way demeaning?" When Elizabeth did not answer, he continued, "As it happens, I have nothing but respect for the individuals in my employ, and I would ask no task of a servant that I would not undertake myself, should it prove necessary." He took a breath, as if pausing to give himself a moment to think. "I beg your pardon. I believe I expressed myself poorly. It is only that I would prefer not to see you scrub pots after all you have been through today. I meant no offence."

Despite her ire, Elizabeth's gaze softened. "I appreciate your concern. But as I said, I am well recovered. It will not take long, and I would prefer to leave things as we found them."

Slowly, Darcy nodded. "Very well, I will concede. But then you must allow me to be of some assistance. May I dry for you? I think I should be able to manage that, even from my position here at the table."

Elizabeth's eyebrows lifted, practically reaching her hairline. Mr. Darcy, drying dishes? It was all she could do to keep her composure. "I... If you wish..." she finally sputtered. When Darcy nodded, she moved to the cupboard, collecting a stack of toweling and bringing it to where he sat. With the two of them working, the chore was finished in very little time. When all was in order, Elizabeth assisted Mr. Darcy to the parlor before heading to the corridor where Thomas had stacked the extra wood. In the small parlor she built up the fire before settling comfortably into one of the two armchairs facing the hearth. Across from her, Mr. Darcy stared into the flames and Elizabeth regarded him from the corner of her vision.

Outside, a harsh wind whistled in the trees, but within the tiny cottage, there was only silence.

Turning towards the hearth, Darcy focused his attention on the hiss and crackle of the fire. The throbbing in his leg was growing progressively worse, but he did not want to consume any more brandy. Being alone with Elizabeth was enough of a temptation without having his mind clouded by drink. His gaze wandered back to the place where she sat, bathed in the fire's amber glow. He wondered what she was thinking. Despite her bravado, the situation they found themselves in had to be unsettling for her— stranded in a cottage in the middle of the woods with a man she vehemently disliked. Heaven knows, if anyone found out, her reputation would be ruined. Darcy sighed. Not that he would have any difficulty doing the honorable thing and marrying her, but for the first time since his failed proposal, the thought gave him little pleasure. As much as he wanted her, knowing he would be forcing Elizabeth into a union she found reprehensible would be his undoing.

You could not have made me the offer of your hand in any possible way that would have tempted me to accept it. I had not known you a month before I felt that you were the last man in the world whom I could ever be prevailed on to marry...

The soft timbre of Elizabeth's voice drew him from his humiliating recollections and he pulled his gaze away from the flames.

"I beg your pardon, Miss Bennet. I was not attending. What were you saying?"

"I was just asking if you were too warm. Your face is flushed. Would you like to move farther from the fire?"

Darcy could feel the color in his cheeks deepen. "No. I am well."

Elizabeth nodded and the conversation lapsed. But after several minutes, Darcy sat forward in his chair.

"Miss Bennet, I realize the predicament in which we find ourselves must be distressing for you. I want to assure you that if it is within my power, no one will learn of this. Thomas will not speak of it, and with any luck we will be returned to the Bell first thing in the morning, with no one the wiser."

To Darcy's surprise, Elizabeth appeared disconcerted by this shift in the conversation.

"Thank you. I suppose I hadn't really considered..." Addressing her comments to his last statement she continued, "I did not think it was in your nature to be deceptive, Mr. Darcy. Did you not tell me once that you loathed disguise of any sort?"

Darcy looked away, squirming in his seat. Leave it to Elizabeth to remember every pompous statement he had ever uttered. Attempting to keep his voice even, he looked back at her, his expression earnest. "I did. But in this case, it cannot be helped. If anyone were to find out we spent the night here unchaperoned, your reputation would be beyond repair, and we would be compelled to marry. You do understand that?"

Elizabeth's eyes grew round and Darcy cleared his throat. When he continued, his voice had lost some of its edge. "Miss Bennet, as we are speaking of honesty, there is a matter that has been weighing on me. I feel I owe you an apology. For something I said to you, in the carriage."

"Oh?"

"Yes. I am afraid I was not truthful with you about my reasons for missing your sister's wedding. It was not business that kept me away."

Elizabeth studied him with an unreadable expression. "No, I did not think it was. But if there is an apology owing, it is to Mr. Bingley and my sister. I already knew you disapproved of the match, so it was no surprise to me that you chose not to attend."

"Is that what you think?"

Elizabeth lifted her hand in a small wave. "Pray, do not trouble yourself about it now. I am only grateful you did not stand in the way of—"

"Miss Bennet, again, you misunderstand. I did not keep my distance as a form of protest. I am very happy for Bingley and your sister. I was wrong about their affection for one another and I should not have interfered. I have told Bingley as much."

"But then, I do not understand..."

Darcy clasped his hands, leaning forward so that his elbows rested upon his knees. "I stayed away because I did not wish to make *you* uncomfortable. After we parted in the spring, knowing your feelings…" Elizabeth flushed a soft pink and Darcy averted his gaze. "It is just that I understood the event would be a special celebration for your family. I did not want my presence to mar your enjoyment of the day."

"But Mr. Bingley asked you to stand up with him! I know he was disappointed when you declined."

Darcy shrugged. "Bingley is the forgiving sort. And I wrote to express my well wishes."

"Still, he wanted you there," Elizabeth repeated. "You should not have stayed away because of me."

"Miss Bennet, I did not tell you this to make you uneasy. I merely wished for you to know that your happiness will always be of great importance to me. This will never change."

"I… Thank you," she whispered.

Darcy leaned his head against the worn upholstery. Briefly giving in to the pain, he allowed his eyes to slip closed for a moment.

"Mr. Darcy, you must still be in a good deal of discomfort. Perhaps some brandy in a cup of tea?"

Darcy opened his eyes. "No, I will save the brandy. But some tea would be welcome, if you will join me?"

Elizabeth nodded. Making her way to the kitchen, she returned shortly with the teapot and another bundle of ice for Darcy's leg. He watched as she poured out the tea, handing him his cup. Taking a small swallow, his mouth turned down at the corners.

"Miss Bennet, what is in here?"

Elizabeth tilted her head, regarding her own teacup. "It is willow-bark tea. I noticed it when I was going through the pantry earlier. My aunt used to make it when any of us were ill. It should help with the pain." She took a sip, attempting to disguise her own displeasure. "I am sorry it does not taste better."

Darcy studied her over the rim of his cup. "No doubt you are missing the lemon," he said, and Elizabeth gazed back at him with obvious surprise.

"I recall that that was how you usually took your tea when we were at Netherfield."

Elizabeth continued to stare before saying, "You are correct, sir. I am inordinately fond of lemons. I used to eat them whole when I was a child, much to the amusement of the rest of my family. However, I now content myself with lemon flavored confections and the occasional slice in a cup of tea."

Darcy took another swallow of the herbal mixture, stifling a grimace. "You seem quite knowledgeable on the topic of medicine, Miss Bennet."

Elizabeth lifted one shoulder. "My aunt's father was a physician. She picked up many useful remedies from him, which she has passed along to me. At Longbourn I am usually the one to assist when anyone is ill or injured. My mother is far too nervous and my father and youngest sisters have never taken an interest in such matters. Mary and Jane are some help, but I am afraid Jane gets faint at the sight of blood. So, you see, that leaves me. But I have always found it fascinating."

Darcy smiled. "Well, as the recipient of your expert care, you have my gratitude."

"And I am happy to be of service to you, sir," Elizabeth replied.

For some time after that, they sat gazing at the fire, each thinking their own thoughts. Darcy continued to sip his tea, slowly growing accustomed to the taste. Whether it was the herbal remedy or the brandy he had consumed earlier he could not say, but he found himself relaxing as the ache in his leg and ribcage gradually receded. As the quiet stretched on, Darcy remembered how Elizabeth had chastised him for his silence during their dance at the Netherfield ball. *I should say something,* he thought. Something to put her at ease.

Casting about for a neutral topic, he roughly cleared his throat. "Miss Bennet, you spoke of your aunt. Do you refer to the relations you are now traveling to visit in Town?"

Elizabeth looked up, clearly startled by this shift in the conversation. "Yes, sir. My uncle owns a business there. Jane and I have spent a considerable amount of time with them, ever since we were quite small. Though I suppose that will change now that Jane is married."

"Oh? Only Mrs. Bingley and yourself?" Darcy inquired. "What of the rest of your sisters?"

"No, only the two of us. It is rather a long story. I would not wish to bore you."

"Please. I would like to hear it."

Elizabeth studied him as if to judge the veracity of his words. "Very well." Nesting comfortably into the corner of her chair, she continued, "I suppose it began when my sister Kitty was born. My mother's confinement was a difficult one... To tell the truth, she was so ill the midwife insisted she have absolute peace and quiet. So, Jane and I were bundled off to stay with our Aunt and Uncle Gardiner in Town. Our younger sister Mary, who was still in the care of a nurse, was sent to our Aunt and Uncle Phillips, so that she might be closer to home. Kitty was delivered safely, but my mother took much longer to recover. Jane and I stayed in Town for the better part of a year, visiting home only briefly.

"Of course, my parents were warned not to attempt another child, but Mamma was determined to deliver a boy, since Longbourn is entailed to Mr. Collins, as you know." Darcy nodded and Elizabeth paused before saying, "By the time Jane and I were ready to return, our mother was increasing again and the situation was much the same. The nurse stayed on to care for Kitty and Mary, and Jane and I remained with the Gardiners who had become almost second parents to us by then. When Lydia was born, the midwife said it was a miracle Mamma survived." Elizabeth took a sip of her tea. "There were no more children after that. Eventually, Jane and I returned home, but by then our family relationships had permanently shifted. I think that is why Jane and I have always been especially close, having at one time been one another's sole companions. It is the same for Lydia and Kitty—Mamma has always doted on them as neither was expected to survive." Elizabeth sighed. "I am afraid poor Mary has always been wedged in the middle. I fear it has been difficult for her." Elizabeth finished her story, staring into the fire.

Darcy followed her gaze. Well, that explained a vast deal. Suddenly, Mrs. Bennet's nerves seemed more than justified. Of course, the woman's manners still left much to be desired, but Darcy could not help but admire her determination—both to produce an heir and then, when that failed, to see her daughters well-settled and adequately cared for. Aloud he said, "I can see how that must have been difficult for you."

Elizabeth glanced up at the sound of his voice. "No, I am grateful for the time I have been able to spend with the Gardiners." Tipping her chin up a notch she added, "They are wonderful people. Jane and I continued to visit them often, even once we had returned to Longbourn to live."

"You were traveling with your aunt and uncle earlier this summer, were you not?" Darcy asked. "I believe Bingley wrote about a trip to the Lakes?"

To Darcy's surprise, Elizabeth flushed.

"I... yes... That is, we were to travel to the Lakes, but my uncle was detained on business, so we were not able to journey quite so far as we had originally planned."

"Oh?"

Elizabeth's finger traced a slow circle around the edge of her cup. "Yes. We only went as far as Derbyshire. My aunt wished to visit the town where she was raised."

Darcy's eyes widened. "Your aunt hails from Derbyshire, Miss Bennet?"

"Yes. From Lambton, sir," Elizabeth answered,

watching as the significance of this statement registered in his eyes.

"But, that is only five miles from Pemberley!" Darcy could not believe what he was hearing. Had Elizabeth been in the nearest village when he had been holed up at Pemberley, despairing of never seeing her again?

"Yes, I know. Although I believe you were from home at the time we visited. At least that is what the house-keeper indicated."

Darcy startled. "You visited Pemberley?" he asked, and Elizabeth nodded.

"My aunt had toured the grounds several times as a girl, but had never been inside the house. She was eager to see it, and she thought I would enjoy the gardens there."

Darcy found himself leaning forward in his chair, the pain that had been practically unbearable a short time ago all but forgotten. "And did you?" he asked, hoarsely. "Enjoy the gardens, that is?"

Once again, Elizabeth's cheeks colored. "Yes, of course! But I think there are few who would not enjoy them. They are amongst the finest I have seen."

"And did you have the opportunity to tour the public rooms?" Darcy pressed, eager to hear everything. "I hope you found them to your satisfaction?"

Elizabeth's eyes brightened. "Oh, yes! The views from the music room were breathtaking. I am certain I would never get any practicing done if I had such a lovely prospect to distract me. And I especially enjoyed the portrait gallery."

At the mention of the gallery, Darcy recalled a conversation with his housekeeper shortly after his arrival at Pemberley the previous summer. Mrs. Reynolds had spoken of a small party that had toured the house the day before, mentioning that a young woman had claimed an acquaintance with him. At the time, Darcy had given the story little credence. He was used to unmarried ladies of the *ton* and their match-making mammas claiming a connection when no such relationship existed. But as he thought about it, he seemed to remember Mrs. Reynolds saying the young lady had taken a keen interest in the gallery, particularly in the portraits of Georgiana and himself.

Darcy looked up in confusion, realizing Elizabeth had been speaking to him. "My apologies, Miss Bennet, what were you saying?"

Elizabeth flushed. "Not at all, sir. I only wished to assure you that we never would have trespassed on your privacy had you been at home. I... I hope the idea of my visiting Pemberley does not distress you."

"On the contrary. You will always be welcome at Pemberley. My only regret is that I was not there to acquaint you with the estate myself. Perhaps another time..." his voice trailed off and Elizabeth looked away.

"Thank you."

The two sat quietly for several moments gazing at each other in the fire's golden glow.

"Mr. Darcy, if you are not feeling too fatigued, perhaps you could tell me a little more about Pemberley?"

"Certainly. What would you like to know?"

Elizabeth indicated that she was happy to hear whatever he was willing to share, and Darcy thought seriously for several moments before speaking.

"You mentioned your enjoyment of the gardens. Had I been present, there is one in particular I would have wished to show you. It is a walled garden some distance from the house, and one that is not open to the public. It is less formal than the gardens you toured, but we grow a wide variety of vegetation there. My mother had it designed when she first came to the estate as a young bride." Darcy smiled. "She spent many happy hours within those walls. She used to call it her refuge."

"It sounds lovely," Elizabeth murmured. After a moment she added, "You were close to your mother. I can tell."

Darcy nodded, his throat suddenly tight. "She was an extraordinary woman. Kind and generous. She adored art and music and nature in all its forms. She would take me on long walks when I was a boy. She taught me the names of all the plants and flowers. Though I learned the management of the estate from my father, I believe it is from my mother that I get my devotion to the land." He paused before continuing softly, "I still miss her very much."

"I cannot imagine the heartache of losing a parent," Elizabeth answered.

Darcy gazed back at her, but his mind was far away. "For many years I could not stand to visit that garden. After my father's death, I locked the gate. It was only this past summer that I began cultivating it again. I think it would make my mother happy to see it returned to its former glory." Darcy did not add that it was Elizabeth's refusal at Hunsford that had inspired him to revitalize his mother's garden. It had given him a purpose, a distraction at a time when he most needed one, and oddly it had made him feel closer to the woman he loved when he worked on it, alongside his gardeners. Somehow, he always pictured Elizabeth there, amongst the brightly colored blooms, her eyes sparkling with laughter. He turned his attention to the flesh and blood Elizabeth who smiled sleepily.

"Tell me more. How long has the estate been in your family?"

"Oh, many generations. My great, great, great grandfather purchased it on the occasion of his marriage. He came here from France…"

Elizabeth eyelids drifted shut, but Darcy continued to speak in a low murmur. The soft hum of his voice mingled with the crackling of the fire, and a profound sense of tranquility settled over the small parlor—as if all was exactly as it should be.

CHAPTER 5

The fire had long since burned down and the room was becoming cold. Darcy glanced over at Elizabeth, asleep in her chair. Several chestnut curls had escaped their pins and now rested against one rosy cheek. Even in repose, she was the most beautiful creature he had ever beheld. His eyes roamed her body, and warmth ignited in his chest. He would have liked to say that what he felt was a chaste sort of tenderness but strictly speaking, that would be untrue. He could not look at her—long lashes impossibly dark against her fair skin, the neckline of her gown slipping from one shoulder—and not feel a certain degree of carnal longing. But to his surprise, there was a stronger feeling holding the physical desire at bay. Watching Elizabeth, a fierce sense of protectiveness surged within him, and he knew in that moment that he would stop at nothing to keep her safe.

He turned his attention to the mantelpiece. The pistol

from the carriage still rested atop the roughhewn surface. He had attempted to press it upon his footman, but Thomas had refused the weapon. Now, Darcy was glad to have it. Elizabeth was under his care, and although he would gladly inflict bodily harm with his bare hands if it came to that, given his injuries, the pistol would make things easier.

His gaze returned to Elizabeth's sleeping form. As he watched, the shadow of a smile hovered at the corners of her lips and a feeling of guilt stirred in Darcy's chest. He should not be staring at her as she slept. Observing her in such a vulnerable state was clearly an invasion of her privacy. Such intimacies were the privilege of a husband— or a lover—and heaven knew he was neither of those. Nor would he ever be.

The muscles in his throat constricted and he forced himself to look away. No, that honor would belong to some other man.

Closing his eyes, Darcy drew a ragged breath. The scent of wood-smoke filled his lungs, mingling with the lingering aroma from their dinner. Ignoring the burning in his ribcage, he inhaled again, this time picking up the subtle hint of wildflowers and lemon. God, he needed to remember that smell!

A log popped against the grate and he opened his eyes. Across the room a fly buzzed, futilely thumping against the sealed windowpane. Fingering the armrests of his chair, Darcy stared at the once-bright colors of the hearth rug, long since faded to a single muted hue. Slowly he adjusted his position, turning to survey the modest parlor.

An old rocking chair sat beside a scarred wooden table and a small writing desk was tucked in a corner beneath the eaves.

It wasn't much, but he felt a sudden uncontrollable urge to memorize every detail. To imprint this place upon his consciousness, to hold it tight within his heart, so that someday, in ten or twenty or thirty years, when he was feeling sentimental, he could call up every sight and sound and smell and touch. Every precious moment of the one night he had been exactly where he longed to be—alone with the woman he loved.

A gust of wind rattled the shutters and Darcy shivered in his seat. The fire had all but gone out. Pulling himself awkwardly to his feet he approached the hearth, feeding logs to the glowing embers. Gritting his teeth against the ever-present pain, Darcy dropped back into his chair, reaching for the flask and draining the last of the brandy.

In the seat opposite, Elizabeth shifted in her sleep and Darcy sighed. He knew he should wake her. It was late and she should get some rest in a real bed. It was wrong to sacrifice her comfort for his own selfish pleasure.

Leaning forward, he softly called her name. When she did not wake, he reached out his hand, intending only to touch her wrist, but instead his fingers brushed against the silken texture of her gown where it covered her curled legs. Warmth radiated up his arm and he promptly withdrew his hand.

"Miss Bennet."

Elizabeth's eyelids fluttered and then opened. She

stared back at him in confusion before straightening her spine, one hand tugging at the neckline of her dress.

"Forgive me, I did not realize I was so tired. How long have I been asleep?"

"Not long," Darcy lied. "But it is late. You should retire."

Elizabeth glanced over at the hearth, the flames dancing in the grate. "Did you tend the fire? You should have woken me!"

"It was no bother. But I am afraid the fire in the bedchamber will have to be lit. Thomas laid it before he left."

Elizabeth stretched, arching her back like a cat, and Darcy nearly levitated out of his chair.

"I will attend to it now," she said, rising to her feet. "But then you must take the bed. You will be more comfortable if you can stretch out your leg."

Darcy shook his head, as much to clear the vision of Elizabeth's gown pulled tightly against the contours of her body as to contradict her words. "That will not be necessary. I am perfectly content here. The bedchamber is yours."

Elizabeth's fingers clenched at her sides. "Mr. Darcy—"

His gaze traveled to her small fists and his mouth crinkled at the corners. "Do you mean to fight me, Miss Bennet? I do not generally engage in fisticuffs with women, though in my current state, you are likely to best me."

Elizabeth's eyes widened. Her lips momentarily pressed together, but it wasn't long before her expression gave way to laughter. "Very well, Mr. Darcy, you win. I certainly would not wish to be responsible for the deterioration of your health."

Leaving the room briefly, she returned with a pot of tea and a thick quilt. "Are you certain you will be comfortable? I am happy to stay a while longer if you would like the company."

For a moment Darcy contemplated accepting her offer, but he could see she was exhausted. "No. I am well. And you should sleep. It has been a long day, and with any luck, our rescuers will be here early tomorrow."

He thought he saw a shadow cross Elizabeth's features. She turned to go, but then stopped, her back to him. "If you require anything, Mr. Darcy, you need only call. I shall leave the bedchamber door open."

Darcy stilled, as a feeling of intense gratitude washed over him. Despite everything she had said that day at the parsonage, she trusted him to behave in an honorable manner.

If she knew how much he wanted to leap out of his chair and take her in his arms! Swallowing hard, he lifted his gaze. "I thank you Miss Bennet. That is most kind, but I will be fine."

Elizabeth nodded, and a moment later, Darcy felt the gentle press of her hand upon his shoulder.

To his dismay, he could still feel the impression of her fingers long after she had quit the room.

Elizabeth was not certain how much time had passed before she woke, but the taper on her bedside table had yet to burn out, so she could not have been asleep for long. The low moaning that had pulled her from slumber began again, drifting in through the partially opened door. Swinging her legs over the side of the mattress, Elizabeth stood, hurrying from the room.

In the parlor, Mr. Darcy was slouched in his chair, shivering violently. Elizabeth quickened her pace, her footsteps reverberating off the hardwood floors.

Darcy's eyes were closed, the covers she had given him clenched tightly in his fists. Even in the low light, she could see the faint sheen of perspiration that dampened his brow. Another moan slid from his throat and Elizabeth rested the backs of her fingers against his forehead.

At the touch of her hand, Darcy's eyes cracked open.

"Mr. Darcy, you have developed a fever," she said quietly. "We need to get you into bed."

Darcy blinked back at her, his teeth chattering.

"Mr. Darcy, can you hear me? We must get you into the bedchamber."

He continued to stare for a moment before answering. "N-n-o. That is n-not n-necessary," he whispered. "Forgive me, d-did I wake you?"

"Shh. Do not distress yourself. But I am afraid it is necessary. We have to get your fever down. Can you stand?"

Darcy jerked his head in a brief nod. "I... I think so..."

"Here, lean on me." Elizabeth lifted his arm, draping it carefully around her shoulders. She tugged to help him to stand and Darcy yelped at the sudden movement, but staggered to his feet.

"Put your weight on my shoulder," Elizabeth murmured, as Darcy stifled a groan.

"I cannot. I am too heavy…"

"Mr. Darcy, I am stronger than I look. Keep your weight off your injured leg. We only have about twenty paces to go."

Darcy gritted his teeth, stumbling forward until they reached the bedchamber.

They made their way slowly across the room before Elizabeth released her hold, carefully lowering him onto the mattress. For the first time, she noticed that he had removed his waistcoat and cravat, and his collar was open at the neck.

An odd feeling settled in her belly.

Darcy's body trembled as Elizabeth lifted his legs onto the bed, pulling the counterpane up and tucking it beneath his chin. Closing his eyes, he rested his head against the pillow, breathing in the fresh scent of citrus that lingered on the bed linen. All at once he realized that Elizabeth had been in this very bed only moments before and his pulse beat a wild rhythm against his chest. He struggled to sit but immediately felt Elizabeth's delicate hands pressing against his shoulders.

"Shh, lie back. I am going to get some fresh tea and a cold cloth for your head."

Darcy moaned, sinking into the pillows.

He must have fallen asleep, because when he opened his eyes again, there were cool compresses draped across his neck and forehead and Elizabeth sat beside him in a high-backed chair. For a moment, he forgot where he was, but when he attempted to shift position, the blistering pain that seared his chest was a harsh reminder.

"Elizabeth," he whispered.

Elizabeth leaned forward, barely reacting to Darcy's use of her Christian name. "Do not try to talk. Here, you must drink as much as possible." She pressed a cup to his lips.

Darcy managed to swallow a few sips of the tepid tea before dropping back onto the pillows. Elizabeth set the cup on the bedside table and moved to return to her seat, but Darcy reached out, catching her hand.

"Miss Bennet..."

"Yes?"

"Thank you," he murmured.

Elizabeth smiled, lightly squeezing his fingers. "There is no need to thank me. Just close your eyes, and try to sleep."

Sometime later Elizabeth awoke from a restless slumber, rubbing the back of her neck which had grown stiff from dozing in the chair. Soft gray light filtered in through a crack in the shutters and a faint rasping filled the air. Before her in the bed, Mr. Darcy lay perfectly still. Dark stubble shadowed his jaw, but beneath that, his skin was deathly pale. But the thing that troubled her the most was the terrifying rattle of his breathing.

"Mr. Darcy?" She reached out her hand, laying it gently upon his shoulder. Again, she called his name, but the gentleman did not rouse. Panic prickled deep within her. Something was wrong. For the first time it occurred to her that perhaps the gentleman had sustained some inner injury that neither of them had been aware of… A shiver rippled up her spine. Mr. Darcy's ragged breathing reminded her of a neighbor who had fallen from the hayloft in his stables. A broken rib had punctured one of his lungs. He had not recovered.

She called out once more, shaking Mr. Darcy harder. After a moment, his eyes opened, but the gaze he fixed on her was glassy and unfocused. His head turned, his attention fixed upon the far side of the room, as if regarding something only he could see.

Elizabeth slipped her hand in his. "Mr. Darcy, can you hear me?"

He did not respond immediately, but after a few seconds, his eyes drifted to her face. "Elizabeth," he rasped, his voice barely above a whisper. "Please. Go."

His entreaty brought her dark brows together. Go? Where would she go? Perhaps he wished for her to fetch something. "What are you in need of?" she asked softly. "Would you like more tea?" She turned towards the cup on the bedside table, but his grip contracted around her fingers.

"No. Please…" He drew an uneven breath and Elizabeth could see it took all his strength to form the next two words.

"Don't. Watch."

Their eyes collided and the air seemed to leave Elizabeth's body—for what she saw reflected back at her was not anguish or even fear, but resolution.

He was going to die, and he did not want her to witness it.

"Mr. Darcy, I am not going anywhere."

He opened his mouth, but this time Elizabeth silenced him, placing a finger against his lips.

His eyes remained fixed on her form, tracking her as she straightened and crossed to the hearth. The chamber had grown cold and she stopped to place several logs upon the fire, fueling the flames. Setting the fire-iron in its rack, she turned back to the bed, but this time she moved to the opposite side. Darcy continued to stare, his breathing labored, as she climbed in beside him, stretching out on top of the quilted counterpane. Their eyes studied each other—Elizabeth's watchful and worried, Darcy's filled with desire... and regret.

Once again, Elizabeth reached for his hand, lacing her fingers firmly with his. His thumb brushed against the sensitive skin on the inside of her wrist and Elizabeth's heart fluttered in her chest. She strengthened her grip.

"Sleep now," she whispered. "I will be here when you wake." Mr. Darcy regarded her for several long moments before closing his eyes.

After that, he did not stir.

Elizabeth opened her eyes. Mr. Darcy lay beside her, as still as death. The rasping sound had ceased. She lurched upright, tugging the bedclothes from his body, her gaze trained upon his chest. Slowly it rose, then fell. Elizabeth crumpled in relief.

He lived.

Reaching up, she placed her fingers to his brow. Cool. Her own breath escaped in a grateful rush. Rising from the bed, she moved to the window, pacing back and forth across the hardwood floor. Perhaps his body had merely been in shock as a result of the trauma he had suffered. Nevertheless, she would feel significantly better when the physician arrived to offer a professional diagnosis.

Returning to the bed, Elizabeth sat. A single lock of hair had fallen across Mr. Darcy's forehead, and she lifted her hand, brushing it back in place. Angling her head, she studied his countenance. Sleep had softened the harsh lines, but she could not help but notice the perfectly straight nose, the full lips, the firm jaw. He was as flawless as a statue. Slowly, as if of their own accord, her fingers trailed down his temple, brushing against the rough stubble of his beard. Darcy murmured in his sleep and Elizabeth quickly withdrew her hand. Good heavens, what was she doing? She was alone in a bedchamber with a man who was not her father. Or her husband...

And yet, strangely, she did not feel anxious or even ill at ease. Still, the impropriety of the situation was not lost on her, and she abruptly rose, smoothing her skirts. When she turned back around, Mr. Darcy's eyes were open.

Elizabeth offered him a shaky smile. "You are awake. How do you feel?"

Darcy did not answer, but struggled to sit.

"No, do not move. I think the worst is over, but you must continue to rest."

Darcy opened his mouth, but a sudden pounding on the front door startled them both. Their eyes locked.

"Our rescuers," Elizabeth murmured. She turned to go, but to her surprise, Darcy's fingers closed around her wrist.

"Miss Bennet," he croaked. "Exercise caution... when opening the door."

Elizabeth nodded and moved to step away, but his grip tightened.

"There is a pistol. On the mantelpiece."

The banging resumed. Elizabeth swallowed. Hurrying into the adjoining room, she scooped up the pistol as a strong voice called out from the other side of the door.

"Mr. Darcy? Is anyone at home?"

At the sound of Mr. Darcy's name Elizabeth's body relaxed. The man called out again, and Elizabeth noted that the voice was deep and male, but she did not recognize it as belonging to Thomas, Mr. Darcy's footman. She twisted the latch, easing the door open, the gun held tightly behind her back.

Outside the world shimmered in the morning light, but snow no longer fell. A red bay gelding was tethered to a nearby tree and an impeccably dressed gentleman stood before the door. Upon seeing Elizabeth, he instantly doffed his hat, bowing low at the waist.

"Good morning, madam. I hope you will pardon my early arrival, but I am looking for Mr. Fitzwilliam Darcy. Is he within? I am Mr. Cartwright, his personal physician."

Elizabeth's eyes grew round as she stepped back, giving the gentleman room to enter.

"Oh! Yes, of course. I beg your pardon, I wasn't expecting... " her voice trailed off as the doctor stepped across the threshold. A blustery wind followed him in and Elizabeth hastened to shut the door. Returning the pistol to its place upon the mantle, she quickly took the physician's coat, draping it over one of the armchairs by the hearth.

"I am very glad to see you, sir," Elizabeth continued, leading the way across the compact parlor. "Mr. Darcy was feverish during the night, and his breathing has been labored, but he appears much improved this morning."

They entered the bedchamber to find Darcy propped against the pillows. To Elizabeth's surprise, when he spoke, his voice was composed, although still weak.

"Cartwright. Thank you for coming so quickly. May I present Miss Elizabeth Bennet? I was escorting her to Town when the accident occurred." After a brief pause he added, "Her maid has only just stepped out."

Elizabeth's gaze immediately darted to the physician, but as far as she could tell he seemed unperturbed at finding his patient alone in a deserted cottage with a young woman, with or without her maid.

Cartwright nodded. "I received the express from your man last night and left before first light. I am glad to see it was not more serious, but I would like to do a thorough examination." He set down his bag and began rummaging through it as Elizabeth moved in the direction of the door.

"Miss Bennet, wait." Turning to his physician, Darcy continued, "I would like you to attend Miss Bennet first. She does not appear to be badly injured but she did hit her head and she has some scrapes along her..." His complexion deepened and he cleared his voice before continuing, "That is, I would feel more at ease if you would examine her."

Elizabeth felt her own cheeks color. "That will not be necessary, sir."

"Miss Bennet, I insist. I will not agree to be seen until you are looked after." He glanced up at her and his tone softened. "Please."

The doctor, who had been dividing his attention between the two of them now turned to face Elizabeth.

"Of course," he said. "I will be happy to wait on you, Miss Bennet. Would you prefer that we postpone the examination until your maid returns?"

Elizabeth bit her lip and looked at Mr. Darcy who seemed to realize his error. He opened his mouth to speak but it was Elizabeth who answered.

"No, sir. It is not necessary to wait."

Darcy made to stand. "I will give you your privacy," he said formally, but Elizabeth held up her hand.

"Oh, no, Mr. Darcy. You will stay here. The doctor can examine me just as well in the parlor." And with that she turned and headed for the door.

Elizabeth had been examined and declared perfectly well and the doctor was attending to Mr. Darcy when the second knock sounded at the door, followed by Thomas's familiar voice.

Elizabeth hurried to allow the footman entry, surprised to find that he was not alone.

The servant offered her a formal bow, introducing the young woman by his side as Miss Wilkins, a maid from the Bell. "Miss Bennet, Miss Wilkins will attend you on our journey back to the inn. I have already secured your belongings and had them removed to the coaching station. The roads are passable and there is a carriage waiting at the end of the lane, so we may leave whenever you are ready."

"I... I thank you, sir," Elizabeth stammered. Goodness, Mr. Darcy's staff certainly was efficient.

The maid offered her a brief curtsy and the three made their way into the parlor where the footman continued, "I saw a horse outside, miss. I assume the doctor has arrived?"

"Yes. I should like to wait for news of Mr. Darcy's condition before we depart, if that is acceptable?" It was still early, and with the weather, Elizabeth was certain her uncle's carriage could not possibly reach the inn for several more hours. She noted with some surprise that the thought of being rescued, instead of filling her with relief, left her with an odd despondency. She should be happy about finally being extricated from such a difficult situation. By nightfall she would be safe and snug in her aunt and uncle's townhouse—and away from Mr. Darcy...

The physician's appearance in the small sitting room jolted Elizabeth from her contemplations and she rapidly stood.

"How is he?"

"I am afraid Mr. Darcy's injuries are quite severe, although under the circumstances he is doing far better than I might have expected. His left leg appears to be broken and I believe he has sustained several cracked ribs. I have given him something for the pain. Once that takes hold, I will set the leg and then I would like him to remain here for a few more days."

Elizabeth nodded. "Do his lungs appear to be affected? He was having difficulty breathing last night."

The doctor regarded her curiously. "Not so far as I can see. The fever and the shortness of breath are not unusual given his injuries, but time will tell. Actually, Miss Bennet, I believe I owe you my thanks. Mr. Darcy told me it was at your suggestion that he removed the boot and kept his leg elevated, and that you used cold compresses to reduce the swelling. Without these measures, I fear things could have been substantially worse."

Elizabeth flushed. "I am glad to have been of assistance. Do you think... That is, will he make a complete recovery?"

"I should hope so. The cracked ribs will heal themselves, and the break in his leg appears to be clean. If he can be persuaded to stay off it for several months I would not expect any lingering difficulties."

Elizabeth released a breath. Somehow, she could not have borne it if Mr. Darcy had been permanently incapacitated. "I am glad to hear it," she answered. Her gaze wandered to the closed door to the adjoining chamber. "Is there any other way I might be of service?"

But before she had even finished speaking, the physician was shaking his head. "No, no. I expect Mr. Darcy will sleep for some time."

Elizabeth nodded, surprised at the weight that had settled upon her shoulders. Moving to gather her belongings, she turned to Mr. Darcy's footman. There was no sense in delaying. It was time to go.

Darcy pulled the covers closer to his body, fighting against the silky darkness attempting to drag him under. He needed to stay awake. He needed to be coherent when Elizabeth came back into the room.

He tried to roll onto his side, but the burning in his chest made moving next to impossible. He turned his head, breathing deeply when his face pressed against the pillow. He could still detect her scent, although it was fainter than before. A contented sigh slid from his throat. She was well. Cartwright had assured him her injuries were minor. That was all that mattered. But even as he thought it, his heart filled with sorrow. She was well, but she was leaving. Never again would they share the intimacy of the last four and twenty hours. She would return to her life, and he to his. Oh, perhaps their paths would cross again through Bingley and Jane, but it would not be the same. She would marry someone else, bear that gentleman's children, grow old—without him.

In the distance, a door slammed, rattling the window-panes. Several moments later Darcy heard the unmistakable clatter of hoof-beats moving down the drive.

She was gone. And she hadn't even said goodbye.

CHAPTER 6

Stars.
Too many to count.
A thousand points of light,
shimmering in an inky sky.
A man,
staring up into the heavens.
The air filled with a deathly rattle,
as her name drifted towards her,
a whisper on the wind.
"Elizabeth…"
Her feet were moving now
…almost there.
The man's head turned
and his eyes
found hers.
"Don't.
Watch."

A shot,
piercing through the silence.
A red stain,
turning the white snow
dark.
She opened her mouth,
and screamed...

E lizabeth's voice echoed off the walls of the bedchamber. A moment later the door flew open, her aunt's hurried footsteps pounding across the hardwood floor. "Elizabeth! What is it? Are you unwell?"

Soft fingers caressed Elizabeth's sweat-soaked skin as she pressed against the carved oak headboard. The mattress dipped as her aunt perched beside her, lighting the taper on the bedside table. Elizabeth blinked.

"Lizzy?"

Shaking her head, Elizabeth fought her way back to the present as bits and pieces of the dream continued to swirl inside her head. Slowly she turned in the direction of the voice. Her aunt's kind eyes gazed back at her, warm and worried.

"I... Forgive me," Elizabeth stammered. "'Twas only a dream."

Her aunt murmured words of comfort as Elizabeth struggled to hold onto the shadowy images, but they were already trickling away. All but one. The man in the snow— Mr. Darcy.

"Sounds more like a nightmare," said her aunt. "Would you like to talk about it? It might make you feel better."

Elizabeth shook her head. "No. That is, I... I do not remember."

Her aunt nodded. "Well, that is for the best, I suppose. Shall I fetch you something to help you return to sleep? Some warm milk, perhaps?"

"No, do not trouble yourself. I am sorry for waking you."

Bending to kiss Elizabeth gently on the cheek, her aunt rose. "It was no bother. Pray, sleep well, Lizzy."

But Elizabeth did not sleep. She could not shake the sense of foreboding that lingered in the dream's wake. Mr. Darcy. Dead. Was the dream some type of premonition? No, surely it was only her own fear-filled memories.

Elizabeth chewed her lip. Ten weeks. It had been ten weeks since her return from Kent, and in that time, she had not told anyone what occurred on that stormy November day. Not about the accident, nor about the subsequent time spent alone with Mr. Darcy. She had considered confiding in her aunt and uncle, but even though she believed her relations to be fair-minded, the consequences of the wrong people finding out eventually decided her against it. But now...

Throwing off the bedclothes, Elizabeth paced to the window, staring out into the moonlit street. There must be some way to know if Mr. Darcy was well. Indeed, she would not rest easy until she was certain of the gentleman's continued recovery.

Her thoughts ran in circles until finally her spine

straightened. Of course! Mr. Bingley would know. Yes, her brother would be able to ease her uncertainty. Tomorrow she would write to Jane and inquire after Mr. Darcy. Certainly, there could be nothing amiss in asking after the gentleman's health?

Returning to her bed, Elizabeth slipped beneath the covers. Yes, as long as she had Jane's assurance that Mr. Darcy was well, she would be content.

Curling onto her side, Elizabeth released a satisfied sigh, once again surrendering herself to slumber.

Somewhere overhead a bell jingled as Elizabeth entered the brightly lit shop, grateful to escape the brisk January breeze. Following her aunt across the polished floors, Elizabeth's eyes swept the spacious room, taking in the bolts of fine silks and linens that lined the walls. Although her aunt often escorted her on shopping expeditions when she visited Town, never had Elizabeth been in any establishment quite as fashionable as this one.

Making her way to one corner of the shop, she examined a pair of evening gloves, longingly fingering the soft leather. What her youngest sisters would not give to own anything half so fine! With a sigh, Elizabeth carefully returned the mousquetaires to their shelf. It had been silly to come inside. The bonnet she had admired in the window likely cost more than her remaining pin money, and next month's besides.

Elizabeth turned away from the display, absently

staring out into the busy street. In the weeks since her return to Town, she had not been able to shake the feeling of melancholy that had followed her from Kent. While Jane had replied promptly to Elizabeth's letter seeking intelligence about Mr. Darcy—assuring her that the gentleman in question was indeed alive and well—her sister could give her no further details beyond what Elizabeth already knew: Mr. Darcy had suffered several broken bones in a carriage accident but was expected to recover. However, despite these assurances, Elizabeth continued to feel inexplicably anxious—and the dreams persisted. And if it ever occurred to her to question her preoccupation with that particular gentleman's well-being, she simply told herself she would feel the same for anyone with whom she had shared such a harrowing experience.

A tug at her elbow pulled Elizabeth from her thoughts.

"Lizzy! Did you see the ballgown over there? Would that not look well on you?"

Elizabeth turned in the direction her aunt indicated. The gown on display was exquisite—a deep sage green with delicate floral embroidery around the sleeves and neckline and Elizabeth could not help but smile at her aunt's enthusiasm.

"Indeed, it is lovely. But I fear I would be quite out of place wearing anything so fine to the Meryton Assembly, even if I had the funds to acquire it."

Her aunt sighed. "I suppose you are correct. Well, you must at least try on the bonnet you were admiring."

In the distance a bell tinkled, announcing the arrival of more customers and Elizabeth watched as a well-bred young lady entered the shop, followed by a genteel-looking woman of slightly more mature years. The girl and her companion made their way to the counter, just as the proprietor entered through a velvet drape.

Upon seeing her newest customers, the modiste hurried over, her lips drawn into a broad smile.

"Miss Darcy! How good it is to see you again. I hope nothing was amiss with the gowns we delivered?"

At the shopkeeper's words, Elizabeth started, her eyes immediately returning to the younger of the two women. Though her bonnet obscured most of her face, Elizabeth noted that the girl was tall and willowy. Her pelisse was well-cut from a rich burgundy wool and she carried herself with a graceful air. Elizabeth's heart pounded as she edged closer, discreetly trying to get a better look. Could this be Mr. Darcy's sister?

"No, not at all," the girl was saying. "They are perfect. But I had hoped to select a pair of slippers to go with the blue evening gown. I believe I saw some when I was in here last that would do well."

The modiste beamed. "Yes, of course. I know exactly the ones you mean. I believe we have something that should fit." The woman retreated behind the curtain, and the girl seemed to feel Elizabeth's gaze, turning towards her and offering a shy smile.

Elizabeth's breath caught. It *was* Mr. Darcy's sister! Although she was several years older, Elizabeth recognized her from the portrait she had seen in the gallery at Pemberley.

Marshaling her expression, Elizabeth crossed the

room. Dropping a polite curtsy, she returned the young girl's smile.

"I hope you will forgive me for being so forward, miss, but I happened to overhear the modiste address you by name. Would you by chance be related to Mr. Fitzwilliam Darcy of Pemberley, in Derbyshire?"

Surprise showed on the girl's face and Elizabeth did not miss the hint of wariness that appeared in her light eyes. "Yes," she answered cautiously. "Fitzwilliam is my brother."

"Pray, excuse my presumption in introducing myself. I am Elizabeth Bennet. I had the pleasure of making your brother's acquaintance when he was visiting his friend Mr. Bingley near my family's home in Hertfordshire. As a matter of fact, Mr. Bingley is recently married to my eldest sister."

All apprehension instantly lifted from the girl's features and her countenance brightened. "Oh! Miss Bennet! Fitzwilliam has spoken about your family often. It is a great pleasure to meet you at last."

Elizabeth felt a warm flush building in her cheeks as she wondered what choice comments Mr. Darcy might have made about her mother and younger sisters. But if he had said anything unkind, it certainly was not evident from his sister's warm reception.

Elizabeth turned to her aunt who had come to stand beside her. "Miss Darcy, may I present my aunt, Mrs. Edward Gardiner?"

The girl dipped a demure curtsy and introduced the woman with her as Mrs. Annesley. The party of four exchanged pleasantries for several moments before Miss Darcy's companion excused herself to examine a display of shawls in another part of the shop.

Gathering her courage, Elizabeth turned back to her new friend. "Miss Darcy, may I inquire after your brother? I had heard he was in an accident some time ago..."

Elizabeth's words caused a shadow to cross the young girl's expression as she nodded slowly. "Yes, Miss Bennet, he was. But he is doing much better now. Oh! But you must come and see for yourself. He is just outside in the carriage."

An electric charge seemed to run down Elizabeth's spine as her gaze darted to the door. Mr. Darcy was here! Struggling to hide her agitation, Elizabeth turned back to face his sister. "That is kind of you, Miss Darcy," she murmured, "but I would not wish to intrude."

"It would be no imposition, Miss Bennet. He would be pleased to see you, I am sure of it. He—" But before she could finish her sentence the modiste returned, a stylish pair of evening shoes dangling from her fingers.

"Oh, yes! Those will do perfectly."

"An excellent choice. Shall I wrap them for you now? Or would you prefer to have them sent?"

Georgiana Darcy turned to her new acquaintances. "Do you mind waiting? I shall just have these wrapped, and then we may go and see Fitzwilliam. Won't he be surprised?"

Alone in the carriage, Darcy altered his position, attempting to better accommodate the leg he had stretched across the squabs. Outside, the London streets bustled with fashionable members of the *ton*, but he barely took notice. As they had been for many weeks, his thoughts were miles away, in a small cottage in the Kent countryside—with Elizabeth Bennet.

Images from their shared night together flooded his mind—Elizabeth cooking in the rustic kitchen, the way her skin glowed as she slept by the fire, the earnest expression in her eyes when she told him the accident had not been his fault. And then there were the things he could only half remember—Elizabeth lying next to him on the narrow bed, her delicate fingers caressing his cheek...

No, surely he had dreamed that portion.

Darcy smothered a sigh. Why did he continue to torture himself? Whatever had occurred, it had meant nothing to her. She had not even spoken to him before she departed.

Before he could ruminate any further on the matter, the carriage door swung open and Darcy straightened as his sister's rosy cheeks appeared inside the compartment.

"William, I have the most wonderful surprise! You will never guess!"

Too late, Darcy noticed a pair of women in his sister's shadow and he groaned under his breath. *This* is why he did not wish to accompany Georgiana on her shopping expeditions. Why he had scarcely left the house in above two months. Blast! He craned his neck, but the footman was blocking his view. Let it not be Caroline Bingley, he thought miserably.

He sought to compose himself as Georgiana stepped back and his heart stuttered inside his chest.

"Miss Bennet!"

From her place on the pavement, Elizabeth colored. "Mr. Darcy. I hope you will excuse the intrusion. My aunt and I happened upon Miss Darcy in the dress shop and she was most insistent that we come and pay our respects."

Darcy stared at Elizabeth, momentarily at a loss for words. How had such an extraordinary occurrence come to be? Why, Elizabeth and his sister had never even been introduced! Yet here they stood side by side, his sister smiling openly, and Elizabeth, looking vaguely embarrassed but every bit as beautiful as he remembered.

A gust of wind tossed the curtains on the carriage windows and Darcy pulled himself from his musings. "It is no imposition, Miss Bennet, I assure you. But pray, come inside out of the cold." Turning to the woman standing slightly off to the side he added, "I would be most happy to make the acquaintance of your aunt."

Elizabeth exchanged a brief glance with her relation who nodded, before allowing Darcy's footman to hand her into the coach. Sliding onto the front-facing seat, Elizabeth waited for her aunt to follow before performing the necessary introductions as Georgiana took the place beside her brother, explaining the circumstances that had led to their unexpected meeting.

The footman latched the door and Darcy pulled his

gaze away from Elizabeth, directing his attention to his sister. "Georgiana, is Mrs. Annesley not with you?"

"Oh! I told her she might take the rest of the afternoon to complete her shopping." Turning to her new acquaintances, she explained, "My companion has a daughter in Cornwall who is nearing her confinement. Mrs. Annesley will be traveling there to help with the babe, and I know there were some purchases she wished to make before she departs." Georgiana moved to face her brother. "You do not mind, do you, William?"

Darcy frowned. In truth, he did not like the fact that Georgiana was so indulgent. Surely Mrs. Annesley had time to shop on her many hours off. But he did not wish to upset his sister nor appear churlish in front of Elizabeth and her aunt.

"Of course not," he answered before turning to face Elizabeth's relation. "Mrs. Gardiner, it is a great pleasure to make your acquaintance. I understand you hail from Lambton, very near Pemberley."

Before the woman could answer, Georgiana slid forward in her seat. "Truly?" she asked and Mrs. Gardiner nodded her confirmation.

"Yes, indeed. I have visited Pemberley many times. Most recently this past summer."

"Oh, I wish we had known! We would have had you to tea, wouldn't we, Fitzwilliam?"

"Undoubtedly," Darcy answered, but when he spoke, his eyes were on Elizabeth.

"That is very kind, Miss Darcy," Mrs. Gardiner continued, "but I do not believe you or your brother were in residence at the time."

"Mr. Darcy, I hope you are in good health?" Elizabeth interrupted, her gaze wandering to the leg he had stretched out along the floor of the compartment.

"Yes," added Mrs. Gardiner, "we heard from Elizabeth's eldest sister that you were in a rather bad carriage accident. I hope you are recovering well?"

"I thank you, madam, I am. Fortunately, I have a wonderful staff and my own excellent sister to see to my every need, although I am still not able to get around as easily as I would like." He paused for a moment before adding seriously, "Indeed, my physician has informed me that the care I received directly *after* the accident is likely the reason my recovery has been so swift."

Elizabeth flushed and briefly looked away, but returned his gaze when he addressed her directly.

"It is a pleasant surprise to find you here in London, Miss Bennet. Have you been in Town for some duration?"

"For several months, sir," Elizabeth answered quietly. "I traveled to Longbourn for a week at Christmas but was persuaded by my aunt and uncle to return with them for the remainder of the season."

"I trust you are enjoying your visit?"

"Yes, sir. Very much."

Silence descended, but after several moments Darcy and Elizabeth spoke at once.

"Miss Bennet—"

"Mr. Darcy I—"

"I beg your pardon, Miss Bennet. Pray, continue."

"Oh. I was only going to say that my aunt and I should let you carry on with your shopping. It was not our intention to take up your entire afternoon."

"Not at all. We are completely at leisure today. As a matter of fact, my sister and I were just about to return home for tea." After a brief pause he cautiously added, "It would be our pleasure to have you join us if you have no prior engagements. Our townhouse is just around the corner."

"Yes, do come!" Georgiana interjected hopefully, while Darcy held his breath in anticipation.

Mrs. Gardiner's gaze settled briefly on Elizabeth's flushed countenance before she turned to face the gentleman on the opposite seat. "We thank you, sir and would be most happy to accept your invitation. My niece and I have no fixed engagements for the remainder of the afternoon."

CHAPTER 7

A short time later, the Darcy carriage pulled up before an elegant townhouse set back from the busy street. Almost immediately, a footman materialized to hand the three ladies down, but when it was Darcy's turn to exit, he waved the man aside, leaning upon a polished wooden cane and limping through the gate.

"Brother, may I assist you?" Georgiana asked, her voice laced with concern, but Darcy shook his head.

"No. I can manage. Pray, show our guests inside. I will join you shortly."

Georgiana nodded before leading Elizabeth and Mrs. Gardiner up the handful of steps and into a tastefully appointed front hall. Upon their entrance, Darcy's butler arrived to collect their outer apparel, and Elizabeth took a moment to study her surroundings. Even from the marble vestibule, it was clear that the home was both large and expensively furnished; however, it did not feel in any way imposing. Turning to follow Mr. Darcy's sister, Elizabeth craned her neck to peer into a lavish dining parlor, before ascending to the next floor. Her feet sank into the thick carpet as the party made their way into a comfortable drawing room, where they were joined a few minutes later by Mr. Darcy.

"Georgiana, perhaps the ladies would like to refresh themselves. Would you show them the way while I ring for tea?"

"Yes, of course," Georgiana murmured, beckoning to her guests.

"That would be most appreciated," Mrs. Gardiner answered, and Elizabeth smiled over her shoulder as she and her aunt followed Georgiana from the room.

Darcy had scarcely made it across the floor when his butler appeared.

"Will you be requiring anything, sir?"

"Ah. Yes, thank you, Stevens. If you would, pray, have Mrs. Guilford send up tea."

The butler nodded, moving to the door.

"Oh! And Stevens, perhaps some chocolate, for the ladies…"

"Very good, sir." The servant turned to go, but paused at the threshold. "Was there something else, Mr. Darcy?"

"Actually, yes. Do you know if Mrs. Parker has made any lemon biscuits?"

Despite his best efforts, the butler's eyebrow twitched. "I shall inquire in the kitchens, sir," he answered evenly.

Darcy nodded. "Er, yes. Good. And Stevens, when you return, there is a package on the desk in my study. If you would be good enough to bring it to me?"

Settling into his chair, Darcy's gaze swept the fashionable front-parlor, taking in the silk wall hangings, the tall French windows, and the crystal chandelier. Everything looked as it always did, but suddenly he was seeing it all through Elizabeth's eyes. Would she be comfortable here? Would she find the furnishings tasteful and refined, or would she consider the décor gaudy and uselessly fine?

Tugging at his cravat, Darcy wished Georgiana had chosen to take their guests to the cozier morning room, but there was nothing to be done about it now.

Muffled footsteps caused him to look up. Elizabeth stood in the doorway, her expression uncertain.

"Miss Bennet!" Reaching for his cane, Darcy hastened to his feet as Elizabeth stepped into the room.

"Forgive me, Mr. Darcy, I did not mean to startle you. Your sister is showing my aunt a painting in the upstairs hall. I expect they will be down momentarily." Moving gracefully across the floor she took a seat as Darcy looked on.

In truth, when he had seen Elizabeth standing there, he had not given a thought to the whereabouts of his sister and Mrs. Gardiner. Now he only hoped viewing that painting took a substantial amount of time.

"Ah, yes," he answered, slowly regaining his seat. "There is a fine likeness of the high street in Lambton outside my sister's sitting room..." his voice trailed off, his gaze fixed upon Elizabeth's heart-shaped face. His eyes moved to her left temple where there had once been a deep gash, but the skin there was smooth and unmarked. Leaning forward in his chair, he said softly, "Miss Bennet, are you well? I hope you have suffered no lingering effects... from your injuries?"

At the allusion to the accident, Elizabeth flushed, her gaze dropping to her lap. "No, I am quite recovered."

"I am glad. I did not wish to inquire earlier. I take it from your aunt's comments that you have not informed them of what occurred in Kent?"

"No, sir. I have not."

Darcy nodded, taking a deep breath. "As it happens, I am pleased to have a moment alone. There is something of yours I wished to return, but I have been unsure how best to accomplish it."

Elizabeth leaned forward in her seat as Darcy retrieved the small parcel from a nearby table. Darting a glance at the open door, Elizabeth rose, crossing to where he sat. Claiming the package, Darcy watched as she returned to her chair, peeling back the plain brown paper.

Elizabeth gasped, staring at the volume bound in rich mahogany leather. *"Gulliver's Travels!"* Raising her eyes, she met Darcy's gaze. "It is exquisite. But you must know I cannot accept this."

"I do not see why. It is not a gift, Miss Bennet. The book belongs to you. As I stated, I am merely returning it."

Elizabeth angled her head, one eyebrow arched in his

direction. "Mr. Darcy, I think we both know that this is not my book."

Darcy briefly looked away, but when he spoke his voice was level. "No, it is true that it is not the exact volume you lost. Although I was able to retrieve your copy from the scene, I am afraid it was ruined by the snow."

Elizabeth nodded. "I thought as much. And I appreciate your efforts, sir. You are very generous. Nevertheless, it would be wrong for me to accept this."

He studied her intently for a moment before speaking. "Miss Bennet, it is only a book. And besides, this volume does belong to you."

He motioned for her to open the cover and Elizabeth did as he directed. There, neatly written across the flyleaf were the letters E. BENNET.

Her bright eyes lifted, and Darcy regarded her with a satisfied smile. "So you see, I cannot return it. Nor would it be prudent for me to keep it here in my own library."

Elizabeth's lips curved at the corners. "There is one small problem, sir. The volume I lost did not belong to me but to my father. And his name does not begin with the letter E."

"Yes, I had thought of that. But I wanted you to have a copy of your own, since I know how much you were enjoying it. I would be happy to procure another for your father, if you would like."

Elizabeth opened her mouth to answer, but stopped at the sound of voices in the outer hall. Hurriedly setting the book aside, she stood as her aunt and Miss Darcy entered the room, directly followed by two maids bearing large silver trays laden with food and drink.

The group exchanged pleasantries as the maids set out the tea. When the servants had finished and left the room, Georgiana stepped up to pour, asking everyone's preferences before turning back to the large assortment of cakes and sweets. "Oh! Mrs. Parker has sent lemon biscuits! You must both try these. They are one of our cook's specialties."

Elizabeth regarded Darcy out of the corner of her vision. "What a coincidence. Lemon happens to be a weakness of mine." Accepting the plate Georgiana offered, Elizabeth lifted one of the glazed biscuits, her expression transforming into one of delight as she took her first bite. "Miss Darcy, these are indeed delicious. I can see why they are a family favorite."

Reluctantly pulling his attention away from Elizabeth, Darcy turned to face her aunt who was calmly sipping her tea. "Mrs. Gardiner, Miss Bennet mentioned that your father was a physician. Did he practice in Lambton?"

"He did, sir. I believe he attended some of the tenants at Pemberley on occasion. Perhaps you may remember him? My family name was Harper."

Instantly, Darcy's face brightened. "Indeed, I do! I had the privilege of making his acquaintance when I was a boy of ten or eleven. My cousin and I were fishing and... Well, it is a long story, but I managed to get a hook caught in my hand. Our family physician could not be reached, and so your father came and looked after me." Extending his palm, Darcy indicated a thin white line near the base of his thumb. "You see? Four stitches."

To Darcy's surprise, Elizabeth's teacup rattled against its saucer and she quickly set it aside. A soft flush made its way up the column of her neck as she peered down at his outstretched hand.

Mrs. Gardiner laughed, breaking the tension. "That must have been quite a traumatic experience, Mr. Darcy. I hope he was gentle with you?"

Darcy withdrew his hand, settling back in his chair. "Yes. I remember he was most kind."

"I am glad to hear it," Mrs. Gardiner answered.

Elizabeth inhaled a shallow breath, turning to face Georgiana who had been sitting quietly throughout this exchange. "Miss Darcy, I hear you are fond of music and that you play the pianoforte exceedingly well. Do you practice often?"

Georgiana raised questioning eyes, darting a brief glance in Darcy's direction before answering. "I would not say I play *very* well, Miss Bennet. But I do enjoy music, and I practice whenever I can. My brother recently purchased a new instrument for me, so I have been playing more often of late." All at once, her expression lightened. "Would you like to see it? The music room is just next door."

Before Elizabeth could respond, Darcy turned to his sister. "Perhaps Miss Bennet would prefer to finish her tea first, dearest," he said gently, causing his sister to blush.

"Yes, of course! I did not mean to rush you, Miss Bennet."

Elizabeth smiled. "Not at all. I should love to see your pianoforte, Miss Darcy. The tea will keep."

Georgiana looked to Darcy and he nodded his consent before flashing Elizabeth a smile of gratitude.

"We shall only be a moment," Georgiana said, rising from the sofa. "Would you care to join us, Mrs. Gardiner?" she asked, but Elizabeth's aunt shook her head.

"I appreciate the offer, Miss Darcy, but I will stay and keep your brother company. This way we may reminisce about Derbyshire without boring poor Lizzy."

Darcy watched as Elizabeth leaned down to kiss her aunt sweetly on the cheek before turning to follow Georgiana into the corridor.

Upon entering the music room, Elizabeth noticed that, like the drawing room, the salon was tastefully furnished. In one corner, an enormous pianoforte took center stage, with several comfortable sofas and chairs arranged in small groupings nearby.

Elizabeth approached the instrument, running her fingers gingerly across the glossy wood, and a sigh of admiration left her lips. Although she was not an accomplished player herself, even she could see that the piano was of the highest quality.

Georgiana grinned. "My brother is far too good to me. And it plays beautifully. Would you like to try it, Miss Bennet?"

Elizabeth lowered herself onto the carved wooden

bench, her fingers tentatively plucking out a simple tune on the ivory keys. Glancing up at Miss Darcy, she smiled. "It is lovely. You are lucky to have such a devoted brother. I can see he cares for you very much." To Elizabeth's surprise, Georgiana paled, briefly casting her eyes to the carpet.

Elizabeth stood. "I beg your pardon, Miss Darcy. Have I said something to upset you?"

"Oh, no! It is only... I have been so worried about Fitzwilliam lately. The carriage accident he was in was quite serious. He... he might have died. And the worst part of it was that I could not even be with him..."

Elizabeth regarded her curiously. "Did Mr. Darcy not return here after the accident?"

Georgiana shook her head. "No. At least not directly. Tragically, the coachman was killed, and William insisted on accompanying the body back to Pemberley—even though my brother's physician warned him he should not travel. I begged to join him there, but he did not wish for me to be on the roads in the poor weather. He stayed at Pemberley a month before returning to Town, just before Christmas."

"I see, Elizabeth murmured. "I had not realized..."

"Yes. It was difficult to be away from him. And since his return, I know he has been in a good deal of pain, but I somehow feel it is more than that. I know he blames himself for the coachman's death. Part of the reason he returned to Pemberley was so that he could settle the man's affairs and offer aid to his widow." Georgiana flushed, lowering her lashes. "I beg your pardon, Miss

Bennet. I should not be burdening you with all of this. My brother would be angry if he knew I had shared so much with you."

Elizabeth smiled, reaching for the young girl's hand. "It is no bother, Miss Darcy. It seems you could use someone to confide in, and I am happy you felt comfortable doing so with me. We need not inform your brother of our conversation."

Georgiana offered up a shaky smile. "Thank you, Miss Bennet. And you are correct. I *have* wished for a confidant. I am afraid I have only Mrs. Annesley, and she is more like a mother than a friend. You are so easy to talk to. And after everything Fitzwilliam wrote to me from Hertfordshire, I feel as if I have known you a lifetime already."

Elizabeth's brow furrowed. "Your brother wrote of me?" she asked incredulously, and Georgiana nodded.

"Oh, yes. Many times." She paused for a moment before continuing. "I am so pleased to have run into you and your aunt today, Miss Bennet. I have not seen my brother this happy for a very long time. He has left the house but once since he arrived from Pemberley and that was only for a brief trip to the booksellers."

"The booksellers?" Elizabeth repeated, a strange sensation prickling at the back of her neck.

"Yes, shortly after he arrived. Given his injuries, I expected he would send a footman to pick up anything he wished for, but he insisted on going himself. I thought at the time it was to purchase a Christmas gift for me, but as you see, I received this lovely pianoforte and no books."

Elizabeth palms dampened as Georgiana continued, "In

truth, I have been worried about William since last spring, when he returned from my aunt's home in Kent. I have never seen him so... lost. I feel something must have happened there but he has refused to speak of it. I am afraid my brother holds a great deal inside. He does not show his feelings easily, even to me."

Elizabeth ran her fingers along the smooth surface of the piano. "I am sure he simply does not wish to burden you. Perhaps there are others he feels more comfortable confiding in."

Georgiana shrugged. "Only Richard; that is, my cousin, Colonel Fitzwilliam. They are extremely close. But Richard is always off with his regiment, so I fear my brother is often left to his own devices."

The clock on the mantelpiece chimed the hour and Georgiana started. "Goodness, we have been absent a long time. We should return or my brother will worry. You were good to listen to me, Miss Bennet," she added, quietly.

Instinctively, Elizabeth reached for the younger girl's hand, giving her fingers a gentle squeeze. "It was my pleasure, Miss Darcy. And you can rest assured—I shall not say a word."

The foursome spent another agreeable half hour over tea, until Mrs. Gardiner glanced at the long-case clock, indicating that it was time to go.

Darcy stood, leaning lightly on his cane. "Mrs.

Gardiner, Miss Bennet, allow me to have my carriage drop you at home. It is late and much too cold to walk."

Mrs. Gardiner smiled. "Do not trouble yourself. We are only going to Gracechurch Street and I am certain a hackney will be available."

Darcy frowned. It was bad enough to think of Elizabeth venturing into Cheapside in the approaching darkness, he certainly was not about to have her riding in a hack when he had a perfectly good carriage to transport her. "Truly, madam, it is no trouble."

While Darcy gave instructions to have his carriage brought around, Elizabeth folded Georgiana in a warm embrace, before turning to Darcy and dropping a brief curtsy. She had almost reached the door when he called out behind her.

"Miss Bennet, you must not forget your book."

Elizabeth paused, a light flush sweeping across her cheeks, but she walked slowly back to the table to retrieve the volume.

Addressing Mrs. Gardiner, Darcy continued, "It is a book I borrowed from Miss Bennet some time ago. I have been remiss in not returning it sooner. Again, you have my apologies, Miss Bennet."

Elizabeth glanced up at him, and Darcy noticed the mischievous smile playing at the corners of her mouth.

"Not at all, Mr. Darcy. Indeed, I must endeavor to lend out Papa's books more often. They do seem to return in better condition than when they left."

CHAPTER 8

Darcy got very little rest that night, and when he did sleep, his dreams were of Elizabeth. He awoke later than was his custom, still warmed by the memories of the previous afternoon. How fortuitous that Georgiana should have run into Elizabeth and her aunt in that dress shop! And to think, he had almost refused to accompany his sister. If this was the result, he was going to take a much more active role in chaperoning Georgiana from now on.

Shaking his head, his thoughts drifted back to Elizabeth, seated in his drawing room. He could hardly believe that it had actually happened. And her behavior towards him had been everything that was kind and courteous. Could her opinion of him be changing? He scarcely dared to hope... and yet it appeared it might be so.

The mere thought set his heart racing, and he swung his legs eagerly out of bed.

"Pierce!"

His valet instantly appeared in the doorway to his dressing room. "Good morning, Mr. Darcy. Would you like me to prepare a bath, sir?"

The broad smile that lit Darcy's countenance seemed to take the valet by surprise, causing Darcy to chuckle softly. "Yes. Thank you, Pierce. And then if you would send word to my sister that if she has not yet broken her fast, I will join her in the small dining parlor in three quarters of an hour."

"William, it is so good to see you up and around. Is your leg giving you less discomfort today?"

Darcy looked up from his plate, smiling at his sister across the table. He could see the genuine pleasure in her eyes and immediately felt badly for his neglect of her over the past couple of months. Since the accident, he had been woefully out of sorts, due in part to the discomfort he was in, but also, he knew, due to the feeling of despair that had settled over him since parting with Elizabeth in Kent. Unwilling to subject his sister to his foul mood, he had chosen to spend most of his time alone—taking breakfast in his sitting room and whiling away the afternoons closeted in his library or his study. He had made a point to dine with Georgiana once or twice a week, and would often seek her out in the music room to listen to her play, but more often than not he left her in Mrs. Annesley's capable hands.

"Yes, Georgiana, I am feeling better today. I apologize for being so inattentive to you in recent weeks. I shall attempt to remedy that in the future."

Georgiana flushed a soft pink. "It is no matter. I know you have been feeling unwell." She continued to eat her breakfast for some moments before glancing shyly in Darcy's direction. "Though I was wondering if your improved disposition might have something to do with our visitors yesterday?"

Darcy struggled to keep his expression neutral as he slowly stirred his coffee. "Yes, well, it was a nice change to have guests in the house," he said carefully.

"Indeed, it was. I liked Miss Bennet very much. And her aunt as well."

"I am of the same mind. They are good people."

"William... might we pay a call on them this afternoon? That is, if you feel up to traveling?"

Darcy lifted his gaze, surprise overtaking his features. He could not remember the last time his sister had suggested calling upon an acquaintance. Even with their own relations, she was generally reticent and would only join him on social calls at his insistence.

"I would be happy to pay a visit with you, sweetling, but I believe we must wait a few days. It would not look well for us to call immediately."

"Oh. Yes, I am certain you are correct." Georgiana paused, and then her eyes lit. "Perhaps we could go early next week?"

The thought of seeing Elizabeth again sent Darcy's

pulse racing, and he could feel a boyish smile stretching his lips. "It would be my pleasure to escort you."

As far as he was concerned, the next few days could not pass quickly enough.

Elizabeth sat in the Gardiners' front-parlor, the new edition of *Gulliver's Travels* resting lightly in her lap. Running her fingers down the page, she stared at the printed words, but her attention was not on the tale. Her mind was more agreeably engaged, as she once again relived the time she had spent in Mr. Darcy's company. Although she was still coming to terms with her changing feelings for the gentleman, there was no denying that the proud and disagreeable man she had met over a year ago in Hertfordshire seemed to no longer exist. As a matter of fact, when she was in his home, she had found him almost charming in his attention to both herself and her aunt.

And then there was his gift. While Elizabeth knew it had been improper to accept the book, she still marveled at the easy manner with which he had convinced her to do so. But was the gesture simply the considerate replacement of her damaged property, or did it signify something more?

A knocking at the door pulled Elizabeth from her musings as the Gardiners' butler entered with the post. Her aunt thanked him, setting aside her embroidery and taking up the stack of correspondence. Elizabeth returned to her book but was soon interrupted by her aunt's voice.

"Oh, Lizzy, there is one for you. I believe it is from Jane."

Accepting the letter, Elizabeth eagerly broke the seal. It had been almost a week since she had last had word from her sister and she was anxious for news from home. Her enthusiasm rapidly dissipated however, for as soon as she began to read, she could tell something was not as it should be. For one thing, the letter was startlingly brief— filling only a quarter of the page. For another, her sister's usually impeccable handwriting was cramped and uneven, causing Elizabeth to have to squint to make out some of the words.

Fine lines furrowed Elizabeth's brow, and Mrs. Gardiner came to sit beside her niece. "It is not bad news, I hope?"

Elizabeth looked up. "I am not certain. Here, perhaps you should read it for yourself." Silently she passed the note to Mrs. Gardiner who skimmed the page.

My dearest Lizzy,

Pray, forgive the hasty nature of this letter, but something has occurred which requires your immediate presence at Longbourn. Be not alarmed, as we are all in good health—however our parents are both desirous of your company as soon as may be. My dear husband has offered to send his carriage, which will arrive on Thursday afternoon. I will explain all when I see you.

Your loving sister,
Jane

Mrs. Gardiner finished reading and Elizabeth caught her eye. "What do you think it means?"

"I have no idea. I suppose we will have to wait until Thursday to find out."

Darcy woke early, hurrying through his morning routine and making his way to the breakfast parlor as fast as he was able. Today was the day he would see Elizabeth! He wondered if it would be possible to call immediately following their morning meal... No, that would look too forward. And besides, he still needed to obtain her aunt and uncle's address. He had planned on sending one of his footmen to Gracechurch Street first thing this morning to seek out the Gardiners' residence.

Darcy entered the room to find Georgiana and Mrs. Annesley already seated at the table. His sister rose to greet him and Darcy was quick to note her wan pallor and the dark circles beneath her eyes.

"Sweetling, you do not look well," he said with concern. "Did you sleep poorly last night?"

Georgiana sank back into her chair, staring down at her barely-touched plate of food. "No, not very well. I believe I shall go back upstairs and rest after breakfast."

Darcy's gaze darted to Mrs. Annesley, but from what he could observe, she did not seem overly alarmed.

"Yes, of course," he answered. "Is there anything I can do for your comfort? Shall I fetch the doctor?"

"Oh, no. I am certain I will be well after some rest. I am only sorry to spoil your plans for the day. I know you wished to call on Miss Bennet."

Darcy waved his hand, even though the mention of Elizabeth made his insides quiver. He would not make his sister feel worse than she already did. "Nonsense, you are not spoiling anything. We can go as easily tomorrow or even later in the week. My only concern is for your health."

"Thank you, William," Georgiana said quietly, and he watched with some concern as she slowly rose and quit the room.

Darcy spent the remainder of the morning attending to business matters in his study, but when his afternoon meal was concluded, he made his way along the third-floor passageway, stopping to knock softly at the entrance to his sister's chambers. After several moments, the door was opened by Mrs. Annesley.

"How is she?" he asked.

"Miss Darcy is resting, sir. I am certain she will be much improved tomorrow."

Darcy stepped into Georgiana's sitting room, turning towards the windows and running a hand through his hair. He did not like seeing his sister unwell. It conjured up too many unhappy memories from his boyhood when his mother remained closeted in her chambers, too weak even to allow him to visit. "Should I not send for the doctor?" he finally asked.

His sister's companion offered him a gentle smile. "I do not think it necessary, sir. I believe Miss Darcy is only... indisposed. It is a common enough occurrence for girls her age."

Suddenly taking the woman's meaning, Darcy colored. "Ah, yes. I see. Well, if you are certain..."

"Pray, do not worry, Mr. Darcy. I will stay with her and if anything changes, I shall inform you immediately. However, I am confident that Miss Darcy will be well enough in a matter of days."

Nodding uncertainly, Darcy bid the woman a good afternoon and returned to his study. He could only hope his sister's companion was not mistaken in her optimism.

The steady beat of horses' hooves drew Elizabeth to the nearby window. Peering down into the street, she was just in time to see the familiar outline of Mr. Bingley's carriage drawing up to the low iron gate. Turning away from the glass, she scanned the bedchamber for any remaining items before moving to the wardrobe to collect her pelisse. A knock sounded and Elizabeth gathered the ribbons of her bonnet, calling out for her aunt to enter. But when the door opened, it was not Mrs. Gardiner who stood before Elizabeth in the corridor.

"Jane!" Elizabeth cried, hurrying to embrace her eldest sister. "Whatever are you doing here? When you wrote to expect Mr. Bingley's carriage, I did not realize you would be accompanying it!"

"I had not anticipated it myself," her sister answered, stepping across the threshold. "But Charles did not like the idea of you traveling with only a footman, and he had some business in Town..." Her voice tapered off but her lips soon lifted into a sweet smile. "In any case, I could not resist the opportunity to keep him company, as this way I could see my dear sister that much sooner."

"Well, I am very glad to see you," Elizabeth answered happily. "Come, let us go downstairs. You and Mr. Bingley must be in want of some refreshment after your journey."

She moved to the door, but Jane did not follow. Elizabeth turned back to face her sister.

"Lizzy, Charles is not here. He has gone to see his solicitor and will return for us later this afternoon. But I would like to speak with you and I... I think it would be better for us to do so privately, before joining our aunt and uncle."

Elizabeth's brow crinkled but she nodded her agreement, taking her sister's hands and leading her to a small sitting area in the corner of her chambers. "Come, sit here by the fire and tell me what this is all about. I confess, I was most anxious when I received your letter, although you stated that no one was ill."

Elizabeth broke off as Jane stared at her lap, twisting her handkerchief. Finally, Jane raised her eyes to meet her sister's concerned expression. "No. No one is ill. It is... It is Lydia. She is to be married."

"Married!" Elizabeth gasped. "To whom? I had no notion..." Suddenly, realization dawned and Elizabeth's eyes widened. "Jane! What has happened? Has she..."

"Oh, no! Nothing like that."

Elizabeth regarded her sister whose countenance bore the telltale signs of her discomfort. She knew both of her sisters well enough to quickly realize that there was more to the story. "Jane, you must tell me everything. What has Lydia done?"

Jane sat still for a moment, her lower lip caught between her teeth. "It appears that she was... seen... with one of the officers. Behind the village hall, during a recent assembly."

Elizabeth sucked in a breath. "Good heavens! And now she is to marry him?"

Jane nodded and Elizabeth's gaze sharpened.

"Jane, what are you not telling me?"

Her sister's chin quivered before her usually serene expression crumbled. "Oh, Lizzy, it was in every way horrible! I have never seen Papa so angry. Of course, he demanded the lieutenant offer for her... and the gentleman... he refused! He said that while he cared for Lydia, he was obligated to marry a woman of means, and of course you know Lydia has no dowry to speak of. Mamma took to her bed in a fit of nerves, and Papa... truly I was afraid for his health." Jane broke down, sobbing softly into her handkerchief.

Elizabeth leapt to her feet, stalking to the window. "What was Lydia thinking?" she spat. "Allowing a gentleman to take liberties when no formal agreement had been reached? And Papa has no one but himself to blame. I always said he was far too lenient with her."

Jane dabbed at her eyes, her expression pained. "I

think Lydia must have believed there was an understanding in place, otherwise she could never have behaved as she did."

"Oh, Jane! You always think the best of everyone. But Lydia has never shown good sense and you know it. I am certain she thought of nothing beyond her own enjoyment." Elizabeth fixed her sister with a steady gaze. "But, I do not understand. You said they *were* betrothed. How was Papa able to change the gentleman's mind?"

Jane's cheeks once again flushed crimson and she turned away before glancing back at her sister. "Charles... Charles offered to settle a sum of money on Lydia." Elizabeth's mouth dropped open and Jane hurried on, "At first Papa refused, but truly there was no other way. It would have been very bad for Lydia, indeed for all of you, if the lieutenant had not married her."

"Jane! How much did Mr. Bingley give her?"

Jane was silent for a moment before answering. "Five thousand pounds," her sister said softly.

Elizabeth gasped.

"He is at his solicitor's offices even as we speak, settling the details."

Elizabeth studied her sister's face, seeing that Jane's eyes glistened with unshed tears.

"My husband truly is the best of men, is he not? He said it was of no significance... But I feel so ashamed that he should have to do such a thing on our sister's behalf."

"And what does Lydia have to say about all of this?"

"Oh! She does not know. And she cannot, Lizzy! No one knows, save Papa and myself, and now you."

Elizabeth nodded. "Yes, you are quite right. Lydia would tell all of Meryton and Papa would be mortified. Not to mention the whole of our acquaintance knowing the gentleman had to be forced to take her." She was quiet for a moment. "When is the wedding?"

Jane sighed. "In three weeks' time—as soon as the banns can be read. Papa was of a mind to force an immediate marriage and Charles even offered to obtain a special license, but Lydia would not have it. She wants as long a betrothal as possible so she may show herself off to all our neighbors. She even petitioned for an engagement ball, but of course Papa refused. He is only granting her the three weeks because we all agreed a rushed marriage might give the wrong impression." Jane smiled tremulously. "My poor Lizzy, forgive me for burdening you with all of this, and for cutting short your stay in Town."

Elizabeth squeezed her sister's hands before pulling Jane into a fierce embrace. "You have nothing to apologize for. And it will be good to be home. Well, at least it will be good to be near you again," she added and her sister responded with a weak laugh. "Now, let us go and find our aunt and uncle. At the very least, we should notify them there will be another wedding in the family."

CHAPTER 9

The journey to Hertfordshire passed at the usual speed. Due to the party's late arrival, Elizabeth spent the night at Netherfield; so it was not until the following morning that she and Jane made the three-mile trip to Longbourn. At the sound of carriage wheels on the gravel drive, the door to the house was thrown open and Mrs. Bennet, Lydia, and Kitty hurried to greet the returning sisters.

"Lizzy! Thank goodness you have come!" Mrs. Bennet cried, fluttering her handkerchief. "There is so much to be done! And your father is no help at all. He has barely stirred from his bookroom these last seven days."

Elizabeth reached out to give her mother a tentative embrace as Kitty rushed forward to tug at Elizabeth's sleeve.

"Lizzy, may I borrow your yellow gown for the ceremony? You know I have nothing half as fine and Lydia has asked me to stand up with her."

Elizabeth sighed. "We shall see, Kitty," she answered, moving towards the house where Lydia stood, her eyes sparkling with mirth.

"La, Lizzy! Do you not wish to congratulate me?" she trilled. "I am certain you had no notion when you went away that you should return to find one of your sisters engaged to be married. And me, the youngest of us all!"

"Hush, Lydia!" hissed Jane, in an uncharacteristic display of emotion. "We are all very happy for you, but we need not conduct this discussion in the courtyard."

Lydia pouted but Jane managed to usher the party into the house to continue their conversation in private.

After retiring to her room to see to her belongings, Elizabeth made her way downstairs, passing the parlor where she could hear her mother's and sisters' voices raised in excited conversation. Arriving at the entrance to her father's library, she tapped softly at the door, twisting the handle at Mr. Bennet's bid to enter.

Crossing into the chamber, Elizabeth made her way to one of the overstuffed chairs opposite Mr. Bennet's desk. Studying her father's face, she could immediately see the effect recent circumstances had taken. In addition to the deep grooves that marked her father's brow, his eyes held a sadness Elizabeth could not recall seeing there before.

"Papa, how are you?"

The clock in the corner ticked off the minutes as Mr. Bennet stared vacantly into the back garden. When he answered, his voice was devoid of emotion. "This is my fault."

Although Elizabeth had expressed similar sentiments in London, seeing her father's anguish, her only inclination now was to ease his suffering, and so she responded gently, "You must not blame yourself. You know Lydia has always been headstrong and determined to have her way, whatever the cost."

Mr. Bennet released a breath, finally turning to face his favorite daughter. "No, Lizzy. It is my own weakness that brought this about. I did not rein her in as I should have done, and now we are all reaping our just rewards. Were it not for Mr. Bingley..." he did not finish the sentence, but instead picked up the tumbler of brandy before him, draining it in one long swallow.

"Yes," Elizabeth answered quietly. "Jane told me of Mr. Bingley's generosity. We must all be eternally grateful for his kind attention."

Replacing his glass, Mr. Bennet removed his spectacles before slowly massaging the bridge of his nose. "It is a debt I am afraid I can never repay."

"Papa, we must remember that Mr. Bingley is family now. I do not believe he expects compensation." When her father did not answer, Elizabeth decided her best course might be to turn the conversation. "But what of Lydia's gentleman? I imagine she is well pleased as he has the good fortune to sport a red coat, but what of his character? I must admit to having some concerns based on the story Jane related."

Mr. Bennet snorted, tilting his head. "From what I have observed, he is as silly as your sister. However, I must confess, although he did balk at Lydia's lack of dowry, he does not appear to be totally mercenary, so I suppose it could be worse. And he does seem quite taken with your sister's... charms." At this, Mr. Bennet smirked, a bit of his usual liveliness returning. "In any case, you may judge for yourself, my dear Lizzy, as your Mamma has invited him to dine with us this evening. Now, why do you not run along and join your sisters. I believe I am in need of a nice long rest if I am to tolerate the upcoming festivities with my usual good grace."

Elizabeth did not heed her father's advice to join the remainder of her family; she too felt incapable of an afternoon spent in Lydia's presence. Instead, she made her escape through the side door, eager to enjoy a long ramble in the countryside after so many weeks in Town. She did not return for several hours, leaving just enough time to dress before joining her mother and sisters who were already gathered in the drawing room. Taking a deep breath, Elizabeth entered the parlor, steeling herself against the commotion that was sure to follow. She was not to be disappointed.

"Lizzy, there you are! It is about time," Mrs. Bennet called the moment Elizabeth had crossed into the room.

"Jane and Mr. Bingley will be here at any moment, as well as Lydia's dear Mr. Hughes," she added, waving her handkerchief in the direction of her youngest daughter.

Elizabeth made her way to a seat near the window, smothering a sigh. "Oh, yes. Heaven forbid we keep the lieutenant waiting."

Across the room, Lydia scowled. "You needn't look so sour about it, Lizzy. It is hardly my fault that men prefer my company to yours, even if I am five years younger."

Before Elizabeth could reply, Kitty spoke. "You forget, Lydia, that Lizzy might have been the first to marry had she accepted Mr. Collins."

"Do not remind me!" cried Mrs. Bennet. "I have not forgiven you, Lizzy. To think, because of your headstrong ways, Charlotte Lucas will one day be mistress of this house. Thank goodness our dear Jane managed to secure Mr. Bingley, otherwise, heaven knows what would have become of us."

"Mamma..." Elizabeth began, but she was once again interrupted, this time by Mary.

"Not everyone believes securing a husband is the key to happiness, Mamma. I think Lizzy did the right thing. She would never have been content with Mr. Collins."

Surprised, Elizabeth turned to face her middle sister. "Thank you, Mary."

Mrs. Bennet opened her mouth, but as luck would have it, she was soon distracted by the sight of a carriage pulling into the drive, so Elizabeth was spared her mother's further opinions on the matter.

❄

Elizabeth lifted her wine glass, draining its contents. Across the table Lydia prattled on about wedding fripperies, while beside her Mr. Hughes sat quietly eating the meal Mrs. Bennet had spent two days planning. Elizabeth studied her soon-to-be brother. To her surprise, her impression of him had been favorable so far. Knowing Lydia, Elizabeth had expected someone brash and bawdy, but instead she found the gentleman quiet and somewhat shy, especially around her gregarious family. And she had once or twice caught him staring at her youngest sister with an expression that could only be described as awe. Elizabeth released a breath. For all her concerns, he was a good deal better than she had reason to expect and far superior to anything Lydia deserved.

Setting down her cutlery, Elizabeth turned her attention to the conversation just in time to hear Mr. Bingley directing a question to the lieutenant, as Lydia had finally stopped speaking long enough to take a bite of food.

"Mr. Hughes, have you and Miss Lydia settled on where you will reside after the wedding?" Bingley asked, and Elizabeth noticed the worried expression that flickered across Jane's face.

The lieutenant opened his mouth, but it was Lydia who answered. "My Uncle Phillips has found us lodgings in Meryton. The house is frightfully small, but I dare say it will do well enough until my darling Hughes can sort out something better. Surely there must be a small estate in the vicinity we might lease."

Bingley coughed, taking a sip of his wine as Jane turned to address her sister. "Lydia, you know very well there are no such properties available. Besides, Mr. Hughes must be near his regiment, and certainly will not have the time to manage his own estate."

Nor does the man have two shillings to rub together, Elizabeth thought, exceedingly glad Mr. Bingley had taken pains to safeguard Lydia's dowry so the money could not be touched until her sister reached her majority. Honestly! Did Lydia never have a concern for anything besides her own selfish desires?

As if to prove Elizabeth's point, Lydia waved her hand in a dismissive manner. "Oh, Jane! We shall have a steward for all that tedious business. But I suppose you are correct. It would be silly to tie ourselves down when we shall be removing to Brighton in a few short months. And then who knows? My dear Hughes was even thinking of purchasing a commission in the regulars, weren't you, Henry?"

Now it was the lieutenant who coughed into his napkin before turning to his betrothed. "I hope to... one day," he murmured.

Elizabeth frowned and shot her sister a look, before turning to her mother to inquire about the next course.

Darcy stepped onto the pavement of Gracechurch Street, glancing up at the modest townhouse. Though not nearly as grand as the homes he was accustomed to frequenting, the façade was freshly painted and the brick walkway leading to the front steps was flanked with neatly trimmed shrubbery. His knock was answered promptly by an immaculately dressed manservant, and after presenting his card, Darcy was shown into a tastefully furnished salon.

Mrs. Gardiner stood when he entered, and although her face showed surprise, her eyes were warm, and Darcy immediately felt at ease.

"Mr. Darcy, this is indeed a pleasure."

Darcy bowed, a quick scan of the room showing him that Mrs. Gardiner was the only occupant. Attempting to hide his disappointment, he took the seat his hostess indicated. "Mrs. Gardiner, I hope you will excuse the intrusion. I happened to be in the area and thought I would stop in to pay my respects."

"It is no imposition, sir. As a matter of fact, you find me quite at my leisure, and I always welcome company."

"I thank you. My sister and I had anticipated calling earlier in the week, but unfortunately, she has been indisposed. I... I trust you and Miss Bennet have been in good health?"

"We have, sir. But what of Miss Darcy? I hope she is not still unwell?"

"No, she is much improved. Though I have encouraged her to rest, else she certainly would have accompanied me." Darcy turned to face the door, twisting his walking stick between his fingers.

Mrs. Gardiner fixed her gaze on his and a smile touched her lips. "Pray, do give Miss Darcy my regards.

And I am certain Lizzy would wish to convey hers as well." She paused for a moment before adding, "Unfortunately, my niece is no longer residing with us. She returned to Longbourn yesterday afternoon."

Struggling to hide his disappointment, Darcy schooled his expression. "Oh? I did not realize... That is, I had understood Miss Bennet was to have stayed in Town for some duration."

"Yes, that was her original intent," Mrs. Gardiner answered slowly. "It was a last-minute decision. My husband and I were sorry to see her go."

Darcy's gaze shifted to the window. "I see. And do you expect that Miss Bennet will return before the end of the season?"

"I do not believe her plans are set, sir."

Conversation faltered until Mrs. Gardiner introduced the topic of Derbyshire and the two spoke for some moments about mutual acquaintances. But when the clock struck the hour, Darcy reached for his stick, slowly rising to his feet.

"Forgive me, Mrs. Gardiner, but I must return to my sister. She is not yet fully recovered and I do not like leaving her alone for an extended period."

"Of course," Mrs. Gardiner answered, rising and accompanying him to the door.

"I pray you would convey my best wishes to your family," Darcy added.

"And mine to yours, sir. I hope our paths will cross again one day."

And although Darcy nodded, he thought such a circumstance very unlikely.

Lydia's wedding day soon arrived, and in an intimate ceremony in the Meryton church, Lieutenant Henry Hughes and Miss Lydia Bennet became husband and wife. Afterwards, the four and twenty neighborhood families along with a smattering of out-of-town relations joined the newlyweds at Longbourn for the wedding breakfast. Although Mr. Bingley had gallantly offered Netherfield for the celebration, Mr. Bennet had steadfastly refused, feeling his son-in-law had done quite enough for the couple already.

Weaving her way through the clusters of friends and relations who had assembled in Longbourn's parlor, Elizabeth approached her aunt and uncle who were presently conversing with Jane and Mr. Bingley.

"I will go up and change," said Elizabeth. "We can be off as soon as Lydia and the lieutenant take their leave."

The Gardiners were quick to agree, but Jane reached for Elizabeth's hand. "I do wish you would stay, Lizzy. You know you are always welcome at Netherfield if Mamma's nerves are too much for you."

Elizabeth laughed. "You are too kind, Jane. But you and Charles are still newlyweds yourselves. I could not impose on you for any length of time. No, I would much rather go back to London with our aunt and uncle."

At this, Bingley stepped forward. "I know your mind is already made up, but I would like to second Jane's offer. You know you will always be welcome wherever your sister and I reside."

Touched, Elizabeth murmured her thanks before taking a breath and turning to her sister. "Jane, I wonder if I could trouble you to accompany me upstairs. There is something I would speak to you about before I go."

"Jane, say something."

It was a quarter of an hour later and Elizabeth was perched on the corner of her bed, her sister staring back at her from the facing window seat.

"Lizzy! I can hardly believe it. You might have been killed!"

Crossing to the window, Elizabeth sank down beside her sister, wrapping her arms around Jane's slim shoulders. "But I was not. As you can see, I am perfectly well."

Jane blinked back at her. "But the carriage was wrecked! And the coachman *was* killed. I remember Charles saying so. Were you truly not hurt at all?"

Elizabeth shook her head. "Just some scrapes and bruises. Mr. Darcy and I were both thrown from the coach. I was extremely lucky."

"But Lizzy, that was *months ago*, and you have said nothing in all this time!"

Elizabeth's gaze fell to her lap. "I know; forgive me. It

was not something I could put into a letter, and Mr. Darcy and I both agreed it would be best if nobody knew. Besides, I did not want to tax you with keeping my secret."

"So instead you have shouldered the burden all alone. Oh, Lizzy, I do wish you had trusted me."

"Well, I am trusting you now. Though apart from Charles, I must beg you to repeat this to no one. I would never require you to keep such a secret from your husband, but my reputation would be in tatters should this be generally known."

Jane instantly bobbed her head, her eyes widening in alarm. "Of course! I would never wish for you to be the subject of gossip." After a moment she continued. "But I do believe Mr. Darcy to be an honorable man. I am certain he would offer for you should such a thing become necessary."

Elizabeth opened her mouth to speak, but her sister hurried to add, "Not that I would ever wish for you to be forced into such a marriage. It is my greatest hope that you will marry for love, and I know how you feel about Mr. Darcy."

Elizabeth slowly nodded. Though in truth she was not at all certain how she felt about Mr. Darcy, nor could she comprehend the gentleman's feelings for her. However, her sister was correct about one thing—Darcy was a man of honor. To Elizabeth's surprise, a feeling of happy anticipation settled over her, and she was surprised to note that she almost wished word *would* get out. So shocked was she by this sudden realization that she barely noticed when Jane quit the room to allow Elizabeth to change.

Goodness, what was happening to her? Did she actually wish to marry Mr. Darcy?

Wandering over to her bedside table, she picked up the book he had gifted her. Carefully lifting the leather cover, she stared at her name, written on the first page in Mr. Darcy's bold hand, and her thoughts drifted back to their time in the cottage. When had she begun to see him in a different light? She knew she had softened towards him when she read his letter. Then, visiting Pemberley, seeing the place that was his home, she had felt she'd come to know him a little better. And it was true that she had wished to see him again, to apologize for her behavior the day of his proposal. But she would not have said she *liked* the man. She had still found him proud and arrogant.

Until the cottage.

Elizabeth tucked the book into her satchel. Perhaps it was seeing him so vulnerable... though she had never been the sentimental sort. Certainly she was not the type to fall in love with a man simply because he had relied upon her for a brief time. No, it was not that. Thinking back, she remembered their recent conversations, and her lips curved into a slow smile. Somehow, when it had been only the two of them, things had seemed different. *He* had seemed different. Even in the carriage, before the accident. And then in Town, when she and her aunt were invited into his home. He had been so genuine and... kind. And he had gone to the trouble of tracking down her book, not to mention taking every precaution to ensure that no word leaked out about their time alone.

Suddenly, Elizabeth frowned. But was that truly to protect her reputation? Or was it simply to ensure he was not trapped into a marriage he no longer desired?

CHAPTER 10

E lizabeth held the gown against her body, gazing into the mirrored glass. Diaphanous layers of sheer muslin floated around her, as weightless as a cloud. Tiny seed pearls shimmered at the empire waist and delicate silver threads embellished the graceful skirt. It was easily the most exquisite article of clothing Elizabeth had ever owned and she still felt wholly undeserving of it. Although the Gardiners claimed it was merely an early birthday gift, Elizabeth knew better. Her aunt had purchased the garment in an attempt to lift her niece's spirits. Releasing a breath, Elizabeth carefully lay the evening gown across the bed.

The last couple of months certainly had been a trial. After more than a fortnight spent at Longbourn for Lydia's wedding, Elizabeth had returned to London, hoping to put the entire affair behind her. Her aunt had told her about

Mr. Darcy's visit, and despite the nagging concern for her reputation in the wake of Lydia's recklessness, Elizabeth still hoped he would once again call at Gracechurch Street. She could not help but think that if she could see him, and talk to him, she would know if his feelings remained unchanged.

But it had now been four weeks since her sister's wedding, and almost two months since she had last seen Mr. Darcy. Of course, she could not be certain the gentleman was aware of her return to Town, but she knew he corresponded with Mr. Bingley, so she had to assume he was informed. Which meant he had likely also been made aware of her sister's marriage—as well as the circumstances preceding it.

Fastening the last comb in her dark curls, Elizabeth stepped into her gown. Despite her low spirits, she was looking forward to her evening at the theater. Although she had seen several productions during her stay, tonight was special. They had been invited to a performance given by a celebrated soprano passing through London on a tour of the continent. Tickets were in high demand but her uncle had been invited to share the private box of one of his business associates. It seemed the man had been recently widowed and had planned to attend the event alone. When Mr. Gardiner mentioned his niece's keen interest in the performance, the gentleman had been quick to invite them to join him.

Gazing pensively at her reflection, Elizabeth's thoughts returned to Mr. Darcy. She didn't know precisely when things had begun to shift, but it had been many weeks since her feelings for him had gone from dislike, to tolerance, to... a feeling she scarcely dared name. And the thought of Lydia's near ruin casting a pall on their blossoming friendship filled her with the deepest regret.

After all of their progress, she simply could not bear the notion that Mr. Darcy was out there somewhere thinking ill of her.

Darcy stood with his chin tipped upwards as his man made the final adjustments to his cravat. Reaching for a brush, the valet ran an expert hand over his master's jacket, but after only a moment, Darcy waved him away with a flick of his wrist.

"Pierce, that is enough fussing. It is merely a night at the theater, I am not being presented at court."

His valet stiffened, casting his eyes to the floor and Darcy felt his shoulders slump.

"Forgive me, Pierce. You have outdone yourself, as always. I am simply in a bad humor this evening."

His valet nodded and Darcy smothered a sigh. In truth, he had been in a foul mood these past six weeks, ever since his visit to Gracechurch Street when he had learned of Elizabeth's departure. Darcy's gaze drifted to the writing desk in the corner of his chambers where Bingley's latest letter sat. When he had received it several days ago, he had impatiently broken the seal, scanning his friend's unruly scrawl for Elizabeth's name. When his eyes had at last lit upon the name *Bennet,* he had practically ceased breathing; but it had only been one sentence notifying him of the marriage of Elizabeth's youngest sister to someone in the local militia.

"Will there be anything else, sir?"

Blinking at his valet, Darcy shook his head. "No, that will be all. And you need not wait up. I shall see you in the morning."

Exiting his apartment, Darcy stepped into the corridor. It was still early. He would look in on his sister before he departed.

Finding the door to her chambers ajar, Darcy knocked lightly before entering. Inside the spacious chamber, Georgiana rested on a chaise near the window, while Mrs. Annesley sat beside the fire, her knitting needles rhythmically clicking, a ball of wool resting in her lap. At the sound of his footfalls, Georgiana lifted her gaze, smiling in his direction. "William! Are you leaving already?"

Moving across the room, Darcy pressed a soft kiss to his sister's forehead. "Yes, dearest. I thought I might walk to Matlock House since the weather is so unseasonably warm. The physician has said I should be exercising my leg and there is no point in taking two carriages when there are so few of us going." He paused for a moment. "Are you certain you would not prefer me to stay? Truly, I would not mind."

"Oh, no! I would feel terrible if you missed the performance on my account. And I know Lord and Lady Matlock and our cousins are looking forward to your company."

Darcy frowned, tugging on his cuffs. "Well, if you are certain…"

In truth, he would much rather be here, sitting quietly with his sister, perhaps reading to her or playing something on the pianoforte in her private sitting room. It concerned him greatly that Georgiana was once again indisposed. Although she had eventually rallied from her previous malady, he did not like the fact that she still seemed drawn and tired.

Walking over to the window, Darcy stared down into the street. As he had done many times before, he found himself reflecting bitterly on the fact that Georgiana was forced to come into adulthood without a mother or a sister to guide her. What good was he, or his cousin Richard for that matter, when it came to understanding the needs of a young girl approaching womanhood? As usual, his thoughts turned to Elizabeth. If only she had accepted him, they would now be happily married and Georgiana would have an elder sister to turn to. Frowning, he studied his reflection in the darkened glass. Well, it was not to be. Elizabeth was gone, and he and his sister would simply have to rely upon Mrs. Annesley to advise them. Perhaps if things did not improve, he would consult Lady Matlock.

Remembering his aunt, Darcy withdrew his pocket watch. If he was going, he had best get started. His uncle never liked to be kept waiting.

Mr. Gardiner's carriage pulled to the curb and Elizabeth's uncle stepped down, turning to hand the ladies to the pavement. They were still a good distance from the theater, but the knot of carriages at the entrance made it impossible for their coachman to get any closer.

"I am afraid we shall have to walk the last stretch," Mr. Gardiner apologized, taking his wife on one arm and his niece on the other.

Elizabeth's face flushed with excitement as she took in the throngs of people milling about in their evening finery. "It is no bother, Uncle. It is a lovely night."

Her aunt smiled, clearly pleased with her niece's enthusiasm, and the small party set out. Joining the mass of theatergoers, they climbed the handful of steps and entered the ornate lobby. Mr. Gardiner surveyed the crowd in an attempt to locate their host.

"It may be impossible to observe one another in this mob, but we shall have a look around. In any case, Mr. Whiting has given me the direction to his box so it is of no great significance if we are not successful in finding him here."

Mrs. Gardiner nodded and the threesome began slowly making their way to the stairs.

Darcy stepped beneath the portico of the Theatre Royal, his gaze fixed upon his uncle's back. Lady Margaret kept pace at his side, her fingers resting lightly on Darcy's sleeve. Arriving at Matlock House earlier that evening, he had been informed that their party had diminished by one more member as his cousin Lord Hazelton, Lord and Lady Matlock's eldest son, had developed a headache and did not feel up to accompanying them—leaving Darcy to escort Hazelton's wife. Not that Darcy minded. Lady Margaret was pleasant enough. Certainly she was beautiful, with a quick wit that reminded him a bit of Elizabeth's. The daughter of a marquess, Lady Margaret possessed flawless manners and always comported herself with the utmost decorum. Yes, his cousin had done well for himself. And although Darcy would have preferred his sister's company, having a companion on his arm would at least cut down on the number of unmarried ladies vying for his attention.

Entering the crowded lobby, Darcy's spine automatically stiffened. Damnation! It looked like the whole of London society was here for this evening's performance. And now that he was to escort Lady Margaret, he would not be able to depart early as he had previously intended. Out of the corner of his eye he felt the stares of those around him, and his skin tingled as their salacious whispers floated in the air.

Lady Matlock turned to say something to her daughter-in-law, before allowing her husband to guide her across the lobby to greet some of their acquaintances. At the slight pressure on his arm, Darcy turned to face the woman by his side.

"There is no need to look so miserable, you know," Lady Margaret whispered. "I would be happy to accompany you to our seats if you would prefer to get out of this crush."

Abashed, Darcy smiled down at her. "Is it that obvious?" he asked, causing his companion to laugh lightly.

"Yes. You look quite despondent. Come, let us go to the box. Lord and Lady Matlock will know where to find us."

Elizabeth trailed behind her aunt and uncle, craning her neck to get a better look at the other ladies in their elegant gowns and jewels. But they had not gone more than a few paces when Mrs. Gardiner stopped short, causing Elizabeth to bump up against her.

"Lizzy, isn't that Mr. Darcy? There, across the lobby..."

Elizabeth felt her pulse quicken as she hurriedly scanned the crowd. It did not take long to spot the gentleman who stood several inches taller than those around him, and her heart leapt at the sight. His dark head was bent slightly as he conversed with someone beside him and Elizabeth's gaze traveled downward. The woman at Mr. Darcy's elbow was possibly a few years older than herself, and exceptionally beautiful. Her copper colored hair was twisted into an elaborate knot showcasing a glittering tiara, and her gown was a brilliant sapphire blue, a perfect match to the jewels resting against her alabaster skin. As Elizabeth watched, she leaned up and said something that made Darcy's mouth lift into a smile. The woman laughed at whatever he said to her in return and Darcy placed a hand on the small of her back. And in one fluid movement, the couple headed for the stairs.

Darcy began walking in the direction of the grand staircase when the sense of someone's gaze upon his person made him turn. Immediately, his steps faltered and his breath froze inside his chest. Elizabeth! She was standing halfway across the crowded lobby beside her aunt and a slightly older gentleman who Darcy took to be her uncle. His gaze swept her form and his insides quivered. My God, she was breathtaking! Their eyes locked and he saw a flash of recognition before Elizabeth looked away. Carried by the crowd, their parties drifted closer together, and Darcy attempted to adjust his expression—it would not do to meet her relations looking like a lovesick schoolboy.

They were within steps of one another when Darcy stopped, executing a deep bow.

"Miss Bennet, this is a pleasant surprise. I did not realize you were back in Town."

"Yes. I returned some weeks ago," Elizabeth answered before turning to her uncle and performing the necessary introductions.

"A pleasure, sir," Mr. Gardiner offered as the two gentlemen exchanged polite bows.

Darcy greeted Mrs. Gardiner warmly before shifting to include Elizabeth and her uncle. "Will you permit me to introduce Lady Margaret Hazelton to your acquaintance?

Lady Margaret, this is Miss Elizabeth Bennet and her aunt and uncle, Mr. and Mrs. Gardiner."

Lady Margaret dropped a graceful curtsy, which Elizabeth and Mrs. Gardiner returned as Darcy's gaze swept the crowded entrance hall. "My own aunt and uncle, Lord and Lady Matlock, are also in attendance, but we seem to have been separated by the crowd." Bringing his attention back to Lady Margaret, he added, "Miss Bennet and I met in Hertfordshire when I was visiting my friend Bingley last year. He is now married to Miss Bennet's eldest sister."

Lady Margaret offered her congratulations, and Darcy turned to address Elizabeth.

"Miss Bennet, I understand your youngest sister is also lately married. I hope you will allow me to wish you joy?"

To Darcy's surprise, Elizabeth's cheeks colored and she briefly looked away.

"Yes, I thank you, sir," she murmured.

Darcy stepped forward, his brow furrowed, but Elizabeth's gaze remained firmly fixed somewhere over his right shoulder. Mr. and Mrs. Gardiner exchanged a glance.

There was a moment of awkward silence before Lady Margaret spoke. "Will you be in Town long, Miss Bennet?"

To Darcy's great relief, Elizabeth turned to face his cousin.

"I have no set schedule, your ladyship, but I will likely remain until the spring."

Mrs. Gardiner touched her husband's arm. "Edward, perhaps we should find our seats," she said softly and the gentleman nodded his agreement.

The group prepared to part, but after a slight hesitation, Darcy turned to address Elizabeth's uncle. "Mr. Gardiner, it would be my pleasure to have you join us in my box. My own party is reduced in number as my sister and cousin were unable to attend."

Mr. Gardiner's brow lifted in obvious surprise. "That is very kind of you, Mr. Darcy—"

"—but we could not possibly accept," Elizabeth finished. All eyes swiveled in her direction, and Elizabeth flushed. "That is, there is a fourth member of our party, sir, and we would not wish to crowd you."

Mr. Gardiner regarded Elizabeth for a moment before continuing amicably. "I am afraid my niece is correct. But I do thank you for your generous offer. Perhaps another time."

"Of course." Darcy bowed. "Enjoy the performance," he answered stiffly before the two parties went their separate ways.

Darcy was not enjoying the performance. Although his gaze was fixed on the stage below, he would have been at a loss to describe a single detail that had occurred since the curtain lifted. Shuffling in his seat, his eyes swept the dimly lit theater, but he could not locate Elizabeth's party. His lips pressed together as he recollected the conversation in the lobby. After everything they had been through together he did not expect Elizabeth to be ill at ease in his presence. Perhaps he had misinterpreted her behavior… No, it was as if she could not wait to get away from him!

His thoughts returned to the last thing she had said before they had left to take their seats. A fourth member of their party. It could mean only one thing.

As soon as the curtain came down at the beginning of the interval, Darcy was on his feet. "May I bring you ladies some refreshment?" he asked, turning to his aunt and Lady Margaret.

Lord Matlock's brows lifted in surprise. "Well, this makes a change. I have never known you to willingly brave the throng if you could avoid it, Nephew."

Darcy flushed. "Yes, well... I feel the need to stretch my legs after sitting so long."

His uncle nodded and the two gentlemen made their way down the sweeping staircase, stopping every few feet to greet various members of the *ton*. Darcy cringed as one particularly effusive matron thrust her young daughter in his direction so forcefully, the girl practically tumbled to the landing. By the time Darcy and his uncle reached the lounge, Darcy remembered in great detail why he never left his box until the conclusion of the performance.

Nodding to an acquaintance from his club, Darcy's eyes scanned the heavy crowd. Much as he hated every moment of this, it would all be worth it for another chance to speak with Elizabeth. Finally, his perseverance was rewarded when he spotted the familiar figure of her uncle standing near the refreshments conversing with a younger gentleman. Darcy's gaze narrowed as he studied the stranger. Though not particularly handsome, the man was well groomed and seemed affable, with a ready smile. Darcy's fists clenched as he continued to scour the room to no avail. Elizabeth must have remained with her aunt in their seats.

Just then, Mr. Gardiner turned, and Darcy spun on his heel.

Conversing with Elizabeth and her family was one thing, but he had no desire to make idle chatter with the competition.

Elizabeth's gaze darted to the entrance to their box. What could be taking so long? She turned back to her aunt, but Mrs. Gardiner was still deep in conversation with Mr. Whiting. Elizabeth sighed. She should have accompanied her uncle to the lounge as he had suggested. As painful as it would have been to see Mr. Darcy's beautiful companion, sitting here wondering about her was proving far worse.

Pretending interest in her aunt's conversation, Elizabeth twisted in her seat. Finally, her forbearance was rewarded when the curtain opened and her uncle entered. But disappointment washed over her as she saw that he was alone. Lowering her lashes, she instantly chastised herself for her foolishness. Of course he was alone! What had she expected, that Mr. Darcy would abandon his companion to pay a social call to her in her box? If she had wished to spend time in his company, she had squandered her opportunity.

Mr. Gardiner stepped forward, offering cups of punch to Elizabeth and her aunt. "Madeline, you will never guess who I ran into while waiting for the refreshments. Do you remember Mr. Clarke? The solicitor I dealt with on that warehouse project last summer?"

"Yes, of course," Mrs. Gardiner answered, taking a sip of her drink. "He was in practice with a son, I believe, was he not?"

"Yes, exactly. And I have just met the son here in the lounge. A fine young gentleman. Very friendly," he added, casting a sidelong glance at his niece.

Elizabeth flushed, turning her attention to her lap. The last thing she was in the mood to endure was her uncle attempting to make a match for her with one of his acquaintances. "Did you... did you happen to see Mr. Darcy?" she asked.

Mr. Gardiner's gaze darted to the side, exchanging a look with his wife. "No, Lizzy, I did not. Although to be honest, the crowd was uncommonly thick, and I was not really attending."

Elizabeth nodded, but as the performance resumed, the thoughts she had been holding at bay came rushing to the surface.

It was done. She need no longer question Mr. Darcy's feelings, as he had made them abundantly evident tonight. He had found a woman of equal standing, one who would bring her own set of noble connections to a marriage and whose family would not be a degradation to the Darcy name. No, Lady Margaret would be a proper mistress for Pemberley, just as his own beloved mother had been...

Tears blurred Elizabeth's vision and she attempted to dash them away with the palms of her hands.

When the curtain fell, Mrs. Gardiner turned to her niece. "Did you enjoy yourself, Lizzy?" she asked and Elizabeth forced a smile.

"Yes, Aunt. And I do thank you for taking me, as it will likely be the last performance I shall see for some time. I have decided I will return to Longbourn by month's end."

CHAPTER 11

It was over. Darcy stared at the rows of books that lined the walls of his richly appointed library, but all he saw were Elizabeth's fine eyes, turned away from him in pity.

... there is a fourth member of our party...

She had found someone else, just as he always knew she would. Someone who did not get tongue-tied when he tried to converse with her. Someone who could fashion a proper proposal without insulting the people she loved.

He took a bitter swallow of his drink. Why had he ever allowed himself to believe her feelings for him had altered? True, she had been kind to him—both in the cottage and afterwards in Town. But why shouldn't she be kind? They had agreed to put the past behind them. To forge a friendship of sorts.

She had never hinted at wanting anything else. No, it

was his own arrogance that allowed him to read more into the situation than was actually there. She had cared for him after the accident as she would have cared for anyone who had been injured. She had made her feelings on marriage perfectly clear when he had offered for her. In that regard, it was evident that nothing had changed.

Everything had changed. Since the night at the theater, Elizabeth had relived her encounter with Mr. Darcy and the sophisticated lady on his arm more times than she cared to count. Fingering the embroidery frame resting in her lap, she once again recalled the look on Mr. Darcy's face when he congratulated her on Lydia's marriage.

Nausea twisted Elizabeth's stomach. He knew. Based on his expression, she was certain of it. No wonder she had not heard from him in all the weeks she had been back in Town. Mr. Bingley must have confided in him, and now he wished to have nothing more to do with her. Any small spark of admiration Mr. Darcy still felt for her had clearly been stamped out by Lydia's folly.

Elizabeth's eyes burned with the effort of holding back tears and she dipped her gaze as a knock sounded at the drawing room door. Brushing her fingertips along the edges of her lashes, she turned to see the Gardiners' butler enter the salon.

"Mr. Bennet has arrived, madam," the servant intoned, and Elizabeth's head snapped up as her aunt met her gaze with a questioning expression. Elizabeth stood, her embroidery falling to the floor. "Papa? Aunt, were you expecting him?"

Mrs. Gardiner shook her head. "No, Lizzy, I was not." Turning to the butler she added, "Mr. Wright, pray, show him in."

It was only a moment before Mr. Bennet entered, bowing to his hostess before his eyes found his daughter.

"Papa!" Elizabeth closed the space between them, but drew back when her father stiffened. "What is it? Is someone ill?"

It seemed to take an eternity for her father to answer, and when he did, there was no mistaking the seriousness in his tone. "No, Lizzy. Everyone is well. But I have come on an urgent matter. There is something I must speak with you about."

"Certainly."

Mrs. Gardiner rose, her gaze shifting between her niece's worried expression and her brother's stony stare. "Pray, make yourself at home, Brother. As you are now here to keep Lizzy company, I will check on preparations for the evening meal. You will dine with us, I hope?"

"Yes. I thank you, Madeline. And some time alone with my daughter would be much appreciated."

As soon as the door closed behind her aunt, Elizabeth spoke. "Papa, I beg you, tell me what is amiss. Is it Jane? Has something happened between her and Mr. Bingley?"

"No, Lizzy, your sister is well, as is Mr. Bingley. As a matter of fact, your brother has accompanied me to Town. He dropped me here on his way to the Hursts'."

"Then what—"

"I have come here to speak with you about a serious matter that has recently come to my attention. Something that concerns you."

Elizabeth's eyes clouded with confusion. She could not for the life of her imagine what would have her usually affable father looking so grave.

Mr. Bennet steepled his fingers, regarding his daughter over the rims of his spectacles. "Now Lizzy," he finally began, "I am going to ask you a question, and I would like an honest answer."

"Certainly, Papa. I have always been truthful with you."

Elizabeth's father regarded her in silence for several moments. "Perhaps. Though one need not speak a falsehood to lie, my dear. The damage done by a deliberate omission can be every bit as great."

At her father's words, Elizabeth felt the first stirrings of comprehension and she briefly looked away. Taking a breath, she answered calmly, "What is it you wish to know? You have my word I will be as honest with you as I am able."

"Very well." Mr. Bennet studied his daughter. "Is it true you spent a night alone with Mr. Darcy last autumn?"

Although the question was not entirely unexpected, hearing her father express it in such a cold, hard manner made Elizabeth cringe. Rising, she paced to the window. "Who told you this?"

"It does not signify who told me. I am waiting for your answer, Lizzy."

Elizabeth turned, squaring her shoulders. "Yes. Although it is not what you seem to assume. I ran into Mr.

Darcy in Kent when I was returning to London. Uncle's carriage had been delayed and I was faced with spending the night in the parlor at the coaching inn as there were no available rooms. Seeing my distress, Mr. Darcy offered to escort me to Town."

"And?" Mr. Bennet prompted.

"There was an accident. Mr. Darcy was badly injured. We were forced to take shelter in an unoccupied cottage while Mr. Darcy's footman returned to the inn for help."

"So, it is true. You were alone with him, just the two of you?" Mr. Bennet scrutinized his daughter, his mouth a hard line. "What were you thinking, Lizzy? I would expect this sort of behavior from Lydia, though I know I am at fault for not restraining her properly. But never from you."

Elizabeth's temper flared. "Papa! I do not know what you are suggesting but the situation is completely different. Mr. Darcy was seriously hurt. And even if he were not, he has always behaved in an honorable manner. I am deeply offended, sir, on Mr. Darcy's behalf as well as my own."

Taking in the stricken look on his daughter's face, Mr. Bennet softened his tone. "Forgive me, Lizzy. I do not mean to suggest that you did not use proper judgment, and I agree that Mr. Darcy has always seemed a decent enough fellow. Certainly, that is Bingley's opinion of him. And I know you claim not to even like the man. But that is not the point! If anyone were to find out about this, you would be ruined, regardless of what actually occurred."

Elizabeth stalked across the carpet, her agitation growing with every step. "That is why Mr. Darcy and I both agreed it would be best if no one knew. He assured me his staff was to be trusted."

"Lizzy, come sit down. To my knowledge, Mr. Darcy's people have revealed nothing. I found out quite by accident. I happened to overhear Mr. Bingley speaking to Jane. They are both quite distraught, thinking they have betrayed your confidence."

Elizabeth made her way back to the settee, perching lightly on its edge. "Poor Jane. But then you see, if no one else has any knowledge of these events, there can be no need for concern."

Mr. Bennet sighed. "But I *am* concerned, Lizzy. If word should get out, I must know the gentleman will do the honorable thing. I must be allowed that assurance."

A sinking suspicion made Elizabeth's heart rate escalate as she regarded her father's somber expression. "Papa, certainly you do not mean to speak to Mr. Darcy about this?"

"That is precisely what I intend to do. I have come to Town for just that purpose."

Elizabeth opened her mouth, but Mr. Bennet lifted his palm. "Now Lizzy, I know you would not wish to be forced into marriage. Hopefully it will not come to that. But if it does, I must have Mr. Darcy's pledge that he will stand by you." Placing a reassuring arm around his daughter's shoulders, Mr. Bennet continued, "Come, let us speak no more of this. I have had a long journey and am in need of sustenance. Bingley and I will seek out Mr. Darcy in the morning."

That night, Elizabeth scarcely slept, and when she did, horrible images from the accident haunted her dreams. Rising at first light, she hurried through her toilette, hoping for as much time as possible to reason with her father before his intended departure. But despite her entreaties throughout the course of the morning meal, Mr. Bennet remained unmoved.

"Papa, if you must speak with Mr. Darcy, at least allow me to accompany you," Elizabeth pleaded, trailing her father to the door.

Mr. Bennet turned, surveying his daughter with a raised brow. "Certainly not. This is no place for you, Lizzy. Mr. Bingley will accompany me."

Elizabeth's stomach lurched as Mr. Bennet retrieved his greatcoat and hat from the Gardiners' butler. She knew Jane's husband would do well as an intermediary; nevertheless, the thought of her father interrogating Mr. Darcy and insisting upon a marriage... well, it did not bear thinking about! It was one thing when she still had some hope that the gentleman continued to hold her in high esteem, but now, knowing that he had no particular affection for her and no inclination towards marriage—at least not with her as the bride. How would she ever face Mr. Darcy again, knowing he would now find himself honor-bound to marry her against his wishes?

Darcy lifted his glass of port, staring at the fire that sizzled and snapped in the iron grate. No matter how hard he tried, he could not shake Elizabeth from his thoughts. Seeing her again at the theater had made him even more aware of the stark contrast between her and the women of the *ton*—the fashionable set, from which he was expected to choose a wife. He grimaced as he pictured them, hiding behind their disingenuous smiles and their feigned laughter—like so many fine gowns all cut from the same pattern.

But not Elizabeth. No, whatever faults Elizabeth possessed, the one thing that could be said of her was that she was always completely and utterly herself. She did not dissemble and she was unceasingly honest. It was one of the things he loved best about her, yet it also made the feelings she had displayed at the theater all the more difficult to face.

A sharp rap at the library door dragged him from his private reverie. "Come!" he called out, setting down his glass.

The door swung open to reveal a grim-faced Stevens.

"I beg your pardon Mr. Darcy, but you have visitors."

Darcy tensed, fixing his butler with a hard stare. "I thought I made it clear I was not at home. To anyone."

"Yes, sir. But it is Mr. Bingley and another gentleman. Mr. Bingley indicated that the matter was urgent."

Darcy inhaled a deep breath, immediately feeling remorse for snapping at his butler. Although he had asked not to be disturbed, Stevens had been in his employ long enough to know that there were always exceptions to be made, most notably for his cousin, Colonel Fitzwilliam, and a few close friends, like Bingley.

Darcy straightened in his chair. He did not recall Bingley mentioning a trip to Town, but he knew for his friend to arrive unannounced the matter must be important. Buttoning his waistcoat, Darcy gave his butler a brief nod. "Very well. You may send them in."

Bowing, Stevens quit the room, returning moments later with Bingley in tow.

Darcy stood. "Bingley, this is a surprise. I hope nothing is the matter..." his words trailed off as he took in the gentleman standing at his friend's shoulder. "Mr. Bennet!" Darcy's countenance paled. "Is someone ill?"

From the doorway Stevens cleared his throat, diverting Darcy's attention. "Will there be anything else, sir?"

Darcy's gaze flicked to his butler as he waved him away. "Thank you, no. I will ring if we require anything."

The servant retreated with a brief bow, closing the heavy door behind him.

Darcy took one uneven step, regarding Bingley who stood just inside the threshold.

"Is it Jane?" he asked before an even more terrifying thought occurred to him, and his blood turned to ice. "Has something happened to Miss Elizabeth?"

Bingley's eyebrows jumped at his inquiry, but it was Mr. Bennet's black look that held Darcy's attention.

Bingley offered an uncertain smile. "No, no. Everyone is well. I beg you to excuse us for calling unannounced, Darcy. It is just... That is, Mr. Bennet wished to have a word."

Once again, Bingley's voice faltered and Darcy turned his attention to the older gentleman who had yet to speak.

"Certainly," Darcy answered. "Pray, sit. Can I offer you a glass of port? Or I would be happy to ring for tea."

Bingley's expression brightened at the mention of port, but Mr. Bennet shook his head. "That will not be necessary. What I have to say should not take long."

Darcy nodded, gesturing towards the sofa and settling back into the armchair he had recently vacated. "Mr. Bennet, how may I be of service?"

Elizabeth's father studied his host, his gaze coming to rest on Darcy's leg, which was stretched out upon the ottoman before his chair.

"I see you are still recovering from your injury, Mr. Darcy. A carriage accident, was it not?"

Darcy started, but swiftly composed his features. "Yes," he answered succinctly.

"And did that not occur in the autumn, on your journey from Kent?" asked Mr. Bennet, raising one eyebrow in an expression very like his daughter. "I believe my Lizzy traveled from there at about the same time."

Darcy stiffened as Mr. Bennet's unasked question hovered in the air. "I am afraid I do not take your meaning, sir." Turning to face his friend, he noted that Bingley was studying the intricate pattern on the carpet.

Mr. Bennet's expression grew grave. "Very well, Mr. Darcy. I will state my question plainly. Was my daughter with you when you traveled from Kent? And did you in fact spend a night unchaperoned with her? I would suggest you think carefully before answering, sir."

Darcy regarded the older gentleman, his expression rigid. "I have no need to think carefully. Indeed, Miss Bennet was with me. I encountered her at the Bell in Bromley and offered to escort her to Town as her uncle's carriage had been delayed."

"Go on."

Darcy leaned back in his chair, wearily massaging his temples. "The accident occurred about an hour into our journey. Mercifully, Miss Bennet was unharmed; however, I was not so fortunate. The weather was severe, so we were forced to take shelter in a nearby cottage while my footman went for assistance." After a brief pause he added, "But you seem to know all of this already. Might I ask how you came upon this intelligence?"

Bingley coughed. "I am afraid that is my fault, Darcy. Miss Elizabeth told Jane, and then Jane relayed the story to me. Unfortunately, I made mention of it within Mr. Bennet's hearing." Bingley's shoulders slumped and he once again averted his gaze.

Darcy turned his attention back to Elizabeth's father. "Does Miss Bennet know?"

"That I am aware of the situation?" Mr. Bennet asked. "She does. I confronted her yesterday and she related a similar tale. What I would like to know, Mr. Darcy, is why I am first hearing of this now, and from someone other than yourself? As her father, did you not think I had a right to know what occurred?"

Darcy narrowed his gaze. When he spoke, his voice was as hard as granite. "What *occurred*, sir, is that your daughter very likely saved my life. I did not wish to repay her by spreading gossip that would only serve to damage her reputation. If you are insinuating that I compromised Miss Bennet in some way, you are mistaken."

Bingley slid forward in his seat. "Now, Darcy, no one is saying anything of the sort. We both know you regard Miss Elizabeth almost as a sister. It is only her good name that Mr. Bennet is considering. You have to admit, if word did get out, it would look quite bad."

Darcy sighed, fixing his gaze on Mr. Bennet. "Forgive me. Naturally I understand your distress, and I apologize for not consulting you on the matter. But I believed this was a decision best left to your daughter. As to our present situation, I do not think there is cause for concern. Only one member of my staff and my personal physician are aware of the circumstances of the accident and I trust their discretion completely. So, unless Bingley opens his mouth again, there is no reason to be worried for Miss Bennet's reputation."

Elizabeth's father frowned. "I hope you are correct, Mr. Darcy, and I see no reason to press the point further at this time. However, I would like your word that if the story does come out, you will behave as a gentleman."

Darcy did not answer, turning instead to face the fire. Oh, the irony! What he would have given a year ago to be in this predicament. A forced marriage. A guarantee that Elizabeth Bennet would at last be his.

Of course, a year ago he did not know that she despised him.

The last man in the world...

Darcy shook his head, trying to clear away the memory.

Then again, that was before the accident. She had been so attentive when they were together at the cottage... But compassion was not love. And he could not forget her behavior the night at the theater. If her heart was engaged elsewhere... The mere thought made Darcy's insides ache. No, he could never do that to her. He would rather die by slow inches than see her trapped in a marriage not of her choosing.

"Mr. Darcy? What say you, sir?" Mr. Bennet's voice broke through Darcy's thoughts and he turned away from the hearth.

"No."

Mr. Bennet's eyes widened. "Forgive me, I do not understand."

"Then I shall be more clear. If you are asking me to force your daughter into a marriage she does not desire, the answer is no."

"You are refusing?"

"Yes."

"Darcy!" Bingley yelped, jumping to his feet and placing a calming hand on Mr. Bennet's shoulder as the older gentleman stepped in Darcy's direction. "It is only a precaution. Of course, none of us expect it shall ever come to pass."

But Darcy shook his head, turning his full attention back to Elizabeth's father.

"Mr. Bennet, I will do everything in my power to protect your daughter and to preserve her reputation. On that, I give you my word. But I am sorry. I will not marry her."

❄

He had refused.

The door to Elizabeth's bedchamber closed with a hollow click and she collapsed against it, borrowing support from the wooden paneling. Sinking to the floor, she stared into the gathering darkness, slowly coming to terms with what she should have realized months ago: Mr. Darcy no longer possessed the feelings he had laid claim to at the parsonage last April. She had been given her chance, and she had thrown it away.

Harsh laughter tickled her throat as she shook her head at her own foolishness. This was her fault, and no one else's. She had sealed her fate when she refused his proposal. No man, especially not one as proud as Mr. Darcy, would ever offer for the same woman a second time.

A sob slipped from her throat, but despite the grief that twisted her stomach, she knew that her punishment was just. She had sown her bitter oats in resentment and conceit, and now she must reap the consequences.

Struggling to her feet, Elizabeth wrenched her trunk from the foot of her bed, tugging gowns from her wardrobe and tossing them inside. She would leave this place, as soon as may be. Indeed, she could not stay in London another moment—not when she ran the risk of crossing paths with Mr. Darcy; or worse, opening a news-sheet and reading of his betrothal.

Casting about for the remainder of her belongings, Elizabeth's eyes landed on the bedside table and she quickly crossed the chamber. Reaching out her hand, she snatched up the fine leather volume. Mr. Darcy's gift. The book she had once believed to be a symbol of his affection and regard.

Suddenly, that gentleman's somber countenance appeared before her and his voice echoed around the chambers of her mind: *Miss Bennet, it is only a book.* Even then, he had been attempting to manage her expectations. The book was not some tender token of his esteem, but merely a replacement of her damaged property.

Opening the cover, she glanced down at the inscription on the gilded page: E. BENNET. Even in this, his meaning had been clear—no fond sentiments, no elegant inscription. Not even her full name.

Grasping the volume, she stalked to the hearth. Flames licked at the glossy leather binding as she held the edges above the blaze. Heat seared her skin. Slowly, she peeled her fingers away one by one.

But despite her best intentions, her grip tightened, and she drew her hand away from the fire. No, she could not burn it. No matter the reason, her conscience would never allow it.

Moving to her trunk, Elizabeth shifted her gowns, burying the book beneath the rest of her belongings. She would keep it as a reminder of her own stupidity. And tomorrow she would return to Hertfordshire and begin anew. Time would heal her injured pride, and when next she found herself in Mr. Darcy's company—as she knew she must—she would greet him with polite civility. Never would he know of her altered feelings or her shattered hopes. Certainly, he was too much of a gentleman to mention her father's visit, and neither would she. They would simply go on as they had before. In time, she would grow accustomed to a life spent without him. Yes, in time, all would be well.

CHAPTER 12

The polished surface of Darcy's desk was no longer visible beneath the mounds of accumulated papers requiring his attention, but he could not bring himself to care. Turning in his chair, he gazed numbly out the window. In the small back garden, the trees were beginning to bud, signaling the end of a long winter and the promise of spring.

It had been more than a month since Mr. Bennet's unexpected visit, and with each day that passed, Darcy sank further into a mire of despair. What had he been thinking, refusing Mr. Bennet's demands? He should have leapt from his chair, acquired a special license, and married Elizabeth on the spot. Surely, she had *some* feelings for him. Could those feelings not have grown into love, if given the chance? But even as his mind formed the thoughts, his heart knew otherwise. She did not love him. She would never love him. She had found another, someone from her own social circles, someone who would make her happy. And he knew now that he could never be content if she were miserable.

A knock sounded at the door to the outer corridor and Darcy called out for whoever it was to enter, glad to have a reason to turn his mind away from such melancholy deliberations. His butler stood at the threshold, an impassive expression on his face. "Mr. Bingley is here, sir. He is inquiring whether you are at home."

Darcy narrowed his eyes in the man's direction. *Not again.* As much as it would please him to see his friend, he knew he could not stomach another confrontation. If Bingley was here with Mr. Bennet, or worse yet with Caroline... "Is he alone?"

"Yes, sir," Stevens answered.

Darcy closed the ledger in front of him, pushing back his chair before offering a single nod. Best to get it over with. "Very well. Pray, send him in."

A moment later his old friend stood before him, offering a warm handshake by way of greeting.

"Bingley, this is a surprise. I had not realized you were once again in Town."

"Er, yes, though only for a couple of days. I had business with my solicitor. I should have written, but it was rather a spur of the moment decision."

"It is of no consequence, it is always good to see you." After a moment Darcy added, "Well, it is *normally* good to see you."

His friend colored, taking a seat on the opposite side of Darcy's desk. "Actually, that is one of the reasons I came. I wished to apologize again for that business with Mr. Bennet. I am sorry to have put you in such an awkward position."

"Pray, do not trouble yourself. You said as much in your letter. I do not blame you—or Mr. Bennet for that matter. It is obvious he cares for his daughter. I am certain I would have the same concerns if Georgiana found herself in similar circumstances. However, I am afraid I must stand by my decision in this matter." Climbing to his feet, Darcy crossed to the window, gazing out through the mullioned glass. "I trust she is well?" he asked, after a lengthy pause. "Miss Bennet?"

"Oh, yes. Quite well. She returned to Longbourn some time ago. Jane is all too happy to have her sister settled close by again."

"And... there have been no more betrothals amongst the Bennet daughters, I presume?"

Bingley angled his head. "No, no. None as yet."

Darcy released a breath, turning away from the window. Well, at least he had that much to be thankful for —Elizabeth had not become engaged to anyone else in the time since he had last seen her. "Did Mrs. Bingley accompany you to Town?" Darcy inquired, grasping for a less volatile topic of conversation.

"No. Jane chose to remain at Netherfield, as my trip was to be of such a short duration. Elizabeth, that is, Miss Bennet is staying with her." Bingley crossed one foot over the other, chuckling softly. "To tell the truth, I think they were happy to be rid of me for a few days. Actually, I was happy to find you at home, Darcy. Are you not normally at Rosings by now?"

At the mention of his aunt's estate, Darcy tensed. "My sister and I will be spending Easter in Town this year."

"Oh?"

"Yes." Darcy paced over to his desk, brusquely rearranging the scattered papers into neat stacks. "Georgiana's companion is in Cornwall for some months. My sister had no wish to travel and I did not feel comfortable leaving her alone."

What Darcy did not disclose was that he could no longer stand to be in such close proximity to Hunsford, where the memory of Elizabeth's refusal was as fresh as ever. Nor did he repeat the tirade he had been subjected to by letter when he had informed his aunt of the change in plans.

Darcy looked up, resuming the conversation. "Speaking of Georgiana, I know she would be unhappy to miss seeing you. Will you stay for tea?"

Bingley accepted the invitation with alacrity, and the two men proceeded to the music room. Georgiana sat at the pianoforte, her head bent in quiet concentration as bright, cheerful notes reverberated in the air. When she finally became aware of their presence, her fingers stilled and she hastily stood, the piano bench scraping against the wooden floor. "Oh! Fitzwilliam! I did not hear you come in."

Darcy closed the door behind them as Bingley stepped forward, offering a warm smile. "I must beg your pardon for intruding upon your practice, Miss Darcy. It was not our intention to interrupt."

"Yes, pray, finish, dearest," Darcy added. "As you know, that happens to be one of my favorite pieces."

Georgiana flushed, glancing nervously from her brother to Mr. Bingley.

Bingley opened his mouth, but Darcy cut off his friend's protestation, "Come, Georgie. I know you do not like to exhibit, but Bingley is practically family. And you must get used to performing in company. You play beautifully and it is a shame not to allow others the pleasure of hearing you."

Georgiana colored even more deeply at her brother's compliment. "Very well," she murmured, as the two gentlemen took seats nearby.

When the last few notes had faded away, both men applauded heartily and Darcy escorted his sister to the sofa. "That was marvelous. Now here, sit down and I will ring for tea."

The three conversed happily until the tea arrived and Georgiana stood to serve.

Taking the cup she offered him, Bingley smiled broadly, gazing at his hostess above the rim. "Miss Darcy, your brother tells me you will be staying in Town for Easter. Are you expecting guests?"

Georgiana poured out her brother's tea, remembering to add the slice of lemon he had recently begun to favor. "No. I am afraid it will only be Fitzwilliam and myself. My cousin Richard could not get away from his regiment and Lord and Lady Matlock and their family have all gone up to Derbyshire." She stepped forward, carefully handing Darcy his tea.

Bingley glanced over at his friend, hastily setting his own teacup on a nearby table. "I have just had the most wonderful idea! I don't know why I did not think of it sooner. You must both come to Netherfield!"

Darcy's breath caught, his fingers automatically tightening around the delicate porcelain handle of his cup. "That is generous of you, Bingley," he answered, "but I am afraid it is impossible."

"Come now, Darcy. You have already admitted that you have no fixed engagements. Jane and I would be pleased to have you. And you needn't worry about Caroline, if that is your concern. She and Louisa have gone up to Suffolk to spend some months with Hurst's family."

Georgiana sat forward in her chair, her eyes sparkling with eager expectation. "Could we not go, Brother? I have not yet had the pleasure of meeting Mrs. Bingley, and I would so love to become further acquainted with Miss Bennet."

At the mention of Elizabeth, Darcy flinched. What he wouldn't give to see her again, even for a moment! But no sooner had hope flared within him than he remembered the look on her face in the theater lobby. No, she would not wish him there. And if what he suspected was true, and there was another gentleman in the picture, seeing her again would be a cruelty—to both of them.

Avoiding Georgiana's gaze, Darcy turned to face his friend. "Forgive me Charles, but it is out of the question. My sister and I could not possibly intrude upon your family with so little notice. Perhaps a visit might be arranged at a later time."

Bingley opened his mouth, but soon closed it again. Darcy was known to be stubborn. Once his mind was made up, there was generally no changing it.

His friend sighed. "Very well. But the invitation stands should you reconsider."

Darcy nodded, but steered the conversation to other things. No, he would not reconsider. Elizabeth had her life and he had his. The sooner he came to terms with that, the better it would be for everyone concerned.

Dinner that evening was an awkward affair. Bingley had declined Darcy's invitation to dine, and Georgiana barely spoke. Darcy suspected she was still unhappy about his refusal to travel to Netherfield, but it could not be helped. He had spent enough time disturbing Elizabeth with his unwanted presence; he would not do so again.

As soon as the meal was at an end, his sister pleaded a headache and retired to her chambers. Darcy adjourned to the library, hoping a glass of brandy and a good book would prove a satisfactory distraction; but an hour later he was still staring at the opening pages of *The Lady of the Lake*. He had just made up his mind to give up entirely when the door banged open to reveal his cousin, Darcy's butler hard at the colonel's his heels.

"Colonel Fitzwilliam," Stevens announced, trying to maintain some dignity as Richard entered ahead of him.

Darcy stifled a smile, closing his book and setting it on a low table. "Thank you, Stevens."

His butler nodded, retreating into the hall and Darcy turned his attention to his cousin, who was already helping himself to a hefty glass of port.

"Richard, to what do I owe this unexpected surprise? I thought you were still in Norfolk."

Settling into a chair by the fire, his cousin grinned. "I have only just arrived. There is a bit of business I must attend to in London and I hoped to take advantage of your hospitality, if you do not mind. The family's gone up to Matlock and I did not relish the idea of rattling around in the townhouse all on my own."

"Of course. You may stay as long as you wish. I only feared you had come to attempt to drag me to Rosings. You should know I am resolved on that score. I will not change my mind."

Colonel Fitzwilliam barked out a laugh. "Oh, no, not I! After the scathing letter I received from Lady Catherine, I would not venture into Kent for all the cognac in France. As you may have gathered from your own letter, our aunt is most seriously displeased."

Darcy scowled, tugging at his cravat. "She will recover."

Taking a swallow of his drink, the colonel sprawled comfortably in his chair. "By the by, I recently received another letter I thought might be of interest. From my friend Westinghouse. In New York."

Darcy who had stood to refill his own glass froze with his hand on the decanter. "Has he news of Wickham?

What have you heard? Do not tell me that blackguard is planning to return to England?"

"Ha! After you threatened him with debtor's prison? Not bloody likely. Even America is better than the Marshalsea."

"Well, what then?" Darcy snapped, splashing brandy into his glass. "Is Wickham complaining about his treatment? Asking for more money?"

"No..." The colonel answered slowly. "On the contrary, it seems he has taken to New York like the proverbial duck to water." After a lengthy pause, Richard continued, "According to Westinghouse, Wickham is engaged to be married. To a local heiress."

Tossing back the contents of his glass, Darcy dropped into his seat. "She has my sympathy, as do the rest of the American people. Though I cannot say I regret my actions. As long as Wickham keeps away from Georgiana and— that is, as long as he stays off English soil, I am content."

"Yes, I believe you made your feelings abundantly clear when you placed him on that ship. I still say you were far too generous with him."

Darcy frowned. "Perhaps. But I would have given far more to ensure he no longer had the opportunity to harm the people I love. I should have sent him away years ago."

In truth, Darcy wished he had rid himself of Wickham before the scoundrel had been able to get his hooks into Georgiana. It was only when he had returned from Rosings last spring and a rumor reached him that Wickham intended to ruin one of the Bennet daughters that Darcy knew he had to act. Regardless of what had occurred between them, he could not abide the thought of Elizabeth or someone she cared for coming to harm when it was within his power to prevent it.

Colonel Fitzwilliam smirked. "Too true. Though I still would have enjoyed running him through. Well, enough of that parasite. I would much rather hear about you and Georgie." His gaze dropped to where Darcy's long legs were stretched out in front of the fire. "You look well. And you are getting around without the cane, I see."

Darcy nodded. "Yes, the break has healed nicely."

"And Georgiana? You wrote that she was lately unwell. I hope it is nothing serious?"

Darcy shrugged, although his lips turned down at the corners. "She seems to have recovered, though as a gentleman I am at a loss to understand such things. And now Mrs. Annesley has gone off to the West Country to spend the summer with her daughter, so I do not even have her to rely upon."

"Well, there is always Mother. Or Lady Margaret, come to that."

"Yes. I will certainly contact one of them should the problem persist." After a moment he added, "Georgiana will be happy to see you, of course. How long are you to be in Town? Will you stay for Easter?"

"No, I am afraid not. As soon as my business is concluded I must rejoin my unit. Rumor has it we will be returning to the peninsula before long."

Darcy frowned. "I wish you would consider selling your commission, Richard. You know I would happily host you at Pemberley indefinitely. Or if you would prefer, we might look into acquiring a smaller property in the vicinity. Georgiana worries about you, and quite frankly, so do I. We would both like to have you settled and out of danger."

Richard stared into the fire, sipping his drink. "I appreciate the offer, Darcy, you know I do. But I could never hang about at Pemberley like some sort of charity case, and I know next to nothing about running an estate." He held up his hand. "And before you say you would teach me, I am afraid I would not be suited to it. Besides, I like soldiering. It is one of the few things I excel at. The military gives me a sense of purpose—training my men, seeing them succeed."

"But don't you ever get tired of it all? Constantly fighting the same enemy with no end in sight? Honestly, I do not know how you stand it."

Richard shrugged. "It is what they pay me to do."

Darcy swirled the amber liquid in his glass. The color reminded him of the flecks of gold that sparkled in Elizabeth's eyes. Stifling a groan, he tipped his head against the back of his chair, closing his eyes. How was he ever to endure a lifetime spent without her? How does one find the strength to carry on when all seems lost...

Darcy did not realize he had spoken those last words aloud until his cousin's deep laugh wrenched him from his thoughts.

"Ah," said Richard. "Well that I can answer in one word: Hope. For even in times of despair, there is always reason for hope. As I tell my men, it matters little if we lose the battle, so long as we win the war."

Darcy lowered his gaze, letting his cousin's words sink in. Hope. When had he given up the hope that Elizabeth might one day be his? Despite how things appeared, had he done all he could to change her opinion of him? Had he made every effort to be a man worthy of her regard? Or had he relinquished her too quickly? She was not betrothed, after all. Bingley had told him as much. And if anyone was worth fighting for, surely it was she?

Perhaps it was not too late.

Setting his glass upon the table with a clatter, Darcy rose to his feet. "Pray, forgive me, Richard, but I have just remembered an urgent matter that requires my attention. You are most welcome to stay at Darcy House for as long as you like, but I am afraid Georgiana and I are for Hertfordshire in the morning."

CHAPTER 13

E lizabeth watched as Jane rushed down the steps of Netherfield Park, the hem of her gown fluttering about her ankles. Behind her, Elizabeth followed at a more subdued pace, a small smile lifting her cheeks. Despite her low spirits, it was difficult to remain unaffected by the sight of her usually sedate sister all aquiver at the return of her husband after an absence of only two days' time.

At the foot of the steps, the Bingley carriage coasted to a stop and the footman jumped from his perch. In a matter of seconds, Bingley had scrambled out, pulling his wife into a tender embrace and kissing her sweetly on the cheek.

Not wanting to intrude, Elizabeth hung back, happy to bask in the reflected glow of her sister's happiness. Attempting to give the couple a modicum of privacy, Elizabeth turned, her gaze drifting to the coach which was still parked in the drive. Expecting to see the footman latch the door, her brows drew together as the liveried servant stepped to one side and a tall figure exited the compartment. As Elizabeth watched, the gentleman reached back to hand down a fashionably dressed lady. Odd, Jane had said nothing about expecting guests. Curiosity pulled Elizabeth forward but she had not gone more than a handful of steps when the man turned, and Elizabeth froze. Mr. Darcy! Astonishment and apprehension drew the breath from her body and she could feel a warm flush creeping up her neck. Fighting to regain her composure, Elizabeth swallowed. The moment she had dreaded had arrived.

Stepping forward to greet the mistress of the house, Darcy sketched a bow, as Bingley turned to Georgiana, stammering through a hasty introduction. Shifting his attention from Bingley to his wife, Darcy frowned.

"Mrs. Bingley, I hope you will excuse our unexpected arrival. I was under the impression that your husband sent an express informing you of our visit, but I can see by your expression that he did not."

A contrite Bingley glanced in his wife's direction. "Er, yes, forgive me, dearest. It was only when I arrived in London and found Darcy and his sister at loose ends that I thought to have them join us for Easter. I did mean to send word first thing this morning, but in my haste to be off, I am afraid I quite forgot."

Jane offered her husband a sweet smile before turning

back to her guests. "I assure you, Mr. Darcy, it is of no consequence. We are delighted to have you both."

Observing the warm look Mrs. Bingley gave her husband, Darcy suddenly felt ashamed of his previous efforts to separate the pair. Clearly, the two were made for one another, and he could only thank providence that Bingley had forgiven Darcy's meddling and returned to Hertfordshire to pursue his happiness.

Not wishing to intrude upon his friend's reunion, Darcy stepped aside, directing his attention to the house, and the hairs at the back of his neck immediately stood on end. At his slight intake of breath, Georgiana followed his gaze and a girlish laugh slid from her lips as she hurried to greet her friend.

"Ah, I see you ladies are already acquainted," said Bingley, taking his wife's arm as Darcy slowly followed behind the rest of his party.

"Indeed," Elizabeth answered. "I had the pleasure of making Miss Darcy's acquaintance some time ago, in Town." Her gaze drifted in Darcy's direction and her smile wavered. "Mr. Darcy."

Darcy offered her a shallow bow. "Miss Bennet."

Bingley glanced nervously from one to the other as Jane began ushering everyone into the front hall. Leading the way to the drawing room, Mrs. Bingley turned to her guests.

"Miss Darcy, Mr. Darcy, you must be fatigued from your journey. I will call for a maid to show you to your rooms."

"I thank you," Darcy answered. "That would be much

appreciated. I am certain my sister would wish to rest before dinner."

Darcy watched as Elizabeth approached her own sister, saying something softly in her ear.

"Oh, Lizzy! Must you?" Jane answered. "There really is no need... "

Elizabeth ventured a glance in Darcy's direction and their eyes caught. "Yes, I am afraid I must. I have monopolized your attention long enough and will now leave you to your guests."

Before Jane could reply, a commotion in the front hall diverted everyone's attention as a shrill voice reverberated off the marble floors.

"Really, Smithers! I do not need to be announced. Just tell me where I might find my brother and... Oh! There you are, Charles."

Caroline Bingley halted at the threshold and Darcy frowned. He fixed Bingley with a questioning glare, but his friend appeared just as astonished as the rest of the party.

"Caroline! What on earth are you doing here? I thought you were in Suffolk." Peering over his sister's shoulder, his mouth fell open in obvious confusion. "And where are the Hursts?"

Miss Bingley sailed through the open door, waving her fingers dismissively. "They are still at Kennelworth. But I could not tolerate one more day in that dusty mausoleum. You know how I abhor the country."

Bingley's eyes bulged, his expression rapidly turning from surprise to alarm. "But... I... Why did you not write to inform us of your plans? Surely you did not travel here on your own?" he stammered.

"Certainly, I did not travel on my own. My maid is with me, as well as two footmen." Suddenly her gaze shifted to where the rest of the party stood, frozen in place, and a small gasp escaped her throat. "Why, Mr. Darcy! And dearest Georgiana! I had no notion *you* would be at Netherfield."

Caroline moved further into the room and Darcy instinctively stepped back, his frown deepening. "It was a last-minute decision," he answered stiffly. "As a matter of fact, we have only just arrived."

"Well! How lucky it is that I decided to alter my plans, else you would have had no suitable company at all." Tearing her eyes away from Darcy, she finally turned to acknowledge her brother's wife. "Jane, dear, you look lovely, as always... Oh! And Eliza. I did not see you standing there."

The thin smile Caroline offered Elizabeth did nothing to mask her disdain, and Darcy felt his jaw tighten.

"Do not concern yourself, Miss Bingley," Elizabeth answered, sweetly. "I was just leaving."

Barely acknowledging Caroline, Jane turned to face her sister. "Are you quite certain you will not reconsider Lizzy?" she asked in a strained whisper, but Elizabeth shook her head. "Very well. If you will excuse me, Caroline, I will see my sister out. When I return, I shall inform Mrs. Bridges that you have arrived unexpectedly and will require a room."

The two women turned to go, but before they could

reach the hall, Darcy called out. "Miss Bennet, I trust we will have the pleasure of your company on Easter Sunday?"

Slowly, Elizabeth turned, and he was surprised to see that an arch smile played across her features.

"Yes, sir. Indeed, you shall have the pleasure of being surrounded by the entire Bennet family, as Jane has invited us all to spend the day."

Behind him, Darcy could hear Caroline Bingley smother a gasp, but his eyes remained locked on Elizabeth's face.

"I shall look forward to that, Miss Bennet," he answered.

The Easter services had scarcely reached their conclusion when Elizabeth's youngest sisters were on their feet, bursting through the doors at the back of the parish church and clattering down the wooden steps.

"La!" trilled Lydia, as soon as they had reached the churchyard. "I thought that rector would never cease speaking! He has grown as long-winded as Mr. Collins!" Pulling her sister Kitty towards the village green, she leaned in to continue in a loud whisper, "Kitty, did you take note of Emma Winthrop's hideous new bonnet? I declare, she looked as if she had walked straight into one of Mrs. Doyle's fruit salads. And I heard Mrs. Long say that Emma sent all the way to London for it, too. As if there are not enough ugly bonnets to be had right here in Hertfordshire!"

Kitty giggled behind her hand as Mary and Elizabeth walked up to them, a disapproving frown marking Mary's face.

"Oh, come Mary," said Lydia. "Even you must have noticed it, as Emma was sitting directly in front of you."

"I noticed nothing of the sort," Mary replied primly. "I was busy listening to the sermon, as you should have been also. And you would do well not to speak so unkindly about one of our neighbors, especially on such a holy day, and in a churchyard, no less."

Elizabeth trailed her squabbling sisters, attempting to hide her embarrassment as Mr. and Miss Darcy joined them on the green. They were presently met by the rest of their party, and plans were soon underway to adjourn to Netherfield.

At the arrival of Bingley's coach, Lydia clutched at her husband's arm, dragging him to the front of the group. "Henry and I shall ride in Mr. Bingley's carriage," she declared with a girlish giggle. "It is ever so much finer than Papa's."

"Certainly," Bingley answered. "It would be our pleasure."

Jane flushed crimson and Caroline looked as if she might be ill.

"Come, Lizzy!" called Mrs. Bennet, as their own conveyance drew up behind the Bingleys' black lacquered chaise and four. "There will not be space for you in Mr. Bingley's coach, and you must sit in the middle as you know Kitty will be unwell if she cannot look out of the window."

Casting a brief glance in Darcy's direction, Elizabeth's stomach twisted. "Mamma, it is such a fine day, I believe I shall walk to Netherfield."

A look of annoyance flickered across Mrs. Bennet's features as she regarded her second daughter. "In your best gown and slippers? Certainly not. It is out of the question."

"Mamma, please! I will take care not to over-exert myself and I shall stick to the lanes. Besides, I have worn sturdier shoes for this very purpose," Elizabeth added, lifting the bottom of her skirt to reveal walking boots.

Frowning at Elizabeth's footwear, Mrs. Bennet opened her mouth to protest further, but Kitty interjected, taking her mother's arm. "Oh, let her walk, Mamma. You know she will be in a poor temper if you do not, and this way there will be more room in the carriage for the rest of us."

Mrs. Bennet continued to pout, but eventually muttered her consent and Elizabeth hastened to take her leave. As she passed Mr. Bingley's coach, her gaze was drawn to Mr. Darcy, who appeared to be studying her with an enigmatic expression. Elizabeth's cheeks warmed, and she quickly turned away, glad she would have at least a half an hour alone before once again surrendering herself to the gentleman's company.

Darcy leaned back in his chair, stretching out his long legs and tilting his face up to the sun. The entire party was gathered on Netherfield's stone terrace, having just finished an extravagant luncheon served in the unseasonably warm April sunshine.

The conversation during the meal had been pleasant enough, with talk of the weather, the current London fashions, and the upcoming May Day ball. Mr. Bennet had been cordial to Darcy, but every now and then the younger man looked up to see Elizabeth's father regarding him with a watchful eye. As for Elizabeth, while Darcy was grateful to see the kind attention she paid his sister, he noted that she had seated herself as far away from him as possible, curtailing any chance at private conversation.

In truth, Darcy had considered offering to accompany Elizabeth on her walk to Netherfield after the morning services, but given the precarious position he was in with Mr. Bennet, he knew such a gesture would not be prudent. As a matter of fact, he had been most concerned about being in the company of Elizabeth's father again after their conversation in London; but Bingley had assured him that due to the continued concealment of Darcy's interlude with Elizabeth in Kent, Mr. Bennet's temper had cooled. Still, it would not be wise for Darcy to put himself in the position of being once again in Elizabeth's sole company.

The midday meal now complete, Mr. Bennet stood, expressing his desire to avail himself of Bingley's library, while Kitty and Lydia, along with Mr. Hughes, set off to call upon Colonel Forster, who was having an informal gathering for the local militiamen.

When those members of the party had gone, Bingley turned to the remainder of the group, dusting his hands together, his expression eager. "Well, what shall the rest of us do? Perhaps a walk around the park? I know Miss Darcy has not had a chance to see much beyond the formal gardens, and it is an exceedingly pretty day."

Elizabeth and Georgiana both consented to the plan, and Darcy was just about to echo his agreement when Mrs. Bennet called out from across the terrace.

"A walk! Goodness, after all that rich food! And Lizzy, have you not walked quite enough for one day? What will Mr. Bingley think with you always traipsing about?"

"Oh, I think it is delightful that Miss Elizabeth enjoys the exercise," Bingley put in hastily, but Mrs. Bennet hardly seemed to be listening.

"Jane, dear, you may go if you wish, but I shall require a rest. I am sure one of the guest chambers must be available."

Jane hurried to her feet. "Certainly Mamma, I will show you upstairs."

As the two women moved towards the house, Darcy quickly voiced his agreement to the proposed outing— Caroline immediately echoing his sentiments; but Mary Bennet rose, indicating that she was not inclined to walk, and would instead join her father in the library.

In due course, the party of six set off through the gardens in the direction of a small pond at the edge of the property. Bingley led the way with Jane and Elizabeth by his side, followed by Darcy and Georgiana. But it was not long before Caroline appeared to stumble, catching

Darcy's arm in a vice-like grip. "Oh! Forgive me, Mr. Darcy. The ground here is dreadfully uneven. I hope you do not mind if I impose upon you for your support?"

Breathing in the overwhelming scent of Caroline's thick perfume, Darcy stifled a grimace. "Not at all." In front of them, Elizabeth glanced over her shoulder and Darcy noted the twinkle in her eye and the half-smile that touched her lips.

The party soon cleared the small formal gardens, and the group was able to spread out, with Georgiana ambling ahead to view the pond with the Bingleys. And although he was unable to extract his arm from Caroline's clutches, Darcy lengthened his stride, pulling his unwelcome companion along. Finally, he reached the spot where Elizabeth stood beneath a flowering blackthorn tree. Studying her serious expression, Darcy held back a sigh. There must be a way for the two of them to have a few moments alone! They had not had an opportunity for confidential discourse since Mr. Bennet's visit to London, and Darcy was unable to gauge Elizabeth's feelings. Perhaps she was concerned about his reaction to her father's ultimatum? If only he could reassure her that he had no intention of forcing her into marriage...

Affording him a brief glance, Elizabeth turned to stare across the water. It was clear she had been avoiding him prior to their walk, and with Caroline pasted to his side and Georgiana, Jane, and Bingley only a few paces away, he was at a loss as to how to begin a private conversation.

Clearing his voice, Darcy fixed his gaze on the little he

could see of Elizabeth's countenance. "It is warm for April," he offered.

Elizabeth's eyes slid briefly in his direction, but she did not comment.

At his other side, Caroline snapped open her parasol—a hideous burnt-orange contraption—swiping at the air in front of her face with an exaggerated frown. "I quite agree. It is utterly stifling. And the warm weather has brought out the insects."

Elizabeth seemed to be fighting a smile, but she continued to stare into the distance.

Ignoring Miss Bingley, Darcy tried again. "I imagine you are enjoying the countryside after your winter in Town, Miss Bennet. Will you be spending the whole of the summer at Longbourn?"

Confronted with a direct question, Elizabeth clearly felt that she could no longer ignore his presence and she turned in Darcy's direction. "Mainly, yes. Although I plan on touring the Lakes with my aunt and uncle in June."

Darcy eagerly grasped onto the proffered topic of conversation. "Ah, yes. The trip you were to have taken last summer. And... will you be stopping in Derbyshire?" he continued, his words hesitant.

Elizabeth's brow lifted a fraction of an inch. "I do not believe our plans are fixed at this time, sir."

Before Darcy could reply, Caroline burst forth, "Oh, how I love Derbyshire! Mr. Darcy, I hope we shall have the pleasure of visiting your estate once again this summer?"

Reluctantly pulling his attention away from Elizabeth,

Darcy responded tersely, "I do not believe your brother has any desire to leave Netherfield, Miss Bingley."

"Oh, I am certain he would make an exception for a trip to Pemberley. He cannot wish to remain in Hertfordshire all summer. If it is this warm in April, the heat during July and August would be positively oppressive."

Once again, Darcy fought for control of his emotions. This walk was not turning out at all as he had hoped. He was desperate for a few minutes alone with Elizabeth, but could not see how such a thing would ever be accomplished.

As if sensing his dilemma, Bingley turned around, waving in their direction. "Caroline! Pray, come over for a moment," he called. "I wish to have a word."

Caroline let out an exasperated huff before recollecting herself and peeling her fingers from Darcy's sleeve. "Forgive me Mr. Darcy, it seems my brother has need of me. I shall return in a trice," she simpered, batting her lashes.

Darcy nodded, hoping his relief was not evident in his expression. As soon as Miss Bingley had gone, he turned towards Elizabeth; but before he could collect his scattered thoughts enough to speak, his sister approached from the opposite direction. "Miss Bennet, did I hear you say you would be visiting Derbyshire this summer?" Georgiana asked.

"I do not believe anything is settled yet, Miss Darcy, but yes, I expect my aunt may wish to spend some time in Lambton."

"Oh! But then you must stay at Pemberley! My brother

and I would be pleased to host your entire party, wouldn't we William?"

Elizabeth lifted her gaze, a doubtful expression in her eyes.

"Certainly," Darcy heard himself respond stiffly. "You would be most welcome."

"Please, say you will come?" Georgiana replied, clearly unaware of the battle her brother was waging with his frayed emotions.

Elizabeth hesitated, slowly beginning to walk in the direction of the others with Darcy and his sister following. "I thank you for the gracious offer," she answered carefully, "but I shall have to discuss it with my relations, as they may have already made other arrangements."

"Of course," Darcy murmured.

The threesome met up with the Bingleys near a small cluster of benches. They had no sooner come to a halt when Caroline sighed, dropping onto the nearest seat. "Charles, I cannot walk another step. I must rest for a while before we return to the house."

Bingley nodded his agreement, settling down with somewhat less flourish on an adjacent bench with Jane by his side. "A fine idea. I think we could all use a rest."

Elizabeth remained standing. "If nobody objects, I should like to walk for a while longer," she said.

Jane smiled, knowing it was not in her sister's nature to be sedentary, especially when out-of-doors. "Of course, Lizzy, go right ahead. We shan't return for at least half an hour."

Elizabeth nodded, making her way towards a small

path that circled the water; but it wasn't long before Darcy's voice arrested her steps.

"Miss Bennet, would you mind if I accompanied you?"

Elizabeth paused, but finally offered him a cursory nod.

Darcy turned to face his sister. "Georgie, would you like to join us?" he asked, but the young girl shook her head.

"No, I think I am also rather tired," she stated, removing herself to one of the benches just as Caroline stood, her eyes fixed on Mr. Darcy.

"Perhaps a stroll would be beneficial after all..." Miss Bingley began, but her brother's voice stopped her in her tracks.

"Nonsense, Caroline. You just claimed to be exhausted and it is still a long walk back to the house. Besides, were you not saying only recently that you longed for Miss Darcy's companionship?"

Darcy took several ground-eating strides, quickly catching up to Elizabeth on the winding path. He wondered if he should offer his arm, but he had the distinct impression that she would not accept it. The two walked for several moments in silence and Darcy began to feel a sense of hopelessness settle over him.

It was obvious Elizabeth did not desire his company, but this might be his only chance to speak with her privately. After tonight they would not be in one another's company for months—and only then if Elizabeth acquiesced to his sister's invitation to visit Pemberley. Thinking back to Georgiana's request, Darcy once again felt the sudden rush of shock and longing. In truth, his sister's words had been so unexpected, they had rendered him virtually speechless, and he had struggled to keep his countenance.

Realizing he and Elizabeth had been walking for some time, he once again peered in her direction. Her bonnet obscured most of her face, but it was clear that she was not best pleased. However, whether her unhappiness was merely the result of his presence or whether it stemmed from some unknown slight, he could not determine.

"Miss Bennet, have I offended you in some manner?" he finally asked.

He could almost feel Elizabeth's body stiffen, but when she turned to look at him, her features gave no hint to her feelings. "No, sir. You have not."

The pair continued on, but after several moments, Darcy let his breath out in a frustrated sigh.

"Miss Bennet, I can see you are upset. But I cannot rectify my mistakes if you will not tell me what I have done."

Elizabeth slowed her steps. "You have done nothing, Mr. Darcy. You have made me no promises and therefore owe me no explanations."

Darcy stopped walking, forcing Elizabeth to draw up beside him. "Miss Bennet... has this to do with the visit your father paid to me in Town?"

Elizabeth's eyes widened. Turning away, she wrapped her arms tightly around her body.

"Forgive me," Darcy continued. "I regret that I have not yet had the opportunity to—"

Elizabeth's raised voice interrupted his sentence. "Mr. Darcy, I assure you, I understand perfectly. However, if you do not mind, I would prefer not to speak further on this topic."

Darcy nodded uncertainly and Elizabeth turned away, lifting her fingers to her temple.

"Forgive me, but I feel the beginnings of a headache. Perhaps I have walked too far today."

Darcy frowned. Now he was certain something was wrong. The Elizabeth Bennet he knew was not prone to sudden headaches, nor would a walk of such a short duration cause her fatigue.

"I would be happy to return with you if that is your wish," he answered.

Elizabeth nodded, but did not take the arm he offered, instead setting off alone in the direction from which they had come, leaving Darcy no choice but to follow after her.

CHAPTER 14

When the evening meal was announced, Mrs. Bennet was the first to reach the dining parlor. Brushing past her eldest daughter, she immediately proceeded to the top of the table, calling out instructions in an authoritative tone.

"Jane, you shall sit at the head of the table, of course, and Mr. Bingley you will sit there, at the other end. Mr. Bennet you must take the place on Jane's right, and I will be here, at her left. Lydia shall sit next to me." Catching a glimpse of Mary out of the corner of her vision, Mrs. Bennet huffed in an exasperated manner. "Mary! What are you doing over there? That is Kitty's seat. You know we will be discussing the upcoming ball and you have no interest in such things. You may go and sit near Mr. Bingley."

Mary's countenance paled and Elizabeth's own cheeks

burned as she darted a glance in Mr. Darcy's direction. "Mamma!" Elizabeth hissed, but before she could say anything further, Mr. Darcy moved past her, coming to a halt at Mary's side.

"Miss Mary, would you do me the honor of sitting next to me? I have not yet had the pleasure of spending time in your company, and I am certain my sister would also enjoy the opportunity to become better acquainted. I believe the two of you have much in common."

Elizabeth stepped back, blinking rapidly, as she watched Mr. Darcy escort a now flushing Mary to the opposite end of the table. Pulling out her sister's chair, he settled her alongside Georgiana before seating himself.

In a flash, Caroline Bingley was across the room, nearly tripping over the hem of her gown in her haste to secure the vacant seat on Mr. Darcy's left. Attempting to conceal her amazement, Elizabeth made her way to the empty chair beside Mr. Hughes.

Once everyone was situated, the footmen began appearing with the first course and conversation flowed in an easy manner. In between bites, Elizabeth continued to glance furtively across the table. She assumed that having done his duty, Mr. Darcy would leave Mary to converse with his sister, but to Elizabeth's surprise, he was animatedly engaged in the two ladies' discourse. Despite her best intentions, Elizabeth found herself drawn to the conversation, and it did not take long for her to overhear Mr. Darcy describing the difficult fingering of one of his favorite piano concertos. Before she knew what she was about, Elizabeth spoke.

"Mr. Darcy, did I hear you correctly? Do you play the pianoforte?"

Darcy's head snapped up at the sound of her voice, and he slowly lowered his fork until it came to rest on the edge of his plate. "I do, Miss Bennet, though not in company. My mother wished me to learn, so I had lessons as a boy, but I have not practiced sufficiently for many years."

Elizabeth watched as Caroline Bingley stilled.

Alerted to Miss Bingley's interest, Darcy redirected his attention to his plate.

"Pray, do not listen to him, Miss Bennet," Georgiana interjected softly. "My brother plays exceptionally well."

"Certainly, he does!" agreed Miss Bingley, and Elizabeth lifted her napkin to cover her smile. Honestly, the woman was ridiculous! Continuing to regard Mr. Darcy, Elizabeth noticed that the gentleman was still studying his dinner, though she thought she detected a slight reddening around his ears.

Taking in the young girl seated across the table, Elizabeth replied kindly, "I am certain you are correct, Miss Darcy."

Ignoring Miss Bingley, Mr. Darcy turned back to Elizabeth's middle sister, broaching the topic of books, and the two soon entered into a lively discussion on what they had read recently, the merits of poetry as compared to prose, and the selection to be found at the local bookshop. Elizabeth continued to eat her meal, but her attention was repeatedly drawn to Mr. Darcy. Was this truly the same gentleman who normally spent his time standing about on the periphery of the room, or with his back turned altogether, gazing out of windowpanes?

Elizabeth sliced into her roast beef, taking a small bite and chewing thoughtfully. What could have precipitated such a transformation? He had certainly made his feelings about her family clear at Hunsford, and yet being in their company now, he did not seem at all disapproving. Stealing another glance in the gentleman's direction, she examined his expression. If she did not know better, she would have almost said that he looked like he was enjoying himself.

Before Elizabeth could reflect any more on the matter, the voice of the newly-minted Mrs. Hughes began rising in volume, pulling Elizabeth from her deliberations and all but silencing the other conversations at the table.

"But I do so wish you could join the regulars!" Lydia whined, addressing her husband. "I am quite certain that were you to take a captaincy, we would have the funds for a proper house like this one, and not have to reside in such cramped quarters."

"Lydia!" Jane cried, while Lieutenant Hughes lifted his glass of wine, draining it in one hurried gulp as Lydia faced her eldest sister.

"Oh, do not be so ill-tempered, Jane. Why should you be the only one to live on a grand estate? My darling Hughes is every bit as clever as your Mr. Bingley." Leaning across Kitty to address her husband, Lydia continued, "I do not see why you cannot purchase a commission like Lieutenant Saunders. Mrs. Forster told me there are balls for the officers all year round when one is in the regulars."

Silence descended, and Elizabeth watched as Mr. Darcy carefully set down his glass. "Mrs. Hughes, I am certain you are correct. My cousin is a colonel in His Majesty's Army and often complains about the many social obligations he must endure. But then, he does not have a charming wife at his side to make them more tolerable."

At Darcy's words, Lydia beamed, while Elizabeth's mouth fell open in absolute astonishment as Darcy continued, "I have also heard the militia is the single best training ground for a position in the regulars. No doubt the lieutenant will find his time here has been well spent."

"There," cried Mrs. Bennet. "You see Lydia, your dear husband will be a fine officer one day and you will both move in the first circles, I am sure!"

Before anyone could comment further, Bingley rubbed his hands together, waving over a footman to commence with the next remove; but Elizabeth's thoughts had already returned to Mr. Darcy's unprecedented defense of her youngest sister. She could not account for it at all!

Suddenly, her mind drifted back to their solitary ramble that afternoon, and she instantly felt a pang of remorse. Clearly Mr. Darcy had wished to assuage his conscience for his refusal to offer for her... She should not have rebuffed his attentions. But she had simply been unable to bear the thought of standing there while he enlightened her as to the precise grounds for his dismissal. For to hear him say that he was attached to another would have been beyond her powers of endurance.

Looking across the table at him now, a sad smile

captured her lips. Surely, Mr. Darcy could see the only way forward was for them to bury the past?

The sun had not yet risen when Darcy woke the following morning, his mind overflowing with thoughts of the woman he loved. He and Georgiana would be returning to London later that day, and although he felt he had succeeded in winning back a little of Elizabeth's goodwill the previous evening, he knew he still stood on shaky ground.

Elizabeth had not yet responded to his sister's invitation to come to Pemberley, and while he might encourage Georgiana to write to her and repeat the offer, he was beginning to think it would ultimately be refused.

Darcy sighed, extracting himself from the bedclothes and retreating into his dressing room. It was too early to bother his valet, so he quickly donned a simple ensemble suitable for riding and headed out of doors. He needed time to think and had always found that was best accomplished in the fresh air.

His feet crunched along the gravel walk as he turned in the direction of the stables. When he reached his destination, he waved away the young groom, preferring to saddle one of Bingley's horses himself as he often did at Pemberley. Something about using his hands, which moved by instinct, always helped calm him and he swung easily into the saddle when he had completed his task. Urging the mare into a slow canter, he headed across Netherfield's west pasture. He had not given any thought to his destination, but as if guided by unseen hands, he soon found himself approaching Longbourn. Pulling back on the reins, he brought his mount to a standstill on a small rise overlooking the house. He was not certain how long he sat there, quietly contemplating the darkened manor, when a door opened and a lone figure emerged. Darcy sat up straighter, straining to see, but he already knew only one inhabitant was likely to be out this early. His heart raced as the caped figure began walking in his direction.

Elizabeth kept her eyes on the path, careful to avoid the ruts left by the recent rains. It was barely daylight and her breath created soft white puffs in the cool air.

Once again, she had spent a restless night, consumed with thoughts of Mr. Darcy. Of course, when she left London, she was well aware their paths would likely continue to cross. But she had been completely unprepared for the feelings that had swelled within her upon seeing him step from the carriage at Netherfield. And while she had initially found herself uneasy in his company, she could not deny that she had been captivated by his cordial attention to her family the previous evening. Not only had her sister Mary, who was always awkward in company, fairly blossomed under his care, but he had been attentive to the rest of her relations as well: flattering

Lydia at dinner, complimenting Kitty on her singing when she had joined Mary at the pianoforte, and even handing Mrs. Bennet into their carriage at the end of the evening. But through it all, it was the intense scrutiny he paid to her that sent Elizabeth's pulse racing and kept her awake late into the night.

Intent on both her thoughts and the uneven ground, Elizabeth did not raise her eyes until she was almost at the top of the knoll. When she finally lifted her gaze, her feet stumbled as she took in the black beast directly in her path.

Swiftly dismounting, Mr. Darcy offered her a hurried bow. "Miss Bennet, I must beg your pardon. I did not mean to frighten you. I was riding past when I happened to see you leave the house."

Elizabeth flushed at having the man who had so recently consumed her thoughts now standing before her. "No, the fault is mine. I was not attending." A slim smile lifted her lips. "Or rather, I was too busy attending to the condition of the path to be fully aware of my surroundings."

Darcy grinned back—a warm genuine smile that somehow made Elizabeth's knees tremble.

"Miss Bennet, I presume you were about to set out on a morning walk. Would you... That is, would it be an imposition if I accompanied you?"

Elizabeth hesitated briefly before shaking her head, nodding to the route she had been planning to take, and Darcy gathered his horse's reins, falling into step beside her.

They ambled along in silence for several moments before Elizabeth spoke. "I am surprised to see you, sir. Were you and Miss Darcy not set to return to London this morning?"

"Indeed, we are. We will leave shortly after breakfast." He turned to smile down at her. "Unlike you, Miss Bennet, my sister is not an early riser."

Elizabeth walked on, but her gaze remained fixed on the ground where Mr. Darcy's footsteps kept pace with her own. "I am glad to see you are able to walk and ride without difficulty," she finally said, taking in his confident stride.

Darcy visibly started at her words, his focus shifting to his leg. "Yes. I was fortunate. The bones set well."

"I am glad."

They continued on for several minutes, Elizabeth still ruminating on Mr. Darcy's conduct the previous evening. It had occurred to her that his altered behavior might simply have been a way to show his respect to the Bingleys, who were hosting him in their home. But regardless of Darcy's reasons, she had been touched by his compassion for her sister, and suddenly felt the desire to tell him so.

"Mr. Darcy, I wished to thank you for your kindness last evening to my sister, Mary. It did not go unrecognized."

Darcy looked over at her, surprise clearly written on his face. "You owe me no thanks, Miss Bennet. I found your sister to be a delightful dinner companion. I enjoyed her company, and I know Georgiana did as well."

"Nevertheless, I noticed the care you took to converse on matters that were of interest to her. Mary can be reserved in company and you did a remarkable job of drawing her out. Indeed, I do not remember when I have seen her so animated, even amongst our immediate family."

"I know how she feels. My own sister was once painfully shy, and I do not perform well to strangers myself, as I believe I remarked to you on another occasion."

Elizabeth tilted her head, contemplating his words. It was true that Mr. Darcy had mentioned his apprehension amongst those with whom he was not well acquainted, but she had never given much thought to what this might mean. Was it possible that what she had seen as pride and arrogance were in fact nothing more than reserve and shyness? And what of Mary? Was it also true that her sister merely felt uneasy in company? A wave of guilt washed over her as she realized she had not been nearly as considerate of her middle sister as she ought. Indeed, it was Mr. Darcy, a virtual stranger, who had gone out of his way to put Mary at ease...

"You are unusually quiet this morning, Miss Bennet."

Elizabeth looked up, her thoughts returning to the present. "You have my apologies, sir. I was thinking about my sister, Mary. I believe it would be good for her to get away from Longbourn for a while. I fear she is too much in Lydia and Kitty's shadow and not enough out in society. Perhaps I will petition my aunt and uncle to allow her to accompany me on our tour of the Lakes."

Elizabeth's voice tapered off and Darcy turned to look at her. "Miss Bennet, I hope you will give some consideration to staying at Pemberley while you are in Derbyshire. I assure you, Miss Mary would be a welcome addition to your party. She and Georgiana appeared to get on well."

Elizabeth studied Mr. Darcy out of the corner of her eye. What was he about? He had made no secret of the fact that he found her family beneath his notice and the behavior of her younger sisters in every way unsuitable. Elizabeth released a weary sigh. Remembering Lydia's remarks last evening, she could hardly blame him. But it was one thing to be solicitous of Mary at dinner, and quite another to encourage a friendship between Mary and his own sister.

Unbidden, an image of Lady Margaret flashed to mind and Elizabeth's stomach clenched. For all she knew, by summer the two might be wed, or at the very least, betrothed. When Elizabeth spoke, her tone was cool. "You are very gracious, Mr. Darcy, but we would not wish to intrude. I am certain you will have more intimate acquaintances at Pemberley this summer."

Darcy's forehead puckered. "I have no plans to host any large parties," he began slowly. "The only other guest would be my cousin, Colonel Fitzwilliam, if he can free himself from his duties."

Elizabeth opened her mouth, and before she knew it, the words that had been tumbling through her head were on her lips. "Oh? Will Lady Margaret not be in residence, sir?"

Darcy's stared back at her, confusion evident in his

expression. "Lady Margaret? Forgive me; I do not understand…"

Elizabeth looked away, staring up into the branches of a nearby cherry tree, a warm flush creeping up her neck. Beside her, Mr. Darcy stiffened. A moment later he rocked back on his heels, clearing his voice.

"Actually, now that you mention it, it *is* possible Lady Margaret will visit. She often accompanies the viscount, Lord Hazelton. However, no plans of that nature have been fixed as yet."

Elizabeth's head snapped around as the gentleman continued, "I regret that I was not able to introduce Lord Hazelton to you that night at the theater, but unfortunately he had taken ill with a headache right before we were to leave."

Comprehension slowly dawned and humiliation of the acutest kind colored Elizabeth's cheeks. "So, the viscount is…"

"My cousin. Colonel Fitzwilliam's elder brother." Darcy paused before adding, "And Lady Margaret's *husband*."

Elizabeth bit her lower lip, raising her eyes to the gentleman by her side. "Mr. Darcy, I…"

Her breath caught as Darcy reached out, lifting her gloved hands. "Miss Bennet, please. Come to Pemberley. My sister does not make friends easily, and it would mean the world to her if you would come."

Elizabeth looked into his eyes, and his expression seemed to brim with tenderness.

No, it was impossible. She could not, *would not*, go to

Pemberley. Doing so would only set her up for further disappointment and heartbreak. She opened her mouth to tell him so.

"Thank you," she murmured. "I will have to consult with my aunt and uncle, but yes. I would like that very much."

CHAPTER 15

The following two months passed swiftly. And while Elizabeth often visited Jane at Netherfield, she remained mostly at Longbourn, which was considerably quieter now that Lydia had removed to her new home in the village. Kitty continued to spend most of her time with her youngest sister, which left Elizabeth quite happily in Mary's sole company. To Elizabeth's surprise, she found that she and her middle sister had much in common, and they passed their days amicably—practicing duets on the pianoforte, reading and discussing books, or quietly sewing. Elizabeth had even begun to coax her usually sedentary sister out of the house, and the two would often take long rambles in the afternoon sunshine, collecting the wildflowers that were beginning to bloom in the Hertford-shire countryside.

It was on one such walk that Elizabeth broached the

subject of Mary accompanying her on her tour of the Lakes, a proposition the Gardiners had readily agreed to and which Mary shyly accepted.

As summer was fast approaching, the local Militia was once again preparing to decamp to Brighton and Lydia was in a fit of joyful anticipation at the prospect of her first trip to the seaside. Although she had begged most urgently for Kitty's company, Elizabeth was gratified to note that her father had refused the proposal—as he did not see Lydia as a fit chaperone, regardless of her marital state—causing no small amount of unrest in the Bennet household. It was eventually decided that instead, Kitty would travel to Kent with Maria Lucas to visit Mr. and Mrs. Collins, as she did not wish to remain alone at Longbourn.

And so, before Elizabeth knew it, she was once again packing for her journey north.

Reaching for the book on her bedside table, Elizabeth admired the glossy leather cover before tucking it inside her satchel. Snapping the clasp, her thoughts drifted to the gentleman who had given her the volume. In only a few days' time she would be in Mr. Darcy's company! Despite her best efforts, her pulse quickened at the thought. Though she would admit it to no one, over the past eight weeks, Mr. Darcy had been often on her mind. When she played the pianoforte, she would wonder if the composition was one that he would favor. When she and Mary discussed a book, she would speculate on what his opinion might be; and at night, she often dreamed of walking the gardens at Pemberley with Mr. Darcy by her side. But despite all this, Elizabeth continued to guard her heart. His relationship with Lady Margaret notwithstanding, the fact remained that Mr. Darcy had refused to offer for her. It would not do to hope for anything beyond friendship.

A knock sounded at the open door, pulling Elizabeth from her reflections, and a moment later, Mary entered the chamber.

"Lizzy, Papa wishes to know if he can send Mr. Hill for our things," said Mary, as Elizabeth turned to close her trunk, tightening the leather strap.

"Yes, I am ready." Lifting her gaze, Elizabeth regarded her sister who stood in the center of the room, clutching her reticule. Elizabeth smiled. If the expression on Mary's face was any indication, one would think they were about to embark on a trip to the gallows rather than a Lakeside holiday.

Crossing the floor, Elizabeth brought her hands to rest upon her sister's shoulders. "I know you are uneasy, dearest," she said gently, "but there is no cause. I will be with you the entire time, and you needn't go out on the water if you do not wish it. It will be a fine adventure, I promise you."

Mary transferred her gaze to the carpet, before offering Elizabeth a small nod. "So you have said. But it is not our trip to the Lakes that worries me. It is the se'nnight we shall spend at Pemberley. I am still not at all comfortable in such esteemed company. What if I should use the wrong fork at dinner? Or fumble at the pianoforte? I have been practicing all week, but—"

Elizabeth pulled her sister into a tight embrace, stemming the flow of words. "Nonsense! Mr. Darcy and his sister are not such severe critics. And Mr. Darcy has assured me there will be no one in residence beyond our own small party and perhaps his cousin, who is very kind."

At Elizabeth's words, Mary seemed to relax a little. It was not until they reached the vestibule that Elizabeth reflected with some surprise on how her perception of Mr. Darcy had changed in the months since the accident.

And though she was loath to admit it, Elizabeth was looking forward to her trip to Pemberley far more than was likely wise.

The clock in Pemberley's entrance hall chimed the hour as Darcy paced past it for the third time. Any moment, she would be here! Tugging at the lapels of his jacket he withdrew his watch, peering at the time before snapping it closed and returning the item to his pocket.

Glancing up at the sound of approaching footfalls, Darcy spied his housekeeper descending the sweeping staircase and hastened in her direction. "Mrs. Reynolds. I trust the bedchambers are all in order? There have been no last-minute complications?"

Darcy could see the glimmer of amusement in the older woman's eyes, but she was quick to assure him that the entire house was in a state of readiness—indeed, had been for many days. Darcy received this information with a distracted nod. Leaving the housekeeper to carry on with her responsibilities, Darcy continued to pace in a tight circle, his fingers idly drumming against the edge of his coat.

"Was there anything else, Mr. Darcy?"

Lifting his head, Darcy noted that Mrs. Reynolds still stood at the foot of the stairs, gazing at him with interest.

"What? Oh, no, no. Pray, return to your duties." His hand moved in the direction of his inner pocket, closing around the cool surface of his watch. Withdrawing the timepiece, he pressed the clasp, holding it up to the light.

A sound that was somewhere between a laugh and a cough emanated from his housekeeper's throat, and Darcy straightened his shoulders. Executing a rigid bow, he turned, walking briskly in the direction of the drawing room.

Crossing the threshold, his gaze roamed the stylishly appointed salon. The terrace doors were open to the outside garden and a warm breeze stirred the air. Breathing in the sweet scent of peonies and lavender, he was instantly reminded of Elizabeth, and he could not help but smile. For a whole week, she would be here, under his roof, just as he had imagined countless times!

Making his way to the far side of the room, he gazed out into the sunny garden. Seven days. It was not much time. Not if he hoped to show Elizabeth that he had become a man worthy of her regard. Darcy sighed, dragging his fingers through the thick hair at the base of his neck. Much as he hated to admit it, women had always been a mystery to him. He had spent his entire adult life trying to avoid the marriage-minded misses who flocked to him for all the wrong reasons. Now, when he finally happened upon a woman whose affection he desperately wanted to win, the irony was not lost on him that he had not the slightest notion of how to go about it.

And this week would be his final chance. If he could not earn Elizabeth's favor here at Pemberley, where he felt most like himself, there was no hope for it at all.

A sudden noise drew Darcy to the tall front windows where a carriage was just beginning its long approach.

His last opportunity was about to begin.

Darcy strode across the marble entrance hall, the sounds of his footsteps echoing in time with the pounding of his heart. Reaching the front door, he barely missed colliding with his butler who appeared from around a corner. Hastings stepped back, allowing his master to precede him in descending the front steps. The carriage pulled up under the columned portico and Darcy shuffled his weight, adjusting his cuffs. A moment later, Elizabeth's uncle exited the coach, turning back to assist the ladies.

Warm greetings were exchanged, and though Darcy did his best to focus on Mr. Gardiner's recounting of the fine condition of the roads, his gaze was repeatedly drawn to Elizabeth. Seeming to feel the weight of his stare, she turned in his direction, a small smile playing at the corners of her lips.

Averting his gaze, Darcy motioned for the party to follow him inside. Leading the way up the steps he called over his shoulder, "Pray, do not worry about the luggage. My men will follow with it shortly."

Entering the hall, Darcy spotted his housekeeper. "Ah, Mrs. Reynolds, allow me to present our guests. I believe you may remember Miss Elizabeth Bennet and her aunt and uncle, as they had occasion to tour Pemberley last summer. And this is Miss Bennet's sister, Miss Mary Bennet."

Pleasantries were exchanged and the housekeeper moved to show the newly arrived visitors to their rooms, but despite his best intentions, when Elizabeth walked past, Darcy found himself reaching for her hand.

At the slight pressure of his fingers she stopped, allowing the others to walk ahead. For a moment, neither of them spoke. Then Darcy leaned down, murmuring quietly in her ear, "Miss Bennet, I am very glad you are here."

A deep flush stained Elizabeth's cheeks and every nerve in Darcy's body trembled.

"As am I, Mr. Darcy." Her low reply was accompanied by a gentle squeeze of her fingers. But all too quickly she released his hand, hurriedly following the rest of her party up the stairs.

After showing the Gardiners to their chambers, Mrs. Reynolds led the Bennet sisters down another long corridor. Pushing open a gleaming mahogany door, the housekeeper stepped back to allow the ladies to enter.

Elizabeth crossed the threshold ahead of her sister and her eyes lit in quiet appreciation. "Oh, how lovely," she breathed, as her gaze swept the sunlit chamber. Turning, she offered Mrs. Reynolds a grateful smile. "Thank you. I am certain Mary and I will be quite comfortable here."

"Oh, no, Miss Bennet. This will be Miss Mary Bennet's chamber. Your own apartment is just down the hall. If you will follow me?"

Elizabeth exchanged a glance with her sister who remained rooted to the floor, her eyes wide.

"Oh! But... Truly, there is no need for us to occupy separate rooms. My sisters and I are quite accustomed to sharing."

"'Tis no trouble," Mrs. Reynolds said simply. "We have ample space."

Elizabeth's eyes darted from the housekeeper to her sister before she finally shrugged, smiling briefly at Mary before turning to quit the room. At the end of the corridor another door was opened and Elizabeth entered, her breath immediately catching in her throat.

The room was, without question, the most beautiful she had ever seen.

Against the far wall, a massive bed hung with a green silk canopy was raised from the floor on a large dais, a long settee at its foot. Opposite the bed, a comfortable sofa and two chairs sat before a marble fireplace, and across the room, graceful French doors opened onto a large stone balcony. A double doorway at the other end of the bedchamber led to a sitting room that was easily as big as Longbourn's front parlor.

As Elizabeth crossed into the adjoining chamber, it was evident that no detail had been overlooked. Vases filled with fresh flowers were placed throughout the suite, and a stack of fine writing paper sat atop an inlaid desk. An assortment of leather-bound books was neatly arranged on the low table nearest the window.

Elizabeth slowly pivoted to face the housekeeper. "Mrs. Reynolds, these chambers are exquisite. But are you certain there has not been some mistake? I cannot see that I should have need of such a large suite of rooms for only myself."

As if to answer her question, a knock sounded at the open door and two footmen entered bearing Elizabeth's trunk and setting it near a large armoire in the corner.

Mrs. Reynolds smiled. "There has been no mistake, Miss Bennet. Mr. Darcy issued very specific instructions as to who should get which room. He selected this apartment specifically for you. I believe he thought you would enjoy the view of the gardens," she added, nodding to the French doors.

Elizabeth followed her gaze, moving across the floor and exiting onto the balcony. Directly below her a sun-dappled garden was in full bloom, and in the distance, rolling hills dotted with the occasional sheep stretched out as far as the eye could see.

From behind her, the housekeeper spoke softly, "I trust I may tell Mr. Darcy you are content, Miss Bennet?"

Elizabeth turned, a wide grin illuminating her features. "Oh, yes, pray do!"

Stepping back into the room, she allowed the housekeeper to show her around, demurring when Mrs. Reynolds offered the services of a maid to assist her in unpacking.

The older woman nodded appreciatively. "Very well. Dinner will be at half-five, and I shall have a maid come to collect you. The house is large and easy to get lost in until you learn your way."

Elizabeth nodded, her feet automatically returning her to the table where she had seen the small assortment of books. Picking one up at random, she glanced at the title: Sir Walter Scott's *The Lady of the Lake*. Elizabeth opened the cover, carefully ruffling the pages. She had heard much praise for Mr. Scott's work, but her father had yet to acquire this particular volume. Reluctantly setting it down, she turned to study the spines of the other books on the table, her pulse instantly quickening as she read through the remainder of the titles.

Robinson Crusoe, The Romance of the Forest, Tom Jones, Clarissa, and a thick volume entitled *Mr. William Shakespeare's Comedies, Histories, & Tragedies,* all stood beside the latest works by some of the world's most celebrated authors.

A wave of emotion swept over her as she lifted the final offering: Plato's *Republic*.

Elizabeth swallowed. Somehow, Mr. Darcy had remembered every book she had mentioned on that long-ago carriage ride and had taken the trouble to see that she had each of them at her disposal. Her throat squeezed and she turned away, hoping Mrs. Reynolds did not see the tears that were already pressing against her lashes.

Unfortunately, Elizabeth was not quick enough for Mr. Darcy's perceptive housekeeper.

"Is anything amiss, madam?" Mrs. Reynolds asked. "I hope you will tell me if there is something I can do to make your stay more comfortable."

Elizabeth laughed, brushing at her cheeks. "Goodness, no! Do not mind me. It is nothing... That is, I am certain if I told you, you would think me quite silly."

"I doubt that very much, Miss Bennet."

Elizabeth lifted her gaze, noting the kindness in the housekeeper's warm gray eyes. Despite her objection, she felt strangely drawn to the older woman and found herself wishing to give voice to her jumbled thoughts. "It is only... When I visited Pemberley last summer, I could never have imagined that one year later I would be a guest in Mr. Darcy's home. Everything is so lush and grand. I suppose I merely feel out of place in the midst of such opulence."

To Elizabeth's surprise, the housekeeper's smile grew. "May I speak plainly, Miss Bennet?" she asked, and when Elizabeth nodded she continued, "Pemberley is indeed a great estate. In my opinion, there is no other in all of England that is its equal. But it is not just the beauty of the land, or the elegance of the furnishings that make Pemberley so fine. At its heart, Pemberley is a home—not just to the master and Miss Darcy, but to scores of others who rely upon it for their living." Squeezing Elizabeth's hand, she added, "It is my hope, Miss Bennet, that on this visit you will come to see it in such a way."

And with that, the elderly woman quit the room, leaving Elizabeth with much to ponder until it was time for supper.

CHAPTER 16

At exactly half past five o'clock, Elizabeth descended the center stairs, her sister Mary by her side and the Gardiners a few paces behind. In the hall below, Mr. Darcy waited, smartly attired in full dress. Beside him stood his sister, equally resplendent in a pale blue satin creation that brought out the color of her eyes. Elizabeth tugged self-consciously at her own gown—a soft yellow silk. It was the nicest one in her wardrobe save the silver muslin her aunt had purchased for her last spring, but it somehow felt inadequate amidst the grandeur of her surroundings. For a moment she regretted not wearing the muslin, but she had purposely avoided it in case there was a more formal dinner arranged for another night during their stay.

When they reached the bottom of the stairs, Mr. Darcy greeted them with quiet courtesy as Miss Darcy blushingly expressed her regret at not being on hand to welcome the party when they arrived.

Elizabeth smiled, hoping to put Georgiana at ease. "There is no need to apologize, Miss Darcy. We are old friends now, and therefore required no formal reception."

Out of the corner of her eye, Elizabeth could see Mr. Darcy discreetly studying his sister, but he soon turned his attention to his guests, leading the way to an intimate dining parlor. The room was well-proportioned and handsomely fitted up, and Elizabeth's eyes widened as she took in the elegantly laid table.

"Pray, sit wherever you are comfortable," Darcy offered, moving to one end of the room.

"Mr. Darcy, I must thank you again for your generous hospitality," Mrs. Gardiner remarked when they were all seated. "Pemberley is as lovely as I always imagined."

"I thank you, Mrs. Gardiner. I assure you it is my pleasure. I am afraid Georgiana and I find ourselves alone much of the time. Pemberley is a house built for entertaining. It is gratifying to see it put to good use."

As Darcy finished speaking, several footmen approached, placing a tureen of soup before Miss Darcy and setting a variety of other dishes along the center of the table. Georgiana served, and animated conversation ensured, but despite her best intentions, Elizabeth's gaze continued to wander to the opposite side of the table, where, to her embarrassment, she often found Mr. Darcy staring back at her.

Towards the end of the first course, Mrs. Gardiner

turned to their host, asking sweetly, "Are you well, Mr. Darcy? You have hardly touched your soup and I believe your footmen are ready with the next remove."

Color infused the gentleman's cheeks and he hastily nodded, turning his attention to his plate and Elizabeth did likewise, vowing to keep her focus on her food for the remainder of the meal.

After dinner, there was the usual separation of the sexes, but it wasn't long before the two gentlemen joined the ladies in the drawing room.

When they entered, Darcy's eyes immediately found Elizabeth, who was seated on a settee beside Mary and his sister. As he watched, Elizabeth laughed at something his sister said and his heart expanded with affection. The simple yellow gown she wore suited her perfectly and her skin seemed to glow in the candle-light. As if sensing his stare, Elizabeth lifted her gaze and a smile played across her countenance. Taking this as an invitation, Darcy left Mr. Gardiner in his wife's company and went to stand at Elizabeth's side.

"Miss Bennet. I am sorry I have not yet had an opportunity to speak with you this evening. I hope you enjoyed your meal?"

Elizabeth lowered her lashes as Darcy settled into a chair he had moved to be closer to where she sat. "I did indeed, sir."

"Good. I am glad. And your chambers? If I can do anything to make your stay more comfortable, you need only ask."

Elizabeth's lips parted and she sat in silence for some moments before finally finding her voice. "The apartment is exquisite. I can hardly think what might be done to improve upon it."

A genuine smile lifted Darcy's features. In truth, he would much prefer to have her installed in the mistress's chambers where she rightfully belonged, but as that was not currently an option, he had seen to it that she had the next best thing. "I am pleased it is to your liking. You may have noticed I took the liberty of having some books brought up, but tomorrow I will acquaint you with the library. You are, of course, welcome to borrow anything else that interests you."

"Thank you, Mr. Darcy. I will look forward to that."

Darcy nodded, then stood. "I believe I will pour myself a drink. What can I get for you, Miss Bennet? Some sherry, perhaps, or a glass of wine? I can also ring for tea... or chocolate?"

Elizabeth grinned back at him. "I thank you. Some tea would be appreciated, if it is not too much trouble."

"None at all. I am certain Georgiana will join you. She often takes tea in the evening." Sketching a brief bow, he crossed the room to speak with a footman who stood silently by the door, before returning moments later with a snifter of brandy.

Nodding her head towards an elaborate floral arrangement she had been admiring, Elizabeth smiled. "These are beautiful, Mr. Darcy, as are the flowers in my chambers. I assume they are from the gardens here?"

"Yes. We grow a wide variety in the formal gardens: roses, peonies, lavender, chrysanthemums... My mother was always fond of flowers. She had them placed throughout the house in the summer months. I have merely continued the tradition."

"I remember your gardens from my visit last summer. I should very much like to reacquaint myself with them."

Just then, the doors to the salon opened and a maid stepped in, bearing a silver tray overloaded with tea and chocolate as well as a variety of pastries and fresh fruit. Georgiana stood, busying herself with serving her guests and Elizabeth appeared to study the young girl for several moments, before leaning in Darcy's direction. "Is Miss Darcy quite well," she inquired softly. "I hope she is not overexerting herself on our behalf?"

Darcy lifted his gaze, watching as his sister reached for the sugar bowl. Elizabeth was right, Georgiana did look fatigued. He knew she had been complaining of not sleeping well, but he wondered if it was something more. Setting down his glass, he shifted his attention back to Elizabeth. "I believe she is only a little tired, Miss Bennet."

His sister approached them then, handing Elizabeth her tea, and Darcy changed the subject. "You were mentioning the gardens earlier," he said, raising his voice to include the others in the room. "It would be my plea-sure to show your party around the park while you are here. I had thought perhaps tomorrow if the weather holds, we might all ride out in the afternoon. There is a particular spot on the north side of the estate where the views are especially fine. There is even a small rotunda where we may picnic if everyone is agreeable?"

The Gardiners quickly approved the plan, and Elizabeth continued to sip her tea before setting her cup back upon its saucer. "I would like that, Mr. Darcy, though I am afraid I do not ride. However, if it is not terribly far, I am happy to walk."

Darcy's gaze widened ever so slightly. "You do not ride, Miss Bennet?"

"No, sir, I do not. I hope that will not prove to be a hindrance. My aunt and uncle are both comfortable on horseback, as is Mary. But as I said, I am quite content to walk."

"No, no... Of course, there is no difficulty. I would be happy to drive you myself in one of the curricles. I am only surprised. You seem like a lady who would enjoy the activity."

Elizabeth offered him a crooked smile. "I can see how it would seem so, as I do enjoy most outdoor pursuits, but I am afraid horses and I have never seen eye to eye."

"Lizzy was thrown when she and Jane were first learning," Mary interjected. "She has not been on horseback since."

Georgiana gasped. "How terrible. Were you badly hurt, Miss Bennet?"

Darcy glanced from his sister to Elizabeth, concern for Elizabeth's welfare mingling with anxiety for any embarrassment her sister Mary's disclosure might have caused, but Elizabeth looked perfectly at ease.

"I broke my arm, Miss Darcy. However, I am afraid the real injury was to my pride." She grinned broadly now, sipping her tea.

"There is no shame in being unseated, Miss Bennet, especially when one is new to the sport. Even William has been thrown, and he has been riding since he could walk."

Darcy flushed, clearing his throat self-consciously before turning his gaze to the amber liquid that filled his glass.

"I have no doubt Mr. Darcy is an excellent horseman," Elizabeth answered, and Darcy picked up his head.

"Oh, he is!" Georgiana agreed. "He taught me when I was very young. Although I had been taking instruction with our stable-master, it wasn't until I went out with Fitzwilliam that I…" Suddenly Georgiana's eyes lit and she turned to face her brother. "I have just had the most wonderful idea! William, perhaps you could instruct Miss Bennet? The way you did for me, when I was first learning. Do you remember?"

Darcy could feel the heat building in his countenance. Avoiding Elizabeth's gaze, he fixed his attention on his sister. "I do not think that would be appropriate, Georgiana. Miss Bennet is not a child. Besides, I would not wish for her to do anything against her will."

"Thank you, Mr. Darcy," Elizabeth answered.

Georgiana turned to Elizabeth. "You would have nothing to fear with Fitzwilliam, Miss Bennet. He would never let any harm come to you."

Mr. Gardiner laughed, joining the conversation. "Good luck to you, Mr. Darcy. I mean no offense, but I do not think anything less than an act of God would get my niece on horseback. Her father and I have tried to do so for many years."

Darcy shifted uncomfortably in his seat as Mary Bennet addressed her sister.

"Perhaps you should try it, Lizzy. Jane and I have always said you would enjoy the activity if you gave it another chance."

"Yes, why not?" echoed Mrs. Gardiner. "After all, it is not every day one has the opportunity to learn from the master of Pemberley. Besides, I have never known you to back down from a challenge," she added with a chuckle.

Elizabeth glanced sideways at Darcy before answering slowly, "I suppose, I might be willing. That is, if Mr. Darcy could be persuaded."

Darcy's pulse quickened and he found himself answering immediately. "I could be."

"Very well, I accept—on one condition. Since I am undertaking an activity that I am far from comfortable with, Mr. Darcy, my stipulation is that you would do the same."

"I beg your pardon, Miss Bennet. I do not take your meaning."

"It is quite simple, sir. You may give me one riding lesson, but in return, you must allow me to instruct you in something at which you are equally unfamiliar."

In spite of himself, Darcy could feel a smile tugging at his lips. "Such as?"

Elizabeth set down her cup. "That is a good question. As you seem to be proficient in most things, I will have to think on it a while."

The sound of Mr. Gardiner's deep laughter filled the air. "Watch out, Mr. Darcy. I would not put it past my niece to school you in the fine art of embroidery if you are not careful."

Darcy could feel the look of alarm that crept across his countenance, and Elizabeth laughed without reserve. "That is not a bad idea, Uncle, except I am afraid my own embroidery skills are severely lacking, so I am not certain I would make the best teacher."

"Perhaps you could instruct him on the pianoforte?" said Mrs. Gardiner, but it was Darcy who spoke next.

"You are all forgetting that I have not yet agreed to this scheme. However, I will submit to a music lesson if that is your wish, Miss Bennet."

Elizabeth stared back at him, raising one perfectly sculpted brow. "That is very generous of you, Mr. Darcy. But *you* forget that I already know you play—and exceedingly well if your sister is to be believed. No, it must be something you are wholly unfamiliar with. I will need some time to consider the matter."

Darcy leaned forward, bracing his elbows upon his knees. "So, you expect me to agree without having the slightest idea of what I am agreeing to?"

"Yes."

"That hardly seems fair, Miss Bennet."

"Mr. Darcy. If I am willing to get on a horse, something I can assure you fills me with no small amount of anxiety,

I do not think you will have cause to complain about whatever activity I should suggest."

"Touché, Miss Bennet."

"Then we are agreed?"

Staring into her bright eyes, Darcy nodded. "Yes, Miss Bennet. We are agreed."

CHAPTER 17

The steady sound of raindrops lashing against her windowpane woke Elizabeth from a restless slumber. Slipping from underneath the bedclothes she padded across the floor, opening the tall French doors. Outside, the sky was a dismal gray and a stream of water cascaded off the roof, pooling on the balcony floor. Elizabeth sighed. There would be no picnic today, but on the bright side, neither would she have to take Mr. Darcy up on his riding lesson. Elizabeth smiled. No, there would be no trip to the countryside, but she was quite certain that a day spent in Pemberley's library would suit her every bit as well.

Elizabeth was the last to enter the breakfast parlor. Upon seeing her standing in the doorway, Darcy immediately rose, Mr. Gardiner following suit.

"Miss Bennet. Good morning. I hope you slept well?" Darcy inquired as the two gentlemen regained their seats.

All eyes swiveled in Elizabeth's direction, causing a becoming flush to infuse her cheeks. "I did indeed, Mr. Darcy. I hope I did not keep you waiting?"

"Not at all—you are welcome to come and go at your leisure. Pray, help yourself to anything you like," Darcy added, gesturing to the sideboard, which was heaped with a vast array of breakfast foods. Darcy watched as she turned to fill her plate. Like him, she did not indulge in any of the heavy cooked dishes, instead selecting scones and jam, as well as a bowl of fresh blackberries. He tried not to stare as she took a seat at the opposite end of the table and sipped her tea before plucking a fat, ripe berry from her bowl and slipping it into her mouth.

Next to him, Mr. Gardiner coughed into his hand and Darcy tore his eyes away from Elizabeth, noting that her uncle was observing him attentively.

"I am afraid the weather will keep us from enjoying the outing you mentioned last evening, sir," Mr. Gardiner said evenly.

Darcy nodded, confirming the truth of the matter, and conversation veered to alternative plans for the day. Mrs. Gardiner stated her intention to call upon one of her acquaintances who lived in the area. Mary voiced her willingness to go along, and Elizabeth was then applied to for her approbation.

"I should love to make Mrs. Driscoll's acquaintance, Aunt, but I had hoped to explore Mr. Darcy's library today. Would you mind very much if I stayed behind?"

Darcy's breath hitched at Elizabeth's words but he forced himself to focus his attention on his plate. Did it signify that she wished to remain here at Pemberley rather than joining her aunt and sister?

"No, of course not," Mrs. Gardiner answered. Addressing her husband, Elizabeth's aunt added, "And what about you, Edward? Will you accompany us?"

Mr. Gardiner chuckled. "A morning spent discussing fashion and the like? I think not. I would much rather stay here and put Mr. Darcy's billiards room to good use. That is, if you have no objection, sir?"

Darcy immediately shook his head. "I hope you will use any part of the house you wish," he answered, but he could not help but wonder if the gentleman's desire to remain at Pemberley was for the sake of billiards or keeping an eye on his niece. Once again, Darcy found his gaze wandering to the opposite end of the table. Elizabeth had finished her pastry and was now returning to the sideboard for an additional helping of fruit.

"I see you are enjoying the berries, Miss Bennet," he said, attempting to keep his tone light.

"Indeed, I am, sir. Do you cultivate them here in your gardens?"

Darcy responded with a shake of his head. "In the gardens, no. They grow wild along the edge of the property. By August there is such a large quantity, we cannot collect them fast enough. But even now, there is quite a surfeit. I think we still have enough for our cook to make a pie or two." Darcy was gratified to see a slow smile animate Elizabeth's features. "If you would like, Miss

Bennet, perhaps we can go picking when the weather clears?"

Elizabeth stared vaguely across the room, worrying the small garnet cross that hung about her neck, before turning to face him with a sparkle in her eyes. "What? Oh, yes, indeed, Mr. Darcy, I would quite enjoy that."

As it was still too early for social calls, Darcy offered to show his guests through the house, a suggestion that was eagerly agreed to by all. And although Elizabeth and the Gardiners had toured the public rooms already, he made a point of taking them to many private areas of the home as well, regaling them with anecdotes from his childhood and recounting stories he had been told by his parents. Even Georgiana seemed to be back in her usual good spirits and joined in with her own reminiscences. Finally, the party reached the front hall, and Darcy led the way to an ornately carved door, stepping back with a flourish to allow Elizabeth to enter. The lady crossed the threshold and stopped. A sharp gasp drew from her lips, and Darcy smiled, following with the rest of the group.

In size, the library was one of the largest rooms in the house—almost half again as big as Pemberley's grand ballroom—and except for the tall windows and the space where the two fireplaces stood, bookshelves lined every wall from ceiling to floor. In the center of the space, the comfortable furniture was arranged in intimate groupings, creating numerous places to curl up and read. But it was the books that formed a muted tapestry of burgundies and browns, forest greens and midnight blues that seemed to draw Elizabeth's attention to the room's perimeter. Approaching the nearest shelf, she reached out her hand, running her fingers reverently along the gilded spines.

After a few moments Darcy followed, coming to a stop just behind her shoulder. "Is anything the matter, Miss Bennet? You are unusually quiet."

Elizabeth turned, delight dancing in her hazel eyes. "I... no... That is, I knew your library would be impressive, but I never imagined anything like this. Goodness, I may never leave!"

Georgiana who had been standing a few steps away thanked Elizabeth for her compliment, but Darcy could feel the blood rushing to his head. If only that were true! He would gladly expand the library to fill the entire west wing if that would be enough to keep Elizabeth here indefinitely.

Clearing his throat, Darcy leaned down, speaking directly into Elizabeth's ear. "I am glad you approve, Miss Bennet. I know how much you love books, so coming from you I take that as the highest compliment."

Elizabeth turned to look at him. "Good. It was intended as such."

Darcy's pulse quickened and his gaze remained fixed on Elizabeth's elegant profile as she pulled a book at random from the stacks. He watched as she caressed the leather bindings, and his entire body burned with longing.

Oh, to have her touch him like that! To feel the softness of her skin while he breathed in her sweet scent. If only he could declare himself then and there! He would do anything; beg her on bended knee to be his, now and forever...

He stepped closer and his hands reached out of their own accord.

The sound of a throat being cleared somewhere nearby arrested Darcy's steps and he pivoted in the opposite direction. His butler stood in the center of the room.

"I beg your pardon, sir, but a letter has just been delivered. It is addressed to the Miss Bennets. I thought you would wish to be informed straightaway."

Darcy instantly stepped forward, as heat rushed to his cheeks. Dear God, he had almost touched her! Right here in the presence of her relations and his own sister! Never had he been so grateful for the prompt delivery of the morning post.

"Yes, thank you, Hastings," he mumbled, taking the missive and briefly glancing down at the flowery hand before extending it in Elizabeth's direction. "For you, Miss Bennet."

Turning away from the bookshelves, Elizabeth took the letter.

Watching her face, Darcy felt the first stirrings of apprehension. "I hope it is not bad news?" he asked as Elizabeth's fingers worked to loosen the seal.

"No... I am certain there is no cause for alarm. But the letter appears to be from my sister Lydia, who I am afraid is not prone to writing unless she has something of a dramatic nature to report."

Hearing her words, Mary and the Gardiners joined the pair as Elizabeth unfolded the single sheet of thick velum.

To give the family some privacy Darcy stood slightly apart from the group, but looked on with concern as Georgiana settled in another corner of the room and pretended interest in a book that had been lying on a nearby table.

As she read, Elizabeth's frown deepened, and it wasn't long before Mrs. Gardiner asked anxiously about the news.

"Forgive me. No one is ill, though the letter is indeed from Lydia. She writes to inform us that her husband has purchased a captaincy in the regulars and they will be relocating to Newcastle within a fortnight."

Mary and the Gardiners expressed their surprise as Darcy rubbed the back of his neck, the first stirrings of self-reproach rippling up his spine. "Are those not happy tidings, Miss Bennet?" he asked cautiously.

Elizabeth turned to look at him. "Yes...," she answered slowly, folding the letter and passing it to Mary.

Mr. Gardiner shook his head. "I have no doubt my sister is heartsick."

Contrition twisted Darcy's stomach. "Yes, I had not thought... That is, I suppose it will be difficult for your family, having your sister settled so far from Longbourn."

Elizabeth fixed her attention on her host, and to Darcy's vast relief, one side of her mouth tipped into a grin. "Oh, no, it is not that. I love my sister, Mr. Darcy, but I have long thought that we could all benefit from a bit of separation from Lydia's... exuberance."

Darcy was about to answer when Mary Bennet let out a most unladylike snort and all eyes turned to her.

"Lizzy, did you take note of this?" Mary inquired, and in a most derisive tone she read aloud: "*'I shall endeavor to write, but you know married women have never much time for writing. My unmarried sisters may write to* me, *as you will have nothing else to do.'*"

Mr. Gardiner barked out a laugh while his wife merely rolled her eyes. The party discussed the letter for several more minutes before the clock struck the hour and Mrs. Gardiner and Mary began preparing for their morning call.

Darcy rang for the carriage and requested a footman to attend the ladies, while Mr. Gardiner again stated his intention to make use of Mr. Darcy's billiards room. An additional footman was called to escort him thither, leaving Darcy, Georgiana, and Elizabeth as the only occupants left in the library. As his sister remained settled with her book, Darcy approached Elizabeth, taking a seat across from her as propriety dictated.

"I beg your pardon, Miss Bennet. I know it is none of my concern, but you did not look entirely pleased when you read your sister's letter. I hope the Hughes' removal from the neighborhood has not caused you any distress?"

To Darcy's relief, Elizabeth shook her head. "No. Truly I am happy for them. It is only… I cannot help wondering where the lieutenant came upon the funds to purchase such a commission." Seeming to realize she had spoken far too plainly, Elizabeth flushed. "Forgive me, sir. I realize that was a highly improper thing for me to say."

Darcy frowned, but when he leaned forward, his voice

gentled. "Miss Bennet, I hope you will consider me a friend, and as such you are most welcome to discuss anything you wish. Nothing you divulge will leave these four walls." Glancing over at his sister who remained engrossed in her book, Darcy continued, "I am certain there are any number of explanations. Perhaps the lieutenant was given the money by some relation... Or mayhap he won it at cards or the like. I believe gambling is quite prevalent amongst those members of the militia."

But Elizabeth was already shaking her head. "Not such a large sum of money. And I do not believe there are any close relations who would be in a position to help him in such a way—at least not on *his* side."

Darcy rubbed at his forehead, causing Elizabeth to sigh.

"Forgive me again for unburdening myself to you, Mr. Darcy, I know I should not."

Darcy looked away. The last thing he wanted was for Elizabeth to worry that someone in her family had unnecessarily depleted their resources. "Are you concerned that your father has purchased the commission?" he asked gently.

To his surprise, Elizabeth widened her eyes, and a laugh slipped from her throat. "Papa? Oh, no! Certainly, it was not him. I believe it must have been Mr. Bingley who supplied the funds. I am afraid there is no other explanation."

Darcy startled. "Bingley? What makes you think so?"

Elizabeth met his gaze before glancing away. "Of course, I cannot know for sure. It is just that Mr. Bingley has come to the aid of our family in the past, and while we have all been exceedingly grateful, in this case such a gesture was entirely unnecessary."

Darcy's forehead wrinkled. What on earth could Bingley have done to help the Bennets? Unless perhaps Elizabeth referred to his friend's willingness to marry Jane Bennet without the benefit of a dowry... Still, it made sense that Elizabeth should suspect her brother-in-law. He was the most likely candidate, and knowing Bingley's generous nature, Darcy felt certain his friend would have purchased the commission if the thought had occurred to him.

Shifting his weight, Darcy carefully chose his words. "Whoever it was, I am certain they would not wish for you or your family to feel beholden to them, Miss Bennet. I have little doubt this individual had ample funds to make the purchase. Pray, do not trouble yourself about it."

"I suppose you are correct," she answered. "I hope you will not say anything to Mr. Bingley. I do not think he would wish for me to know."

Darcy released a breath, squirming uncomfortably in his chair. "Of course."

A knock sounded on the open door and Darcy and Elizabeth both turned to face the footman who had come to convey Mr. Gardiner's invitation for Darcy to join him in the billiards room. A request that under the circumstances, Darcy was all too happy to oblige.

Darcy did not know how long he had been sitting at his desk, his attention fixed upon the worn volume that had become one of his most cherished possessions.

After engaging in several rounds of billiards with Mr. Gardiner—who to Darcy's surprise turned out to be quite an accomplished player—that gentleman had expressed a desire to rest, and Darcy had returned to his study. But it was not long before his correspondence was put aside, and his hands were reaching for the book he kept hidden within his desk.

Sitting forward in his chair, he brushed his fingers over the cracked leather bindings and his heart pounded inside his chest. He ruffled the pages and several sheets came loose from the broken spine. Darcy peered at the smudged print before lifting one of the pages. Probably it was only his imagination, but he thought he could detect Elizabeth's fragrance within the fabric of the paper.

Setting the page aside, Darcy released a breath. It was wrong of him to have kept her book. He hadn't intended to. When he had come up with the notion of replacing the volume—an idea that had so consumed him he had traveled to three separate booksellers to find just the edition he wished to give her—his plan had been to return the damaged copy along with his purchase. Although no longer legible in places, he knew the book belonged to her father and possibly had sentimental value. But when it came time to wrap the parcel, he found he could not part with it. Somehow, the worn volume had become a sort of talisman, his one last connection to the woman he loved.

And despite the impropriety of his behavior, he was exceedingly glad to have it.

The sudden echo of footsteps in the outer hall snapped Darcy from his musings and he hastily buried the book beneath a stack of correspondence. Scooping up the loose pages, he folded them into a neat square, slipping them into the pocket of his coat as a soft knock sounded at the door.

"Enter," he called, and seconds later his sister's face appeared around the doorjamb, causing him to smile. "Georgie! Pray, come in." He pushed back his chair, motioning her forward.

His sister came to stand before his desk and Darcy noticed with relief that she looked less fatigued than he had seen her in some time, but her expression was serious.

"Fitzwilliam, I have been sent to fetch you. There is an urgent matter in the kitchens that requires your attention. You must come at once."

Darcy pulled his gaze away from Georgiana's flushed countenance and his forehead wrinkled. The kitchens? That area of the house was strictly his housekeeper's domain. As a matter of fact, Darcy could not remember ever being summoned below stairs for a consultation, in all his time as master. "Is it not something Mrs. Reynolds can handle?" he asked.

Georgiana immediately shook her head. "No. I am afraid not."

"Well, whatever it is, I am happy to discuss it, but I do

not believe Mrs. West would welcome my presence in her kitchens. I shall send for her to attend me here."

Darcy moved in the direction of the bell-pull, but to his surprise, Georgiana reached across the desk, staying his hand. "No, William, it cannot be discussed here. And it cannot wait. You must hurry."

Still confused, but seeing his sister's resolve, he allowed himself to be propelled out of the room and along the corridor to the back stairs. Following his sister's steps, it occurred to him that he had not been in this part of the house in... actually he could not remember the last time he had been in this part of the house. Certainly, it had been years.

Feeling like an interloper, Darcy tentatively entered the kitchens on Georgiana's heels—and froze.

The large room was empty save three people, but Darcy only had eyes for the one who stood directly before him, a crisp white apron covering her sprigged-muslin gown.

"Miss Bennet!" He looked around in confusion. "I hope you have not lost your way?"

A smile brightened Elizabeth's features and her eyes sparkled with barely suppressed mirth. Behind him, Darcy could hear his sister's throaty giggle.

"No, Mr. Darcy. I have not. But pray, do come in. We only have the use of the kitchens for a scant two hours before your staff must return to begin preparing for the evening meal, so there is little time to dawdle."

Darcy stepped farther into the room, his questioning eyes darting to Mrs. Reynolds, who stood slightly to one side, but she only smiled and walked over to take a seat on one of the chairs that surrounded a long wooden table at the back of the room.

"Miss Bennet, I am afraid you find me at a loss. Might I ask you to enlighten me as to the purpose of this meeting?"

"Certainly, sir. I am going to instruct you on the proper preparation of a pie. Blackberry, to be exact," she added, reaching for the basket of berries sitting on the nearby sideboard.

Darcy's eyebrows lifted and Elizabeth's smile broadened.

"I see," he answered, causing Elizabeth to laugh with the exuberance of a girl half her age.

"I must confess that at first I had trouble devising a task upon which I could educate you, Mr. Darcy. However, I then remembered that you are not so practiced in the kitchen." Her expression turned serious before she continued, "And I did promise most faithfully to bake for you one day. Do you not remember?"

Darcy swallowed, tugging at his neck-cloth which suddenly seemed far too tight. The memory of their time in the cottage's small kitchen played out in his mind's eye and he kept his gaze locked on hers when he answered. "Yes, Miss Bennet, I remember."

They stood looking at each other for a long moment before Elizabeth stepped away, pulling an apron from one of the pegs along the wall. When she spoke again, her voice was light. "I suggest you remove your coat, sir. I would not wish to get into trouble with your valet."

Darcy blinked back at her, struggling to process the shift in the conversation. "You want me to... That is, I assumed this would be a demonstration of some sort..." he stammered, but at the look on Elizabeth's face he reached out his hand, his fingers closing around the rough cloth.

Elizabeth studied him before addressing Georgiana over her shoulder. "Miss Darcy, perhaps you can assist your brother with that apron. He seems unsure of how to utilize it."

Snapping out of his shock, Darcy waved his sister aside before tugging off his coat and slipping the smock over his head. "That will not be necessary, Miss Bennet."

Elizabeth offered a wry smile, reaching for his discarded coat and moving to hang it on a rack in the corner. Suddenly, Darcy remembered the pages of the book, secreted away in his pocket. What would she say if she found them? Would she realize where they had come from? But Elizabeth was already crossing back to where he stood, causing Darcy to release his breath. Tying the apron strings, his gaze darted to the back of the room. Besides Mrs. Reynolds, one of the kitchen maids lingered near the entrance to the pantry, her eyes wide.

Darcy rubbed his neck, glancing uneasily around the kitchen.

As if sensing his discomfort, Elizabeth looked up from her preparations, her gaze following his. "Oh, forgive me, Mr. Darcy. I hope you do not mind a small audience. Mrs. Reynolds wished to observe the process, and I am certain you know Sarah," she added, nodding to the scullery maid. "She has volunteered to stand by in case we should require assistance."

Elizabeth grinned up at him then, causing Darcy's heart rate to escalate. To calm himself, he turned his attention to the young maid, noticing that she immediately dropped her gaze. In truth, he was not certain he had ever been introduced to the girl—Pemberley had a large staff, and he generally did not come in contact with those who worked below-stairs. Seeing the maid's obvious discomfort at being in the presence of the master, even if he was standing before her in an apron and shirtsleeves, Darcy smiled, attempting to put her at ease. "I thank you, Sarah, for allowing us to invade your workspace. I hope we do not prove to be too much trouble."

Darcy watched in amusement as the girl's eyes formed round circles and a slight flush colored her cheeks. "Oh, no sir! 'Tis no trouble!"

"Good. I am pleased to hear it." Allowing his smile to remain, he turned to face Elizabeth. "Very well, Miss Bennet. I await your expert tutelage. What would you have me do?"

Elizabeth regarded him over the curve of her shoulder. "I suppose you might begin by sorting these berries," she said, indicating the basket in front of him with a tilt of her chin. "Meanwhile, Miss Darcy and I will mix the ingredients for the crust."

Darcy looked from the basket to the bowl in front of him. "Er... sort them? Pardon my ignorance, Miss Bennet, but can we not just pour the desired amount into the crust?"

Elizabeth cocked her head. "No, Mr. Darcy, we cannot."

Stepping over to where he stood, she reached across his body, her fingers brushing his wrist as she began picking through the basket of fruit. Her proximity made Darcy's stomach tumble. Steadying his breathing, he forced himself to focus on what she was saying.

"...and as you can see, some of these are not sufficiently ripe." Elizabeth held up a pale blush-colored berry for his inspection. "Others have become slightly squashed in transport," she continued, picking out another berry and showing it to him, before popping it into her mouth.

Darcy felt a smile twitching at his lips. "And is it also my job to consume all of those damaged berries, Miss Bennet?"

Elizabeth gazed back at him seriously. "You may do as you wish, Mr. Darcy. However, it *is* important to taste the fruit; otherwise you will not know how much sugar to use. Here," she added, plucking a fat purple berry from the basket. For a moment Darcy stilled, thinking she intended to place it into his mouth, but instead she simply held it out to him. When he did not react immediately, she took his hand, turning it over before placing the berry lightly in his palm.

Darcy swallowed, lifting the fruit.

"Well?" Elizabeth asked as Darcy chewed.

"It is... very good."

"Yes. But you will notice that it is also slightly tart, though it is fully ripe. That is due to the earliness of the season. In a month's time, the fruit will be much sweeter.

This is why you must taste and adjust the sugar accordingly."

"I see."

"Now, any of the berries that are not fit to use, you may put here, in this bowl. Oh, and you must not worry that they will go to waste. While I would not wish to make use of them in the pie, they are perfectly adequate for preserves or sauces."

Darcy lifted his gaze, staring at her intently. "I assure you, Miss Bennet, I was not worried."

Suddenly, Georgiana looked up from where she was slicing into a slab of butter, enthusiasm lighting her features. "William, perhaps if Mrs. West uses the leftovers to make preserves, we might put together baskets with fresh bread and bring them to the tenants. Do you not think that a fine idea?"

"Certainly not," Darcy answered, and Georgiana's smile faltered. "Really, Georgie," Darcy continued, "would you have me give the tenants jam made from inferior berries? No, it cannot be done. We will simply have to eat the preserves ourselves, no matter how horrible they are."

Georgiana's mouth dropped open and she stared back at her brother, her eyes as wide as saucers. Out of the corner of his vision, Darcy could see Elizabeth biting back a laugh.

"I believe your brother is teasing you, Miss Darcy," Elizabeth said, gently squeezing the girl's shoulder. "Now, enough of this gadding about. Let us concentrate on our work, or we will never have this ready before the servants return to begin the dinner service."

Dinner was a jovial affair, with Mrs. Gardiner sharing stories from her morning call and Elizabeth joining in on a discussion of the local sights with Mary and Georgiana. When dessert was finally presented in the form of a steaming blackberry pie complete with fresh whipped cream, Elizabeth grinned with obvious delight.

"Mr. Darcy, this pie is delicious," Mr. Gardiner stated a few moments later. "Quite the best I've had as a matter of fact. You must give my compliments to your cook."

Darcy's gaze found Elizabeth, who laughed outright.

"I believe you just have, Uncle," she said brightly before Georgiana shared the story with the rest of the table.

"Ah, so this was Mr. Darcy's lesson, was it not?" Mrs. Gardiner replied.

"Well done, Lizzy," added Mr. Gardiner. "Although I hope you have not given your aunt any ideas." At which Mrs. Gardiner swatted her husband playfully with her napkin.

Darcy cleared his throat, feeling a telltale flush warming his neck. "I enjoyed myself immensely, as it happens," he said, his eyes remaining fixed on Elizabeth's. "But let us not forget, Miss Bennet that we still have your riding lesson to look forward to."

"I have not forgotten, sir," she answered. "I have given my word. I assure you, I do not intend to back down."

CHAPTER 18

The following morning, Elizabeth stood before the looking glass in Georgiana's chambers. Much to her dismay, the day had dawned sunny and clear, leaving no good excuse for her to postpone her riding lesson with Mr. Darcy.

Frowning at her reflection, she turned to speak to Georgiana who was adjusting the train of Elizabeth's habit. "Is this really necessary, Miss Darcy? Would not one of my own gowns do?"

Georgiana gazed up at her and Elizabeth noticed that the young girl's face appeared pale and drawn, but Georgiana's mouth lifted in a determined smile. "No. You will need something looser in the skirt. Besides, you would not want to get one of your own gowns dirty. And I have more than enough to spare, though it is lucky that we are close to the same size."

Elizabeth nodded, plucking at the folds of her skirt.

She could not imagine how such an excess of material would be beneficial, unless it was to pad her fall. She shuddered at the thought, turning away from the mirrored glass.

"There," said Georgiana, coming to her feet. "Now, we just need to get you a pair of boots."

"You needn't trouble yourself, Miss Darcy. My walking boots will do well enough," Elizabeth answered.

"Oh, 'tis no trouble. And you must have proper boots for riding, walking shoes will not do at all. I will have one of the maids bring several pairs for you to try." Georgiana moved in the direction of the bell-pull, but she had not taken more than three steps before she doubled over at the waist.

Elizabeth hurried to her side. "Miss Darcy, are you unwell? Shall I send for your brother?"

Georgiana gasped, but quickly shook her head. "No! I pray you do not. Forgive me, Miss Bennet, it is only a cramp. It will subside in a moment. And I would not wish to worry Fitzwilliam."

Elizabeth looked back at her uncertainly. If Miss Darcy was truly ill, her brother would not thank Elizabeth for keeping it to herself. Before she could speak, Georgiana straightened and a bit of her natural color returned to her cheeks. "Truly, I am well. Now, let me ring for those boots. We would not want to keep my brother waiting."

Elizabeth entered the stables and blinked, her eyes slowly adjusting to the low light. Taking a steadying breath, her lungs filled with the overpowering aroma of hay and horses and a shiver rippled down her spine. From somewhere nearby, one of the animals whinnied and Elizabeth instinctively stepped back. *This was a mistake. I cannot go through with it.* Lifting her skirts, she spun in the direction of the door.

"Miss Bennet. Welcome."

The deep voice that came from somewhere behind her made Elizabeth freeze. Slowly, she turned around, just in time to see Mr. Darcy step from the shadows. Despite her anxiety, Elizabeth noticed that he was impeccably attired in buff-colored breeches, high boots, and a fitted jacket. Swallowing past the tightness in her throat, Elizabeth opened her mouth to speak, but before she could form the words, he had come up beside her.

Regarding Elizabeth with a steady gaze, Darcy lightly cupped her elbow, steering her towards the door. "Come. The horses are already outside."

Elizabeth nodded, allowing Mr. Darcy to draw her into the hazy sunshine. Once they had stepped clear of the stables, her breath came easier and her gaze shifted to the nearby paddock—which was noticeably empty. Feeling slightly more tranquil now that she was out in the open air, Elizabeth turned to her companion. "Exactly where are these mythical horses, Mr. Darcy? I do not see then anywhere in the vicinity."

To her surprise, the question made him visibly uncomfortable and he stiffened slightly before fixing his eyes on a small copse of trees in the near distance.

"I had a groom take them on ahead. We will have our lesson in one of the adjacent pastures and I thought you might prefer to walk there rather than ride. I hope that meets with your approval?"

Elizabeth felt her heart quicken at the intensity in his expression. "I... yes. Thank you. I would prefer to walk for a while."

Darcy nodded, extending his arm and Elizabeth slipped her hand into the bend of his elbow.

They continued in silence for a while before Mr. Darcy spoke. "Miss Bennet, I wondered if you might enlighten me as to your previous riding experience. I think it would help me to better know how to proceed with our lesson."

Elizabeth turned away, her upper lip catching between her teeth.

"Come now, it can't have been that bad. Tell me, how old were you when you had your first instruction?"

"I was seven, sir."

Darcy nodded, thoughtfully. "Georgiana was only a bit younger when I began tutoring her. And... were you afraid?" he asked. "Horses can often sense fear and it can make things more difficult for some."

Elizabeth shifted to look at him. "Oh, no! It was Jane who was anxious, though she is more than a year older. So, you see, it is quite ironic that she took to it so easily while I... did not."

"Will you tell me what happened?" Darcy asked gently. "The day you fell?"

Elizabeth sighed, but nodded. "From as far back as I can remember, it was my fondest wish to learn to ride and to have a horse of my own. I am afraid I pestered my poor father mercilessly until he finally relented, purchasing a lovely pony and engaging an instructor to teach both Jane and me how to ride her. Every day, I would wait in the stables and watch as our grooms saddled the pony, and then the instructor would arrive and Jane and I would take turns riding around our back pasture. Of course, Jane, being a most obedient child, was perfectly content with this arrangement. But every day I would beg to be allowed to leave the enclosure. At night, I dreamt of galloping across gently rolling hills, the sunlight on my cheeks and the wind in my hair... So you see walking around our fenced paddock was not exactly to my liking." Elizabeth paused and a smile played across Darcy's countenance.

"In any case, things continued in this manner for about a fortnight when one morning I decided I could not plod around that pasture one more time. I woke early and slipped into the stables. By this time, I knew how to saddle Jade—that was the horse's name—and I quickly mounted her and set out. At first, I kept the pony to a walk. But when I reached the open fields, I kicked her as hard as I could, slapping her neck with the reins for good measure. Before I knew it, we were racing across our fields, just as I had in my dreams... But it wasn't long before I lost control. The pony was going faster and faster. I pulled back on the reins to slow her down but I lost my balance and fell—hard." Elizabeth shuddered at the memory and Darcy's grip strengthened on her arm.

"That must have been frightening."

Elizabeth lifted her shoulders before letting them drop. "Actually, I believe I was in a state of shock. My arm hurt, badly. I couldn't move it at all. But I went and fetched the pony—she hadn't gone far—and walked back home. Of course, when my parents found out, Mamma took to her bed in a fit of hysterics and Papa forbade me from going anywhere near the stables again." When Darcy looked at her in confusion, Elizabeth hurried to clarify, "Oh, he did not forbid me to ride, he only wanted to ensure that I was not so reckless as to take the pony out alone. Everyone assumed that once my arm healed, I would go back to my lessons, but I never did. The pony became Jane's after that, and I decided to stick to using my own two feet to get where I was going."

Elizabeth had just finished her tale when the pair came around a bend in the road, exposing a large pasture where two horses, one gray and one chestnut-brown, were grazing in the tall grass. Elizabeth stopped walking.

Darcy looked down at her, his gaze tender, and Elizabeth felt herself momentarily calm.

"Thank you for telling me that story, Miss Bennet. I hope you know that I would never allow any harm to come to you. However, if you have changed your mind, I would understand. You need not do anything against your wishes."

Elizabeth stared into his dark eyes. "I know," she answered.

As they stood looking at one another, a young groom

rose from where he had been sitting in the grass and began walking in their direction.

Removing his cap, the boy nodded to Mr. Darcy before turning to stare at Elizabeth, his eyes round.

Darcy cleared his throat, garnering the boy's attention. "I trust the horses are prepared as I instructed?"

Again, the groom nodded, and Darcy continued, "Good. You may go now, James. We will return them to the stables later this afternoon."

The boy darted a curious glance at Elizabeth before doffing his cap and hurrying off.

Darcy stepped over to their mounts, collecting the reins and leading them to the edge of the pasture.

Elizabeth watched as he approached, tilting her head slightly to one side. "Mr. Darcy, neither of these horses seem to be fitted with a side saddle."

Darcy instantly colored, his gaze slipping away. "No."

"So... you expect me to ride... astride? *This* is your mysterious teaching method?"

The chestnut gelding whickered, tossing his head, and Darcy fingered the reins. "I beg your pardon, Miss Bennet. I should have asked you if you would be willing to undertake such an endeavor before we set out. If you are truly opposed, we can return to the stables for a different saddle, of course."

Elizabeth carefully stretched out her hand, her fingers coming to rest on the smooth muzzle of the dapple-gray. "Is this one to be mine?" she asked.

Darcy nodded. "Yes. This is Calypso. My father purchased her for Georgiana's tenth birthday. She is one of the gentlest animals I have ever come across. You will be quite safe in her charge."

Elizabeth did not answer, but she continued to stroke the mare's velvety nose.

"And that one is yours?" she finally asked, lifting her chin in the direction of the other horse.

"One of mine, yes. This is Poseidon."

Elizabeth turned to pat the chestnut gelding but after a few seconds Calypso stepped forward, pushing her nose under Elizabeth's arm.

Darcy grinned. "She is jealous." Pulling a carrot stub from the pocket of his jacket, he placed it into Elizabeth's palm. "Here. These are her favorite."

Elizabeth cautiously extended her hand, laughing when the horse's lips tickled her fingers.

Darcy rubbed the mare's neck. "I think you have made a friend, Miss Bennet. And I can assure you, once Calypso has formed an attachment, she is exceedingly loyal."

Elizabeth angled her head, gazing into Mr. Darcy's eyes. They stared at one another for several seconds before Elizabeth looked away. "Very well, Mr. Darcy."

The gentleman's brow lifted in obvious surprise. "Then... You are willing to ride... in this manner? It will not make you uncomfortable?"

Elizabeth's mouth turned up at the corners. "On the contrary. I have always thought riding astride would be a good deal easier. Safer, too." Soft laughter bubbled in her throat as she turned back to her companion. "Though now I understand why your groom was looking at me with such curiosity."

"I will admit that is why I thought it best to have our lesson here, away from the stables."

Taking Calypso's reins, Darcy led the gentle mare over to a tall oak tree and Elizabeth followed. Lifting her hem, she carefully slipped the toe of her boot into the stirrup.

"Here, place your hands on the pommel, Miss Bennet, and then pull yourself up."

Elizabeth did as he instructed, but her right leg became hopelessly tangled in the seemingly endless material of her skirts and she dropped back onto the ground, grumbling in frustration. "Oh, bother," she muttered, gathering the material of her gown in her free hand and hitching it up around her knees.

Immediately, Darcy looked away.

Calmly adjusting her skirts, Elizabeth gazed down at him as the horse shifted beneath her. "It seems your plan would have been better executed had it involved a pair of breeches, Mr. Darcy," she called, amused at the deep flush that had settled upon the gentleman's countenance.

Darcy coughed, busying himself with handing Elizabeth the reins, but she could see a smile twitching at his lips. Lifting himself into his own saddle, he drew his mount up alongside Calypso, giving Elizabeth some basic instruction before the two set out at a slow walk. After a few minutes, Darcy nudged Poseidon with his left thigh. Bringing the gelding in close, he reached out, lightly taking Elizabeth's gloved hands.

"Miss Bennet, here. Loosen your grip, like this. And press in with your legs; that is what will keep you on.

Although I promise, you have nothing to fear. She will not bolt."

Elizabeth glanced nervously in Darcy's direction, but she breathed deeply, forcing herself to calm. *"Nothing beautiful without struggle."*

She had not even been certain she had spoken aloud, until Mr. Darcy leaned in, replying seriously, *"Those who don't know must learn from those who do, Miss Bennet."*

Elizabeth glanced back at him, her eyes wide. Was Mr. Darcy quoting Plato to her? The fact that he had recognized the source of her quip was surprising enough, but to have him return it shocked her to such an extent that she forgot her anxiety altogether. As they rode, Elizabeth continued to ponder the subject. Of course, she knew Mr. Darcy to be an educated man, but aside from her father, she had never met anyone with such a ready intellect. As a matter of fact, she could think of no other gentleman of her acquaintance who was as knowledgeable or as well-read as the one by her side. Nor could she think of any man whose disposition and talents would suit her half as well…

They continued on in silence for some time before Mr. Darcy glanced in her direction. "How are you feeling?" he asked.

"Better than I expected. I think you are correct about riding in this manner."

Darcy nodded, sitting back in his saddle. "When Georgiana was small, I noticed she never wished to ride at any pace faster than a walk, although she loved the activity. When I asked her about it, she said she always felt as though she would slip off, despite the pommel. And I have to say, having ridden that way myself last November, I now know exactly what she meant."

Elizabeth stared at him in confusion until an image of Mr. Darcy perched upon the carriage horse in the aftermath of the accident flashed to mind. Wondering at his ability to tease her over something that had caused him such distress, she slowly shook her head. "I am not certain that is a fair comparison, sir, as you were injured at the time, not to mention riding without the benefit of a saddle."

"True. But I still prefer riding with one leg on each side of the saddle."

Elizabeth flushed and looked away, before turning back to ask, "And does your sister continue to ride in this manner, sir?"

Darcy laughed easily. "No. She gave it up some years ago and has become quite proficient with the side-saddle. I am certain she would be happy to teach you if you ever decide to make the switch."

"Perhaps someday," Elizabeth answered. "Though I have learned the hard way that one must walk before they can be expected to run."

CHAPTER 19

The next hour slipped by as Darcy and Elizabeth crisscrossed Pemberley's lush pasture. With each turn, Darcy noticed that Elizabeth seemed more at ease, and before long he was gratified to see that she was able to keep pace beside him at a steady trot.

Not wanting to tempt fate, Darcy suggested they leave the remainder of the lesson for another day, and the pair dismounted beneath the great oak where they had begun, settling in the shade to enjoy the refreshments that had been left for them. When Darcy produced a wine bottle, Elizabeth's eyes widened, but she laughed heartily when he moved to pour and it was not wine but lemonade that flowed into her glass.

The soft ripple of Elizabeth's laughter still hung in the air when Darcy felt a slight tremor beneath them, followed by the unmistakable sound of hoofbeats pounding on the hard-packed earth. Turning his head, Darcy saw James, his stable lad, galloping in their direction at a breakneck pace. Dropping his glass, Darcy stood, fear settling like a stone in the pit of his stomach.

"What is it? What has happened?" he demanded as the groom reined in his mount.

"'Tis Miss Georgiana, sir. She's taken ill. Mrs. Reynolds sent for the doctor, and Mr. Hastings says you're to come right away."

Before the boy had finished speaking, Darcy was already yanking at the knots that tethered Poseidon's reins to a low hanging branch. *This was his fault.* He knew Georgiana had been feeling unwell. He should have insisted that a physician be summoned weeks ago!

"James," he barked over his shoulder, "escort Miss Bennet back to the house, and then deliver Calypso to the stables." Freeing the reins, Darcy turned to Elizabeth, softening his tone. "Forgive me, Miss Bennet, for leaving you this way. James will return you safely to the house." He prepared to mount, but Elizabeth reached for his arm, holding him in place.

"Mr. Darcy, wait. I will come with you."

"I appreciate the offer, Miss Bennet, but I am afraid I intend to ride at a rapid pace. I fear even if you were up to the task, Calypso is not." He turned away, but Elizabeth's fingers tightened around his arm.

"Can your horse accommodate two riders, sir?"

Darcy stilled. "What?"

"I shall ride with you, if you will allow it."

"I... Are you... That is, are you certain?" he stammered, but Elizabeth was already reaching for the saddle.

"Quite certain. Although I may need some assistance in mounting. Poseidon is quite a bit taller than Calypso."

Darcy blinked back at her.

"Mr. Darcy? Please, hurry. We are wasting time."

Snapping out of his torpor, Darcy immediately stepped forward, placing his hands on Elizabeth's slim waist and easily boosting her into the saddle. Swinging up behind her, his pulse raced as her back pressed against his chest, her soft curls brushing his cheek. Filling his lungs with her light floral scent, he grasped the reins in his right palm before sliding his left arm securely across her body. Pulling the horse about, he stared down at his wide-eyed groom.

"James, take Calypso back to the stables and then collect Poseidon from the east side of the house," he called, before kicking his mount into a brisk trot.

Anchoring Elizabeth firmly in place, Darcy rested his chin gently on her shoulder so he could speak into her ear. "Are you well, Miss Bennet?" he asked, raising his voice slightly to be heard over the pounding of the horse's hooves.

Elizabeth nodded. "Yes, as long as you keep your arm around me I am quite well. However, I am certain you intend to travel faster than this!"

Heat rushed through Darcy's bloodstream like a wildfire, and it was all he could do to keep from touching his lips to the pale column of Elizabeth's neck. Instead, he dug his heels into the gelding's flanks and Poseidon took off at a run. Elizabeth remained pressed against him, but her posture was relaxed, not stiff with tension as he had expected.

Once again, Darcy sent up a prayer of thanks that he had requested Poseidon for today's lesson. In truth, he generally rode his newest stallion, Apollo, but he had specifically selected the elder, more docile Poseidon for his outing with Elizabeth. Apollo was an excellent mount, but he could also be headstrong and temperamental, and Darcy had wanted to leave nothing to chance.

As they galloped through the fields, a tempest of emotions swirled inside his body—terror for his sister and what he might find back at the house mixed with the sheer ecstasy of racing across his estate, Elizabeth Bennet wrapped tightly in his arms. Briefly, he wondered how one person could feel such diametrically opposed sensations, but all too soon, the familiar stone edifice was upon them, causing him to focus solely on the task at hand.

When they neared the east terrace, Darcy yanked abruptly on the reins, and Poseidon skidded to a halt, pitching them forward in the saddle. Automatically, his arm tightened around Elizabeth's waist and he shifted slightly, studying her face. But although her cheeks were stained a deep pink, she did not seem in any way frightened.

Darcy moved to dismount, gathering Elizabeth in his arms and carefully guiding her to the ground. And although the urge to embrace her had never been stronger, he immediately released his hold, taking a step backwards.

Remembering his sister, apprehension turned his stomach and he reached out to squeeze Elizabeth's hand in a gesture of farewell. His long legs had carried him halfway to the French doors before he realized that Elizabeth's fingers still clung tightly to his own. Glancing over his shoulder, he saw she was hurrying after him, easily matching his pace. His grip increased around her hand, and heat shot up his arm. Jerking open the door to the conservatory, he began weaving his way through the room, pulling Elizabeth behind him. When they reached the front hall, he turned towards the grand staircase, stopping short when he saw his butler.

"Hastings! Where is Miss Darcy?" he called, his voice tight with emotion.

"In her chambers, sir. Mrs. Reynolds is attending her."

With a brief nod, Darcy took to the stairs, Elizabeth following at his heels. At the door to his sister's apartment he came to a halt, taking a moment to steady his breathing before entering, only remembering to release Elizabeth's hand as he crossed the threshold.

Mrs. Gardiner moved from her position at the window as they entered and Darcy strode in her direction. "What has happened?" he demanded.

"I am afraid Miss Darcy collapsed a short time ago. She is resting now, although I believe she is still in a considerable amount of pain."

Bile rose in Darcy's throat and he quickly turned away, but it was Elizabeth who spoke.

"I am to blame," she whispered, causing Darcy to

swing around to stare at her with no small amount of surprise.

"I believe she had a similar episode this morning, when she was helping me to dress," Elizabeth continued. "I wanted to send for you, but she insisted it was nothing of consequence."

Darcy dropped his gaze, raking his fingers through his hair. "No. This is not your failing, Miss Bennet. It is mine. Georgiana has been complaining of these pains for some time. I should have sent for a physician months ago." Pacing to the window he murmured, "If anything happens to her, I will never forgive myself."

Squaring his shoulders, Darcy turned, pulling at the door to his sister's bedchamber. Inside the adjoining room, Georgiana was curled into a tight ball on the large bed. Mrs. Reynolds sat on the edge of the mattress, a damp cloth pressed against the young girl's brow.

Seeing Mr. Darcy enter, Mrs. Reynolds stood, making way for him as he neared the bed.

"How is she?" he asked.

As if to answer his question, Georgiana groaned, peering up at him with frightened eyes. "William," she breathed. "It hurts so much."

Darcy sat, stroking his sister's cheek with the backs of his fingers. "I know, sweetling. The doctor is on his way." His eyes found Mrs. Reynolds and his mouth tightened. "Where is Prescott?" he hissed. "He should have been here by now!"

"I cannot imagine, sir. I dispatched a rider over an hour ago."

Before Darcy could respond, a knock sounded on the sitting room door. "Mr. Darcy," Elizabeth called softly, beckoning him with a slight tilt of her head.

Darcy reached out, squeezing his sister's fingers. "I will return directly," he told her gently before following Elizabeth into the adjoining room, pulling the door closed behind him.

An unknown gentleman stood near the entrance to the outer corridor.

"Mr. Darcy, this is Dr. Grant."

Elizabeth crossed the room and Darcy's eyes narrowed as the gentleman sketched a bow.

"Mr. Darcy. I had hoped we would have had the chance to be formally introduced under more pleasant circumstances, however I understand—"

"Where is Prescott?" Darcy snapped. "We sent for him over an hour ago."

The physician's eyebrows lifted, but he answered evenly, "My apologies, sir. I am afraid Dr. Prescott has been called away on another matter. However, I am happy to attend your sister." Reaching into his breast pocket, he withdrew a folded sheet of parchment, holding it out to his host. "If I may."

Darcy took the note, rapidly scanning the brief missive. When he finished reading, he handed it back and began to pace in tight circles before coming to stand before the unfamiliar gentleman.

"You are a physician?"

"Yes, sir. I am also a trained surgeon."

A muscle tightened in Darcy's jaw and he stifled a

snort. "My sister does not require a surgeon," he said, his gaze hardening. "What is your age?"

The gentleman offered a slow smile. "Five and twenty, sir."

"And your training?"

"I was educated at Oxford. I have spent the past three years apprenticing in Paris for one of France's most prominent surgeons. I have been practicing with Dr. Prescott since the spring."

Darcy rubbed the back of his neck, stalking to the window and staring out into the gardens.

Behind him, Grant spoke quietly. "Mr. Darcy, I understand your hesitation. But I can assure you that I am perfectly qualified to examine your sister. As the letter from Dr. Prescott indicates—"

A sharp cry from the next room redirected everyone's attention and Darcy flinched.

"Mr. Darcy, your sister appears to be in some distress. If you will grant me permission to see her, I may be able to help."

The room was silent for several moments before Darcy offered a curt nod. "Very well. But I wish to be present."

Grant's eyebrows lifted. "I beg your pardon, sir, but I do not believe that would be... That is, I intend to do a thorough examination. I would of course be happy to have any of the ladies of the household present."

At the physician's words, Darcy instantly colored. "Yes... I... Forgive me. My housekeeper is with her." His eyes wandered to Elizabeth. *No. I could not ask it of her...*

As if reading his thoughts, Elizabeth came to stand

beside him. "Mr. Darcy, I would be happy to stay with your sister if you wish it."

Before Darcy could respond, Mrs. Gardiner placed a hand on her niece's shoulder. "I do not think that is wise, Lizzy. The sickroom is no place for an unmarried lady. I will go, if Mr. Darcy has no objection?"

"Nonsense," Elizabeth answered. "I have been in many a sickroom before, and likely will be in many after today. Though I am certain Mr. Darcy would be happy to have you accompany me." Turning to Darcy she added, "If you are agreeable, we shall both go."

Mrs. Gardiner offered a small frown, but she did not object, and Darcy quickly gave his approbation. "Thank you. I would be most grateful." Leading the small party to his sister's chamber, Darcy crossed to the bed before making the necessary introductions.

"You will notify me as soon as the examination is over?" he asked, turning to Grant.

"Of course."

A brusque nod served as Darcy's reply, and, with one last look at his sister, he headed for the door.

The latch clicked, and the ladies retreated to the foot of the bed. Georgiana huddled deeper beneath the covers, her expression wary, but Elizabeth noticed that a warm smile crinkled the corners of the physician's eyes.

"Miss Darcy, I can see you are in a good deal of discomfort. If you will consent, I would like to examine you to see if I might be able to determine the cause of your distress, and hopefully offer you some relief. Pray, can you tell me exactly where you are feeling the pain?"

Georgiana flushed, lowering her gaze. Pulling one hand from beneath the bedclothes, she used it to gesture to her abdomen and Dr. Grant nodded.

"Mrs. Reynolds," he said softly, "if you would be so kind as to lay Miss Darcy on her back. You may cover her to the waist, but lift her gown enough so that I may see the middle-section of her body."

Mrs. Reynolds nodded, moving to the side of the bed as the doctor stepped away, motioning for Mrs. Gardiner to accompany him. Without waiting to be asked, Elizabeth followed her aunt and the physician to a small alcove near the windows.

"May I be of some assistance, sir?" Mrs. Gardiner asked when they had reached their destination.

The physician's eyes darted from one lady to the next, settling briefly on Elizabeth before returning to her aunt. "Yes... I... forgive me, Mrs...."

"Gardiner."

"Yes, forgive me, Mrs. Gardiner... I am not certain how well the two of you are acquainted with the family, but I was wondering, that is, is there any chance Miss Darcy might be... with child?"

Mrs. Gardiner drew in a breath, and her lips parted in surprise. Exchanging a glance with Elizabeth, she turned to study the gentleman. "I am afraid I do not know the lady well, sir. We are merely guests in Mr. Darcy's home..." She paused for a moment. "However, if you are asking my opinion, I do not think it likely. In addition to the fact that it would seem most out of character, I believe Miss Darcy has been experiencing these symptoms for some duration. Since the winter, at least."

The doctor appeared thoughtful, then nodded slowly. "I see. Thank you, Mrs. Gardiner; I appreciate your candor. And pray, forgive me, Miss Bennet. I do apologize for raising an uncomfortable topic. As you can imagine, I did not feel I could ask her brother, and I would prefer not to bring up the subject with Miss Darcy herself... at least for the time being."

Before either of the women had a chance to answer, Mrs. Reynolds interrupted to inform the physician that Miss Darcy was ready for the examination to proceed. Grant nodded, moving to the bed and smiling down at his patient.

"Miss Darcy, I am going to apply a small amount of pressure to your abdomen. Pray, let me know if anything I do causes an increase in pain."

Georgiana nodded her understanding, staring resolutely up at the silk canopy. Her countenance remained a mask of indifference until the doctor pressed down in one particular area, causing her to cry out in obvious distress. Removing his hands, Grant pulled on the hem of her gown, covering her exposed skin.

"Forgive me, Miss Darcy. We are almost finished." Sitting beside the bed, the physician reached for her hand. Turning it palm-side up, he carefully pressed his thumb against the inside of her wrist.

"I noticed a beautiful pianoforte in the next room, Miss Darcy. Do you play?"

Georgiana picked up her gaze, looking to Elizabeth for a moment before turning back to the physician. "Yes, sir. I do. That instrument was a gift from my..." Georgiana gasped. "...from my brother, several years ago."

"And do you favor a particular composer?" the physician inquired.

"I... I am fond of Mozart. And Bach."

Grant smiled. "Ah. I am an admirer of Mozart as well. But I must confess to a preference for Beethoven. I had the privilege of hearing him play several years ago in Vienna and it was an unforgettable experience." Releasing Georgiana's wrist, he rested his palms on the edge of the mattress, leaning down to press one ear against her chest. Georgiana drew in an uneven breath at the unaccustomed proximity to a gentleman who was essentially a stranger.

"I understand he is no longer performing, which is a shame," Grant continued easily. "You may just breathe normally, Miss Darcy." A moment later the doctor stood, tucking the covers beneath Georgiana's chin and lifting his bag. "I thank you for your forbearance. If I might only ask you a few questions?"

The doctor's inquiries caused even Elizabeth to flush with embarrassment, but Georgiana answered everything that was asked of her with a sincerity and straightforwardness that belied her seventeen years.

Finally, the interview was over and the doctor stood to leave. "I will only be a moment, Miss Darcy and then I will return with something that should help with the pain."

Georgiana nodded, and Elizabeth could not help but notice that the fear in the young girl's eyes was replaced with something altogether different as she watched the physician quit the room.

In the adjoining chamber, Darcy continued to pace across the carpet, his hands clenched as tightly as the knot that had taken hold inside his chest. When the door to his sister's bedroom finally opened, it was all Darcy could do not to pounce on the young physician.

"Well? How is she?" he demanded. "Have you determined what is the matter?"

The doctor crossed the room with a measured stride, settling into a chair near the hearth and clasping his hands beneath his chin. He sat for several moments before answering. "Forgive me, Mr. Darcy, I wish I had better news. But I believe what is ailing your sister is of a serious nature. From my examination and what she has told me, I believe Miss Darcy is suffering from a blockage of some sort. Most likely a stone in her bladder. Needless to say, this can be extremely painful."

Nausea churned the contents of Darcy's stomach and he quickly looked away. He would sooner walk through the fires of hell than have any suffering visited upon his sister. Turning back to face the physician, he struggled to compose his features. "Assuming you are correct, what can be done?"

There was a long pause before the doctor answered.

"The best prognosis would be for her to undergo a procedure to remove the stone."

"What type of procedure?" Darcy asked warily, his gaze narrowing.

The physician's eyes lowered briefly. "Not an easy one, I am afraid. I have a book at my residence detailing the technique. I shall send for it. But for now, I would like to give your sister something for the pain, if you will agree?"

Darcy readily consented, concern for his sister momentarily driving all other thoughts from his mind.

Grant looked on impassively as Darcy slammed the volume closed, his expression black with rage.

"Have you taken leave of your senses? Do you honestly believe I would allow my sister to undergo such a vile method of treatment?" Surging to his feet, Darcy paced to the window of his study, attempting to regulate his breathing as fury roiled within his gut. Dear God! The drawings in that book would rival any of the lewd images he had seen bandied about at Eton or snickered over by the rogues and reprobates who frequented his clubs.

Behind him, Grant spoke, cutting into Darcy's thoughts. "I know it can appear quite shocking. But I assure you it is a practice that has been used effectively for well over a hundred years, and to be—"

"I do not care if it has been performed on the Prince Regent himself!" Darcy growled, yanking out his chair and throwing himself into it. "And who would carry out such an operation? You? It is completely indecent!"

Grant had the courtesy to flush, but when he spoke, his voice was calm. "I am a trained surgeon, sir. I have performed this procedure dozens of times."

"On women? On unmarried young girls, for God's sake?"

"Yes, sir." Grant paused for a moment before continuing, "Mr. Darcy, I understand your concern. Truly. But if we do not operate..." he stopped there, but his meaning was clear.

Darcy rubbed a hand across his face, playing for time. "And if you do operate? Can you guarantee that she will recover?"

"No, sir. As I am sure you are aware, I cannot."

Darcy stood again, moving to the window. "And these other patients... the ones on whom you have performed this procedure. Have they all survived?"

Grant hesitated a moment too long.

"I want another opinion," Darcy snapped. "Where the devil is Prescott? He has been attending Georgiana since her birth."

"He is with a patient in Chesterfield. Even if we sent for him now, he would not arrive for several days."

Darcy returned to his seat, pulling out pen and paper. "Do you have his direction?" When Grant nodded Darcy began to write. "Good. And if he cannot come, I will send for my London physician."

Grant leaned back in his seat, tenting his fingers. "As you wish. But I will remind you that should my diagnosis be confirmed, neither of them would be qualified to operate."

Darcy's fingers tightened around his quill. He did not know what the answer was. What he did know was that no young, single gentleman would perform such an operation on his sister if Darcy could in any way avoid it. "We shall deal with that issue once they have made a diagnosis," he said through gritted teeth.

Grant remained silent as Darcy wrote, waiting patiently while the butler was summoned to dispatch the letters. When the door had closed again, Grant continued, "Mr. Darcy, I am happy to wait for the arrival of one of your own physicians, but I hope you will allow me to remain in residence. I would like to be here should my assistance be required."

Darcy's stomach clenched but he eventually offered the surgeon a grim nod. "You may stay."

"Thank you. And, in the meantime, there is one other thing I should like to try."

Darcy's brow lowered, and Grant smiled. "You needn't worry; it will not require a knife. And in truth, I do not believe it will be successful. Still, if we are to wait..."

"What is it? I will agree to anything if we might avoid the type of operation you are suggesting."

"Well, we might try flushing the stone. Barley water or birch leaf tea may be beneficial, and I have heard of some herbs that might be used."

"Anything. Just tell me what you require and I shall see that you have it."

Grant nodded. "I will speak with your housekeeper, but

I do not wish to raise your hopes, Mr. Darcy. I still believe surgery to be the best way."

"Thank you," Darcy choked out. "My sister means the world to me. If there is anything you can do to relieve her suffering, I will be forever in your debt."

The physician stood. "Very well, Mr. Darcy. Let us go and see what might be accomplished."

CHAPTER 20

Darcy entered his sister's bedchamber to find Georgiana in a deep slumber, clearly still under the influence of the laudanum she had been given earlier by Grant. Beside the bed, Elizabeth sat quietly, an open book resting in her lap. On the far side of the room, one of Pemberley's chamber maids was laying a fire, though the air was still warm.

Elizabeth looked up when Darcy approached, closing her book and setting it on a table near the bed. With a start, Darcy recognized it as the volume he had given her last winter. An unexpected warmth coursed through his veins as he crossed to her chair. "It is good of you to sit with her, Miss Bennet."

Elizabeth smiled up at him. "I am happy to do it." After a slight pause she added, "Has the doctor left, sir?"

At the mention of Grant, Darcy grimaced. When he spoke again, his words were clipped. "No. Mrs. Reynolds is preparing a room. I have sent for my own physician and for my cousin, Colonel Fitzwilliam, who is Georgiana's second guardian. But Grant will stay until we can determine what is to be done."

"I see." Slowly, Elizabeth stood. "Forgive me, I do not wish to intrude on your time with your sister."

Darcy's gaze flicked to the maid who was just finishing up at the hearth. "Miss Bennet... There is something I had hoped to speak with you about. If I might request another moment of your time?"

"Of course. Perhaps we might step into the sitting room? I am certain we will hear your sister if she wakes."

Darcy nodded gratefully and gestured for her to precede him, after ensuring the maid would stay until he returned.

Entering the parlor, Elizabeth settled comfortably onto the sofa and Darcy took a chair several feet away, glancing absentmindedly out the window. Somehow the plan that had seemed so reasonable only a few moments ago now felt arrogant and ill-conceived, and Darcy's resolve wavered.

"You wished to ask me something, Mr. Darcy?" Elizabeth finally prompted when the silence had stretched out for longer than was comfortable.

Shifting his gaze to Elizabeth's face, Darcy smiled, releasing a heavy sigh. "In truth, I have no right to ask anything of you, Miss Bennet. You have already been far more gracious than I have any call to expect. It is just that my sister is not accustomed to being on her own, especially when she is unwell. Normally her companion, Mrs.

Annesley, occupies the chamber on the other side of this sitting room, but now... well. Of course, Georgiana is attended at all times," he hastened to add, "but a maid or a nurse is not the same as... That is..."

Elizabeth listened to Darcy's halting speech, her lips lifting slightly at the corners. "Mr. Darcy, are you asking me if I would be willing to move into the room adjacent to your sister's?"

Darcy nodded self-consciously, his gaze briefly dropping to the carpet. "I know you are only to remain at Pemberley a few more days, and naturally, you would not have to do anything for her care. But I believe my sister would be happy to have the companionship of another lady close to her own age, and I know she has come to view you as a friend..." his voice tapered off as Elizabeth's smile grew.

"I would be only too happy to oblige you, sir."

Darcy felt his shoulders relax as an unexpected lightness filled his body—like a hot air balloon cut free of its moorings. "Truly? It would not be an inconvenience?" When Elizabeth shook her head, he continued, "Of course I will speak with your aunt and uncle to be certain they have no objections."

Elizabeth answered with a wave of her hand. "I am certain they will not. But you may do so if it would put your mind at ease."

Darcy climbed to his feet, and Elizabeth followed.

And for the first time in the past four and twenty hours Darcy felt that perhaps in time, all might yet be well.

✻

That night's meal was a quiet affair. Darcy joined his guests, but remained mostly silent, staring down the table to where Elizabeth was deep in conversation with Grant. A frown pulled at Darcy's lips as he pushed the food around his plate, drinking more wine than was customary. When the last course had finally been consumed, the doctor returned upstairs to check on his patient, and the rest of the party adjourned to the sitting room. Within a half an hour's time, however, Darcy excused himself.

Crossing into Georgiana's chambers, he found his sister awake, propped against her pillows.

Grant sat in a chair beside her bed, speaking softly, but upon Darcy's entrance the physician clambered to his feet.

"I beg your pardon," Darcy said stiffly, halting inside the door. "I hope I am not disturbing your work."

"No, not at all. I have just brought your sister some more tonic. But I will leave Miss Darcy to rest."

Darcy nodded and Grant bowed before quitting the room.

Excusing Georgiana's maid, Darcy crossed to his sister's bed, taking the seat Grant had vacated. "How are you feeling?" he asked gently.

Georgiana attempted a smile, but Darcy could see that her eyes were fogged with pain. "I am well. That is... I am not feeling any worse than I did before."

Turning away, Darcy struggled to tamp down the torrent of emotions that coursed through him. His gaze settled on the tray that rested upon a nearby table and he looked back at his sister. "Sweetling, you have hardly touched your supper. Can I have Mrs. Reynolds bring you something else? Some broth, perhaps?"

Georgiana shook her head. "I am not hungry." After swallowing a few sips of the herbal remedy left by Grant, she directed her attention back to her brother.

"William, as you are here, there is something I wished to speak to you about."

"Of course. Anything."

Georgiana bit her lip, her gaze briefly darting across the chamber. "It is to do with Miss Bennet," she finally began.

Darcy started. "Miss Bennet? Are you not pleased she has agreed to take the chamber next door? You must forgive me if I have overstepped in offering it to her, I only thought..."

"Oh, no! It is not that. I am very happy to have the company."

Darcy relaxed slightly in his chair as Georgiana stared across the room. "William... Are you... That is, are you fond of Miss Bennet?" Darcy's eyebrows dipped but Georgiana hurried on, "It is only that I have never seen you show a preference for any young lady before, but when you look at her... well, I have seen the way you look at her," she said softly, her cheeks flushing a delicate pink.

Darcy tugged at his cravat, his throat constricting uncomfortably. Although a part of him wished to share his feelings with his sister, it would not do to give Georgiana false hope.

"I think Miss Bennet is a fine young lady, but there is no attachment between us, if that is what you are asking."

"Oh."

Georgiana lowered her lashes and Darcy reached out, stroking her hand. "Georgie, do not distress yourself on my account. You must only concentrate on getting well."

To his surprise, a single tear slipped down his sister's cheek. "I know. I had only hoped..."

"Hoped what, dearest? Pray, tell me what has you so upset?"

Georgiana drew an uneven breath. "It is just that if anything were to happen to me, I would not wish for you to be alone, and I thought, Miss Bennet..."

Darcy quickly stood, moving to sit at the edge of his sister's bed. "Georgiana, nothing is going to happen to you. I will not allow it."

His sister smiled up at him with tear-filled eyes. "There are some things even you cannot control, Fitzwilliam. And if the worst should happen..."

"Shh. I will not have you speaking that way," Darcy answered, but he could feel his chest constricting painfully. His sister's eyelids fluttered and Darcy stood. "You are tired. I will send for your maid to come sit with you."

Georgiana sank back against her pillows. "William, will you not play something for me before you go?"

"Of course, if you wish it. Although it has been some months since I practiced, so you will have to forgive any flaws in the execution."

Georgiana smiled sleepily. "You always play beautifully," she said softly, sliding deeper beneath the counterpane.

Darcy crossed to the outer chamber, settling himself onto the piano bench. Raising the cover, he ran his fingers lightly over the keys. "Is there anything in particular you would like to hear?"

Georgiana started to shake her head, but suddenly stopped. "Could you play something by Beethoven?"

Darcy turned to study his sister through the open door. He did not generally play works by that particular composer and did not know any pieces by heart, but he was happy to attempt it if it would raise his sister's spirits. Lifting the stack of sheet music, he shuffled through the pages until he came upon Beethoven's Sonata "Quasi una fantasia." He studied the notes for a minute, then propped the music on the stand and began to play.

Elizabeth slipped out of the Gardiners' apartment, turning in the opposite direction and padding down the corridor to Pemberley's family wing. Entering her bedchamber, she made her way to the dressing table, settling upon the padded seat. Catching a reflection of her surroundings in the mirrored glass, Elizabeth smiled. While nowhere near as grand as the apartment she had previously occupied, the room was still significantly larger than the bedchamber she had shared with Jane at Longbourn. Like all the rooms at Pemberley, it was decorated with an understated elegance, the emphasis on comfort over fashion. Turning her attention to her own image in the glass, she slowly began removing the pins from her hair, allowing it to tumble around her shoulders. Hoping her aunt and sister had finished readying for the night, Elizabeth moved in the direction of the bell-pull. She would need her aunt's maid to assist her in removing her gown. But she had only made it midway across the carpet when she was surprised to hear the soft strains of the pianoforte drifting in from the adjoining chamber. *Georgiana must be feeling better,* she thought, stopping mid-stride, her hand poised to pull the satin cord.

Changing direction, she made her way closer to the door. The music that seeped into the chamber was hauntingly beautiful and expertly played, and Elizabeth found herself pressing up against the polished wood. She had heard that Miss Darcy was talented, but if what she was listening to now was any indication, the stories hardly did the lady justice. Twisting the handle, Elizabeth eased the door open the smallest crack, and a stifled gasp slid from her lips.

For it was not Georgiana sitting at the pianoforte, but Mr. Darcy.

Struggling to calm her pounding heart, Elizabeth stared, riveted by the sight of his fingers moving with practiced grace across the ivory keys, melancholy notes reverberating in the air. The room was softly lit, and his face was half in shadow, his head dipped slightly to his task, one rebellious lock of chestnut hair falling across his brow. He glanced briefly at the sheet music in front of him, and Elizabeth watched as the tempo changed, his fingers fairly flying across the keys to tease the suddenly-lively notes from the instrument. As if in a trance, she stood fixed to the spot letting the evocative music wash over her before fear of discovery caused her to slip back inside her chamber, reluctantly closing the door.

The following morning Elizabeth rose early. Making her way to the dressing table, she loosened her plait and ran her fingers through her thick curls, letting her mind drift back to the previous evening when she had stood at the door listening to Mr. Darcy play. She now realized that to say the gentleman was proficient at the pianoforte was a vast understatement. However, it was not just his technical mastery at the instrument that had struck her so acutely, but rather the depth of emotion with which he performed. In truth, she had never heard anyone play half so well.

Her thoughts progressed to the time she had spent at Rosings, how she had played for him there and how he had stood beside her and then complimented her afterwards.

No one admitted to the privilege of hearing you can think anything wanting.

She flushed now to consider her playing as compared to his. If only she had known of his superior skill, she never would have agreed to exhibit in his presence.

Pulling her hair into a simple knot, Elizabeth began inserting the pins that would hold it in place. It was interesting to note that Lady Catherine had not impressed upon her nephew to perform, and Elizabeth could not help but wonder if the lady in question was even aware of Mr. Darcy's talent. Elizabeth rather doubted it, and upon further reflection, thought it possible that no one besides his sister and a handful of servants had ever had the pleasure of hearing him. For some reason, this struck her as unbearably sad and her hands stilled as a wave of emotion swept over her. Swallowing down the lump in her throat, she studied her appearance in the glass. Eyelids swollen, nose red, curls sticking out in all directions. Goodness, she looked a fright!

A sudden knock sounded at the door and Elizabeth called for whomever it was to enter. A moment later she turned to see her aunt step into the chamber.

"Good, you are awake." Mrs. Gardiner smiled, crossing to where Elizabeth sat.

"I am. As a matter of fact, I was just about to see if I might procure the services of your maid." Elizabeth gestured to the back of her gown and Mrs. Gardiner stepped behind her, fastening the hooks. When she had finished, Elizabeth's aunt lowered her chin, bending over her niece's shoulder to finger the loose curls framing Elizabeth's face. Their eyes met in the mirrored glass.

"Can it be salvaged, do you think?" Elizabeth asked.

Her aunt looked back at her, her expression serious. "Oh, I think most things can be salvaged if one is willing to put forth the effort," she answered.

Elizabeth blinked up at her, suddenly feeling they were no longer speaking of her hair.

Giving her niece's shoulder a gentle squeeze, Mrs. Gardiner crossed to the fireplace, retrieving the curling tongs Elizabeth had left there to heat. "How is Miss Darcy? Have you seen her this morning?" Mrs. Gardiner asked, returning to Elizabeth's side and leaning down to twist several locks around the hot metal.

"I have not. I hope she is feeling better. I know Mr. Darcy is concerned."

"Yes, I am certain he is." Mrs. Gardiner hesitated for a moment. "Actually, Lizzy, that is what I came to speak to you about. Your uncle and I have been discussing the matter, and we both feel we should not continue to trespass upon Mr. Darcy's hospitality. He has enough to worry about without houseguests underfoot. To that end, we have decided to leave for the Lakes ahead of schedule."

Elizabeth sat perfectly still, her eyes once again finding Mrs. Gardiner's in the beveled glass. "What? When?"

"Tomorrow morning. We would leave today, but we have already accepted an invitation to dine with the Driscolls."

"I see."

Pinning the last of Elizabeth's curls into place, Mrs. Gardiner shifted position, studying her niece. "You are not pleased."

"No. It is not that. I know you are likely correct, and I do not wish to impose upon Mr. Darcy's kindness."

"However...?"

Elizabeth expelled a gentle breath. "It is only that I cannot help feeling that I am abandoning them. Mr. Darcy has been so worried, and Miss Darcy is without her companion..."

Mrs. Gardiner came to perch on the corner of Elizabeth's bed. "Your feelings do you credit, Lizzy, but the Darcys are hardly alone—they have a doctor in residence as well as a house full of servants." She paused for a moment before adding, "And you are not Miss Darcy's companion."

"No. But I would like to be her friend. If I leave now, I would be letting both of them down."

"Well, there is no possibility of you remaining if the rest of us depart."

Elizabeth tilted her head and Mrs. Gardiner's eyes grew round.

"Lizzy! Certainly not! Your uncle would never allow it."

"Might we at least ask Mr. Darcy if he would wish for me to stay?"

"It is not about what Mr. Darcy wishes. You cannot stay alone with an unmarried gentleman and no chaperone. It is out of the question."

Elizabeth's thoughts immediately drifted to the cottage and she could feel the heat rising to her cheeks. If only her aunt knew this would not be the first time she and Mr. Darcy had been alone together.

"But surely you trust Mr. Darcy? And I would be staying as Georgiana's guest as much as his. Besides, you know that he and Mr. Bingley are as close as brothers, and as Charles is now family, are the Darcys not practically relations as well?"

Mrs. Gardiner shook her head, but Elizabeth could see that she was struggling to suppress a smile. "I think you stretch the facts, Lizzy. However, I will speak with your uncle. But I must have your word that you will adhere to whatever he decides."

"Of course," Elizabeth answered.

She did not let her aunt see she had crossed her fingers behind her back.

Later that afternoon, Elizabeth entered the library with no small amount of trepidation, taking a seat on the brocade sofa opposite her uncle's chair. "You wished to see me, Uncle?"

Without preamble, Mr. Gardiner answered. "I did, Lizzy, and I am certain you must know what this is about." Settling back in his seat, the gentleman continued, "Your aunt has informed me that you wish to remain at Pemberley rather than journeying on to the Lakes as we had planned."

"I do, sir."

"Then I will speak plainly. I am not in favor of the plan."

Elizabeth's stomach plummeted. "Oh, I see."

"You must understand that in your father's absence, you are under my protection, and I do not believe he would thank me for leaving you here without a chaperone." Mr. Gardiner paused for a moment, studying his niece's downcast expression, and his own countenance softened. "However, I do agree that Miss Darcy could use a friend. Indeed, I think they both could."

Elizabeth's eyes lifted and she felt her heart lighten as a glimmer of hope took hold.

"I have just spoken to Mr. Darcy," her uncle resumed, "and he also approves of you staying—"

"Oh, thank you!" Elizabeth cried, but Mr. Gardiner lifted his hand.

"Hold on now, Lizzy, I have not finished. I am going to give my blessing, but only with certain explicit stipulations."

"Of course," Elizabeth immediately answered. "Whatever you wish."

"First, you will move back into the guest wing of the house and a maid will be assigned to you."

"But uncle, I do not need a—" At her uncle's expression, Elizabeth studied the toes of her slippers, catching her lower lip between her teeth.

"The maid will stay with you in your chambers at night and will act as your companion during the day. You will dine with Miss Darcy in her chambers or in your own sitting room. At no time will you be alone with Mr. Darcy. Is this acceptable to you?"

Elizabeth nodded, lifting her gaze. "It is. Except... how will this look to Mr. Darcy? Will it not appear that we do not trust his honor?"

To Elizabeth's surprise, Mr. Gardiner chuckled. "I think not, as these were his own suggestions. Oh, and one other thing. With Mr. Darcy's permission, I have sent an express to your sister Jane asking that she and Bingley travel to

Pemberley. With any luck, they should be here within the week. Once your sister arrives, you will be free to come and go as you please."

Elizabeth jumped up then, wrapping her arms around her uncle's neck and showering him with kisses. It was only much later that she stopped to consider the fact that she was once again missing her long-awaited trip to the Lakes.

Yet, strangely, she could not find it within herself to feel any regret.

CHAPTER 21

T he voice was a low hum, coming to Darcy as if from a great distance. He attempted to turn in the direction of the sound, but something was pressing against his cheek, holding him in place.

"Mr. Darcy."

Summoning his strength, he attempted to move his head, but his body refused to obey.

"Sir?"

With great difficulty Darcy forced his eyes to open.

Hastings stared down at him, his forehead crinkled and Darcy jerked upright in his chair.

The butler took a polite step backwards. "Forgive me for waking you, sir. I thought you would wish to know that your guests have returned. They have retired for the evening, as has Mr. Grant."

Darcy sat straighter in his seat, tugging at his sleeves and dragging his fingers through his tousled hair. God, he must look a mess! How long had he been asleep at his desk? "What time is it?" he asked.

"Past midnight, sir."

"And my sister?"

"I believe Miss Darcy is sleeping. One of the housemaids is with her."

Darcy nodded, wincing at the twinge in his neck. He would feel significantly more at ease if he had been able to retain the services of a nurse, as he had intended. But when he broached the topic with his sister, Georgiana had begged that he would not. Much like himself, his sister was never easy in the company of strangers, and the idea of having someone completely unknown to her in her chambers day and night, attending to her in a most intimate manner had agitated her to such a degree that Darcy finally relented, agreeing to make do with the services of Georgiana's maid. All in all, he could not say he blamed her. It was bad enough she had to suffer the attentions of an unfamiliar physician.

Frowning, Darcy rose from his chair. "Has there been any word from my cousin or Prescott?"

Though it was almost imperceptible, Hastings stiffened. "No, sir. The entire staff has been alerted to notify you the moment either of them arrives. I was just about to lock up, but one of the footmen will remain at the door in case anyone should reach Pemberley during the night."

Again, Darcy nodded, chagrined. "Of course. Thank you, Hastings. I might have known you would have the matter well in hand." Bidding the faithful servant a good night, Darcy made his way up the stairs and along the corridor, pausing when he reached his sister's chambers. When his soft knock produced no reply, he eased the door open and peered inside. Several candles were still burning, and in the soft light he could see Georgiana tucked up in her bed, sleeping soundly. In a corner of the room near the window, one of the maids was curled into an armchair, also asleep.

Darcy crossed to where the young maid sat, placing a hand lightly on her shoulder. The girl jumped, her eyes flying open in alarm.

Lifting a finger to his lips, Darcy stepped back, motioning for the maid to follow him out into the passageway.

The moment the door closed behind them, the girl spoke, the pitch of her voice rising in agitation. "Mr. Darcy, I beg your pardon! I was only resting my eyes for a moment. It will not happen again!"

Darcy opened his mouth, but the maid pressed on. "I did not mean to fall asleep! I beg you, do not inform Mrs. Reynolds. She will sack me for sure!"

Despite the girl's distress, Darcy could not help the smile that touched his lips. Perhaps he would need to have a word with Mrs. Reynolds. He had never seen the older woman as a harsh task-master, but the housekeeper appeared to have this poor girl quaking in her boots!

"Pray, do not concern yourself... Polly, is it?"

The girl nodded.

"I have no intention of notifying Mrs. Reynolds, and I am not angry. I only wished to tell you that you may retire. I will sit with my sister now."

"Oh, no sir! I could not go to bed. I was told that I'm to stay with Miss Darcy until Logan returns in the morning. Mrs. Reynolds won't like it if I leave."

Smothering his amusement, Darcy stared down at the young girl with feigned solemnity. "I appreciate your concern, Polly, but *I* am telling you that you may withdraw. Unless of course you feel Mrs. Reynolds outranks me?" he asked, causing the girl to blush furiously.

"N-no sir! But... shall I send one of the other maids to take my post? You cannot mean to sit up for the remainder of the night?" As soon as the words were out of her mouth, the girl's cheeks flamed and she began to stutter an apology.

Darcy waved his hand. "Be easy. I am not especially tired. Now, go. And if you encounter Mrs. Reynolds, pray, tell her you left on my orders."

Darcy slouched in his chair, an unopened book held loosely between his fingers. In the large bed across the room, Georgiana continued to doze, occasionally mumbling incoherently in her dreams. The clock on the mantelpiece ticked out a steady rhythm and despite his best intentions, Darcy's eyelids grew heavy. Stretching his legs, he allowed his head to tip back against the cushions. The intoxicating lure of slumber tugged at his consciousness, pulling him under...

Without warning, a blood-curdling shriek split the air and Darcy leapt from his chair. His book hit the floor with a loud *thwack* and his gaze flew to his sister's face. But he realized almost immediately that the sound had not come from her. His head snapped in the direction of the adjoining chamber.

Elizabeth!

Darcy was instantly across the room, racing through the adjacent parlor. His knee connected with some piece of furniture and he muttered an oath. The voice cried out again, high-pitched and laced with terror.

Reaching Elizabeth's door, Darcy pounded on the paneling, stopping after a moment to listen for a response. The unmistakable sounds of weeping crept through the heavy wood and Darcy's stomach clenched. Making up his mind, his fingers found the brass knob, which turned easily in his hand.

Moving through the open door, Darcy stepped into the chamber. A sliver of moonlight fell through a gap in the draperies, guiding him as he slowly approached the bed. Elizabeth sat upright amongst the tangled sheets, her breathing rapid. Darcy moved closer and Elizabeth launched herself into his arms, clinging to his neck and whimpering against his collar.

His composure splintered and he wrapped his arms around her trembling shoulders, gathering her close. Through her thin nightdress he could feel the curves of her body and a familiar ache settled in his chest. He swallowed hard, lifting one hand to lightly stroke her hair.

"Shh... It was only a dream. You are safe, Elizabeth. You are at Pemberley, and you are safe." Holding Elizabeth gently in his arms, Darcy was reminded of all the times he had done the same for Georgiana when she had awoken from a nightmare after their father's death. But embracing Elizabeth now, he was acutely aware that she was neither a young girl, nor was she his sister.

Closing his eyes, Darcy breathed in Elizabeth's sweet scent. Continuing to murmur softly in her ear, he allowed himself to envision a time when he might have the right to comfort her as a husband comforts his wife. To always be by her side, offering his protection.

He knew the moment Elizabeth became fully aware of her surroundings. Her body stiffened and Darcy immediately released his hold. Slowly straightening his spine, he allowed her arms to slip from around his neck. His eyes had adjusted to the darkness by now, but he could not read Elizabeth's expression. Moving away from the bed, he turned to light the candle sitting upon a nearby table.

Elizabeth clutched the covers to her chest and Darcy took another step back, giving her space. "Pray, forgive my intrusion, Miss Bennet. I was sitting with my sister when I heard you cry out. I am glad to see it appears to have only been a bad dream."

Elizabeth continued to grip the counterpane blinking in the flickering light. She stared wordlessly at him for several moments but after a while she seemed to recover her equilibrium, and when she spoke, her voice was low, but steady. "Pray, forgive me for worrying you. Indeed, it was only a dream, and I am quite recovered now."

Darcy inclined his head, offering her an awkward bow. "I will leave you to your privacy, then." He walked halfway to the door before turning. "Is there anything you require before I go? I can ring for one of the maids to come sit with you, if you would like?"

"Oh, no! Do not disturb anyone at this hour. I... I think I will read for a while and then attempt to return to sleep."

Darcy nodded, his eyes soft. "As you wish. Sleep well, Miss Bennet."

Walking back into his sister's chamber, Darcy could not help feeling somewhat relieved to know that Elizabeth would be moving back into the guest wing on the morrow. Clearly having her in such close proximity was not as good an idea as he had previously thought.

The following morning Elizabeth woke with the sun, still reeling from the night before. Hurrying to dress, she sat before the mirrored glass, studying her flushed countenance as her late-night encounter with Mr. Darcy played out inside her head: the dark room, Mr. Darcy holding her, his hands warm against her back, his soft voice whispering words of comfort... Good Lord! How was she ever to face him again after such an incident? Perhaps she should join her aunt and uncle on their trip to the Lakes after all.

Pushing back her chair, Elizabeth rose and headed for the door. It was still early. She would take a walk in the gardens. She needed time to clear her head, and she could not bear to face anyone until she had come to a decision.

Hurriedly descending the stairs, Elizabeth padded across the vaulted entrance hall, hoping Mr. Darcy's always efficient staff had already put out a pot of tea. But as soon as she reached the breakfast parlor, her feet ground to a halt. There, alone in the room, sat the one person she would have moved heaven and earth to avoid.

His head was bowed over his paper, but as if by instinct, Darcy lifted his gaze, rising when he spotted her standing in the doorway.

"Miss Bennet. Good morning."

Elizabeth stared back at him, but her feet remained pinned to the carpet. She could feel a blush spreading from her neck to her hairline and would have liked nothing better than to turn and run, but of course now that he had noticed her, that was no longer an option. Attempting to regulate the hammering of her heart, she schooled her features and slowly entered the room.

"Good morning, Mr. Darcy," she answered, hoping her voice was reasonably steady. Making her way over to the sideboard, she selected the first thing she saw—a roll and butter—and filled a cup with freshly brewed tea. Feeling Mr. Darcy's watchful gaze, she stood uncertainly for a moment before choosing a seat farther down the table.

"I trust you are well this morning, Miss Bennet?"

Elizabeth tensed, her eyes darting to the footman stationed near the door.

"Yes. I thank you, sir," she murmured, immediately fixing her attention on her food.

Darcy frowned, then turned to address the footman. "Andrew, would you be good enough to go to the kitchens and speak to Mrs. West about preparing a basket for our guests? I am certain they will wish to depart shortly after breakfast and I would like everything to be ready."

The footman bowed and promptly removed himself from the room.

Once the door had closed behind him, Darcy drew his chair in Elizabeth's direction. "Miss Bennet," he said softly, but Elizabeth's focus remained on her plate. "Elizabeth, will you not look at me?"

At the use of her Christian name, Elizabeth's eyes widened and her gaze snapped in his direction.

Seeming to realize his blunder, Darcy colored. "I beg your pardon, Miss Bennet. I can see you are upset. I only wished to ask—"

But before he could complete his sentence, the sound of raised voices in the vestibule silenced them both, and Darcy hastily moved his chair back to its original position. The Gardiners, Mary Bennet, and Grant entered the breakfast parlor, and Darcy stood. After greetings were exchanged and everyone had helped themselves to food, Mr. Gardiner looked across the table at his elder niece.

"Well, Lizzy, I see you are up early as usual."

His gaze swept the edges of the room, clearly noting the absence of the footman, and Elizabeth flushed.

As if reading her thoughts, Mr. Darcy turned in his seat. "Mr. Gardiner, I have taken the liberty of sending my man to the kitchens to ask my cook to prepare some provisions for your journey. I assumed you would wish to depart shortly, although of course you are welcome to stay as long as you would like."

"That is most considerate of you, Mr. Darcy," Mrs.

Gardiner replied, casting a glance at her husband. "And yes, we will leave as soon as we have broken our fast. My husband has already sent word to ready our carriage."

Mr. Darcy nodded and Elizabeth lifted her teacup, studying him out of the corner of her eye. She could not help but notice how well he looked this morning, his still-damp hair curling against the collar of his jacket.

A sudden image of him standing in her bedchamber wearing only shirtsleeves and trousers flooded her mind and she promptly lowered her lashes. How could she stay on in Mr. Darcy's sole company after what had occurred the night before? But more to the point, how could she bear to leave?

Elizabeth stood beside the Gardiners' carriage as her uncle offered their host a cordial bow. "Mr. Darcy, we thank you for your hospitality. I hope you will extend our best wishes to your sister. We will be praying for her speedy recovery."

"I thank you, sir," Darcy answered, reaching out to grip Mr. Gardiner's hand. "I am sorry your stay was cut short, but I wish you a pleasant journey."

Elizabeth stepped forward as Mary and her aunt approached the carriage.

"You haven't changed your mind, have you?" Mrs. Gardiner whispered, wrapping Elizabeth in a light embrace.

After only a second's hesitation, Elizabeth shook her head. No, she hadn't changed her mind. Despite all that had occurred, she could not shake the feeling that her place was at Pemberley.

"Very well. Just remember, you are not a prisoner here, but you must take care. We will see you within a fortnight."

"Yes, Aunt," Elizabeth said softly as her uncle stepped forward to assist the ladies into the carriage.

Watching as the Gardiners' coach disappeared down the drive, Mr. Darcy offered Elizabeth his arm. Escorting her back inside the house, he turned to address his butler who was waiting in the front hall. "Hastings, would you be good enough to locate Mrs. Reynolds? I would like to have her acquaint Miss Bennet with the maid who will be acting as her companion."

Hastings hurried off to do his master's bidding and Darcy shepherded Elizabeth across the hall to the library. Settling her onto a silk damask sofa in the center of the room, he moved to take a nearby chair.

Elizabeth sat twisting her handkerchief, her gaze fixed mostly on her lap.

After several moments of awkward silence, Darcy leaned forward. "Miss Bennet, I beg your pardon. I wished to apologize—both for the way I addressed you at break-fast this morning and for... last night. I hope you know I would never have entered your chambers if I was not worried for your safety. If I caused you any embarrass-ment, I assure you that was not my intent."

Elizabeth picked up her head, her cheeks pink. "I know that, Mr. Darcy, and I thank you for your concern." She paused for a moment before continuing, "I hope I did not disturb your sister when I... when I called out."

"No. My sister is a sound sleeper, even when not under the influence of laudanum." He smiled, but then his expression grew earnest. "Would you care to speak about it, Miss Bennet? The dream, that is?"

"No, sir. Again, I appreciate your concern, but I would rather not."

"Forgive me, I did not mean to pry. I merely thought... I wondered if it might have had something to do with the accident."

Elizabeth startled. "The accident? But that was more than six months ago, Mr. Darcy." Suddenly a thought occurred to her and her eyes widened in alarm. Good heavens! Had she spoken in her sleep? The idea that, in addition to seeing her in the privacy of her chambers, Mr. Darcy might also be privy to the personal nature of her dream was utterly humiliating. She looked away. "What made you think so?" she asked.

Darcy's shrugged offhandedly. "It is not uncommon for the effects of such a traumatic experience to linger. I have dreamt of the accident myself, on occasion," he added quietly.

Elizabeth turned to study him. "Have you?"

"Yes."

Hoping to move the conversation away from herself, Elizabeth continued, "I had meant to inquire... about the coachman. How is his widow faring? I am certain this has been a difficult time for her."

Out of the corner of her eye, Elizabeth could see Darcy tense.

"She is... as well as could be expected. While I have assured her that she will always have a home at Pemberley, she has gone to spend some time with her son and his family." Before Darcy could elaborate, a knock sounded at the open door and Mrs. Reynolds entered, a maid in tow.

Darcy and Elizabeth rose.

"Ah, Mrs. Reynolds. And Polly." Darcy smiled as he turned to address the young maid standing in his housekeeper's shadow.

The girl's eyes grew round, but she dropped a polite curtsy, stepping forward at Mrs. Reynolds' prodding.

"Miss Bennet, Polly will attend you for the remainder of your stay. I have freed her from her other duties, so she is completely at your disposal."

"That is kind of you, Mrs. Reynolds, but I am certain that will not be necessary. At home, I share a maid with all my sisters and am accustomed to managing mostly on my own."

The housekeeper glanced over at Mr. Darcy but it was he who spoke.

"Miss Bennet, I assured your uncle that I would provide you with a companion. You would not have me go back on my word, now would you?"

"No, Mr. Darcy, I would not. Though I assume I shall not have to rely on Polly's *companionship* while I am in the company of your sister?"

"No, of course not. Georgiana is attended at all times,

so there is no need to trouble any of the other maids if you are with her."

"Good." Facing the maid, Elizabeth continued, "In that case, you may have some time to yourself, Polly, as I intend to sit with Miss Darcy for the remainder of the morning."

She turned to go, but Mr. Darcy's voice arrested her steps.

"Miss Bennet, I will see you later, I hope?"

Elizabeth paused, but after a moment she nodded before hurrying from the room.

When Elizabeth reached Georgiana's chambers, she found the physician at the girl's bedside; however, upon her approach, the gentleman stood, bowing deeply and edging towards the door.

"Pray, do not leave on my account, sir. I should be happy to keep myself occupied with a book if you and Miss Darcy wish to converse."

To Elizabeth's surprise, the doctor flushed. "No. I have other things to attend to." Directing his gaze back to Georgiana he said softly, "Pray, drink as much of that draught as you are able, Miss Darcy. I will return to check on you later this afternoon."

Georgiana nodded and Elizabeth turned to the young girl in the bed. "How are you feeling, Miss Darcy? If you would like to sleep, I can also return later."

Georgiana shook her head. "No. I would prefer the

company. It helps to distract me. However, Miss Bennet...
Would it be impertinent for me to ask that you call me
Georgiana?" Before Elizabeth could answer the girl's
cheeks colored and she hurried to add, "It is only that you
feel more like a friend than an acquaintance now, but I do
not wish to make you uncomfortable."

"I would be delighted to call you by your given name. I
would consider it a great honor. And of course, you must
call me Elizabeth."

A small smile lifted Georgiana's cheeks. "I thank you,
Elizabeth. I would like that."

"Good, that's settled then. Now, shall I read to you? Or
I am happy to play the pianoforte if you prefer, though I
must own that I play very poorly compared to you and
your brother."

"I am certain that is not true... But if you would like to
read, there is a book there on the table."

Elizabeth spent the next hour reading aloud until
Georgiana fell into a restless slumber. Shortly afterwards,
Mrs. Reynolds appeared with a pot of tea and a light meal
of cold meats and cheeses, which Elizabeth ate curled
upon the couch in the adjacent parlor. She must have
fallen asleep, because the next thing she knew, she was
being shaken awake by Georgiana's maid. Opening her
eyes, Elizabeth took in the woman's worried expression
and was instantly on her feet.

"I beg your pardon, ma'am, but Miss Darcy is awake
and I think she is unwell. She did not want me to fetch
anyone but—"

Elizabeth was already across the room, heading for the

door to Georgiana's chamber. "No, you did the right thing, Miss Logan."

Entering the next room, Elizabeth hurried to the bed. Georgiana lay on her side, her legs drawn up to her chest and her breathing uneven. It was clear to see that she was in unspeakable pain. Sitting on the edge of the mattress, Elizabeth reached to brush a lock of hair off the girl's forehead and startled at the warmth of her skin. Continuing to stroke Georgiana's hair, she turned to the maid who was now hovering near the foot of the bed.

"Logan, pray, go and fetch Dr. Grant and Mr. Darcy," she said softly. The maid quickly fled and Elizabeth continued to speak soothingly to her friend. "Shh, all will soon be well. I have sent for the doctor."

Tears coursed down Georgiana's pale cheeks as Elizabeth sat beside her, gently rubbing her back. Moments later the door burst open and the doctor entered, his long strides moving him to the bed.

Elizabeth rose, but in her haste to step aside, the heel of her slipper snagged the trimmings of her gown. Without warning, she pitched forward, her arms stretched out in an attempt to break her fall. In a flash, the doctor was before her. Feeling her body collide with his, Elizabeth gasped and then quickly looked away, struggling to regain her balance. "I beg your pardon," she stammered as she felt his hands settle at her waist.

A sudden movement behind them captured her attention and she turned to see Mr. Darcy glowering in the doorway.

Darcy's eyes narrowed as fury roiled within his gut. How dare Grant put his hands on her! And here, in his sister's sick-room, no less! Watching Elizabeth step back, Darcy advanced into the chamber, his fingers tightening into fists, but Georgiana's pained whimper stayed his course.

Darting a venomous look in the doctor's direction, Darcy moved to the far side of the bed. Kneeling at his sister's side, he reached for her hand and all thoughts of Elizabeth and Grant vanished.

Georgiana's eyes were haunted, and when Darcy stared into their depths, it was not his sister's face he saw before him, but his mother's, just as she had looked before death had claimed her. A silent scream began climbing up Darcy's throat and he struggled to compose his features. "Georgie, I am here," he whispered. "Is the pain very bad?"

Fighting back tears, the girl nodded, before letting out a strangled sob. On the opposite side of the bed, Grant reached for his bag.

Darcy lifted his gaze. "What are you doing?"

"Giving her another dose of laudanum. There is nothing more to be done besides managing the pain." After a pause he added, "Unless you have changed your mind?"

Looking away, Darcy felt the terror he had been holding at bay cinch tightly around his heart. He opened his mouth to speak but before he could answer, Georgiana cried out, a chilling high-pitched wail that propelled Darcy to his feet.

"I... excuse me," he choked, before rushing past Elizabeth and out of the room.

Darcy's footsteps pounded through the front hall, carrying him across the threshold of his study. Striding towards the fireplace, he grabbed a decanter from the mantelpiece, splashing brandy into the nearest glass and consuming it in one swallow. The fiery liquid burned its way down Darcy's throat but he was oblivious, immediately refilling his glass. He did not notice the soft footsteps that crossed the room until he felt a gentle hand just above his elbow.

"Mr. Darcy, is there anything I can do?" Elizabeth asked.

Darcy's arm jerked at her touch and he spun to face her. The ferocity that he knew must be reflected in his eyes would have sent most men scurrying for the door, but Elizabeth stood her ground. Darcy turned away. "Unless you know of some magic potion that will relieve my sister's suffering, Miss Bennet, no, there is not."

Elizabeth stepped back, clearly startled by the coolness of his tone. "Forgive me, I know it is none of my affair but... Dr. Grant mentioned you changing your mind. Has he suggested some remedy for what is ailing Miss Darcy?"

Darcy glared back at Elizabeth, his eyes like granite. "Oh, yes, Miss Bennet, the *doctor*, if he can be called such a thing, has a particular remedy in mind." Grasping the decanter, he poured himself another drink, taking a large draught.

Elizabeth waited as Darcy lowered himself into the chair behind his desk. "What sort of remedy?" she finally asked.

Darcy stared vacantly across the room. "Nothing I can discuss. Not with a lady."

Elizabeth stepped closer, taking a seat on one of the chairs opposite the desk. "I am not so delicate as all that, sir."

Darcy took another swallow of brandy. After a moment he spoke, but his eyes remained fixed on a point across the room. "He wants to cut her open. In a most... vulgar manner." Just thinking about the operation made his fingers tighten around his glass.

"Oh, I see. I... I understand how that would be upsetting to you."

Darcy turned his head, fixing Elizabeth with an inscrutable stare. "Do you?"

Elizabeth lifted her chin. "Yes, Mr. Darcy, I do. However, if it is your sister's best chance at a full recovery..."

Darcy's fist slammed against the surface of his desk, making Elizabeth jump.

"It is out of the question. Besides, there is not even any guarantee that it would work."

Elizabeth regarded him quietly. "No, sir. There are never any guarantees."

Darcy looked away, draining the remainder of his drink, and his expression shifted from anger to agony. "I cannot lose her," he whispered. "I have lost too much already. She is all I have left."

Elizabeth leaned forward, her hand closing around his fist which still rested upon the desk.

Darcy stared down at her delicate fingers, her fair skin so much softer than his own. He understood that she meant to offer him comfort, but he could not accept her pity. This was not how he wished to appear before her—weak and afraid.

Suddenly, all the grief and anguish he had held inside for far too long came crashing to the surface. He knew he was perilously close to tears and the thought of her witnessing such a display filled him with horror. Slowly, he withdrew his hand.

"I beg your pardon, Miss Bennet, but I think I would prefer to be alone." As he watched, the light in her lovely eyes flickered and went dim. Her body stiffened and she rose haltingly to her feet.

"Of course," she responded stiffly. "I shall return to your sister."

Darcy blinked, suddenly registering the hollowness in her tone. Drawing a sharp breath, he shoved back his chair. "Miss Bennet, wait…"

But it was too late. She had already gone.

CHAPTER 22

By the time Darcy composed himself and returned to his sister's chambers, it appeared the crisis had passed. Georgiana was sleeping fitfully, though Grant was quick to warn him that the next time they might not be so fortunate. Releasing Grant from his post, Darcy spent the remainder of the night at his sister's bedside, leaving only when her maid appeared early the following morning.

After a brief trip to his own apartment to change clothing, Darcy entered the breakfast parlor, relieved to find it empty. At her uncle's instruction, Elizabeth would be dining in her chambers, but Darcy was in no mood to encounter Grant. Helping himself to a cup of strong coffee, he had just taken a seat when his attention was drawn to a muffled commotion in the front hall. Darcy shoved back his chair, but he had hardly taken a step before his cousin burst into the room, Hastings trailing closely behind him.

His butler came to an abrupt halt just inside the door. "Colonel Fitzwilliam has arrived, sir."

"Yes. Thank you, I can see that Hastings."

Ignoring the butler altogether, Richard crossed the room in hurried strides. As he got closer, Darcy could see that his cousin's uniform was splattered with mud, his dark eyes troubled. "How is she? I left the moment I received your express."

Hastings bowed, withdrawing from the room. Narrowing his gaze, Darcy took in his cousin's harried expression, relieved once again that his sister had rallied from her crisis of the previous evening. He would not have wished for Richard to see her in that condition.

"As of this morning, she is much the same, but no worse," Darcy answered carefully. "Richard, come sit down before you fall down. Have you been riding all night?"

The colonel pulled out a chair, collapsing into it as a footman approached with a fresh pot of coffee. "I stopped for a few hours' sleep. I would have been here sooner if Baron did not need to be watered and rested. What news? Has Prescott arrived?"

Darcy lifted his hands to rub his temples. "Not yet, but I expect him at any time. The surgeon is still here," he added with a grimace. "I will acquaint you with his diagnosis as soon as you are settled."

Richard nodded, rising from his seat. "Very well. I will go to Georgiana now, if I may?"

"Yes, of course. But, pray, take some breakfast first." Darcy's gaze swept his cousin's rumpled form. "And you cannot go looking like that. You will frighten her out of her wits."

Richard began to protest, but a knock interrupted his speech. Both gentlemen turned to see Darcy's housekeeper in the doorway.

"Ah, Mrs. Reynolds, come in. As you see, Colonel Fitzwilliam has arrived and will wish to bathe after he has broken his fast. I trust you will see to those arrangements?"

"It has already been taken care of, sir. Colonel, your usual room has been prepared and Mr. Pierce is at your disposal."

Darcy nodded, grateful for the capabilities of his dedicated staff.

Turning in his direction, the housekeeper continued, "Mr. Darcy, Miss Bennet and Miss Georgiana have already breakfasted and the doctor awaits you in your sister's chambers. The matter is not urgent, but he would speak with you when you have a moment."

Richard's gaze sharpened, and Darcy coughed into his hand. "Er, yes, thank you, Mrs. Reynolds."

The housekeeper nodded, quitting the room and Darcy dropped into his seat. Reaching for his coffee, he took several swallows before finally turning to face his cousin, who was still studying him with rapt attention.

"Darcy, you did not mention you had guests. Would Miss Bennet be Miss Elizabeth Bennet of Hertfordshire by chance?"

Darcy's jaw tightened and he looked away. Blast! He should have anticipated his cousin's meddling and planned accordingly. Keeping his expression neutral he answered, "Yes. Forgive me, Richard, I have not had the opportunity to inform you before now. Miss Bennet was traveling through Derbyshire with her relations. I invited them to stay at Pemberley while they were in the vicinity."

"I see. And where are these relations now?"

There was a brief pause before Darcy answered. "The Gardiners and Miss Mary Bennet departed several days ago for the Lakes. Miss Elizabeth Bennet was kind enough to stay on. She and Georgiana have become close."

Colonel Fitzwilliam shot back a grin. "Ah, she stayed for Georgie. Of course."

"Don't start, Richard. This is not the time. And I am warning you, I will not have you making Miss Bennet uncomfortable with your tactless insinuations."

"Very well. In light of the circumstances, I will desist. But you should know that I have every intention of continuing this conversation later. For now, cousin, you have been granted a reprieve."

One hour later, Darcy and the colonel entered Georgiana's chambers to find Grant perched comfortably on the chair beside her bed. To Darcy's dismay, Elizabeth sat immediately to his left, their shoulders touching and their heads bowed in quiet conversation.

Darcy forcibly cleared his throat and Grant jumped to his feet. Georgiana looked to the door, and her gaze lit. "Richard! William did not tell me you were expected!"

Colonel Fitzwilliam stepped further into the room, offering her an easy smile. "What, can a fellow not pay a surprise visit to his favorite cousins?" Crossing the thick carpet, he bent to place a kiss on Georgiana's brow, while Darcy turned to stare at the physician.

What was the man about, sharing confidences with Elizabeth when he should be attending to Georgiana? "Mr. Grant, may I present my cousin, Colonel Fitzwilliam, with whom I share guardianship of my sister?"

The two men bowed to one another and Grant replied, "Your servant, sir."

"Likewise," answered the colonel before turning warm eyes on Elizabeth, who had risen from her seat and now stood at the doctor's side. "Miss Bennet. How good it is to see you again. Darcy mentioned you were visiting."

"The pleasure is mine, colonel."

Darcy cleared his voice, but before he could think of anything to add, Mrs. Reynolds entered.

"Mr. Darcy, Dr. Prescott has arrived. Shall I show him up, or would you prefer that Mr. Hastings direct him to your study?"

Darcy turned to face his housekeeper. *About damned time!* The elder physician was going to hear a few choice words about keeping his sister waiting with no one to care for her but a young upstart straight out of the schoolroom.

"Pray, show him up, Mrs. Reynolds. I am certain he will wish to examine Miss Darcy. We can speak afterwards." Mrs. Reynolds nodded, departing from the room, and Darcy turned towards his sister. "Georgie, Richard and I will await Prescott below stairs." He glanced at Elizabeth who made to follow, but his sister's soft voice called out before they reached the door.

"Miss Bennet, that is Elizabeth, would you... Do I ask too much to inquire if you would remain here with my maid?"

A muscle twitched in Darcy's jaw as his eyes slid from Elizabeth to Grant. "Georgiana, I do not think we can—"

"I would be happy to," Elizabeth interrupted "That is, unless you disapprove, Mr. Darcy?"

Darcy stiffened. As far as he was concerned, Elizabeth had already spent far too much time hidden away in this bedchamber with Grant and no better chaperones than a maid and his sister, who could barely sit up. He opened his mouth to protest, but it was Georgiana who spoke. "Oh, William would not mind... would you?"

Darcy released a sigh of defeat. "No. Of course not." Darting one last caustic glance in Grant's direction, he turned to his cousin. "Come, Richard, let us leave the doctors to their duties."

The soles of Darcy's boots echoed off the varnished floor as he paced his study. "So, you approve of this scheme?" he hissed, fixing Prescott with a scowl.

"I know it is unsettling, Mr. Darcy, but after examining your sister I agree with Dr. Grant. Miss Darcy is obviously in distress and I believe a lithotomy is your sister's best option."

Darcy turned to face his cousin who sat beside

Prescott. "And you, Richard? Surely you do not wish to expose Georgiana to such an ordeal? It is utterly obscene!"

Colonel Fitzwilliam frowned. "Naturally I do not wish anything of the sort, but you have heard Prescott; it is the only thing likely to relieve Georgiana's suffering. I know she was putting on a brave face for my benefit, but quite frankly I was shocked by how ill she looked. She is clearly in a great deal of pain, and without this operation…"

Richard's voice trailed off, but Darcy could not mistake his cousin's implication.

"Without it she might die," Darcy finished, his tone flat.

"I will not sugar-coat things, Mr. Darcy," Prescott replied. "It is a distinct possibility."

Darcy's stomach twisted. He was backed into a corner and he knew it. But how could he subject his sister to the type of procedure Grant proposed? On the other hand, could he live with himself if he did nothing and Georgiana died as a result? Playing for time, he turned to face his family physician, glad the younger doctor had remained above stairs. "And what of Grant? I know nothing about him. How am I to determine whether he is the person most qualified to perform the operation, should I agree?"

Prescott sat straighter in his chair. "I hope, Mr. Darcy, that you do not think I would bring another physician into my practice without thoroughly checking his qualifications. I know he is young, but Dr. Grant comes with the highest possible character. It is rare to find a physician who is also a skilled surgeon. In truth, Grant is thought to be a bit of a prodigy. I was lucky to secure him. Moreover,

I have never met anyone with such a profound under-standing of the human body. He has read every medical text worth noting, and his ability as a surgeon is unmatched. If it were my own wife or daughter requiring such a procedure, there are few others I would trust to perform it."

At the end of this speech, Colonel Fitzwilliam released a low whistle. "Well, Darcy, you cannot get a stronger endorsement than that."

Pacing to his desk, Darcy released his breath in a heavy sigh. "Very well, I can see I am outnumbered. If Richard agrees, Grant may operate."

CHAPTER 23

D arcy slept fitfully that night and woke early. He was dreading speaking with his sister about the planned surgical procedure, but now that the decision had been made, he was ready to have it over with. Summoning his valet, he dressed quickly and strode the short distance to Georgiana's chambers. The door was ajar but he knocked to announce his presence before entering the room.

His sister lay in the vast bed, her head propped up upon a stack of pillows, her eyes closed. Darcy studied her from across the room, taking in her unnatural pallor. He could tell by the deep furrow between her brows that she still suffered. Beside the bed, Elizabeth sat reading aloud from a book of poetry. Taking in the scene, Darcy felt a knot forming at the back of his throat. His heart ached for his sister, but at the same time it swelled with gratitude and admiration for the benevolence Elizabeth continued to demonstrate.

When she became aware of his presence, Elizabeth ceased reading and stood, closing the book and setting it on the bedside table.

The room grew quiet and Georgiana opened her eyes. "Elizabeth, why did you... Oh, William, I did not hear you come in."

Darcy stepped closer to the bed, pulling his gaze away from Elizabeth and forcing a smile. "Good morning, poppet. How are you feeling?"

Georgiana's cheeks lifted slightly at the long-unused endearment. "I am well. There is still some pain, but I am certain I will be feeling better soon."

Darcy and Elizabeth exchanged a glance before Elizabeth excused herself and Darcy eased into the chair she had relinquished. His gaze wandered the room's perimeter before coming back to rest on his sister's countenance. "Has Grant been in this morning?" he asked, stalling for time.

"No. Dr. Prescott was here earlier. I have not seen Dr. Grant since last evening."

Darcy nodded, briefly looking away. Even though he'd had an entire night to work out the best way to break the news, now that he was here, Darcy found the idea of putting such a subject into words damn near impossible. Taking a breath, he reached for Georgiana's hand, covering her fingers with his palm. "Georgie, I have been speaking to Mr. Grant... about your treatment. I... That is, Grant believes—"

A sudden knocking sounded at the door and Darcy drew in a harsh breath that was equal parts frustration and relief. "Enter," Darcy called, and after a slight hesitation, the door swung open on its hinges.

Grant stood at the threshold, but the gentleman did not cross into the chamber. Instead, his eyes darted in Georgiana's direction before settling upon her brother.

"Mr. Darcy, might I have a word?"

Darcy lifted his gaze, glowering in the doctor's direction. It was not lost on Darcy that the other man had barely spared a glance for his sister. Should the physician not have been in long before now to see to his patient's well-being?

"Can it not wait?" Darcy virtually snapped and Grant shifted where he stood.

A shadow seemed to settle upon the doctor's features. "No, sir. I do not believe it can."

Darcy's mouth tightened. "Very well." Turning to his sister he added quietly, "I will have your breakfast sent up. Pray, try to eat a little. I shall return shortly."

The two men proceeded in silence to Darcy's study. Upon entering the room, Darcy was startled to see Prescott and his cousin already seated within.

"What is going on?" he asked, turning to face the younger physician.

Grant cleared his throat. "Forgive me, Mr. Darcy, but I do not believe I can operate. Prescott has agreed to attempt to locate another surgeon in the area; or if you would prefer, we might send to London, although that will likely take several days."

Darcy stared back at the physician as if Grant had just expressed his intention to fly around the cosmos. "What do you mean you cannot operate? You are the one who convinced me to go through with this procedure in the first place!"

Grant did not answer immediately, but paced to the nearest window, staring out at the grounds for several moments before turning to address his host. "I beg your pardon, sir, but I would prefer not to elaborate. I will only say that I do not believe it would be to your sister's advantage for me to operate. I am very sorry."

Darcy's spine stiffened. Turning to his cousin he barked, "Did you know about this?"

"No. This is the first I am hearing of it."

"And you?" he asked, fixing his gaze on Prescott.

The older physician glanced towards Grant before turning his attention back to Darcy. "Dr. Grant informed me of his decision early this morning. I am not at liberty to say more, but I believe he is indeed acting in your sister's best interest."

Good God in heaven, had they all gone mad? "How can this be in Georgiana's best interest?" Darcy thundered. His head snapped around to face Grant. "I agreed based on the fact that you have performed this operation many times." Shifting his gaze back to the old family retainer he asked, "Do you know of another surgeon in the vicinity who has done anything like this before?"

"I do not. But if you would be more comfortable, we can send to London for a new surgeon as Dr. Grant proposed."

"And waste another week while my sister suffers? I do not want another surgeon. I want to know what the devil is going on here!"

Before anyone could answer, a loud pounding sounded at the door. Without waiting to be given leave to enter, Hastings pushed into the room, his complexion ashen. "I beg your pardon, sir, but it is Miss Georgiana. I think you had better come."

The butler had scarcely finished speaking before Darcy was on his feet, racing for the stairs. His long legs carried him up to the landing and down the corridor in a matter of moments. Bursting into his sister's chambers, his eyes flew to the bed as Grant, Prescott, and the colonel crowded in behind him.

Georgiana lay perfectly still, her fine features damp with sweat, her eyes shut. Beside her, Elizabeth sat cradling her hand.

Darcy's heart plummeted to his boots. "Miss Bennet is she..."

Elizabeth's eyes found his. Her own face was leached of color, but he saw relief reflected in her gaze.

"I believe the worst is over," she said quietly. "But perhaps one of the doctors might examine her, as I am hardly an expert."

Prescott stepped forward. "I will do it. Miss Bennet, if you would remain?"

Elizabeth nodded. "Of course."

"I do not understand. What has happened?" Darcy attempted to approach the bed but his cousin had already taken hold of his arm.

"Come. We will wait next door," said Richard, steering Darcy to the adjoining chamber. Following his cousin's lead, Darcy turned, surprised to see that Grant was directly behind him. "Shouldn't you be in there?"

"No," the young physician replied concisely and Darcy frowned.

The small party moved into the parlor and Colonel Fitzwilliam shut the door between the chambers. Pacing to the window, Darcy pulled his fingers through his hair. "I do not understand," he repeated. "Has she recovered?"

Grant sighed, moving to take a seat. When he spoke, his voice was devoid of emotion. "My guess is that the stone has passed. Dr. Prescott will be able to tell us more after his examination."

"So, she is well? She will not need the operation?"

"If I am correct, then no, she will not. If she has passed the stone, there may still be small fragments left behind, but those should not pose a problem."

Darcy expelled a breath, collapsing onto a nearby chair and dropping his head into his hands.

When Prescott finally entered, Darcy surged to his feet. "Well?"

"She is exhausted, but she has passed the stone."

"Thank God!" Colonel Fitzwilliam released a cry of jubilation, coming over to clap Darcy on the shoulder.

Prescott's weathered cheeks lifted in a smile. "Indeed. Although I believe we also owe our thanks to Dr. Grant. It was likely his herbal draughts that helped to flush out the obstruction. Though rare, I have seen such results before."

Darcy turned to Grant. Despite his reservations about the man, gratitude coursed through Darcy's body. "I do thank you, sir. I am forever in your debt."

To Darcy's surprise, the younger man paled, climbing to his feet. "I am very glad for your sister's recovery, Mr. Darcy, but I assure you, you owe me nothing. Now, if you do not mind, I would like to look in on Miss Darcy, and then I will leave you to your privacy. Again, I am happy for you both."

Grant bowed, crossing to Georgiana's chamber, but Darcy's voice stopped him in his tracks. "Grant... Truly, I am exceedingly grateful for all you have done. I hope we might call on you again, should we have the need?"

The physician stilled. Slowly, he turned to face his host. "If Miss Darcy requires anything further, Dr. Prescott will attend her." And without further discussion, he quit the room, closing the door behind him with a decisive click.

Standing at the tall library windows, Darcy stared out at the gathering darkness. Although his body was exhausted, his mind was at peace for the first time in many days. Georgiana would be well. Raising a snifter of his best brandy, he took a long swallow before glancing over his shoulder. Behind him, Richard sat in a club chair by the hearth. And though his cousin's posture was relaxed, his eyes bore into Darcy with unnerving intensity. Turning back to face the moonlit garden, Darcy's thoughts suddenly shifted, and his happiness crumbled.

His sister had recovered, and for that he would be eternally thankful, but his chances with Elizabeth had never appeared more bleak. They had barely spoken since the day he had snapped at her in his study—the day she had come to him offering comfort, and he had turned her away. He could still see the hurt in her eyes... How she must detest him now.

And then there was Grant. Although Darcy had done his best to discount the signs, it was painfully clear that the physician had developed a *tendre* for Elizabeth. Did she return his affections? Was Grant the real reason she had chosen to remain at Pemberley?

A noise from the other end of the room pulled Darcy from his tortured thoughts and he turned away from the window. Forcing the physician from his mind Darcy crossed the carpet, settling into the chair opposite his cousin. "Very well, Richard. We may as well get this over with."

"Pardon? I am not sure I take your meaning, cousin," Colonel Fitzwilliam drawled, but there was a familiar glint in his eyes.

"You take my meaning well enough, I would imagine. You have been staring at me like that since dinner. I assume this is about Miss Bennet?"

Colonel Fitzwilliam grinned. "Well, now that you bring up the matter," he began.

Darcy groaned. He had no wish to discuss Elizabeth with his cousin, but he knew Richard well enough. He was like a dog with a bone, and there would be no peace until Darcy let him have his say.

As if to corroborate these thoughts, the colonel continued, "I do find it intriguing that the young lady decided to remain at Pemberley in the absence of her relations. What did it take to get them to leave her here?"

Darcy bristled at the implication behind his cousin's words. "I have already told you, she stayed out of kindness to Georgiana. If you are insinuating that anything improper occurred—"

Colonel Fitzwilliam released a roar of laughter. "Ha! I know better than anyone that you are not that sort."

Darcy frowned, unsure if this was a compliment or a slight. "Good."

"But that does not change the fact that you are in love with her."

Darcy's arm jerked up, and brandy sloshed onto the Persian carpet. "Blast! Honestly, Richard, I have no wish to discuss this. I have told you as much once before."

"Indeed—the day we left Rosings. At that time, you intimated that Miss Bennet did not hold you in any special regard. In fact, you seemed to think the lady actually disliked you. Yet here she is, a year later, living in your home, caring for your sister."

"She is not *living* here, she is *visiting*."

"Visiting. And she stayed when the rest of her family departed."

Thinking back to Grant, Darcy's fingers clenched around his glass. "She did not stay for me."

Richard snorted. "You truly believe that?"

"Yes."

"Then you are blind as well as dim-witted."

Darcy blanched before taking another swallow of his drink. "You do not know what you are speaking of."

Colonel Fitzwilliam stared back at him, narrowing his gaze. "I know her eyes light up whenever you enter the room. I know she studies you when she thinks you won't catch her out. In fact, if I was a betting man, I'd say she was half in love with you already."

"You are wrong."

"How do you know?"

"I just do."

"How? No offence cousin, but you have never been particularly adept at gauging the feelings of the fairer sex."

Darcy sprang to his feet, stalking to a nearby table to pour himself another drink. With his back to his cousin, he answered, "I know because I offered for her and she refused me. Are you satisfied now?"

Colonel Fitzwilliam started. "What? When?"

Darcy turned. "When we were at Rosings."

"That Easter?"

Darcy nodded, the agony of her rebuff as fresh as if it had happened yesterday.

Colonel Fitzwilliam leaned back in his chair. "Well, that does put an interesting spin on things. May I ask why?"

Darcy frowned. "Why?"

"Yes, why. Why would a woman of little means and inferior social standing refuse one of the most eligible bachelors in the kingdom?"

"Such financial trappings mean nothing to her. And I have already told you, she despises me. Or... at least she did."

"Ah-ha! So, you admit her feelings have changed?"

Darcy walked slowly across the room, lowering himself into his seat. "Yes, but not in the way you imply. Since we met again by chance last November, I have done everything in my power to erase her earlier prejudice... and I think I have succeeded, to a point. I imagine she has come to view me as a friend—and for that I will always be grateful. But to my shame, I have not been especially kind to her of late. I do not believe there can ever be more between us."

The colonel was silent for a moment. "Do you still love her?"

Darcy stared into his glass before giving his cousin a single nod.

"Have you told her?"

"It is too late. Too much has happened."

Richard frowned, but before he could respond, a soft knocking at the door caused Darcy to start. "Enter!" he called out, his breath catching a moment later when Elizabeth walked into the room.

The two men rose. Colonel Fitzwilliam cast a wry smile in Darcy's direction before turning to Elizabeth. "Miss Bennet! What perfect timing."

Elizabeth's gaze shifted between the two gentlemen. "I beg your pardon, I hope I am not interrupting?"

Ignoring his cousin's chuckle, Darcy answered, "Not at all. Pray, come in."

Elizabeth hesitated, wrapping her shawl more tightly around her shoulders. "Thank you. I will only be a moment. Miss Darcy was asking for a book, and I thought I would retrieve it for her in case she wished to read before bed."

Darcy nodded and Elizabeth made her way towards the shelves. Clearing his voice, Colonel Fitzwilliam followed. "Miss Bennet, I am glad to have an opportunity to see you again this evening. I wished to say my goodbyes as I will be leaving at first light."

Elizabeth turned. "So soon? But you have only just arrived."

"Yes, I am afraid duty calls." With a smirk in Darcy's direction he added, "Besides, I can tell when I am no longer needed. Now, if you will both excuse me, I must prepare for my departure."

Darcy opened his mouth to protest, but it was too late. His cousin was already out the door.

Elizabeth flushed, diverting her gaze to the nearest bookshelf and Darcy swore under his breath. Damn Richard! Did the man never have a care for the consequences of his actions? It was one thing to take perverse amusement in leaving the two of them alone, but it was quite another to put Elizabeth in a situation that would clearly bring her distress.

Fighting his own embarrassment, Darcy crossed to the hearth. Taking up one of the fire-irons, he stirred the flames, glad to have something to distract him from the sight of Elizabeth running her fingers over the spines of his books.

"Were you searching for something in particular?" he finally asked.

Elizabeth acknowledged that she was, giving him the name of the author. Replacing the poker in its rack, Darcy made his way across the room, stretching up to reach for a volume on one of the higher shelves. Removing the book from the stacks he turned, placing it into Elizabeth's hands. His fingers grazed her palm and their eyes locked.

"Thank you," Elizabeth murmured.

"Not at all."

"I should go."

She moved towards the door, but Darcy called out, halting her progress. "Miss Bennet..."

"Yes?"

"I feel I owe you an apology."

Elizabeth paused. When she did not reply, he continued, "I had no right to speak to you the way I did the other day, in my study. You were only trying to help, and I am afraid I was impossibly rude."

"You were upset. Understandably so."

Darcy sighed. "As usual, you are too generous with me. Indeed, I was upset, but that does not excuse my behavior."

Elizabeth closed the space between them, reaching for his hand. When their fingers met, a chill raced up his spine.

"You owe me no apology," she whispered.

Darcy took a tentative step forward. Their bodies were almost touching now, and he could feel her warm breath against his skin. Inhaling her familiar scent, he lowered his head.

Somewhere in the house a door slammed and Elizabeth stepped back. "I should go," she repeated.

Darcy nodded, swallowing hard. "Yes."

"Goodnight."

"Goodnight, Miss Bennet. Pleasant dreams."

CHAPTER 24

Morning light streamed through the casement windows in Darcy's study, illuminating the single letter on the silver tray. Leaning against the back of his chair, Darcy lifted a hand to massage his temple. He had not slept well. Images of Elizabeth and their near-kiss in the library kept him awake late into the night, and when he did finally slumber, his dreams offered little relief.

Rising early, he had attempted to clear his head with a morning ride, but returning to find the letter had done nothing to improve his mood. Picking it up now, he stared at the name inscribed upon the heavy parchment. *Miss Elizabeth Bennet.* A gentleman's hand, Darcy was sure of it. He turned the letter over, examining the unfamiliar seal pressed into the deep red wax. Of course, it could be from Elizabeth's father, but somehow the handwriting did not seem to be that of an older gentleman. It was certainly not from Bingley, as this was not his seal, nor did the precise penmanship match his friend's unruly scrawl.

Unbidden, Grant's image once again found purchase in Darcy's mind. He had not missed the look of repressed longing the physician had directed at Elizabeth before taking his leave. Dropping the folded paper, Darcy's fingers clenched. No. It was impossible. No single gentleman would have the audacity to pen a letter to an unmarried young lady. His conscience prickled. Of course, *he* had done it... But that had been a totally different situation! And he had not sent his letter by post. He had placed it directly and discreetly into Elizabeth's hands.

Before he could consider the matter further, soft footsteps diverted his attention and he glanced up to see Elizabeth and her maid crossing the front hall. Setting the letter back upon the salver he rose and made his way to the open door.

"Miss Bennet!" Elizabeth turned and Darcy continued, "I was just on my way to seek you out. A letter arrived for you a short while ago."

Elizabeth quickened her steps, hurrying in his direction. Her maid, Polly, followed a few paces behind. The two women entered his study and Darcy turned over the letter. "I hope it is not bad news," he said, watching as Elizabeth broke the seal.

"I do not know. I thought it might be from Jane, but the handwriting is my uncle's."

To Darcy's embarrassment, relief flooded through him as Elizabeth turned her attention to the letter, quickly scanning the single page.

"Oh! My uncle has been called back to Town. He writes to tell me that they have had to curtail their travels. He and my aunt will return to collect me within the next few days."

The solace Darcy had felt only moments before instantly turned to dread and he struggled to disguise his distress. "I see." Darcy paused. "Could you not wait and travel with Mr. and Mrs. Bingley? I am certain they would wish to spend some time with you after such a long journey."

Elizabeth looked up, slowly shaking her head. "I would like that, but I am afraid my aunt and uncle will expect me to return with them."

"Of course." Darcy nodded, fighting against the rising panic that twisted his stomach.

Still gripping the letter, Elizabeth sank into one of the chairs before the wide mahogany desk. Her shoulders trembled, and Darcy drew closer to where she sat.

"You are chilled," he murmured. "Let me get a servant to make up the fire."

Elizabeth stared back at him, an unreadable expression in her eyes. "No, I thank you but there is no need. In any case, I should let you return to your work."

She rose slowly to her feet, but Darcy held up his hand. "No, stay." Shifting his gaze, Darcy turned to the maid who still hovered near the door. "Polly, pray, go and fetch a wrap for Miss Bennet."

Elizabeth looked like she might object but returned to her seat, fixing her attention on the maid. "Thank you, Polly. I believe I left my shawl in the music room."

The maid curtsied but remained where she was.

Propping one hip on the corner of his desk, Darcy smiled. "It is all right, Polly. I believe Miss Bennet will be safe enough for a few moments while you retrieve her shawl."

Blushing furiously, the maid dropped another brisk curtsy, darting from the room. Darcy followed her to the door, closing it just enough to give them a small degree of privacy.

Behind him, Elizabeth folded her letter, reaching to place it upon the tray in the center of the desk. Her sharp inhalation caused Darcy to turn, his own breath freezing in his chest.

Elizabeth's stared back at him. "Mr. Darcy, is this not my book?"

Darcy's gaze fixed on the worn volume in Elizabeth's hands. How could he have been so careless? To have left the book on his desk, in plain sight! Well, there was nothing to be done for it now.

Slowly, he retraced his steps. "It is."

Elizabeth pulled her eyes away from his face, flipping through the pages. "But... Did you not say that it was ruined?"

"It is ruined, Miss Bennet, as you see."

"And yet you kept it..."

"Yes."

"Why?"

"I..." Darcy paused, rubbing his face. "Initially I thought to have it repaired, but the damage was too great, so I purchased a replacement. But you are correct. I should have returned the original."

Clutching the book tightly to her chest, Elizabeth stood, making her way around the desk. "You needn't apologize. I do not mind that you kept it, I only wish to know why."

Gazing into Elizabeth's upturned face, Darcy's chest contracted as the words he longed to say swirled inside his head. *Because every time I see it, I am reminded of you. Because when I hold it, I feel your joy. Because I love you.*

A noise from the vestibule caused them to jump apart and they turned in tandem to find Elizabeth's maid standing in the doorway.

"Your wrap, miss."

Coming forward, the maid presented the Indian shawl, and Elizabeth's cheeks colored. "I thank you, Polly."

The clock on the mantelpiece struck the hour and Darcy stepped away, clearing his throat. "Forgive me, Miss Bennet, but I find I am late for an appointment with my steward." Crossing in front of Elizabeth he bent to murmur softly as he passed, "Take the book, it belongs to you."

Elizabeth watched him go before turning her attention to the worn volume in her hand. She remained in that position for several moments before returning the book to its place on Mr. Darcy's desk and following him from the room.

Elizabeth stopped at the door to her chambers. Twisting the handle, she slipped inside, making her way across the Aubusson carpet. A small fire crackled in the hearth, chasing off the morning chill. Draping her shawl upon a nearby chair, she paced to the far corner of the room. Stooping beside her trunk, Elizabeth loosened the straps, tipping back the lid and deftly running her fingers along the smooth bottom.

Her thumb bumped against the tiny lever and she pressed down, causing the door to the hidden compartment to spring open. Reaching into the small space, she pulled out the familiar envelope with its red wax seal. The once crisp vellum had softened to a supple buttery-texture, and Elizabeth was careful not to cause any further damage as she extracted the two sheets of parchment, written through in a very close hand. Rising to her feet, she returned to the comforting warmth of the fire before glancing down at the words she had long ago committed to memory.

Her eyes skimmed the page, phrases leaping out at her to once again wreak havoc with her heart.

Be not alarmed, madam, on receiving this letter...

... I write without any intention of paining you, or humbling myself, by dwelling on wishes which, for the happiness of both, cannot be too soon forgotten...

... pardon the freedom with which I demand your attention; your feelings, I know, will bestow it unwillingly...

... ignorant as you previously were... detection could not be in your power, and suspicion certainly not in your inclination...

... I will only add, God bless you.

Fitzwilliam Darcy

Swallowing back a swell of emotion, Elizabeth turned to stare out the adjacent window. However, when she gazed through the mullioned glass, it was not Pemberley's rolling hills she saw, but Mr. Darcy's countenance—the serious expression in his dark eyes the day he had handed her his letter.

... I write without any intention of paining you, or humbling myself...

And yet he *had* humbled himself. Not only in penning this missive—laying his heart bare and confiding his deepest family secrets—but in all the months that had followed, with his every courtesy to her and her family, despite what had come before. Her throat tightened as tears prickled at the corners of her vision. Propping her elbow upon the mantelpiece, Elizabeth held the letter loosely between her fingers, her gaze coming to rest upon the final line:

I will only add, God bless you...

After the word *add*, she could just make out a splotch of ink upon the fine linen parchment, as if he had held the tip of his pen there overlong before completing the valediction. Had he intended to write some other words in that space, besides his blessings? Elizabeth shook her head. If he had, she would never know. His pride and her prejudice had destroyed any hope they might have had of building a future together.

... *the happiness of both...*

How very different her idea of happiness was now, from what it had been then. In Hunsford, she had sworn that Mr. Darcy was the last man in the world that she could ever be prevailed on to marry. Now, she would give anything just to hear him express the sentiments she had scorned back then.

Her fingers tightened around the letter, a silent sob tickling her throat.

Heaven help her, she loved him. If only she hadn't discovered it far too late.

CHAPTER 25

Apollo's hooves drove into the densely packed earth, but no matter how hard and fast Darcy rode, he was unable to outrun the thoughts that continued to clatter inside his head. Despite his sister's illness, the days he had spent with Elizabeth at Pemberley had been amongst the happiest of his life. But like sand through an hourglass, their time together was slipping away, and he was no closer to declaring his feelings. He had almost done so that night in the library, when Elizabeth had been so close he could smell the intoxicating scent of citrus and wildflowers that always surrounded her—when he had looked into her eyes and thought he'd seen, for a brief moment, a reflection of his own desire.

But in the end, he had done nothing. He had simply let her walk out of the room. Darcy released an anguished sigh.

In the beginning, having Elizabeth at Pemberley had

seemed like a dream, and for a while it had been. But then Georgiana had become ill and he had turned into a man he hardly recognized—his behavior worse even than it had been in Hertfordshire—and Darcy cringed to remember it.

Unbidden, Grant's face entered Darcy's consciousness and his thoughts returned to the times he had witnessed Elizabeth with the young physician: talking animatedly at dinner, sitting side by side in his sister's chambers, Grant holding Elizabeth in his arms... Darcy's fingers tightened around the reins and he shook his head to clear it of the image.

As much as he was loath to admit it, Grant would be a good match for her. The physician was intelligent and kind; he possessed an attractive countenance, and made a comfortable living. He was closer to Elizabeth in age, and of her social sphere. But even thinking about Elizabeth with another man made Darcy's stomach roil and he closed his eyes against the pain.

Then there was that blasted book. He had expected Elizabeth to be angry when she found it, but she had only appeared mildly confused. He was certain she would be grateful to have the volume finally restored to her, but when he had returned to his study, it still sat upon his desk. She had left it for him. But what did the gesture signify? Was the book intended as a keepsake? Or did she simply wish to sever their connection, once and for all...

Yanking on the reins, Darcy allowed the stallion to slow his pace. It was time to make a decision. To figure out what he wanted and to attempt to make it so, otherwise he would spend his whole life wondering if his misplaced pride had cost him the only woman he would ever love.

Relaxing in the saddle, Darcy stared into the distance. So, what did he want? Well, that was simple. He wanted Elizabeth. He could not remember a time when he had *not* wanted her. In the year since his disastrous proposal, his need for her had not abated—it had continued to grow. When he had offered for her at Hunsford, he had desired her. He had been charmed and captivated by her. He had even believed himself to be in love with her. Thinking back on it now, harsh laughter tickled his throat. For just as a shadow is to the solid object it reflects, what he had felt then was a pale facsimile of what he felt now.

But as much as he wanted Elizabeth, there was something he desired even more. He desired her happiness. And if that was with Grant, or any other man, Darcy would step aside. It would be tantamount to torture, but seeing her well-settled and happy—truly happy—meant more to him than his own life.

Your selfish disdain for the feelings of others…

Suddenly, Elizabeth's words echoed inside his head and a sad smile pulled at his lips. She had been correct, of course. It was not *her* feelings he had considered back then, but his own. It was his happiness he sought. Now it was time to seek hers.

Pressing his heels into Apollo's flanks, Darcy tugged on the reins. It was time to set things to rights, once and for all.

❄

Elizabeth wandered through the sunlit gardens, the birds singing in the trees and the fresh scent of newly cut grass filling her lungs. Saying goodbye to the colorful blossoms for a while, she ascended to some of the higher grounds, where an opening in the trees gave way to views of the valley below. A narrow stream meandered beside a low wall, and Elizabeth followed the water until it ended at a small pond. Stopping, she rested her elbow on the stone partition. Pemberley's lands stretched out before her—high woody hills and rolling fields as far as the eye could see. In the near distance, majestic oaks and Spanish chestnuts created a natural border for the more manicured gardens closer to the house. Her throat constricted as she realized all this might have been hers—along with the love and admiration of the best man she had ever known—if only she had not been so foolish and stubborn as to have thrown it away.

Taking a ragged gulp of air, Elizabeth pulled a handkerchief from the pocket of her gown. Lowering her lashes, her gaze fell to the wild lavender growing at her feet. A pair of bumblebees bounced from one blossom to the next, echoing the thoughts that continued to buzz inside her head. But although her mind was in turmoil, one irrefutable fact continued to rush to the surface: Mr. Darcy had kept her book.

When she had glimpsed the volume peeking out from underneath a stack of correspondence on the gentleman's desk, her astonishment had been absolute, and she had seen Mr. Darcy startle when he turned to observe her holding it in her hands. Could he have merely forgotten the item was in his possession? But if that was the case, why had he appeared so uneasy to see that she had discovered it? Had he kept the volume as some sort of token?

Elizabeth's stomach fluttered at the idea, but a moment later her thoughts sobered. Even if he had, that did not necessarily indicate that his feelings had changed. True, there were times—such as the other evening in the library—when she was almost certain he still possessed a degree of affection for her... But that did not alter what she knew to be true.

Mr. Darcy did not wish to make her his wife.

Darcy strode across the wide expanse of lawn bordering the formal gardens. Merging onto the gravel path, he ascended a small rise, and a sudden movement caught his eye. His footsteps stilled. There, not twenty paces away, Elizabeth stood alongside the pond that separated the rose garden from the south pasture. She faced away from him, one knee slightly bent, her weight resting on the ivy-covered wall. Her chestnut curls were uncovered and her pale gown seemed to almost glow in the hazy morning sun.

He must have made a sound, because she turned to face him. He could see what might have been a kerchief clutched tightly in her fist, but she tucked it inside the folds of her gown before moving in his direction.

"Mr. Darcy. Good morning."

Darcy bowed slightly at the waist before walking the

remaining distance to where she stood. "Miss Bennet. I am glad to see you are enjoying the park."

"Yes." Elizabeth's gaze returned to the horizon and when she spoke, her voice took on a wistful quality. "I shall miss it when I leave."

Darcy shifted his weight, his heart contracting at the mere thought of Elizabeth's departure. Attempting to lighten the mood, he glanced around at the empty lane. "I see you are once again without your maid. I hope you have not misplaced your shawl?"

Elizabeth flushed at his tease. "No, sir. Polly is not a great walker and I felt the need for some time alone. I hope you will not give me away?"

Darcy offered her a smile. "You may be assured of my secrecy. Though if it is solitude you seek, perhaps I am intruding?"

"No, not at all," Elizabeth answered. Then, seeming to take in his apparel she added, "Although it looks as if you were planning to ride? Pray, do not allow me to keep you."

"No, I have just returned. I thought I might walk for a while, if you would care to join me?"

When Elizabeth nodded her agreement, Darcy offered his arm, and a feeling of satisfaction settled over him when she took it without hesitation. The two set out. They continued along the well-worn path, neither speaking. Elizabeth appeared to be content to examine the views of the surrounding countryside, but after some moments, Darcy broke their silence.

"Miss Bennet, I wished to thank you—for your kindness to my sister and for staying on to offer her companionship. I am sorry you missed your trip to the Lakes."

Elizabeth looked up at him, as though surprised by his choice of conversation. "It was my pleasure, sir. I am happy to see Miss Darcy restored to good health. And the Lakes will always be there. Perhaps next summer..." Her voice trailed off and they walked for several more minutes before she added, "I have enjoyed my stay. It was good to see your cousin again, and I was pleased to make Mr. Grant's acquaintance, though I am sorry for the circumstances that brought him here. He seems very kind."

At the mention of Grant, Darcy felt his body stiffen.

Elizabeth stopped walking. "Mr. Darcy, is anything the matter?"

"What? No. Why do you ask?"

Elizabeth looked away. "It is nothing. I only thought..."

Darcy's sighed. "Pray, forgive me, Miss Bennet. It was not my intention to make you uneasy."

"You do not make me uneasy. I only wondered if perhaps *I* had made *you* uncomfortable."

"Of course not. Why would you think so?"

Elizabeth lifted her shoulders and it was Darcy's turn to look away. It was time to do the right thing, no matter how painful. If he loved her as much as he said he did, he needed to let her go.

Drawing a breath, Darcy resumed their walk, his gaze fixed on the landscape in front of them. "I believe you are correct, Miss Bennet. Mr. Grant does seem like a good man. I... I am certain he will make an excellent husband."

Out of the corner of his vision, Darcy could see the slight quirk of Elizabeth's brow, and a flush warmed his cheeks. "Forgive me, it is obviously none of my concern, but I... I thought perhaps you had formed some... attachment to the gentleman."

Elizabeth slowed her pace. She regarded him for several moments before appearing to make up her mind. "To be truthful, Mr. Darcy, I *have* formed an attachment, but it is not to Mr. Grant."

Elizabeth's words hung in the air like a dark cloud eclipsing the sun, and Darcy swallowed down the bile climbing up his throat. So, it was true. He was too late. Remembering the gentleman he had seen at the theater, Darcy answered flatly, "Oh. I see. There is... someone else, then? Someone in Town?"

"Yes," Elizabeth answered, and Darcy's stomach plunged.

This was a mistake. He could not stand here and listen to the woman he loved profess feelings for another. Desperately he looked around, wondering if he could claim a sudden megrim and return to the house. He was so consumed with his own thoughts he neglected to notice the hint of a smile that played at Elizabeth's lips. He realized she was speaking again and forced himself to look at her.

"... that is, the gentleman does have a home in London. But I believe he prefers to spend most of his time at his country estate." She hesitated for a moment before adding, "In Derbyshire."

Darcy's feet stumbled to a halt and he shook his head,

wondering if he had heard her correctly. Hardly daring to breathe, he answered slowly, "Forgive me, Miss Bennet. I do not take your meaning."

Elizabeth simply looked up at him, her dark eyes luminous.

"Miss Bennet, you are too generous to trifle with me. If your feelings are what they were at Hunsford, tell me so at once. My affections and wishes are unchanged." Darcy paused, running his fingers through his hair, and when he spoke again, his voice was heavy with emotion. "No. That is not true. My feelings *have* altered. I find I love you far more now than I did then. More now than I ever thought possible."

Elizabeth's eyes grew wide. She opened her mouth, but immediately closed it again.

Darcy gazed down at her before reaching for her hands, slowly running his thumbs across the knuckles. "This cannot come as a surprise to you?"

"I... I confess, it does. That is, I suspected you felt... gratitude... for my assistance after the accident, and for my friendship with your sister but..."

Darcy stepped closer, and Elizabeth's breath fanned his cheek. "Elizabeth. I feel gratitude when my valet draws me a bath, or when my cook serves lamb instead of pheasant. What I feel for you is not gratitude. It is not infatuation. It is a deep, abiding love."

"I do not understand. After your refusal... I thought..."

Darcy lifted her hand, placing a soft kiss upon the outside of her wrist. "Forgive me, Miss Bennet, but I believe *you* are the one who refused *me*. Not that I blame you in the least," he hurried to add. "Not after the way I spoke to you on that occasion."

"You mistake me, sir. I did not mean... I was referring to the conversation you had with my father. In Town."

Darcy's frown deepened. "But... surely you cannot think that I did not wish to marry you?"

Elizabeth looked away.

"Good God. I should have realized..." Abruptly Darcy released her hand, pacing away several feet before returning to her side and gently taking her elbow. "Come. Let us sit," he said, indicating a cluster of benches beneath a nearby oak and guiding her in that direction.

When they were both settled, Darcy leaned forward, resting his forearms upon his knees, but he sat in silence for some minutes before speaking.

"Elizabeth, when your father came to see me in London, the... friendship that you and I had forged was still new, and I did not sufficiently comprehend your feelings for me. You see, it had not been long since your refusal of my offer, and I am afraid the words you said to me on that occasion were still fresh in my memory."

Elizabeth looked away, tears forming at the corners of her eyes. "Do not remind me. I behaved abominably to you then."

"No more so than I deserved."

"So... that is why you refused?"

"Yes. Well, no... As I said, I did not refuse. That is, I only refused to marry you *against your wishes*. As much as I longed to make you my wife, I could not bear the thought of forcing you into an arrangement that would make you unhappy."

To Darcy's dismay, Elizabeth trembled. One of the tears that had been hovering at the edge of her lashes slipped down her cheek. He reached up, brushing it away.

"Elizabeth, I must beg your forgiveness. Never did I imagine that you might misinterpret my feelings, or the reason for my refusal." Sliding across the bench, he folded her in his arms, but it was only seconds before he felt her body stiffen. Releasing his hold, Darcy looked down to see her eyes were filled with tears.

"Mr. Darcy, it is not my intention to cause you any more pain. But I feel I must be honest. I cannot marry you."

"Tell me why. You must know by now that your happiness means everything to me. You need only speak, and I will do whatever you ask."

Elizabeth shook her head. "I believe your sentiments are genuine, and if there was only myself to consider... But I know your opinion of my family. I could never force you to connect yourself with those you feel are so far beneath your notice."

"Elizabeth, do not make yourself uneasy. Were we to marry, they would no longer be *your* family."

Elizabeth's expression shuttered, all animation draining from her features. "I comprehend your feelings, sir, and I assure you I know their faults better than anyone. But I love them dearly, and I will not give them up. Not even for you."

For a moment Darcy looked away. "Forgive me, Elizabeth, I am afraid I phrased that poorly. What I meant to say was that should we marry, they would no longer be *solely* your family. They would be mine as well. And I assure you, I am fiercely loyal to those entrusted to my care."

"But... at Hunsford... you said..."

Darcy lifted his hand to touch her lips, quieting her with his fingers. "Pray, do not speak of it. Everything I said to you on that day was an abomination. Upon reflection, I had no right to make disparaging comments about your relations when members of my own family have behaved far worse. The one true thing I said to you that day was that I loved you." Slipping his hand into hers, he gently pulled her to her feet. "Come. I think it is high time we erased that horrible afternoon from both our memories."

CHAPTER 26

S till holding Elizabeth's hand, Darcy made his way
along the avenue that circled the formal gardens.
Turning onto a smaller footpath, he continued past
polished marbles and neatly trimmed topiaries until he
could finally see the high stone wall, covered almost
entirely in thick vegetation. Stopping beside the iron gate,
Darcy reached into the pocket of his coat, removing a
small brass key and twisting it in the lock. The gate
squealed open on its hinges, and Darcy stood back,
allowing Elizabeth to enter.

Stepping into the enclosed space, he watched her
freeze, a small gasp escaping her lips.

Directly at the garden's center, water from a marble
fountain cascaded into a circular pond, producing a
soothing murmur, while all around them flowers of every
variety blossomed, creating a riot of color. Sunlight filtered
through the surrounding trees and the scent of honey-

suckle and lavender floated on the breeze. Nestled between the blooms, several stone benches sat on a carpet of bright green grass.

Elizabeth turned in a small circle, her eyes shining. "Your mother's garden," she whispered.

Darcy nodded. "Yes. I have wanted to show it to you since you arrived, but there did not seem to be the opportunity, and then Georgiana became ill…"

"It is magnificent!"

Darcy smiled at her obvious delight. "I have kept it locked since my mother's passing. Besides the gardeners, only my sister and I possess the keys." He paused for a moment. "I have never brought anyone here before."

Elizabeth turned to face him. "Thank you for showing it to me."

Settling his palm at the small of her back, Darcy led the way to one of the benches opposite the fountain. He waited for her to sit and then took the spot beside her.

Somewhere in the trees a sparrow called, and another one answered.

Darcy hesitated, collecting his thoughts, before turning to her with a solemn expression. "Elizabeth, there is something I need to say, and I hope you will be kind enough to allow me to express myself without interruption."

Elizabeth nodded her agreement, and after a moment, Darcy began to speak. "Before I met you, I had always considered myself to be an honorable man. I was raised with good principles by two excellent parents who were very much in love. In fact, seeing their devotion to one another made me understand that I would not be happy in a marriage of unequal affection."

He paused and the expression on Elizabeth's face made him believe she saw the sadness he carried.

"But then my mother died, and soon afterwards my father. By the time I reached my majority, the world had become a place where I no longer felt comfortable. I realized that the people who sought my favor saw me only as a commodity. I was highly coveted by women of the *ton*, but not for who I was. No, it was my position, my standing in society, and my money these women wanted—not me.

"By the time I came to Netherfield with Bingley, I had closed myself off to all but a few trusted friends, certain I would never find a woman who could touch my heart.

"Unfortunately, when I first encountered you at that assembly in Meryton, I did not behave honorably. In fact, it pains me to recall the things I said. I do not know why... but I'd like to think it was because I saw something in you, felt something, and I was afraid. Afraid to let down the carefully constructed walls. Afraid to stand up to my family, who I knew would not approve of the match. Afraid to be hurt. And so, I behaved badly. Not just to you, but to everyone in the neighborhood. I was proud and arrogant and I deserved their censure, and yours. To safeguard my heart, I convinced myself that you were unsuitable, and I fled, hoping to put you out of my mind.

"And it worked, for a time.

"But then I saw you again at Rosings, and I realized I could no longer fight my attraction, and so I offered for you. Dreadfully. Yet in my vanity and conceit, I never doubted that you would accept me."

Elizabeth opened her mouth, but Darcy held up his hand. He swallowed hard, staring out across the garden. "No. Pray, let me finish."

"Your rejection of my offer—of me—was one of the lowest moments of my life, but it made me take stock of my imperfections. When you refused me, you spoke of my selfish disdain for the feelings of others, and in that you were correct. I realized when I offered for you, I thought only of my own needs, my own feelings, my own desires. Not yours. I observed myself clearly for the first time, and I did not like what I saw.

"When I left Kent that spring, I did not believe our paths would cross again. Indeed, knowing your feelings for me, I made every effort to see that they did not. Yet I still wished to improve myself. To be a man worthy of your regard, even if your affection was something I could never hope to attain."

Elizabeth flushed, lowering her lashes. "But we did meet again," she said softly, and Darcy nodded.

"Yes, by the grace of God, our paths crossed on that cold November day. And over the past nine months I have had the privilege to be once again in your company. To bear witness to your kindness, your intelligence, and your strength... and I have been awed and humbled by the experience.

"So, here we are, and I now know with absolute certainty that we are not equals. You are my superior in every way that matters." Reaching out, Darcy lifted Elizabeth's hand, brushing a kiss upon her knuckles before sinking to his knees. "Elizabeth, the love I feel for you defies expression. I love you wholly, without reserve. If you refuse me now, I know that I shall never marry, for there is no other woman who could fill the space in my heart that belongs to you.

"So, I will ask you one last time, the way I should have asked you all those months ago. Elizabeth Bennet, will you do me the great honor of becoming my wife?"

As Darcy stared up at the woman he loved, tears welled in Elizabeth's eyes. She opened her mouth and then visibly swallowed, offering him a shaky nod.

"Yes?" Darcy whispered, hardly daring to breathe. "You are accepting me?"

Elizabeth nodded, more forcefully this time. "I am accepting you, sir."

Darcy started to rise, but to his amazement, Elizabeth fell to her knees in front of him, wrapping her arms around his neck.

Instinctively, his own arms slipped about her waist, and he pulled her body firmly against his. His eyes began to sting as he hoarsely choked, "Elizabeth, tell me you will never leave."

"I will never leave."

His palms traveled up her arms, coming to rest upon her shoulders. He lifted his fingers to caress her cheeks, dipping his chin until their faces were inches apart. Elizabeth's mouth opened ever so slightly and his heart raced as his lips brushed hers for the first time. He kissed her delicately, reverently. A small sound slipped from her throat, somewhere between a sigh and a moan and Darcy was overcome with the brightest joy. Dear God, how had he lived his entire life without this feeling? He pulled back to gaze into her fine eyes before once again capturing her lips. Her kisses were as sweet as honey and as intoxicating as the strongest drink. Time seemed to slow and then stop altogether, and Darcy was in no hurry to have it start up again.

He wanted the kiss to go on forever, but after several moments he broke away. He knew he had already gone well beyond the bounds of propriety and he did not wish to overwhelm her. After all, they had an entire lifetime to look forward to.

He opened his eyes to find Elizabeth staring up at him, but this time a mischievous smile brightened her expression.

Reaching for her hands, he rose to his feet, pulling her with him. "Is there something you find amusing, Miss Bennet? Most gentlemen do not like to be laughed at when they have just kissed a lady for the first time."

To her credit, Elizabeth blushed. "Oh, it was not the kiss I found amusing. The kiss was lovely."

Darcy smiled, exposing deep dimples. "Good. I am pleased to hear it."

"It was only that I was thinking about everything you said to me here in this garden, and I believe, Mr. Darcy, that is easily the longest speech I have ever heard you utter. Until today, I would have thought such a thing quite impossible."

The beginnings of a laugh rumbled in his chest, but

Darcy answered seriously, "I will endeavor to do better in that regard, though I doubt I will ever be as loquacious as you. It is simply not in my nature." After a moment, he briefly turned away. "Elizabeth, as gratified as I am by your acceptance, I feel I must ask... What of your father? Will he grant us his consent? I know he was not best pleased with me after our meeting in Town."

Elizabeth lifted her shoulders in a shrug, but Darcy could see that her eyes were troubled. "I do not require his consent. I am of age."

"Perhaps. But I could never marry you without his blessing. Not now. Not knowing how much your family means to you."

Elizabeth reached up, her soft fingers caressing his cheek. "Mr. Darcy, I have made my decision. Now that we have reached an understanding, nothing in this world would keep me from marrying you."

Darcy studied her face. He knew that she believed this to be true, but he also knew that he could not live with himself were he to separate Elizabeth from the one member of her family who held her heart. Forcing his uneasiness aside, he captured her hand, lifting it to his lips.

"Elizabeth, might I request a favor? As we are now betrothed, would it be too much to ask you to address me by my given name? At least when we are not in public?"

Elizabeth's cheeks turned a rosy shade of pink but her mouth and her eyes were smiling. "Yes, I think that can be accomplished. Fitzwilliam."

The sound of his name on her lips made Darcy's

insides quiver and it took him a moment before he was composed enough to speak. "Thank you. But you may prefer to call me William. Most of my relations do, as Fitzwilliam is a family name and it can grow confusing."

"Very well, William," Elizabeth said, leaning up to brush her lips against his jaw.

Darcy closed his eyes and his breathing once again grew ragged. "Elizabeth, I think we should return to the house. We have both been absent a good while and I would not want to give the staff any cause for concern."

"As you wish, my love," Elizabeth whispered and Darcy was certain he had never known such bliss in the entirety of his nine and twenty years.

CHAPTER 27

When Darcy entered Pemberley's great hall with Elizabeth on his arm, the elation he felt in every cell of his body fairly radiated from his being. Elizabeth Bennet had agreed to be his wife! Never in his life could he remember feeling such unadulterated joy.

But the joy twisted into dread at the sight of Grant pacing across the marble floor, his expression grim.

Advancing in the physician's direction, Darcy dropped Elizabeth's arm as a weight settled in the pit of his stomach. "What has happened?" he barked. "Is it Georgiana? Is she ill?"

At Darcy's approach, Grant looked up, appearing momentarily confused. "No. That is, yes." He shook his head. "Forgive me—Miss Darcy is not ill. But I... I hoped I might speak to you about a matter of some importance, concerning your sister."

The knot inside Darcy's stomach loosened slightly, but his heart continued to pound inside his ears. "She is not unwell? You are certain?"

Grant nodded. "Your sister is in good health. At least, I have no reason to think otherwise."

Darcy released a breath, willing himself to relax.

"I will excuse myself," Elizabeth said quietly, already moving towards the stairs; but Darcy reached out, catching her hand. "No. Stay." Turning to Grant he continued, "Anything you have to say about my sister may be said in front of Miss Bennet. She and Georgiana have become close, and I value her opinion."

The doctor shifted his focus from Darcy to Elizabeth before nodding his agreement. "I have no objection."

The small party made their way to Pemberley's library in silence. But the moment the door was closed behind them, Darcy turned to face the physician. "What is this about?"

Elizabeth proceeded to cross the room, taking a seat on a small settee beside the hearth. Regarding a nearby chair, Grant briefly sat, then stood. Pacing to the fireplace he gazed into the empty grate before abruptly returning to his seat and pushing his fingers through his hair. "Mr. Darcy, you may remember that prior to your sister's recovery I expressed some... reluctance to perform the procedure I had initially proposed."

At the physician's words, Darcy lifted a hand to rub his jaw. Reluctance? The man had flat out refused! "I do," he answered.

"Yes. Well. At that time, I did not explain the reason behind my decision. I would like to do so now."

Darcy exchanged a glance with Elizabeth. "I cannot see how it is relevant at this point… unless there is something about my sister's health you are not telling me?"

"About her health, no. As I said, your sister is well. I have every reason to expect she will make a complete recovery."

"Then I do not understand."

"I know." Grant stared morosely at the carpet before straightening his shoulders. "Mr. Darcy, the reason I did not wish to perform the operation was because I realized I no longer possessed the objectivity a doctor should have when dealing with a patient. In short, I had developed… feelings for your sister, and I could not in good conscience perform such a procedure under those circumstances."

Darcy's jaw tightened as a spark of rage ignited in his chest. Good God! As if the idea of any gentleman performing such a procedure on his sister had not been disturbing enough, to think that a man who believed himself in love with her… That he would have… Darcy's cheeks burned and an involuntary shiver raced down his spine. But the more rational side of him recalled that Grant had not gone through with it. Even before his sister had recovered, the surgeon had bowed out. "Are you telling me that you and my sister have formed an attachment?" he finally asked.

"I am telling you that I have come to care for Miss Darcy a great deal."

"And does my sister return these sentiments?"

Grant studied the tips of his boots. "I am unaware of your sister's feelings. I have not made mine known to her, nor do I intend to."

"Why are you telling me all this?"

Grant lifted his gaze. "Because you are the closest thing she has to a father. And because I felt you had a right to know."

Spinning on his heel, Darcy paced to the window and then back to where Grant sat. "She is not even out yet," he hissed. "She is but seventeen years of age!"

Across from him, the physician flinched and Darcy felt a twinge of remorse. In truth, his sister was fast approaching her eighteenth birthday; certainly any number of young ladies were married at such an age. But he was not ready to let Grant escape so easily.

"I understand," the physician answered. "As I have already stated, I do not intend to pursue a courtship. Even if her age were not an issue, I am well aware that I am not of her station."

Darcy frowned, and although he did not turn in her direction, he could feel Elizabeth's gaze. "You think this is why I disapprove?"

Now it was the doctor's turn to show surprise. "Is it not? Obviously, Miss Darcy will have the pick of gentlemen from the first circles when she enters society. It is only right that you should wish for her to make the best possible match."

Slowly, Darcy moved to face Elizabeth. Her expression was placid, but he could detect the slightest hitch to her brow. *She is waiting to see how I handle this.* Darcy lifted his hand, massaging the bridge of his nose before answering carefully, "In truth, it has always been my hope that Georgiana would make an advantageous match. And a year ago, I would have agreed that such an alliance would by necessity involve a gentleman of equal social standing. But now..." His voice trailed off and Grant sat forward in his chair.

"Now?"

"I have but one wish for my sister—that she be happy." Once again, he shifted to face Elizabeth and their eyes locked. "As it happens, I have recently been taught that happiness can be found in the unlikeliest of places."

"Then... are you saying I have a chance?" Grant asked, redirecting Darcy's attention. "You will allow me to court her?"

"At present? No. As I have said, she is not out and too young to enter into such a relationship." Beholding Grant's crestfallen expression, Darcy continued, "However, I will give you leave to... spend time in her company. To get to know her, properly. When she makes her debut next season, if her feelings have grown to match your own... well, then we shall see."

Grant sprang from his seat, a euphoric smile transforming his features. Grasping Darcy's hand, he pumped it enthusiastically. "I thank you, sir. Very much."

"There is no need to thank me. It will be up to Georgiana to determine how things progress from here," Darcy answered.

But despite his best intentions, his mouth curved into a smile.

✳

For the second time in as many weeks, Darcy stood atop Pemberley's stone landing as the Gardiner carriage trundled up the drive. Turning his head, he smiled down at Elizabeth, who waited by his side. He longed to take her hand, or at least offer her his arm, but he had already determined that this would not be the wisest course. Instead he merely inclined his head, and the two walked side by side to the carriage, which had just come to a halt at the base of the steps. In a matter of moments the entire party had exited the chaise, rejoicing at the sight of one another.

Darcy stepped forward, offering Elizabeth's uncle his hand. "Mr. Gardiner, welcome back."

"I thank you, sir. I trust you received my express? I hope it is not too much of an inconvenience to have us return so soon?"

"Not at all. My sister and I are happy to receive you."

Mrs. Gardiner turned from where she and Mary had been speaking with Elizabeth a few steps away. "Pray, how is Miss Darcy? She has been in our thoughts."

"That is very kind, madam. And I am happy to report that my sister is much recovered. She has been resting in her rooms these past few days, but I am hopeful that she will be well enough to dine with us this evening."

Before the Gardiners could respond, the steady clip of horse's hooves drew everyone's attention and all turned to see another carriage rapidly approaching. The vehicle drew closer and Darcy's smile widened. Beside him, he heard

Elizabeth's sharp intake of breath and watched as she lifted her skirts and hurried to meet the slowing coach. Darcy strode after her, arriving just in time to clap Bingley on the back as his old friend jumped to the ground, his wife following in a more dignified fashion.

After a flurry of greetings, the group began making their way towards the house, Bingley falling into step beside his friend as Mr. Gardiner followed with the ladies.

"I hope you will forgive our delayed arrival, Darcy. We had anticipated a speedier journey but Jane has been feeling a bit fatigued, so we limited our travel to only a few hours each day." For a moment Darcy thought he saw Bingley color, but his friend had already turned to look back at his wife.

Glancing over his shoulder, Darcy noted that Jane Bingley did appear somewhat weary, but she was presently arm in arm with Elizabeth and a happy smile lit her features.

"Of course, do not concern yourself," Darcy answered. "I believe your usual rooms have been prepared, unless you and Mrs. Bingley would prefer separate chambers? The Gardiners are in the Rose Rooms, but there are several other apartments available."

To Darcy's surprise, Bingley's flush deepened. "Oh, no, no... do not trouble yourself. Jane and I will be most comfortable... That is to say, my usual chambers will do very well."

Darcy turned away to hide his amusement. "I had thought as much. I will leave it to you to show your wife the way. We dine at half past five."

❄

The dining room was awash with candlelight as the extended party gathered for the evening meal.

Entering the parlor with Elizabeth on one arm and Georgiana on the other, Darcy noted that his sister still looked tired, but her eyes sparkled in a way he had not seen in many weeks. His gaze drifted to Grant who stood awkwardly to one side, briefly wondering if the doctor's presence had anything to do with his sister's heightened spirits. It had been Elizabeth's idea to extend the invitation to the physician, and Darcy was glad he had taken her advice. To see his sister well and happy was something he would always go to great lengths to accomplish.

Settling Georgiana into her seat at the head of the table, Darcy moved to his usual place at the opposite end, his hand resting possessively on the small of Elizabeth's back. As he pulled out her chair, he noticed that Mr. Gardiner followed his movements with keen interest, and Darcy quickly turned away. Propriety be damned! This was one meal where he would have the woman he loved by his side.

Out of the corner of his vision he took in Grant standing uncertainly to his sister's left. Lifting his head, Darcy offered a brief nod—surprised at the warmth that washed over him at the look of happiness he saw reflected in Georgiana's expression.

When the entire party had been seated, Darcy once again rose to his feet, immediately garnering everyone's attention. "If you would indulge me for a moment, I would like to propose a toast." All eyes were fixed upon him as Darcy raised his glass. "I hope you will join me in drinking to my sister's good health, and to Dr. Grant, for his expert care." He turned to face the physician, swallowing down the knot that tightened his throat. "I will be forever in your debt."

Georgiana and Grant both colored as everyone around the table murmured their good wishes, but when the footman approached, Darcy waved him away.

"Before we commence with the meal, I have one other brief announcement. Yesterday, I made an offer of marriage to Miss Elizabeth Bennet, and to my delight and, quite frankly, my amazement, she has accepted me." Darcy rested one hand on Elizabeth's shoulder, and she smiled up at him. "As we have not yet had the opportunity to obtain Mr. Bennet's blessing, I hope you will respect our wish to keep this a private matter for the time being, but we wanted you all to share our joy."

There was a moment of stunned silence, and then the table erupted, with everyone present seeming to speak at once.

"Oh, William, what wonderful news," Georgiana gasped. "I had hoped this would come to pass! I could not wish for a better sister," she added, her gaze falling on Elizabeth, who was at that moment being enveloped in a tight hug by Jane, who had leapt from her place farther down the table.

"Lizzy, I am so happy for you," Jane breathed, laying a hand lightly on the swell of her waist. "I believe we will have many things to celebrate over the coming months."

Elizabeth's eyes widened at the light flush creeping up her sister's cheeks, before Jane said softly, "We shall speak later."

On Darcy's wave, the footmen finally began making the rounds with the first course, as Mary surprised everyone by remarking, "And here I was feeling sorry about you missing the Lakes, Lizzy. But it seems you had plenty here to occupy your attention."

Darcy choked on a swallow of wine, as Mr. Gardiner regarded him from across the table.

"Yes, I look forward to hearing all about it, Mr. Darcy."

The party did not separate after the meal, instead repairing to the music room where Mary, Elizabeth, and Georgiana took turns exhibiting on the pianoforte, much to everyone's delight. However, it was not long before Jane expressed fatigue, and Elizabeth offered to accompany her sister to the Bingleys' rooms.

The door had barely closed behind them when Elizabeth swept her beloved sister into a light embrace. "Oh, Jane, you are positively glowing!" Pulling back slightly, she studied her sister's face. "But are you certain you should be traveling? I would hate to think that you have put your health in jeopardy on my account."

Jane flushed, loosening herself from her sister's gentle hold. "No, I am well. Charles has been taking very good care of me, and I still have some months to go before my confinement. But come, I wish to hear all about you and

Mr. Darcy. I am so happy for you, Lizzy! Charles and I have long thought the two of you were remarkably well-suited."

Elizabeth could not suppress the smile that lifted her cheeks as she led her sister over to a small sofa by the window. "Yes, I believe we are. Although it took me some time to come to that conclusion."

"Oh, won't Mamma be pleased," cried Jane. "A babe on the way and three daughters married!"

To Jane's obvious confusion, Elizabeth's smile faded.

"Lizzy? What is it? Are you not happy with your decision? Tell me what is amiss, for I can see something is not as it should be."

Settling into the seat beside her sister, Elizabeth sighed. "You know me too well. There is something I would speak to you about, though it is nothing to do with Mr. Darcy." Elizabeth studied her reflection in the darkened glass before reaching to smooth the fabric of her skirt. "Actually, it is about Lydia."

"Lydia?" echoed Jane, her brow lifting in surprise.

Elizabeth nodded. "I trust you have heard the news about the lieutenant's new commission and their subsequent removal to Newcastle?"

Jane returned her sister's nod. "Of course. Lydia wasted no time in notifying us of her good fortune. Mamma took to her bed for two days, but was soon persuaded that the event was to be celebrated, even if it did mean her youngest daughter would now reside at the opposite end of the kingdom. But what is troubling you, Lizzy? I know you cannot be regretting having our dear sister settled so far from home."

Elizabeth pursed her lips. "No, in that you are correct. What does concern me is the manner in which Mr. Hughes came to purchase his commission."

"Yes, I *had* wondered about that…" At the expression on Elizabeth's face, Jane's eyes grew round. "Oh! You think Charles was responsible?" When Elizabeth did not speak, Jane continued, "I cannot say I blame you for thinking so, but I must assure you that he was not."

"But… how can you be so certain? You know better than anyone Mr. Hughes had no fortune when he and Lydia wed. And Mr. Bingley has stepped in before…"

Jane flushed. "You are correct, of course. But Charles swears it was not him. And I know he would not lie to me, Lizzy."

"No, of course not. But that is so strange. If it was not Mr. Bingley, and it could not have been Papa, then who was it?"

To Elizabeth's surprise, Jane's flush deepened and she pressed her lips together, as if to keep herself from speaking.

"Jane? What is it?"

"Well, of course, there is no way to be certain… but Charles thinks… well, Charles guessed that perhaps it was Mr. Darcy."

"Mr. Darcy! But he is in no way connected with Mr. Hughes. Why would he do such a thing?"

Jane's eyebrows lifted, and it was Elizabeth's turn to blush. "Certainly not! We had not even reached an understanding when this occurred."

To Elizabeth's dismay, Jane just smiled.

"But how would he have known..."

"Why, from Lydia's own lips, of course. Do you not remember her going on about it when we dined together at Netherfield? Charles reminded me that Mr. Darcy intervened, saying he was certain that an opportunity would present itself."

Elizabeth shook her head. "No, he was only trying to turn the conversation—to keep Lydia from further embarrassing herself."

"Perhaps. But Charles says it is just the type of thing Mr. Darcy would do to please you."

Elizabeth shook her head, as if to better make sense of what her sister was suggesting. "But... then why would he not tell me of it?" Suddenly Elizabeth's jaw dropped as she remembered she had conversed with Mr. Darcy on this very topic the day Lydia's letter arrived. Searching back, Elizabeth struggled to remember Mr. Darcy's exact words. Had he not agreed with her that it was most likely Mr. Bingley who had purchased the commission? No, he had not agreed exactly, he had only said that whoever had done so was likely able to afford it. Elizabeth felt her face pale as her sister's worried eyes fixed on hers.

"What is it, Lizzy? Are you unwell?"

Before Elizabeth could answer, a sharp rap sounded at the door and Mr. Bingley poked his head inside the room. "Ah! My apologies," he said, moving to withdraw. "I can see you are still conversing..."

Elizabeth hurried to her feet. "No, pray, come in. It is late and Jane needs her rest. Have the others retired?"

Charles entered the room, coming to kiss Jane sweetly on the cheek before turning to face his newest sister.

"Yes. Grant took his leave some time ago. The rest of us have only just come up." Lifting his hand to affectionately rub his wife's shoulder he continued, "I must say, I enjoyed making the doctor's acquaintance. He is a fine fellow. I wonder... Do you think he might be a suitable match for Caroline?"

Elizabeth pulled in a quick breath, struggling to hide her alarm. She could not imagine a more unlikely pairing and was fairly certain Caroline Bingley would never consider the physician as a potential suitor, even if the gentleman could be persuaded. It was bad enough to imagine Miss Bingley's reaction when she realized Mr. Darcy was no longer on the market.

"I do not believe it would be wise to raise your sister's expectations," Elizabeth answered cautiously, "as it would appear Mr. Grant's affections are already engaged... elsewhere."

"Oh?" Bingley studied Elizabeth for a moment before his eyes grew wide. "Oh! You cannot mean...? And Darcy has agreed to the match?"

Again, Elizabeth chose her words with care. "He has agreed to the possibility of a courtship, if his sister desires it. Although nothing will transpire until next season when Miss Darcy is out."

Bingley released a low whistle. "Well, I'll be! I never thought I'd see the day... A physician! I believe you are a good influence on him, Elizabeth."

Elizabeth smiled, leaning down to kiss her sister good night.

"I take very little credit for it, sir. I believe Mr. Darcy's feelings on such matters shifted some time ago. And as we all know, for a man to conquer *himself* is the first and noblest of all victories."

With a last glance at Mr. Bingley's puzzled expression, Elizabeth left the room.

CHAPTER 28

R eaching the outer corridor, Elizabeth hesitated. She knew she should return to her chambers, but her mind was still reeling from her conversation with Jane, and the desire to speak to Mr. Darcy was strong. Chewing the inside of her cheek, Elizabeth glanced down the passageway. Surely it was too soon for him to be asleep, and they *were* betrothed, after all. Besides, her aunt and uncle would wish to depart early on the morrow, so if she did not seek him out now, she would likely have little opportunity before they met again in Hertfordshire.

Squaring her shoulders, Elizabeth turned away from her rooms and began walking in the opposite direction. Passing Georgiana's chambers, she continued on until she reached the last door at the end of the corridor, the one she knew led to Mr. Darcy's apartment. For a moment her courage wavered, but before she could lose her nerve she lifted her hand, tapping softly upon the burnished wood.

When there was no response, Elizabeth stepped back, unsure if she should knock again or submit to her reservations and turn back. But the decision was taken out of her hands when the knob twisted, and the door opened.

Mr. Darcy stared back at her, his eyes wide. Taking a step forward, his gaze swept up and down the corridor, before settling on Elizabeth's face. "Elizabeth! Is anything the matter? You are not unwell, I hope?"

"No; I beg your pardon, I know I should have waited until morning. I... I only wished to speak to you... That is, to ask you..." Her voice faltered and she was certain her cheeks must be the brightest shade of scarlet.

She made to step away, but Darcy reached out, capturing her hand and gently guiding her across the threshold.

Entering the expansive chamber, Elizabeth's eyes instantly fixed upon the enormous four-poster bed in the center of the room and her face burned.

Closing the door, Darcy briefly held a finger to his lips. "Wait here. I will return in a moment," he murmured, and Elizabeth watched as he moved to the far corner of the room. Reaching the entrance to an adjoining chamber, he stopped, and to Elizabeth's horror, addressed someone inside.

"Pierce, you may go down. I have decided to answer some correspondence before retiring."

A gasp slipped from Elizabeth's throat. Mr. Darcy's valet, of course! How could she have been stupid enough to think he would be alone? Her eyes widened as a man's voice answered from the next room.

"I can wait, if you would like, sir."

"No, that will not be necessary," Darcy answered evenly.

"Very well. I bid you a good evening then."

Panic forced the breath from Elizabeth's lungs, and she leapt for the door, wrenching it open. But before she could make her way into the corridor she heard the sound of another door closing and Darcy's hand was on her shoulder.

"Don't go."

Darcy reached out, closing the door with a soft click. Elizabeth's gaze lifted for a fleeting moment before flitting across the room. When she finally spoke, her eyes were on the carpet. "Pray, forgive me, Mr. Darcy. I used very poor judgment in coming here."

Lightly touching his fingers to Elizabeth's chin, Darcy tipped up her gaze. "Elizabeth, I wish you would call me by my given name, especially here. I would prefer not to be *Mr. Darcy* in my bedchamber."

Elizabeth's eyes grew round and a deep flush colored her cheeks. "Oh, God! Whatever was I thinking? It did not even occur to me that your valet... Do you think he heard me at the door?"

Darcy tilted his head, a grin tugging at his lips. "I do not believe so. You knocked very quietly. And even if he did, he would have assumed it was Georgiana coming to bid me a good night, as she often does." His smile deepened. "Although I will say, we are both lucky that I happened to be closest to the door. If Pierce had been the one to answer, I am quite certain you would have given the poor man an apoplexy."

Elizabeth's hands flew to her cheeks and her eyes closed in abject mortification. "Mamma has always said my wild ways would get me into trouble one day, and now I can see she was correct."

As Darcy watched, tears formed along her dark lashes and his heart melted. Gently wrapping his arm around her shoulders, he guided her into the adjoining parlor, settling her on a leather sofa in front of the hearth.

Elizabeth let him lead her, but refused to meet his gaze, instead staring into the empty grate. "What must you think of me?" she whispered. "Coming to your bedchamber in the middle of the night. Risking your reputation and my own..." Abruptly her eyes flew open. "You must have thought I came here to—"

Darcy flinched, holding up his hand. "Elizabeth. Pray, allow me to speak." He paused, studying her face as he collected his thoughts.

"First, let me say that finding you outside my chambers was indeed unexpected. However, it was also one of the most delightful surprises of my life. As for what I thought you were doing here," he continued, reaching for her hand and entwining his fingers with hers, "I was under the impression that you came to speak with me, as you clearly stated when I opened the door. It never occurred to me to think otherwise.

"Now, as far as reputations go, while I care very little

about my own in these circumstances, I do care about yours. But as we are already betrothed, in the unlikely event that anyone should find out about this visit, I would happily marry you tomorrow." Pausing for a moment Darcy felt a smile overtaking his features, and he leaned forward, his voice a low hum. "As for your *wild ways*, I must own that I am quite partial to them. Remind me to tell your mother so, the next time we meet."

Elizabeth stared back at him. "Then, you are not angry with me?"

"Angry with you? Whatever for?"

"For... embarrassing you, in front of your servant. We cannot be certain your valet did not hear my voice."

Despite his best efforts, Darcy's gaze traveled her body. "Elizabeth, I can assure you, *anger* is the furthest thing from my mind right now. And as for Pierce, even if he did hear, he is paid to be discreet." For a moment he paused. "Elizabeth, I do feel I should ask, what of your maid? Did she not see you leave your own bedchamber?"

For the first time since she entered the room, one side of Elizabeth's mouth kicked up into her usual arch smile. "No, I dismissed her earlier in the evening. As my aunt and uncle are now in residence, I did not feel there could be any objection."

The air filled with the deep rumble of Darcy's laughter. "Well, we shall have to take care in returning you to your chambers, nonetheless. Now, as I think we have exhausted the topic of you coming here, would you like to tell me what you wanted to speak with me about?"

Once again, Elizabeth colored. "It is so trivial, I do not think I am brave enough to tell you after all of this."

"If it brought you here, I am certain it was not trivial. I believe you said you wished to ask me a question?"

"Yes, I..." Elizabeth's voice trailed off and she glanced nervously around the room. Taking a deep breath, she began again, "It is about Lydia. I was speaking with my sister, and according to Jane, Mr. Bingley did not purchase Mr. Hughes' commission."

At Elizabeth's words, Darcy tensed. "No," he finally answered. "I did."

Elizabeth's eyes widened, but before she could speak, Darcy continued, "Forgive me for not saying anything sooner."

"But, why would you do such a thing? Lydia does not deserve that type of consideration. And why did you not tell me of it when I questioned you after receiving my sister's letter?"

Darcy sighed. "Again, I must beg your pardon. I assure you I had the best intentions, but I can see now that it was not my place to make such a gesture. Not without consulting you first." Looking into Elizabeth's eyes, he willed her to understand. "As for why... While it was a privilege to help the lieutenant, and I had hoped Mrs. Hughes would also be pleased, I must admit that I thought mainly of you."

"I am afraid I do not understand. How was this to please *me*?"

Darcy squirmed slightly in his seat. "Again, I realize it was wrong, but when we spoke in Hertfordshire this spring, you indicated that Miss Mary and Miss Catherine might benefit from having some distance placed between themselves and Mrs. Hughes. Of course, you must know that I would never have taken such a step if I did not think Mr. and Mrs. Hughes would benefit equally from the arrangement."

Elizabeth looked at him, her eyes wide. "But the cost!"

To her obvious surprise, Darcy laughed. "Forgive me if I sound arrogant, Elizabeth, but the cost does not signify. It was comparatively little to ensure the happiness of all concerned."

"And can you tell me why you did not inform me of this when I received Lydia's letter?"

At her question, Darcy withdrew his hand, tugging on his cuffs and looking contritely about the room. "The money was given anonymously. It never occurred to me that you would question where it came from. I did not wish for you to feel indebted to me."

Elizabeth frowned and Darcy's stomach sank.

"I beg you would forgive me. You have my word that nothing of the sort will occur again."

Elizabeth regarded him with a serious expression. "Meaning that in future you will consult me before throwing money at my family?"

Darcy smiled at her teasing. "I will."

"Very well, then. I forgive you."

"Thank you," he breathed, leaning forward to press his lips against her brow. "If I had lost you over this…"

"You will never lose me." Pulling back, Elizabeth gave her head a clearing shake. "In truth, I still cannot understand how I have managed to regain your affections. After your behavior at the theater, I was certain you wished to have nothing more to do with me."

"Yes, I realize now that I should have been more precise when I introduced you to my cousin. It was never my intention to cause you any distress."

"I am embarrassed to admit that seeing you with Lady Margaret elicited feelings that would do me no credit to recount. But I was actually referring to your reaction to Lydia's marriage. I could feel your censure when you spoke of it that night, and I imagined you must have been congratulating yourself on escaping any connection to my family."

Darcy blinked back at her. "Forgive me, but I do not understand. Why would I take issue with your sister's marriage? From what I have observed, she and the lieutenant—nay, captain—seem very happy."

Elizabeth instantly paled. "So, you do not know?"

"Know...?"

Elizabeth looked away. "My sister's marriage was a patched-up affair. Lydia was discovered in a compromising position and the lieutenant refused to offer for her. He was only persuaded to do so when Mr. Bingley increased my sister's portion." She paused. "Mr. Bingley settled five thousand pounds on Lydia to bring the marriage about. I assumed you knew."

Slowly, Darcy shook his head. "No. Bingley keeps his own counsel these days, as well he should. Though now I understand why you suspected that he purchased the lieutenant's commission."

"There is something else. Mr. Bingley has offered to increase my own dowry, as well as that of my other sisters, by an equal sum. While Mary and Kitty may do as they please, I have already refused him. So, you should know that if you still wish to marry me, I come to you with nothing."

Darcy gazed back at the woman he loved, taking in the defiant tilt to her chin, and his heart swelled with pride. Reaching out his hand, he caressed Elizabeth's cheek, tucking one loose curl behind her ear. "Elizabeth," he whispered, "that is a gross misrepresentation. You come to me with *everything*."

Elizabeth stifled a sob and her face crumpled as Darcy folded her into his arms. "I have no need of money," he murmured.

After a moment she pulled away, smiling through her tears. "Yes, I know. I have it on good authority that you are worth ten thousand a year."

Darcy grinned. "Actually, it is closer to twelve, but that was not my meaning. *What I meant* was that I would gladly give it all up—Pemberley, my standing in society, and every shilling to my name—if that is what it took to secure you as my wife."

Elizabeth opened her mouth but Darcy lifted her chin, staring into her eyes. "Do not doubt me, Elizabeth." When she did not answer, Darcy frowned. "What is it? If there is anything else troubling you, pray, tell me. We have had too many misunderstandings already."

Elizabeth nodded. "I agree. And that is why I also wished to tell you... about the dream. The one I had when

I was staying in your sister's apartment." After a moment she continued softly, "You were correct when you guessed that it was about the accident."

"I thought as much."

"It was also not the first time I'd had it."

Darcy's forehead puckered and he lifted her hand, placing a kiss upon her palm before saying tenderly, "I am so sorry, my love. That something I am responsible for has made you uneasy. That you should fear for your safety, even now..."

To Darcy's shame, Elizabeth's eyes filled with tears, but she was already shaking her head. "You misunderstand. My safety was never a concern. For while the dream does end in death, it is not my own... it is... yours."

"Mine? You dreamed I died in the accident?"

Elizabeth responded with a jerky nod.

"And this affected you in such a way?"

Again, Elizabeth nodded, but this time a small sob accompanied the gesture. "I... I dreamed you were killed, and I never got to tell you..."

"To tell me...?"

"That I loved you."

Darcy's heart exploded at her words, and despite his best intentions he slid forward, gathering Elizabeth into his embrace. "Shh... As you said, 'twas only a dream." Drawing back, something occurred to him and he studied her face. "You said you had had the dream before. When did you first have it?"

"In London, directly following the accident."

"Elizabeth... are you saying that you had feelings for

me all that time ago? That you cared for me, back in November? Why did you not say anything? When we ran into each other outside that dress shop... or when I saw you at the theater, or later at Netherfield..."

"Surely, you are not serious? What could I say? It is not a lady's place to tell a gentleman that she loves him. And after the way I treated you when you offered for me, those things I said..."

Closing the space between them, Darcy pressed his forehead to hers. They stayed like that for several seconds before Darcy's light laughter filled the chamber.

Elizabeth pulled back. "Why are you laughing?" she demanded as Darcy attempted to smother his grin.

"Forgive me. I just find it humorous that we seem to be particularly adept at misunderstanding one another. When we first met, I was convinced you teased me to show your regard, when in truth you despised me—"

"I did not despise you." A smile pulled at the corners of her mouth. "Oh, very well, I will admit I did not like you very much. But that was only because of the comments you made at the assembly when we were first introduced." Elizabeth deepened her voice and her face took on a severe expression, "*She is tolerable, but not handsome enough to tempt* me."

Darcy felt the color drain from his face. "You heard. I thought you might have. Good God, no wonder you hated me."

Elizabeth reached up, caressing his cheek. "I did not hate you. I think even then I was drawn to you, although I was too proud and stubborn to realize it."

"It was unpardonable of me to have uttered such a thing aloud, let alone in public. Especially when it was completely untrue."

Elizabeth leaned forward. "You are forgiven," she whispered.

"I do not deserve you. But I am going to spend the rest of my life attempting to be worthy of you, just the same." Moving to press a soft kiss to her cheek, Darcy stood. "Give me a moment. As you are here, there is something I wish for you to have."

Elizabeth watched as Darcy crossed into his bedchamber, returning a few minutes later with a flat velvet case. He resumed his seat, but sat contemplating her for some moments, the box unopened in his lap. When he finally spoke, his eyes were far away, lost in another time and place.

"When I was a boy," he began quietly, "my family spent several months of every year in Town. I never liked going there, mainly because there were often social obligations that took my parents away from me. But whenever they went out, my mother always came to bid me a good night, and I would admire her in her fine gowns and jewels. I thought she was the most beautiful woman in all the world." Darcy smiled, his expression softening. "One particular evening, she and my father were on their way to a ball... I had to have been about twelve or so; Georgiana was just a babe. My mother came to see me in my chambers. She was wearing a blue silk gown embroidered with tiny rosebuds and the jewels around her neck sparkled against her skin. The necklace she wore was not as grand or as showy as some of her other pieces, but it looked beautiful on her, and I told her how much I admired it. I remember she smiled, and leaned down to kiss me on the cheek.

"In any case, time went by, and I did not think any more about it after that. Then, one day, months after my mother's passing, a package arrived addressed to me. Inside it was a jeweler's box. This box." Darcy passed the case to Elizabeth. "Pray, open it," he continued, when Elizabeth hesitated.

Raising the lid, Elizabeth sucked in a breath. Reaching inside, she lifted the delicate chain, examining the blush-colored jewel that sparkled in the candlelight. Surrounding the circular stone, tiny diamonds formed leaves and vines that radiated from the center, giving the impression of a flower opening to the sun.

Next to her, Darcy spoke softly. "It is a pink sapphire. I am told the stone is quite rare." Studying Elizabeth's face, he added, "Of course, if it is not to your taste..."

Elizabeth looked up, tears blurring her vision. "No! It is exquisite. But... shouldn't this go to Georgiana?"

"No. Georgiana has the bulk of my mother's jewels, aside from the Darcy family heirlooms which will go to you after we are married. But this piece... actually there is a note."

Reaching back inside the box, Elizabeth retrieved a single sheet of paper, brittle with age. Before unfolding it, she glanced at Darcy, who nodded. Turning her attention back to the note, Elizabeth read:

William,

This necklace has been my most cherished posses-sion since your father presented it to me on the eve of our wedding, and I can think of no better legacy for you to pass along to your own bride one day. Choose wisely, and I know you will be as happy in your marriage as I have been in mine.

All my love,
AD

Elizabeth looked up at the man she loved. The man who would soon become her husband. "It is perfect."

Reaching for the jewels, Darcy slipped them around her neck. "You are the only woman I could have given this to. I have known that for quite some time."

Still clutching the note, Elizabeth wrapped him in her arms, kissing the edge of his jaw, and then the corner of his mouth. A deep groan reverberated in Darcy's throat before he turned his head, capturing her lips.

Within moments they were both gasping for air. Darcy was the first to pull away, holding Elizabeth at arm's length as he attempted to regulate his breathing. "Oh

God, Elizabeth, how I wish you were my wife already! But as you are not, I think you had better go. If you stay much longer, I am not sure I can be responsible for my actions."

Elizabeth stared up at him, her expression one of complete trust, and Darcy could not resist the urge to pull her soft body against his chest, kissing her hair as his hands caressed the length of her back. His fingers swept the row of buttons that ran down the bodice of her gown, and he moved to study her face.

"How will you manage with all these buttons, now that you have sent your maid away?" he murmured, causing Elizabeth to flush.

"With difficulty, I suppose."

The clock ticked as they studied one another's eyes.

"Turn around."

Elizabeth blinked.

"Turn around," Darcy repeated. Elizabeth hesitated before slowly doing as he bid.

Darcy's fingers grazed the nape of her neck, which was warm to his touch. Steeling his resolve, he deliberately gathered the silky material, working the long line of tiny buttons. Elizabeth shivered and Darcy stilled. When he had finally finished, neither of them moved. Then, very gradually, Darcy dipped his fingers beneath the neckline of the gown, drawing it past her collarbone and along the slope of her shoulder. Elizabeth gasped as the fabric slipped from her slim form, and Darcy's eyes slid closed. He remained motionless, attempting to master his self-control before leaning down to feather light kisses along the curve of her body. *Dear God.* The feel of her flushed skin against his lips was electrifying!

His heart began to pound with longing, and it was with great difficulty that he lifted the edge of her sleeve. Placing his hands on her shoulders, he carefully turned her back around. "There," he rasped. "That should make things easier."

"Thank you."

Squeezing her hand, Darcy rose, pulling Elizabeth to her feet. "Come. I think it is time you returned to your bedchamber. And let us pray no one sees you in this state, or your father will be well within his rights to call me out. His consent will be the least of our worries if I do not live to see our wedding day."

CHAPTER 29

"So, you wish to marry my daughter?" Mr. Bennet peered over the tops of his spectacles, an unfathomable expression shadowing his eyes.

Across from him, Darcy straightened in his chair, tugging at his neckcloth. "I do."

"Well, I must say, this is an interesting development. You may recall that when last we spoke on this topic, you refused to even consider offering for my Lizzy. Your opinion on the matter seemed quite fixed."

Darcy swallowed. "Yes, I am afraid I owe you an apology for that. Although strictly speaking, you are correct, I realize now that I did not make my thoughts entirely clear. My refusal was based solely upon my belief that your daughter was already decided against me. And it was never my wish to force Miss Bennet into marriage, no matter how much I desired it."

"What made you think she would have refused you?"

Darcy looked down for a moment before answering. "It was not conjecture, sir. I had offered for her once before, and on that occasion your daughter did indeed refuse me. Most emphatically. When you came to see me in London, I did not have sufficient reason to believe her feelings had altered since that time." Darcy studied the expression on the older gentleman's face and his stomach clenched. "She did not tell you."

"No, she did not." Mr. Bennet continued to regard Darcy with a serious expression. "But now my daughter has accepted you?"

"Yes."

"Well then, Mr. Darcy, I am afraid I must ask: What has changed? Presumably, Lizzy's reasons for rejecting your suit would be the same now as they were then. Which leads me to wonder exactly what occurred on her visit to your home? Have you seduced her in some way? Offered her some type of monetary compensation? Or was seeing your grand estate too great a temptation?"

Despite his best intentions, Darcy felt an over-whelming rage building inside his chest. It took all his willpower to calm himself enough to reply. When he did, his voice held an icy edge. "Normally, I would not dignify such vile suppositions with a response, but as you are Elizabeth's father, I will answer you. First, I have never seduced any woman, least of all your daughter. I have a young sister who is entrusted to my care, and I treat all women as I would wish her to be treated. Alongside my sister, Elizabeth is more precious to me than any other individual on the face of this earth. I would sooner rip out my own heart than hurt her, nor would I ever force her to do anything against her will." Darcy paused for a moment to steady his breathing. "As to your second point, if you know your daughter at all, you must be aware that no amount of money or material advantage could ever persuade her to accept me. Miss Bennet is the least mercenary woman I have ever encountered. To insinuate otherwise is a slight against her character that I will not tolerate."

Darcy stared back at Elizabeth's father, expecting to see righteous indignation in the other gentleman's expression, but to his surprise, Mr. Bennet's eyes sparkled with amusement.

"Well said, sir! If nothing else, at least I know you may be relied upon to defend my daughter's honor. However, you have not answered my question. If she refused you once, why has she accepted you now? Surely there is some explanation?"

Darcy expelled a sigh, glad to see that he had not fatally offended the man who held the key to his future happiness. "That I cannot answer. What I can say is that it was not the work of a moment. I am afraid when I first expressed my... affection for your daughter, I did so poorly. Unbeknownst to me, Miss Bennet had already formed a negative opinion of me, and to my shame, my manner of address on that occasion did nothing to alter her opinion. However, since last winter, I have had the good fortune to be in your daughter's company on numerous occasions. I have seen firsthand what a warm, compassionate person she is, and I have struggled to be worthy of her. To my good fortune, it seems she was willing to give me a second chance."

"I see."

"Of course, this is only speculation on my part. As the question concerns Miss Bennet's feelings, perhaps you would be better served in applying to her."

Again, Mr. Bennet grinned. "Rest assured, Mr. Darcy, Lizzy has made her feelings for you perfectly clear. In fact, she came to me not long after her return from Derbyshire and told me of her great love for you."

Darcy's cheeks grew warm and he briefly looked away before confusion wrinkled his brow. "I am afraid I do not understand. If you had already spoken to Elizabeth..."

"I had. And while it was comforting to know her sentiments, it was important for me to know yours. Pray, forgive me, Mr. Darcy, for putting you through your paces today, but I needed to be certain. Lizzy's happiness is of paramount importance to me and I do not believe she would be content in a marriage without affection—on both sides."

"Then... we have your permission to marry?"

"Elizabeth is two and twenty, sir. You do not need my permission to wed her."

"That may be true, but I know she would not wish to enter into a marriage without your blessing."

Again, Mr. Bennet smiled. "Then you have it. Along with my best wishes."

Darcy's breath left his body in an audible rush. "I thank you, sir. But I do have one more question. Given your concern for Elizabeth's happiness, how is it you would have forced her into a marriage solely for the sake of propriety?"

"Ah, you speak of my visit to you in London?"

"I do."

"Well, that is simple. You see, Mr. Darcy, I may not be as outspoken as my wife, but I know my daughter. When you were in Hertfordshire that autumn, I observed the two of you together, and I believed Lizzy had formed a strong attachment to you."

At Mr. Bennet's words, Darcy's flush deepened. Of course, he had once labored under the same misapprehension, but he knew now that he had been utterly mistaken. "Forgive me, sir, but what made you think so? When Miss Bennet engaged me in conversation, it was only to argue."

Mr. Bennet barked out a laugh. "Ah! But you see, that is how I knew. Lizzy rarely speaks unkindly to anyone. If she truly disliked you, she would have ignored you altogether. The fact that she argued with you meant her feelings were engaged. I have never seen her behave in such a way with any other gentleman."

"But, what of my sentiments?" he asked. "Just now you stated that you would not see Elizabeth marry a man who did not love her in return, and yet you did not hesitate to force me to offer for her, not knowing whether my own feelings were engaged."

"Indeed, you are correct. However, I had every reason to believe they were. Not only did I watch Elizabeth when the two of you were together, but I studied you as well. I am a man, after all, Mr. Darcy, and not such an old one that I do not recognize the look of a gentleman in love.

The expression on your face when you danced with Lizzy at the Netherfield ball spoke volumes."

"But then... today..."

"Ah, yes, today." Mr. Bennet leaned back in his chair, steepling his fingers. "When I traveled to London, I was convinced that you and my daughter were well-suited, though perhaps both too stubborn to recognize that fact and act upon it. That is why I attempted to force your hand. However, when you refused, I began to doubt my conviction—and your affections. While my assumption regarding my daughter's feelings proved to be correct, I knew I must make certain of your own. I am glad to see I was not mistaken."

For the first time that day, a smile shattered Darcy's cool reserve. "You were not."

Mr. Bennet rose, extending his hand and Darcy accepted it with gratitude.

"You have my blessing, Mr. Darcy. I expect you will treat my daughter well. If not, you will answer to me."

"I would expect nothing less, sir."

CHAPTER 30

The day of Darcy and Elizabeth's wedding dawned bright and clear. Although Darcy had given Elizabeth the choice of waiting for banns to be read and marrying at any date of her choosing, in the end she was as anxious to begin their life together as he, and the two were married by special license on a beautiful summer morning a mere seven days from the day Darcy obtained Mr. Bennet's blessing.

The ceremony finally over, Darcy stood on Netherfield's stone terrace watching his bride move amongst their guests, saying her goodbyes. Seeing Elizabeth approach his aunt and uncle, Darcy tensed, but his lips lifted in a genuine smile as he watched Lady Matlock gather Elizabeth into a tight embrace.

"She has charmed them already, I see," Colonel Fitzwilliam drawled, coming up to stand at Darcy's side.

Turning to face his cousin, Darcy's smile widened.

"She has. And I have you to thank. I know Lord and Lady Matlock would never have attended the nuptials had you not insisted upon it."

The colonel grinned. "They did take some convincing, especially given the short notice. But I thought it important for them to form their own opinions about Miss Bennet—forgive me—*Mrs. Darcy*, rather than believe the lies Lady Catherine has been bandying about."

Darcy's expression darkened and Colonel Fitzwilliam snorted in reply. "Oh, do not look so glum. You know Mother will waste no time in regaling the *ton* with tales of your bride's worthiness. By the time you return from your wedding trip, I have no doubt the whole of London will be falling at Elizabeth's feet."

Darcy nodded, hoping his cousin was not overestimating Lady Matlock's powers of persuasion. "Your mother has my gratitude. Not only for her kindness to Elizabeth, but for allowing Georgiana to stay with them while the two of us are away."

Colonel Fitzwilliam reached for a glass of wine from a passing servant, taking a lengthy swallow. "She needs no thanks for that. She loves having Georgie with her. But speaking of your wedding trip, where exactly are you going? You have been quite mysterious about it all."

"I was wondering the same thing," said Bingley, overhearing the last bit of conversation and coming to join them. "Jane has been trying to wheedle it out of me, but I told her you have not said a word."

"No. Nor do I intend to."

Bingley let out a laugh. "Good man! I do wish I had

thought of that before Jane and I took our trip to Bath. A letter arrived from Mrs. Bennet nearly every day, and Jane felt compelled to answer them all. It was most vexing." Pausing for a moment, Bingley continued, "Oh! Speaking of the Bennets, I completely forgot. Mr. Bennet wished to have a word with you before you depart. I believe you will find him in the library."

Darcy smiled. It did not surprise him that Elizabeth's father would choose the solace of Bingley's library over the chaos of a garden full of guests, especially when that chaos was continually punctuated by Mrs. Bennet crowing to all and sundry about how clever her second daughter was to have refused Mr. Collins.

"Thank you, I shall seek him out directly," Darcy answered, taking a step towards the French doors that led to the conservatory. "Oh, and Bingley, I also wished to express my thanks for hosting the breakfast and for allowing so many of our guests to reside at Netherfield. It was exceedingly generous of you."

Bingley waved his hand in a dismissive manner. "Think nothing of it. It was the least Jane and I could do to spare Mrs. Bennet's nerves. 'Tis good to see you and Elizabeth so happy, Darcy."

Colonel Fitzwilliam reached for Darcy's hand, simultaneously clapping him on the back. "I second that," he said, before leaning in closer to add, "It certainly took you long enough."

"Well, Mr. Darcy, now that you have succeeded in securing the heart and hand of my favorite daughter, I am certain there will not be a sensible conversation to be had at Longbourn for the foreseeable future. I hope you realize your good fortune."

Darcy crossed the floor of Bingley's library, settling into the chair opposite his wife's father. "I do. And I thank you again for your blessing. I hope you know that Elizabeth means the world to me. I intend to dedicate my life to making her happy."

Mr. Bennet nodded and after a moment, Darcy continued, "However, if you will allow me to say so, I do not believe you give Miss Mary and Miss Catherine enough credit. I have found them both to be intelligent and capable. Perhaps all that is lacking is a bit of guidance. I think with some slight direction, they may both surprise you."

Mr. Bennet rubbed his chin. "Hmm… Perhaps you are correct. With Lydia now in Newcastle, I may have a fighting chance after all."

At length, Darcy reached into the pocket of his coat, extracting a thick sheaf of papers. "Actually, I am glad we have found a moment alone. There is something I wished to give you." Mr. Bennet looked at him questioningly, and Darcy added, "It is your copy of the settlement agreement."

"Ah. I thank you, sir."

When Darcy did not immediately release the documents, Mr. Bennet tilted his head. "I trust nothing has changed since we signed the papers in my brother Phillips' offices?"

Darcy replied with a slow shake of his head. "With the original settlement, no. However, I have had my solicitor draw up an addendum to that agreement. I have already showed it to Elizabeth, but I wanted to make sure I had your approval as well."

Looking baffled, Mr. Bennet said, "I will be happy to read it, though I think it unlikely that I would not approve. You have already been extremely generous with my daughter."

Darcy frowned. "I do not see it as generosity, sir. As I have previously stated, as my wife, Elizabeth will share in all that I have. However, this amendment does not specifically pertain to Mrs. Darcy. Perhaps you would like to read it, and then I would be happy to answer any questions." Darcy handed over the folded parchment. "It is the document at the back."

Quiet filled the room as the older gentleman perched his spectacles upon his nose, separating the last sheet from the stack. When he had finally finished reading, he refolded the papers and removed his glasses, raising his eyes to the young man who was now his son. "Mr. Darcy, I do not know what to say."

"You needn't say anything, other than to state your consent. Pray, know that it is my fervent hope that your good health continues for many years. But, as Longbourn is entailed to Mr. Collins, I wanted you to rest assured that Mrs. Bennet, as well as Miss Mary and Miss Catherine if they do not marry, will always be well provided for. I will leave it to you to decide whether you wish to disclose the information in that document, but

Elizabeth and I both felt it would give you peace of mind to know."

"Indeed, it does, Mr. Darcy, and I thank you, from the bottom of my heart." Mr. Bennet paused, but it wasn't long before his playful smile returned. "As to whether I should choose to share this intelligence with my wife and daughters, I think it best we do not. If Mrs. Bennet were to see the amount you have agreed to settle upon her at my death, I believe I may run the risk of being poisoned in my sleep."

Before too many more hours had gone by, Elizabeth found herself on Longbourn's circular drive, watching as the last of her belongings were secured to the back of Mr. Darcy's carriage. Glancing down at her attire, she wondered again if she ought to have changed, but her gown—an intricately embroidered ivory muslin of Jane's that had been hastily made over as a wedding present to her sister—was so beautiful it had seemed a shame to wear it for so short a time.

Before she could think any more on the subject, her husband was at her back, slipping his arms around her waist and bending to kiss her lightly on the cheek.

"Well, Mrs. Darcy, are you ready to depart?"

Elizabeth grinned, relaxing into his embrace. "I am." Turning her head she added, "Are you still intent on keeping our destination a secret? Or might I now learn where we will be spending our first night as husband and wife?"

Darcy looked down at her and his cheeks dimpled. "It remains a surprise, for now. However, I may be persuaded to tell you once we are inside the carriage." His lips brushed the nape of her neck, and Elizabeth shivered. Turning to face her family who had begun gathering in the drive, Elizabeth began walking in her father's direction, but she had not gone two steps before Mrs. Bennet rushed past, her eyes fixed on Mr. Darcy's lacquered coach.

"Oh, Lizzy! How grand you are, traveling in such a fine carriage! I am certain it will be like riding on a cloud! You will hardly notice the bumps in the road with a conveyance such as this!"

Elizabeth shifted her gaze, attempting to hide her embarrassment. Out of the corner of her eye, she studied her new husband, but to her surprise, his smile remained firmly in place.

"I am glad you approve of it, madam. It would be my pleasure to have a similar conveyance at your disposal whenever you wish to visit Pemberley, so you may travel in comfort."

At Darcy's offer, Mrs. Bennet's eyes grew round and for a moment Elizabeth thought her mother might actually swoon. Instead she merely nodded numbly before wandering closer to the coach and continuing to extol the benefits of marrying a gentleman in possession of a good fortune.

Shaking her head, Elizabeth turned to her father who bent to kiss her on the brow. "Goodbye, Lizzy. Be well."

Elizabeth nodded, her throat tight, but she was spared having to reply by her husband, who was once again at her elbow. "You shall see each other very soon. At Christmastime, certainly, but you are welcome at Pemberley whenever you choose. Elizabeth and I hope you will visit often."

Swallowing down the emotion that washed over her, Elizabeth moved on to her sisters, hugging each one of them in turn. It was strange to think that Mary and Kitty would be the only two left at Longbourn now, but Elizabeth knew that Jane would watch over them, and hopefully without Lydia's disruptive influence, her sisters would continue to thrive.

"You must both write to me often and tell me all the news," Elizabeth whispered. Mary and Kitty nodded, and then Darcy was beside her, handing Elizabeth into the carriage, and with a lurch they were on their way.

Darcy watched as Elizabeth leaned out the of window, waving until they reached the lane. When her family home was no longer visible, she settled against the squabs, and Darcy slid forward in his seat. "Are you well, my love?" he asked softly.

Elizabeth smiled back at him. "Yes. Just a little bit sad. But I will see them often."

"You shall," Darcy agreed. "However, I was referring to... That is, I realized this is the first time we have been alone together in a carriage since the day of the accident."

"Oh. Yes, I suppose I had not realized..."

Pulling himself to his feet, Darcy moved from the rear-facing seat, taking the place beside his wife. "Do you mind if I sit with you?" he asked.

Elizabeth immediately shook her head, absentmindedly fingering the jewels that sparkled against her collarbone. Darcy studied her with a pensive smile. "The necklace looks beautiful on you."

A slight flush colored Elizabeth's cheeks. "Thank you. I will cherish it, always. And I hope someday to pass it down to our own son's betrothed. Perhaps it will become a family tradition."

"My mother would have liked that."

Reaching out, Darcy took Elizabeth's hand, locking her fingers with his and squeezing tight.

Elizabeth's fine eyes sparkled up at him. "It was good to see Georgiana looking so well. She is fully recovered, I hope?"

"She is, thank heavens."

"Does she... That is, have you had an opportunity to speak to her? About Mr. Grant?"

Darcy paused. "Yes. We spoke of it at some length on the journey to Hertfordshire."

"And? What are her feelings on the matter?"

Darcy sighed, turning briefly to gaze out at the passing scenery. "She appears to favor the gentleman, though she has only Wickham to compare him to. It remains to be seen whether or not they are truly suited for one another."

"Well, whatever happens, I am proud of you for allowing them the opportunity to become better acquainted." After a slight pause Elizabeth added, "William, I know you do not like to speak of Mr. Wickham, and you have my word that after today, his name shall never pass my lips, but I feel I must ask: Did you have something to do with his disappearance? I have already worked out that you covered his debts."

Darcy frowned. "You are correct. I do not wish to speak of him, especially on our wedding day. However, I will not keep secrets from you. Yes, I covered his debts. And yes, I was responsible for his... disappearance."

Elizabeth paled. "You did not...?"

Darcy pulled back, studying her face. "No! Of course not. Did you think you had married a murderer?"

Elizabeth flushed and Darcy continued, "No, I paid for his passage to the Americas and gave him money besides. It was a small price to pay to have him out of my life and away from the people I love. I also made it clear that if he ever returns, I will not hesitate to have him thrown in debtor's prison, though I do not believe we have to worry about that now. He seems quite happy with his new life."

"I am glad he is gone, for all our sakes," Elizabeth replied, and Darcy smiled as she snuggled against his shoulder.

Gazing down at his wife's treasured countenance, Darcy felt an overwhelming surge of love. No matter what fate threw at them now, with Elizabeth by his side, he knew there was nothing they could not conquer.

Pulling Elizabeth close, he murmured softly, "I meant what I said earlier, about my sister. I will allow her to follow her heart. Given my own experience, I could hardly do otherwise. If Grant brings her joy, I will not stand in his way. I only wish…"

Elizabeth sat up. "You wish…?"

Darcy sighed. "I know Grant is not Wickham, but I wish I could be assured that his interest in her is not mercenary. The fact remains, we know little of him, and Georgiana is in possession of a substantial dowry."

Elizabeth grinned back at him. "I do not think you need worry on that score."

Darcy's eyes widened. "Elizabeth, what do you know?"

She laughed wholeheartedly then, before finally saying, "Only that should Mr. Grant and Georgiana marry, our sister will not be destitute. It seems the good doctor has recently inherited some property in Yorkshire. The acquisition of that estate is the reason he returned to England this past spring. He wished to be nearby so he could more easily oversee its management."

"What? In Yorkshire? Where?"

"I believe he said it was near Sheffield."

Darcy's brow lifted in surprise. "Not Hyland Hall?"

"Yes! I think that was the name. Do you know it?"

Darcy's thoughts spun and he slowly nodded. "I do. My parents and I attended a house party there when I was a boy. Though not as large as Pemberley, it is a substantial estate on a vast piece of property. I remember it being very beautiful."

How had Elizabeth learned all of this? As far as Darcy could remember, Grant had not divulged one morsel of personal information the entire time he was at Pemberley. Suddenly, an image of Elizabeth and Grant seated beside one another in Georgiana's chambers, their heads bowed in quiet conversation flashed to mind and Darcy flinched. God, he had been such a fool!

"But why did you not tell me all of this earlier?" he asked. "For that matter, why didn't Grant? Surely he must have known that information would go a long way towards securing my approbation?"

Elizabeth lifted her shoulders. "I cannot speak for Mr. Grant. *I* did not tell you because I did not want this to be the thing that swayed your opinion. If you were to accept the gentleman, I hoped it would be on his own merits. But if I had to venture a guess, I would say that the physician's reasons were likely the same."

Darcy pulled Elizabeth close, caressing her hair. "Did I ever tell you how much I love you?"

Elizabeth laughed. "Once or twice." Sinking back against the cushions, she continued, "Now that that is settled, might I be allowed to know where we are going?"

Darcy smiled down into her sparkling hazel eyes. "You may. Right now, we are traveling to London. We will spend the night at Darcy House and then, in a week's time, we will journey to the Lakes. It has not escaped my attention that you have been longing to tour that area for quite some time."

The broad smile Elizabeth offered him in response to this news filled Darcy with pleasure.

"So, we shall spend a week in Town?" Elizabeth asked, and Darcy turned away before answering.

"No. Tomorrow morning we will leave… for Kent."

"Kent! You cannot wish to go to Rosings? Not after the

letter your aunt sent when we announced our engagement?"

Darcy's expression darkened. "No. I made it abundantly clear that I would not be visiting Rosings, nor would I offer any help with that estate, until we received a full apology. I also made certain my aunt knew she was no longer welcome at Pemberley, or anywhere else you and I reside."

Elizabeth angled her head, her eyes troubled. "I hate it that I am to be the cause of unrest amongst your relations."

"Pray, do not let it upset you. Lady Catherine would have been unhappy with my choice of wife no matter who I offered for, so long as it was not Anne. My aunt will come around."

"Do you think so?"

Darcy smiled. "I am certain of it. If only because she cannot manage Rosings on her own, nor will she expend the money to have someone else do it."

Elizabeth laughed. "Very well, if we are not to go to Rosings, then where? It is unexpected to learn you have a fondness for Kent."

"Indeed, I do not have a fondness for that part of the country as a whole, but there is one particular cottage I find I am exceedingly partial to."

"Surely not! You would not wish to go to the place that was the cause of so much suffering!"

Seeing the look on his wife's face, Darcy's stomach sank. "Forgive me, Elizabeth. It never occurred to me... Of course, if you do not wish to go there, we will not. But I thought... sometimes the best way to rid oneself of painful memories is to replace them with good ones. Despite what occurred that day, I find the cottage holds a special place in my heart. It is where I fell in love with you all over again, and where I first began to conquer my pride, and to hope that one day I might become a man worthy of your affection."

"But how did you find out who it belonged to? And how did you get the owners to agree to let us use it?"

Darcy flushed. "I had my solicitor track down the proprietors long ago, shortly after the accident. I wanted to compensate them for any damage we caused—breaking the window to gain entry—and for the food we consumed. Once you agreed to marry me, I contacted them again, to see if they would be willing to sell it to me."

"You purchased it? But why, when we only had need of it for a short time?"

Darcy shrugged. "I wished to own it. It is part of our story now. I did not like to imagine anyone else living there."

Elizabeth blinked up at him. "Isn't it a bit... rustic?" she finally asked. "Certainly, it is too small to have any servants accompany us."

"You are correct. It is."

"So... we will be alone there?"

"We will."

A smile touched Elizabeth's expression. "And I suppose I will cook for you?"

Darcy grinned back. "No. I have had my staff see to it that the kitchen is well stocked with prepared foods. I have also arranged for a couple to come once a day to cook and to do the necessary chores. I would not have you wait on me. Though I was hoping perhaps we might do some of those things together."

Elizabeth's smile grew. "Mr. Fitzwilliam Darcy of Pemberley, cooking meals, scrubbing pots, laying fires?"

Again, Darcy colored. "Well, perhaps not scrubbing pots. But I have found I rather enjoy doing many of those things, especially if you will be there to do them with me."

Elizabeth pressed herself close, circling her arms around his neck. "I will always be there."

"So, you do not mind? Returning to the cottage? Tell me the truth. I do not wish to do anything that will make you unhappy."

Elizabeth looked up at him, her eyes shining in the fading light. "I am not unhappy. And I think you are correct. When I left the cottage that day, I was already beginning to suspect that I loved you, but I had no hope you could ever return my feelings. It felt like an ending. But now, it is as though everything has just begun."

"So, it has," Darcy whispered.

And then he kissed her.

THE END

THANK YOU

Thank you so much for reading! I hope you enjoyed this alternate path to Darcy and Elizabeth's happily ever after.

If you feel so inclined, please consider leaving a review on the site where you purchased this book. Reviews help readers find stories they'll love, and assist authors with marketing and distributing their work.

Whether it's a few words or a longer reflection, your thoughts truly make a difference.

With heartfelt appreciation,

Jennifer

ALSO BY JENNIFER ALTMAN

Faults of Understanding

"I have faults enough, but they are not, I hope, of understanding."
—Mr. Darcy, Pride and Prejudice

When Fitzwilliam Darcy makes an impetuous offer of marriage to Miss Elizabeth Bennet, he is convinced they have as good a chance as any for a harmonious life together. That is, until an overheard conversation changes everything, and Darcy realizes he is now joined in perpetuity to a woman who loathes the very sight of him.

Elizabeth Bennet's expectations for matrimonial accord were never very high, having accepted Mr. Darcy's proposal in a fit of pique, not love. Still, she is determined to make the best of her situation, despite having tied herself to such an arrogant, disagreeable man.

But life at Pemberley is not at all what she imagined, and Elizabeth soon finds herself with more questions than answers about the enigmatic gentleman she agreed to wed.

Trapped in a marriage founded on misunderstandings, Fitzwilliam and Elizabeth Darcy struggle with deepening attraction while confronting self-doubt and old betrayals. But is love enough to heal the wounds of the past? What will it take for two people bound by duty to find their way home to one another?

More Than You Know

Fitzwilliam Darcy has spent years guarding a secret—one that could cost him everything.

Resigned to a solitary existence, Darcy has long accepted that love and marriage are luxuries beyond his reach. But when a chance encounter on the Yorkshire moors proves impossible to forget, the life he has so carefully constructed slowly begins to unravel.

Years later, drawn into Hertfordshire society by his friend Charles Bingley, Darcy crosses paths with Miss Elizabeth Bennet —clever, spirited, and unafraid to challenge him at every turn. Yet as his attraction to Elizabeth deepens, so does the fear that winning her affection would mean exposing a truth he has long kept hidden.

Unable to endure the agony of watching Bingley pursue the woman he loves, Darcy flees—but fate has other plans. When unexpected circumstances bring Elizabeth to Pemberley, his restraint is tested like never before.

Torn between duty and desire, Darcy must decide: will he cling to the barriers he has spent a lifetime building, or risk everything for the one woman he cannot forget?

Some Little Alteration

What if you had a second chance to make a first impression?

When Elizabeth Bennet suffers an unexpected accident while visiting her friend Charlotte Collins in Kent, she wakes to a world subtly—yet profoundly—altered. Friendships, family ties, and first encounters are no longer as she remembers: Mr Darcy is a stranger she meets for the first time at Rosings, Jane's circumstances have taken an unexpected turn, and a mysterious locket hints at a future she cannot fully comprehend.

As Elizabeth struggles to reconcile memories that refuse to align, she is drawn into a world both familiar and strange, where every exchange with Mr Darcy offers new insight into the man she once thought she understood. Yet each revelation brings the disquieting awareness that her former life is slipping away. And the harder she clings to her fading recollections, the more swiftly they recede.

Caught between two realities, Elizabeth must discover which truths to trust—and whether love can endure across the fragile boundaries of time.

Some Little Alteration is a spellbinding *Pride and Prejudice* variation, perfect for readers who enjoy stories that blend mystery, romance, and the enduring power of love.

ACKNOWLEDGMENTS

Anyone who has ever attempted to pen a novel knows that writing is not a solitary endeavor. The book you are holding in your hands would not exist without the support, generosity, and input from the following people:

First and foremost, my eternal gratitude goes to Joana Starnes, my JAFF fairy godmother, who proved to me in countless ways that not all superheroes wear capes—some of them wear bonnets. Only the most fortunate writers have someone in their corner to read revisions, offer advice, answer endless questions, and then declare: "That was fun!" Joana, from day one, you have been my biggest cheerleader. You believed in this book, and in me, long before I believed in myself. If there is a kinder, more selfless person on this planet, I haven't come across them. I am forever in your debt, and I feel luckier than you will ever know to call you my friend.

To the other half of team TCP, Jami Dragan: Thank you for being with me every step of the way, for your unwavering encouragement, optimism, and good humor. I'm not sure if I could have made it through this process without you—but I do know that it wouldn't have been nearly as much fun.

An enormous thank you to my copy-editor Jenny Ferguson for taking this project on in the midst of a cross-country move, teaching me how to make an em dash, and saving me from horse Twitter. Thank you for giving this book its final polish. Any errors that remain within the text are undoubtedly my own.

To Susan Adriani at CloudCat design for creating my beautiful cover and for your never-ending patience. You truly were a joy to work with.

Thank you to the following readers who caught mistakes, offered suggestions, and generally made this a better book: Krista Merle Anderson, Anji Dale, Diana Doncaster, Kelly Garcia, Claudine Pepe, Sarah Pesce, and Regina Silvia. Whether you read the complete novel or just a chapter, this book would not have been the same without you. You have my gratitude.

To my ARC crew: Thank you for taking a chance on a new author. Your positivity and enthusiasm have meant so much.

A very special thank you to my friends and family for sticking with me on this long and winding path to publication. Thank you for encouraging me, for believing in me, and for not asking (too many times): "Are you still working on that book?"

A gigantic shout-out to my Pitch Wars posse—I can't imagine being on this writing journey without all of you by my side. To steal a cheesy line from *Titanic*: "Getting into Pitch Wars was the best thing that ever happened to me... it brought me to you."

My thanks also to all of the other Austenesque authors

out there writing such creative, captivating novels. I wouldn't be doing this if it weren't for you. Thank you for the years of entertainment and for teaching me, without realizing it, what a good variation looks like.

And finally, to you, the reader, for allowing me to tell you a story.

ABOUT THE AUTHOR

Jennifer Altman is a novelist, an anglophile, and a lover of all things Regency. After a long career in the television industry, Jennifer shifted to book publishing in 2016 and hasn't looked back. She currently makes her home just north of New York City, where she lives with her Cavapoo, Penny. When she's not writing, Jennifer can be found reading, watching British period dramas, and not cleaning her house.